I0822791

DOMME & DOMMER

FILE BETWEEN BIBLES AND BUTT PLUGS

SOPHIA DOMINA

Cover design: Sophia Domina & Amelia Kohr

ISBN-13: 979-8-218-45421-0

Dad, you blasted off too soon, but I know you're watching from that great gig in the sky. I'm rocking on like I know you'd want me to. This novel is for you.

Mom, thank you for nurturing my creativity and instilling an inextinguishable spirit in me. You're my best friend. However, please DO NOT READ THIS BOOK.

Contents

CHAPTER I

Island Fever

STELLA ARCHED HER BACK in anticipation of the warm rush she hoped would flood her pelvis like a blessing... *Any. Minute. Now.*

Fissures forming in her brow, she tried to focus on anything other than the fact that Adam had massaged her once-ecstatic knob into paralysis. That sweet pang of pleasure never felt so close nor so far away. *La petite mort* would not come. And neither would she.

Stella slid a few sweaty inches away from Adam on the bed. It was December but the tropical heat had not let up. Everything about life on Guam irritated her.

An unspoken query peppered the creases of Adam's stubbled face. His handsome jaw settled into a dejected frame. Within the depths of his mossy green eyes was an interrogatory neither wanted to confirm. He could stroke her for days and nothing would happen. The couple hoped against that awful fact every time they made love.

"Sorry. Maybe I'm just stressed," Stella offered as tears gathered like spilt milk in the chocolates of her eyes. She looked away. "I have to get dressed."

She rose from the double bed, feeling his glance fall admiringly on her Botticellian behind. He reached for her hand. She reciprocated his affection with a gentle squeeze of the alligatored skin of his palm.

She retrieved a modest dress from her small closet while Adam slid a stack of books into a briefcase, stopping to thumb through the wafer-like pages of a worn leather Bible.

A few minutes later, Stella plopped dejectedly into their Civic. She flipped down the mirror to smooth her frizzy brown curls and finish winging her eyeliner. The morning sun streamed through the fronds of the beetle palms lining their dirt road, dappling light on Adam's freckled face as he drove. At 52, he was still handsome in a Clooney-meets-Carell sort of way, but the equatorial sun had inked his coffee-splattered cheeks even darker. *Island life.* They were both battered from these seven years in the remote Pacific territory.

At times, the reflection she saw in the mirror more resembled 48 than 38. They rode in silence, Stella contemplating how to sit through another service without wanting to scream.

*****

"Now, brothers and sisters," a rump roast of a man implored the 100 churchgoers on yet another dreadful Sunday morning. A cheap fan clicked and whined as it oscillated at his side. Like she and Adam, the speaker had relocated from the States to be a missionary. Their organization pressured them to be "exemplary in all things," but this elder was far from an example of health. *Hypocrite,* thought Stella.

"If the son of man had nowhere to lay his head, what should that tell us about how much we should give for our ministry?" he continued, shaking his Bible emphatically. "Ask yourself, 'Am I holding back? Can I do more?'"

Stella rolled her eyes and leaned over to Adam. "More?" she whispered. "Have you noticed that every talk is about doing more?"

Adam nodded, keeping his eyes fixed on the pork sausage of a speaker.

Stella could no longer ignore the greed pouring from the pulpit. If the message wasn't about spending more time going door-to-door, it was about donating more money. Had the doctrine changed or had she been hoodwinked all along?

The congregation stood to sing "Kingdom Melodies" while a sapless piano bleated as if it was playing from the basement of a serial killer. Stella could only pretend to sing. Having grown up with a blues guitarist father who gifted her a legacy of musical appreciation, the "Kingdom Melodies" tested her faith. At the tender age of 19, she had rebelled a bit and become a music journalist, so she was justifiably offended at the lack of lyrical quality and melodic complexity.

Next on the program was an interview with a gangly teen who admitted to a faith-threatening porn addiction. Had he been taken by ISIS, the confession could not have looked more forced.

"Brother Taitano, tell us how your addiction escalated."

The Chamorro boy cleared his throat. The microphone twitched in his slick palms. He scratched distractedly at a smattering of pimples on his chin. "I, uh, it started with soft-core images and then before I knew it, I was paying hundreds of dollars a month to watch, um, live… cam… girls." His voice squeaked with the humiliation of pubescence. He couldn't have been older than 16 and he had never been off the island. "I hated myself," he confessed with a question mark. This had been rehearsed ad infinitum. "I knew I was sinning in such a gross way against Jehovah."

It was mortifying. Stella wanted to stand up and scream, "Leave him alone!" His reputation now a conflagration of imposed shame, she wanted to sweep into the burning building and rescue him, to triage him from the contempt of an entire congregation.

The horror continued with a new animated video for kids about the evils of homosexuality. Stella knew the series well. It had been hokey at best, soft-pedaling the Bible's message of fiery destruction at Armageddon like some Flintstones vitamins quietly laced with arsenic. It began with a *Children of the Corn*-esque sing-a-long by a chorus of young voices.

The first scene opened on a boy of six at school. His fellow student shared that she had two daddies. Righteously shocked, the Witness child returned home and related the conversation to his mother.

"Jehovah doesn't like that," the mother explained in the patterned passive-aggressive tones the religion had perfected. "It's a gross sin for two men to be married. But they can change. Jehovah wants everyone to get into the new system. That means we have to leave our bad ways and do what he commands."

Stella turned to Adam once more, but he pretended not to notice. She wanted to rouse in him not only sympathy for her, but critical thinking about the whole damn organization. How could he ignore all the sex shaming and homophobia?

She leapt up in a fury.

As she pounded towards the last row, a woman stopped her with an outstretched arm.

"I can see your thong," the old lady claimed loudly. Pinned into the lapel of her natty tweed was the symbol of their organization, a Watchtower, that brooch an imagined badge of the chastity police. The decrepit flesh of her nose wrinkled with pleasure. The insult was meant to turn heads.

"My thong?" Stella replied. "I'm not wearing a thong."

"Your dress is practically sheer. I can see right through it! I can see your *thong,"* the old bag insisted even louder.

Stella's blood boiled. She had been a model of modesty, first by remaining a virgin until marriage at 26, then by suffering her husband's lack of sexual prowess without a single indiscretion on her part. Had she been tempted dozens of times? Of course. She was a Monroe; all jello on springs. Even in her religious frocks, she was a vintage pinup. She refused to don the sad potato sacks the organization prescribed for women. And men noticed with a slimy-toothed lust. It didn't matter how much she covered up, Stella was a siren.

She wanted to retort in defiance: "Joke's on you! I wear granny panties larger than the state of Alaska. My derrière eats thongs for breakfast!"

"Dear," the sister continued with affectatious concern. "You don't want the brothers distracted at the meetings. They're trying so hard to resist the temptations of this world."

"No one has been more faithful to God and man than me," Stella retorted, jabbing her chest angrily just as Adam appeared. "Ask my husband. He knows."

Adam made a feeble excuse to the accusatory party, took Stella by the hand, and solemnly drove her back to the isolated serenity of their island bungalow.

"My stepfather had X-ray vision," Stella complained as she sat on the bed watching Adam wrap a fresh tie around his collar. "Ask me how many sweaters I wore just to get from my bedroom to the kitchen! How am I responsible for any man's lust?"

"You're not. But don't blame the brothers, dear. We are in the last days. Satan wants you to give up. He will do anything to discourage you from serving Jehovah."

"Like sending an attack fleet of old bitches to body shame me."

"Stella." He paused to offer her a look of correction.

She didn't care that her language offended him.

"And I'm sick of hearing that I need to do more. How much more? Twenty-five years of sacrifice is not enough? Free labor, donations, giving up education and a full-time career, moving to Guam on our own damn dime… Do I have to climb up on the stake and hammer the nails in myself?"

"You know the Bible says to seek first the kingdom. We can always do more for Jehovah. He's done so much for us."

"*I've* done so much for us. *I* have been supporting us. Not Jehovah!"

"And he appreciates your efforts. He's obviously blessing us."

"And where are your blessings, Adam? Where is your career?"

"I'm doing what I can." His tone was familiar, sheepish, maddening.

"Driving for Uber is not a career, Adam!"

"That's so I have time for the ministry. That's what's important. That's why we are here. I wish you would come out in service with me," he said, stroking her arm as she lay paralyzed on the bed. "Look, I love you. Why don't I make dinner when I get home?" he said, parroting his usual placations.

Stella rolled over to face the window. A few yards away, two goats locked horns in a puckish battle. A rooster crowed. Adam leaned down to kiss her on the head like a parent soothing a child from a tantrum. A day late and a dollar short. That was Adam's M.O. His solution for a bullet wound was a Band-Aid. He left without another word.

Stella hadn't been able to sit through a service in months. She was still attending the meetings to appease her husband and, far off in Texas, her mother too. She knew she needed to pull the ripcord and get out.

Instead, she masturbated.

The small vibrator came from Amazon in an unmarked box. It was her first. She retrieved it from behind her meeting dresses in the back of the single closet she and Adam shared.

The initial twinge of guilt she felt from touching herself had ceased to plague her. The organization twisted every natural inclination into something vile, but as she distanced herself from it, the brainwashing began flaking off like chipped paint.

She opened her computer and scrolled to a private folder. She flicked on the tiny vibrator. The toy buzzed with a meager hum, but terrified of discovery, she muffled it with a pillow. Adam would have been appalled.

As Stella's eyes moved greedily along the image of a bikini-clad babe, she felt a gush under the pulsating head of the wand. Women turned her on. Big, bouncing breasts. Nipples of all shapes and colors. Oiled. Squeezed. Sucked. Pummeled. And what was the real harm in it? She wasn't cheating. It wasn't as if she was looking at another man.

She edged herself, alternating between watching the laptop screen and admiring her juicy ass in the mirror. She stared into her large, brown eyes. "You're a slut. Take it like a whore with your big stupid tits."

With this dirty talk, she came hard and strong. The release was unlike anything she had experienced with her husband.

Stella checked the time. Adam wouldn't be home for another hour. Plenty of time to watch *Sex and the City,* her new guilty pleasure. Cloistered from society, she was a few decades behind media trends, but this was the show that most spoke to her desires for sexual expression, unapologetic feminism, and the life she was starting to believe she was born for. She had been forced into the church at age 12, however, there were accessible parts of her pre-indoctrination psyche. The beautiful bohemian upbringing her hippie parents provided lived in her still.

"I will not be judged by you or society. I will wear whatever I want and blow whomever I want as long as I can breathe and kneel..." The oversexed Samantha delivered the line with bravado to her well-heeled friends. Was real life really like this?

Earlier than expected, Stella heard the crackle of tires over gravel. "Shit!" She shoved the vibrator under her pillow and slammed her laptop shut.

She ran out to kiss Adam, but as usual the needle of her sexual Geiger counter failed to flutter. She needed more.

"Let's take a walk," she said, grabbing his hand with mustered enthusiasm.

He agreed in his typical obliging manner, setting down a rainbow bouquet of flowers for Stella.

As they rounded a dusty trail past a dozen chickens, she excitedly pulled him behind a tree, pressed her chest against his, and ran her fingers along the crotch of his suit. "Let's have sex. Here. Now."

"What if we get caught?" he asked, swiftly moving her hand away, his eyes darting.

"Caught?" Her heart dropped. "We're married."

He pushed past her. "Someone could see us. C'mon, Stella. Let's go inside."

It was pointless. Adam couldn't expand. He had been raised as a Jehovah's Witness and served 20 years as an unpaid "volunteer" at their billion-dollar headquarters in New York. No one was more lobotomized. She had married a 40-year-old virgin with no money and no career. But he was a spiritual man, respected in the organization, and that was enough to convince her he was "the one."

Adam had been her cheerleader in most endeavors, but when it came to the piercing scream of her doctrinal doubts, he was abjectly avoidant.

"I'm going for a run. I need to clear my head." Stella took off, pounding across the dirt. She took refuge in the tropical tangle. She ran hard, kicking up the dust, jumping across a familiar brook and past an abandoned shipping container until the tears came so hard she collapsed.

Due to her increasingly tempestuous moods, Adam had encouraged therapy, an act discouraged by the organization. He was clearly desperate. They named her psychotic breaks "the vortex" in order to define and manage them. They thought that uttering the words could snap her back into reality, like a hand reaching down into the abyss to pull her to safety, but nothing was safe about her world. Every few months she was blindsided by thunderous forces that left her exhausted and ashamed in front of her impotent husband and their punitive god. She blamed herself for caving under the pressure.

She craved color and light and expansion and *freedom*. Thoughts of suicide had been creeping into her meditations with alarming frequency. The things she wanted were contrary to everything she knew, but how could she live another day in this prison?

The balmy air gradually chilled. She had been gone for hours when a voice in the distance called to her. A beam of light bounced along the brush.

"Stella, honey! Where are you?"

As Adam trod through the tall grass, she could see his look of worry.

"It's late. Aren't you cold?" he asked, looking down at her sitting toddler-like in the dirt.

"Adam, I can't do this anymore. I'm miserable. You're miserable." She wiped the snot from her nose with the back of her hand.

"I'm not... *miserable.* Things could be better..." He said, extending a hand to pull her up.

"We can't just accept it," she bemoaned, dusting off her thighs. "I don't want to live like this."

A tense twilight filled the air between them as the jungle stirred in preparation for nightfall.

"Draw close to Jehovah again," Adam pleaded, taking her shoulders in his hands.

"I've done all that," she said, wriggling out of his embrace. A turbulent spirit gathered steam inside her like a locomotive barreling towards destruction. "I've martyred myself for this cause. Don't you see we are being manipulated? We aren't slaves for Jehovah. We're slaving for a group of white men sitting pretty in their sterilized offices in New York!" she roared. "Don't you see how they are milking us for everything we've got?"

"Don't say that. The brothers are the only ones there for us," he defended, his voice fractured with defeat.

Stella's eyes went wild. She felt the terror of the vortex like a hand from the crypt grabbing at her ankles. She bolted towards the house. Adam shuffled dejectedly behind. She flung the front door open and began fishing madly under the bed for her suitcase.

CHAPTER 2

Meeting Marlene

STELLA SPED DOWN a winding road towards the gleaming turquoise waters of the tourist strip. Ten minutes later, she slammed her car into park in front of a 50-story high-rise. Her job as a media director for a top hotel was the single bright spot in her life. Taking the position a year ago had raised many eyebrows in the organization, for it required late shifts, not to mention rubbing elbows with "worldly" entertainers. With Adam's lack of career skills, she had no choice but to step up as the breadwinner. The Witnesses sure as hell didn't give them a dime.

Stella loved the career challenge. It was her first full-time job, for she had devoted the bulk of her youth to going door-to-door at a punishing pace of 90 hours per month. She was something of a wunderkind, having no university education, yet developing creative skills at every agency where she was employed.

Stella rolled her bag up to the front desk of a grand marble lobby. The concierge eyed her curiously.

"You and Adam on the outs again?" asked the chubby-cheeked woman of forty.

Stella laid her head on the cold counter. "Yes, Akina. Same old."

Akina patted her sweetly. "Can't be worse than my husband. You know he gave his cousin $15,000 of my hard-earned money for a surgery in the Philippines he don't really need!" Akina sighed. "You'll get through it, Miss Stella. This just life with men."

"That's a lot of money. How can you stand for that?"

"What choice I have? We living on family land in his aunty's house. Until the military seizes it, we don't got that many bills. It's the Chamorro way, you know. We help our own. Don't matter if we want to or not. Not like you haoles who only looking out for yourself."

"I might as well be Chamorro the way my paycheck is hacked to pieces for everyone else."

Akina slid a room key across the counter. "You're in luck. The penthouse suite is vacant for a couple days."

"Akina, you're a real friend. Thank you."

Stella rode the high-speed elevator to the top floor and flopped onto the bed of the luxury suite. It was late but she couldn't sleep. After tossing and turning for hours, she rose in the pre-dawn twilight and strolled out to the beach in her nightgown like a specter, sidestepping the hermit crabs animating the white sand. She had felt like a shell of a person for years; dead on a vine that threatened to choke her out and end her.

As the first rays of sun burst over the mountains, she returned to the hotel to dress for work. A well-known Japanese dance troupe was performing and she was in charge of producing the show. Her years of training as a public speaker and Bible instructor had prepared her to manage people and entertain groups with aplomb.

Life isn't all bad, Stella thought as she stretched her legs out from the shade of the thatched roof into the benevolent morning sun. She preferred to work poolside. The staff always saved her a little spot on the veranda closest to the ocean. She coated her lips with a frothy cappuccino and opened her laptop to edit a video.

Out of the corner of her eye, she noticed a stately, fair-skinned woman seated a few tables away. She was dressed to the nines, an unusual character, for Guam was most often touristed by young Asian travelers. She and the stranger stole a few curious glances.

"That's beautiful. Whatever you're working on," the woman said as she shimmied over to Stella, pointing at her laptop.

Stella turned to look the stranger in the eye. She was stunning. The dotted net of her green beret coiled seductively over her rich burgundy waves, styled à la Veronica Lake. Her lightly freckled skin stretched like silk across the altissimo of her cheekbones and her lips were precision-painted in femme fatale red.

"Sorry," said Stella as she swallowed a heaping chunk of raspberry scone. She hurried to wipe a mess of cream from her lips. "Thanks."

"Did you shoot it?"

"Yep. I run the media for the hotel."

"Oh, you live here. How romantic it must be. I'm Marlene. And I *love* what you're wearing," she said, gesturing to Stella's dress, a navy A-line that hugged her Coke bottle curves and never failed to upset all the dowdy elders' wives despite her having altered the neckline to reveal less.

Stella introduced herself and smiled.

"I just loathe the casualness of Americans. Everyone should dress for the tableau." Marlene gestured dramatically to the sparkling blue water of the infinity pool. The ruffles of her polka dot blouse rippled like a sea of anemones in the breeze, while her lean legs stemmed like a champagne flute from a pair of pedal pushers.

Stella nodded. "Or maybe we are just overdressed."

"No such thing."

It was true. They were the prettiest peacocks in the place, dressed in '50s silhouettes while the rest of the crowd wore cutoffs.

"I'd love to photograph you." Stella was shocked as the words left her mouth so suggestively. Would the woman think she was flirting?

"I hear that from photographers quite often…" Marlene paused. A smirk populated the conspiratorial corners of her mouth. "I'm itching for a good Naked and Famous. Know of a place?"

"Um, no," Stella replied, the valves of her heart fluttering like the staccato wings of a hummingbird. "I've never shot *nudes,"* she whispered.

Marlene laughed. "No, dear. Naked and Famous is a cocktail, but I like how your mind works!"

Stella was mortified. "Oh! I thought it was something else... to do with photography, but cocktails, yes! I'm off at six. We could meet at the bar…" she offered tentatively.

"Lezzz do," Marlene cooed as she stood up.

Stella watched her strut all the way through the sliding glass doors.

She returned focus to her computer, but after a few hours of fierce determination, she could not concentrate. Marlene was endowed with a circumscribed vitality that captivated Stella and left her buzzing.

She shut her laptop and stared into the sea. The beach was teeming with filial families and googly-eyed lovers. It really did *seem* to be such a happy place. But under the veneer of Americana was a throat-grabbing imperialism that choked out indigenous culture. She knew all too well how difficult it was for a Chamorro dance troupe to make it into the hotel's showcase. She felt a pang of guilt every time she had to reject them in favor of splashy Polynesian dance falsely billed as indigenous. This indignation had been her inspiration to produce a film about the cultural renaissance on the island. Directing her first short gave her a newfound reason for living there. It had even garnered a few laurels in indie film festivals.

Her phone rang. It was Adam for the third time that morning. She silenced it and then strode into the lobby, scanning for Marlene. No sign. She went up to her room and swore she heard a voice from the hallway just as the door was closing.

"I thought I saw you as I was coming up. Oh, you have a penthouse suite. Fabulous," Marlene said, poking her head past the threshold of the door.

"When one is available. When I need an escape."

"Escape from what?"

"Wanna come in?" Stella opened the door wide.

"Sure. Let me see this balcony." Marlene dropped her square vintage handbag on the bed and pushed open the glass doors like a Hitchcockian muse stepping into the 35mm frame of a director gliding in on his crane.

Stella followed her out. Marlene slid the small of her back along the balcony and spread her hands across the rail. She eyed Stella intently for several moments without speaking.

"So, you're an escape artist?" Marlene asked, arching a brow dramatically.

Stella chuckled. "A wannabe!"

"Boy troubles?"

"Man troubles. A husband."

"I've never had one of those. Plenty of wives though."

"Plenty?"

"Figuratively speaking. Many girlfriends. One fiancé. We met in the circus and bonded over a love of drag."

"Oh, wow." Stella blushed.

"Women are a different kind of agony but agony nonetheless."

Stella wanted nothing more than to tell this mystery Marlene all her troubles, but she had been programmed never to complain to an unbeliever about her marriage, the organization, or anything that would bring shame on Jehovah's name.

"You know, I bet I could get the bar to send up that drink you like," Stella offered, moving towards the phone.

"Naked and Famous. Yes, do that."

Stella dialed room service and soon they sat on the bed, toasting the afternoon sun.

"So, what brought you here?" Stella inquired as she choked back the tart cocktail with an inelegant cough. "Sorry, I never drink…"

Marlene took a sip and nodded in approval. "My sub has business here so I'm enjoying a vacation while she slaves away."

"Your sub… subcontractor? So, you manage a company?"

"My submissive."

"Oh, um."

Marlene stared penetratively. Stella knew she could see the hamster running double time behind her eyes. Marlene let Stella's confusion hang in the air like a hunter setting a trap.

"Sorry, but I truly do not know what that means," Stella confessed with a slump of her shoulders.

"I'm a Dominatrix," Marlene said, elongating her beautiful neck as she cocked her chin heavenward. Her hazel eyes seemed to flash at the bombshell disclosure.

Stella was dumbfounded. The database of her mind generated so few references to such a mythical creature. Minus a porno featuring a mean Amazonian jackhammering a vibrator between the writhing thighs of a busty bound blonde, she didn't know the term well at all. Was Marlene a cruel beast with savage instincts? She appeared so genteel, cut from the pages of a vintage *Vogue* not the din of a Berlin dungeon.

"Really?"

"Really."

Before her sat a real-life *Dominatrix*. She should have recoiled, but she found herself thrilled to the core at all the word suggested.

Marlene spent the next hour bringing Stella out of the bunker. With her limited understanding of even vanilla sex, everything Marlene described was a revelation.

"Is D/s the same as BDSM?" Stella asked as she propped herself up on the pins of her elbows like a hungry disciple at the foot of a master.

"D/s means Dominance and submission. BDSM stands for bondage, discipline, sadism, and masochism," Marlene said with a scripted exhalation. She leaned back onto a pillow and draped her arm over her head as if exhausted from what must've been the millionth recital to the uninformed.

"But what kind of person wants to be beaten and tortured? Is that healthy?" Stella's aversion to violence could not be veiled. The real query on the tip of her tongue was about Marlene's proclivity towards abuse. "My stepfather was very dominating. He would chase me through the house, pin me down, and beat me. Never anywhere visible. He knew how to avoid getting caught."

"That's abuse. To be clear, what I'm describing is consensual. It's a type of slaughter submissives desperately seek and don't easily find." Marlene spoke with the prim formality of one giving a triple X TED Talk. "That's a common misconception about kink. Submission starts in the mind. It's a psychological power exchange before it has anything to do with the body."

"I've been a slave of God for 25 years. I know all about submission of the mind."

"Submission is very tied to worship. I have hacked through the jungle to the shrouded lost cities of my submissive's hearts. They dig deep into the hollows of their treasuries, laying gold at my feet. They worship me."

Who actually spoke like this? Much of what Marlene said sounded like a double entendre, a literary allusion, some mystical metaphor. It wasn't just *what* she said, but how she breathed it out—her dramatic intonation, velvety tenor, the arch of a perfectly drawn eyebrow, and her impossibly erect posture. She was every bit the Zelda Fitzgerald, something of an imaginary creature Stella could not believe she had the fortune of knowing so intimately. With each interaction, Stella was seduced further into Marlene's world of psychosexual discovery.

"Wow. So, people worship you." A couple of cocktails in, Stella found herself admiring Marlene in a way she had never admired a woman. With each tick of the sun towards the horizon, she was more and more drawn in by Marlene's warmth. She found Marlene to be an empathetic confidant, and in the way she lived her life, a hero.

"It sounds like my marriage," Stella confessed. "Adam waits on me hand and foot. Whatever I ask, he does… short of earning a living. My therapist told me I don't need a 1950s housewife and I think she's right."

"There are as many types of submissives as there are people. My preference is for an alpha submissive if they are cis-gendered. For domestic servants I don't mind a beta male."

Stella's face wore her thread-bare confusion, so Marlene continued. "Alpha submissives are otherwise dominant in their lives, work, etcetera, but sexually they are submissive."

"And betas are just submissive/submissive?"

"In general terms, yes. Broad brushstrokes. People are complex."

"I think Adam is a beta."

"And that could work if you made it a high-protocol dynamic with more formal instruction. Your husband bows to you naturally. Same with my houseboy. They know no other response to a dominant woman. But it's all communicated and consented to, unlike most vanilla relationships where all these power dynamics are at play but never discussed."

"Yeah, we don't talk about it because in my religion I'm supposed to be submissive to my husband—to every man—but Adam is lost without my direction. It's so frustrating."

"What kind of sex do you have?"

Stella took a swallow of her drink and nearly choked again. She had never talked about sex with anyone other than Adam, not even her Christian "sisters."

"Uh, I was a virgin when I married him. So was he. A 40-year-old virgin like Steve Carell. Can you believe it?"

"Girl! I'd love to have Carell between my legs."

"Me too, but oral sex is forbidden. So many things are. Even masturbation. We didn't kiss until *after* our wedding."

Marlene's face dropped. "Of all the tragedies I've heard. No oral sex? Ever? Tell me, what is at the crux of your most refined fantasies?" She swirled her pinky suggestively around the melted ice in her tumbler.

"I can't remember what you said you did for work..." Stella probed, treating Marlene's question as rhetorical. She was curious just who this feline femme was outside of her fantastical sexual world.

"I am an expert in the art of living fabulously!" Marlene sang with an upturned palm. "Professional diva."

Stella paused, anxious to know Marlene's true profession, but no further explanation was anted up.

Instead, Marlene, in the stealthy slow motion of cats of prey, began crawling across the bed. "And you..." She paused just inches away and cupped Stella's heart-shaped face in her hands. "You're a Baby Domme."

Stella felt a psychic thud. A sort of wrecking ball tearing through her. Tears gathered in her eyes.

"You already knew, didn't you?" Marlene asked.

Stella nodded. "It feels so natural to lead, but I always thought of domination as negative."

"I know. I see you so clearly," said Marlene sympathetically, letting Stella's tears trickle onto her hands.

Like some divine truth bestowed by a priest, it was a christening, a naming of her nature.

Stella wiped her face and sucked back a bit of air, finally gathering the courage to speak. "Oh shoot, my makeup."

"Why are you worried about that?"

"I have acne. It's so embarrassing," she said, bowing her head.

"You look beautiful. Tears moisturize the face," Marlene said, tenderly wiping specs of mascara from the delicate skin under Stella's eyes.

"I want to leave, but will anyone ever love me like Adam? What if no one else finds me attractive?"

Marlene pressed her face to Stella's, absorbing her tears with her cheek. Stella had never smelled a woman in such close proximity, never felt skin so soft against her own. She was both electrified and woozy at the touch.

Marlene then looked her deep in the eyes. She paused then brushed her wet lips against Stella's, moving them just a hair back and forth. Languid and deliberate. A cautious kiss; a test; a dip of the toe in the waters of newborn desire.

Stella parted her lips, inviting deeper contact. Marlene flicked her tongue against Stella's, her saliva sweet and tart with gin. Stella's heart fluttered again, this time with the pomp of a petite cavalry. Without a second thought, Stella kissed her with reciprocal tenderness, her insides a glorious tangle of bliss.

Marlene pulled away first, gradually, as if to let her genie return gently to its bottle, the embers of her sexual energy still charging the air between them.

Stella smiled with satisfaction. *I kissed a girl and I liked it.*

"If your right eye makes you stumble, tear it out…" Stella nervously resumed conversation, attempting to conceal the cataclysmic thrill of such a sinful act. Her pilot light suddenly reignited after countless dim winters, the mezcal waltzing in her head, the mechanical buzz in her most succulent parts… She felt like a spectator of herself, surprisingly unfettered by guilt, so she tried to conjure some up by quoting the very scripture that condemned her. "...That's what the Bible says. And so I did. I tore out all my desires."

"And look at you now. Ready to inhabit the skin you were born in!" Marlene sat back on her ankles in positive appraisal.

"I've been so submissive, I don't know if I can actually break free," Stella argued, her heart still racing with desire for Marlene's touch.

"You are discovering yourself! Find the distillate of your desire."

"I don't know how." Stella could barely get the words out, her voice cracking under the pressure of Marlene's call to action.

"I will teach you." Marlene leaned forward. Her face glowed brightly as if an incandescent bulb had been lit within. There was a sudden urgency in her offer as she enveloped Stella's hands in hers. "The creative kinship I feel for you has been a long time coming. If you only knew how many days I've spent in meditation, burning candles and praying with my head to the south, calling in creative partnership year after year to no avail."

"And you see that with me?"

"I do. You're a fucking queen, running your marriage, your hotel entertainment, this whole missionary life!"

Marlene stroked her hair and Stella felt the sting of her tears again. Their attraction was exo-scripture, without precedent. There was no tradition for this connection—this Dominatrix and her Baby Domme.

"Come with me," Marlene implored, a beam of sunshine moving with a brilliant throb of affection across her cheeks.

Stella searched Marlene's face to assess the seriousness of her proposal. "To Los Angeles?"

"Yes! We'll trace a ladder to the stars!" she insisted with the kind of poetry that stirred Stella's heart. "You never have to dim your light with me. I welcome it and will only reciprocate the beacon."

Marlene's words awoke in Stella the *joie de vivre* of that wildly creative and bossy little girl she was before the cult stripped her of individuality. That child was the byproduct of a strong-willed Sicilian mother who, even in her lack of self-esteem, raised a ballbuster in Stella. They lived near the poverty line, buoyed slightly by food stamps, the evidence of which was Stella's tetherball—nothing more than a plastic milk carton filled with rocks and tied to a street sign. Stella spent many years dancing atop a beat-up Buick in the backyard of their 200-year-old brownstone in Cincinnati, lip syncing to Madonna, imagining herself a star. She kept that magical cosmos embossed in her memory as if crystallized on Kodak paper in that nostalgic '80s shade of brown. Her first decade on this earth was practically "the one who got away," she was filled with such deep longing to feel it again. Marlene's self-indulgence, her love of fashion and cinema, her bright eyes and bossiness was a language Stella understood, even if it was a tongue buried deep under the brimstone of Bible sermons.

Stella slid back towards the headboard and sighed defeatedly. "I can't leave."

"You can. You want to," Marlene insisted.

"I want nothing more, but Adam would be gutted," she said, her voice quivering. She looked past Marlene at the rapidly retreating sun. The walls and furniture took on a monochromatic pallor. The room felt still. She began biting at a hardened sliver of skin around her fingernail.

"Truth hurts!" exclaimed Marlene.

Stella continued picking at the hangnail until a pearl of blood bubbled up. "And what will I do? Where will I live? How will I survive?"

"Stay with me. I suspect you always land on your feet, *el gato.* You're supporting a man in Guam! Imagine the heights you will reach with the freedom to focus on yourself for once."

Marlene's tone and confidence were galvanizing, but Stella had not let herself dream the big dream yet. She had grieved endlessly for lost parts of herself, but betraying her family was too much. She uncoiled the thread of skin on her finger and let the metallic taste of blood soak her tongue.

"It might kill my mother. She's old and feeble, stuck in an abusive relationship."

"And so are you," Marlene retorted.

"What?" Marlene's challenge landed dangerously near to insult, reminding Stella that "worldly people" were not inclined towards self-sacrifice.

"*You* are stuck in an abusive relationship. Did you consent to supporting your husband?"

"No, but…" Stella started defensively.

"Did you consent to all your time and vitality being spent on this island?" Marlene built her offense with litigious conviction. One could imagine her with arms locked arms upon the stand of a courtroom jury, arguing for the sentencing of some notorious felon, pleading for sympathy towards his innocent victims.

"Well, kind of…" said Stella, contemplating whether she should feed her angry surge of resistance. "There are just some things you don't—you couldn't—understand!" Stella pushed herself off the bed in a huff and began relocating the empty cocktail glasses—more than she remembered consuming—to a low credenza near the door.

"Explain them to me." Marlene stood and smoothed the fine linen of her capris.

Stella turned towards her squarely, her eyes animated with a snarling pain. "Will God smite me if I leave? I know you probably don't even believe in God."

"Honey, no, he won't. And yes, I do believe in God. Very much. How could he not want you to live your own truth though? Why would he punish you for that?"

"Because there's only one truth and the Witnesses believe they have it with a capital T! If you leave 'The Truth,' you will be destroyed at Armageddon. But first, guess what!" Stella yelled, pacing across the room in a frenetic gait. "My entire family, all my friends, everyone I've known and loved, they will never talk to me again!"

"And that's exactly why I think you're in a cult."

Stella stopped in her tracks. The word "cult" made her twitchy. It undermined not only her entire paradigm but her intelligence. It implied brainwashing, coercion, drinking the Kool-Aid. Could the misogyny and homophobia of her religion really be compared to the murderous ministry of some madman on a banana republic?

She couldn't deny that she needed to break free from it all, but was she willing to trade everything she knew and everyone she loved—even life itself—for a proverbial 15 minutes of fame? Would that be enough to chew off her leg and break free?

Nothing in her life had ever felt as risky or alluring as Marlene's gamble.

CHAPTER 3

One-Way Ticket from Paradise

STELLA HELD HER BREATH as she slid her key into the front door. Adam sat slumped on the couch, his face a pallid portrait of exhaustion. Her 24-hour absence had taken its toll. A wave of guilt crashed over her.

"I was just working at the hotel," she offered solemnly, rolling her banged-up suitcase across the tile with a clickety-clack.

"I wish you'd answer my calls. I was worried." He exhaled a familiar sigh.

"I know." Stella bowed her head apologetically.

Adam stood and embraced her. Could he smell the rosy tones of Marlene's perfume which had been intoxicating her the whole drive home? She was still buzzing from the day before, though Adam's touch dampened her desire like a wet blanket.

"What if I rough you up a little?" she said, wrapping her fingers around his neck and digging her nails in. "Let's try something new."

"What? No. That hurts." He broke free from her grip and returned soullessly to a mess of papers on the coffee table. "I'm making crew assignments for the Kingdom Hall construction project," he said, rubbing the crenulations of her nails from his neck.

"Great. I can't wait to do slave labor in the blazing sun all summer," she smarted.

Adam shot her a disappointed look. "We came here to help. Jehovah appreciates our hard work. And if we just increase our donations for the next six months, we can help even more with the construction materials."

"But we're already giving a lot."

"You know the brothers here don't have the resources. We are fortunate. Another thousand dollars a month would do so much."

"Adam, are you crazy?" She stared at him incredulously. "No way. I'm working full-time because we need that money ourselves. The cost of living here is killing us."

"We have savings, Stella…" he trailed off, looking away.

"Adam." She inched towards him, her jaw hardening into a tense pack of muscle. "What are you not telling me?"

"I didn't think you'd mind, but…" He backed a nervous foot away. "I already wrote the check to the brothers."

Stella's limbs began to twitch as if seized by some seismic quake. Before she could scream the retort rumbling through her body, a polite knock came at the door.

"Who is that?" Stella startled.

"Dear, please. I invited Brother Johnson over. He's concerned about you."

"But I didn't ask for a shepherding call." Stella felt a sickening undulation in her gut.

"My privileges are on the line with your recent behavior. You rarely go to meetings, your outburst the other day… The brothers have even questioned whether I should be serving as an elder."

"So, this is about you?"

Adam opened the front door and there stood two men in suits holding briefcases. It was too late for Stella to flee. The elders were already greeting her with tepid smiles. She knew the drill. They were there to chastise her under the pretense of "spiritual encouragement."

After a bit of small talk, she was reluctantly bowing her head in prayer, an act she had given up months ago. Why call on a god who never answers? Her faith had shriveled to less than the size of a mustard seed.

"Sister, we're concerned for your spiritual well-being," Brother Johnson said, leaning his broad torso forward on the worn couch. "We've missed you out in field service, we don't hear you commenting at the meetings, and Adam says you've been working overtime quite a bit."

"I have to. We can't afford to serve here if I don't," Stella replied, crossing her arms defensively.

"We were informed of a conflict with a faithful older sister Sunday," the elder continued. "It seems you had an angry outburst towards her. Is it possible that the spirit of this demonic world is rubbing off on you at work?"

Stella looked at Adam with disbelief. He cleared his throat. She desperately waited for him to rise to her defense. He looked down and began tracing the embossed type on his *New World Translation* Bible with the tip of his finger. Silence.

"Um, I… Wow, I don't know what to say. I have been so faithful to Jehovah. You know I'm supporting us, right? And I was humiliated by that sister for no reason. It's shocking that I'm being blamed for any of this."

"Dear, you're not being blamed. The elders just want to help," Adam interjected as Brother Johnson reached for his Bible.

"Let's open to Matthew 6:33," said the bespeckled man of sixty, his voice weary with his own struggles as a missionary. Stella could read his dispassion in the descending altitude of his brow as he flipped to the familiar scripture. They all knew it by rote.

"I'm sorry. I really don't want to talk about this. I know what Matthew says. I am seeking first the kingdom. I can't possibly do more. Please talk to Adam about doing more to help me. I'm exhausted."

"Sister, Adam is working hard as an *elder,*" the old man said condescendingly. "We all value the support you give him so he can focus on the assignment at hand."

"But what about his God-given duty to provide for his household? Isn't the man who fails to do that worse than a person without faith according to 1 Timothy 5:8?" Stella challenged.

She had never spoken to an elder with even an ounce of defiance. It gave her a terrifying rush. Brother Johnson shifted his heavy frame and pursed his lips, his piercing gray eyes communicating a stern warning.

Stella stood, leaning against the chair. "Thank you for stopping by, but I'm not feeling well."

She spun on her heels and left the room. From the bedroom, she could hear Adam apologizing while the elders moved towards the front door.

As soon as the door shut, Stella bounded back into the living room.

"Adam, please tell me you did not donate six thousand dollars. You—you—you did that without consulting me?" Her breathing bordered on hyperventilation as she scratched her scalp with a shell-shocked itch. "No, no, no!"

"Dear, calm down."

"I will not! I spent my life on this—this corporation! No one has sacrificed more than me! But taking—no, stealing—my hard-earned money! Do you know how many millions of dollars are going to child abuse settlements? There's a reason they tell us never to read the news about Jehovah's Witnesses!" A familiar panic took over. Her mind was feral and unchained. She wanted to hit Adam, to break glass, to tear the room apart like an ill-tempered rockstar.

Instead, she stomped towards the bedroom and began packing. Her lungs heaved as if weighed down by a boulder. When the accordion of her tissue finally expanded, a primeval roar escaped through her throat like a demon. Eyes bleary, she clawed at handfuls of clothes and smashed them into her suitcases.

Wheeling her bags into the living room, she exhaled with a surprising calm. "I'm leaving. For good."

"Leaving? Stella, no." Adam's anxious eyes swept across her like searchlights hunting for survivors of a catastrophe. He frantically flipped open his laptop and began playing a religious video. "Please sit down. Watch this." Stella was not only his wife, but his parishioner and the video his last little vigil to save her soul.

Cloying music played in an '80s light rock style so insipid it made Hall & Oates sound like Ozzy Osbourne. A montage of images portrayed a couple going door-to-door then returning home only to erupt into a violent screaming match. "Where did this couple's Christian principles go?" a mustachioed member of the "Governing Body" queried judgmentally from his podium.

It was unbearable. Stella pushed past Adam towards the door. "I was going to give you one more day, talk things through, but this is too much," she said.

"Dear, please," Adam pleaded with outstretched arms. "Where are you going?"

"I don't know!"

She barreled through the door and stuffed her luggage into the car. The godforsaken music of the religious propaganda still played from the laptop. "Satan will do anything to divide us from our mates, but we must resist these sinful and selfish urges..."

She slumped into the driver's seat. Adam clung to the car door. His skin was sallow and his green eyes appeared dishwater gray.

He seemed to have admitted defeat save one last meager salvo. "Stella, do not forget you are my wife."

* * * * *

Stella's hands jittered wildly. They were slick with sweat and she could barely maintain her grip on the steering wheel. Typhoon season had yielded a terrible storm with water nearly up to her car door as she rounded the corkscrew curves of the cliff. But soon, an army-green airport came into sight, perched like Mecca on the top of the mountain. She parked her car outside the Departures terminal.

"What the hell am I doing?" She flopped onto the wheel. The ferocity of her frustration had brought her this far but without a plan, her pragmatism anchored her like an albatross. How could she leave everything behind? She still believed some of the slow drip doomsaying of the organization and her mother would be horrified.

Still, she had to take her chances. With a burst of confidence, she tucked the car keys under the floor mat and grabbed her bags. She would text Adam once she boarded the plane.

She called Marlene and it went straight to voicemail, but the airport was small and she was determined to find her. There were only a few flights a week to Los Angeles. Her heart thumped with a military cadence as she marched through the sliding doors of the terminal. She wiped the rain from her forehead and tried to tame her wild Sicilian waves. The stiffness of the air conditioning chilled her feverish brow. Would she find Marlene? What would she say?

"All passengers on United Airlines flight six departing for Los Angeles, please proceed to gate 5B," rang out a voice on the PA.

Stella hurried towards the ticket counter. There was a long line. She wouldn't make it in time. Her body started to shake. Chills again. *Fuck it.* She rushed up to the desk.

"Hi, can you help me?" Stella asked, wallet in hand.

"Ma'am, there's a line," replied a stern Japanese man in a heavily starched uniform.

"I know. I'm sorry, but this is an emergency."

"What is your emergency?"

"I don't have a ticket but I need to get on that Los Angeles flight," she said, panicking as she went to pull out her missing credit card. Had Adam taken it?

"That's not an emergency. There are other passengers ahead of you. Please go to the back of the line and I will attend to you when it's your turn."

"It's her turn," spoke up a woman from behind.

Stella's head swiveled so fast it appeared to be on a crank. "Marlene!" she blustered, taking in her confident countenance and immaculate figure.

"Sir," Marlene started with a hand pressed on her hip, drawing a crisp line between her Burberry trench and her svelte black jeans. "This woman is in need of a ticket ASAP. She's with me and I am a priority passenger. Would you be so kind as to help her?" Marlene cocked her head and smiled contemptuously.

The agent rolled his eyes. "Ladies, I simply cannot do that. You should have purchased a ticket long ago. Now if you'll move aside, I need to attend to this line of *ticketed* passengers."

"It's an emergency!" Marlene pounded on the counter. "This woman is escaping a cult!"

Stella gulped with embarrassment. A murmur rippled through the crowd.

Marlene leaned towards the ticket agent. "We must get her out of here this instant," she said in a quiet command, sliding her ticket across the counter. "Seat her next to me in first class."

The middle-aged man scowled and began peevishly clacking on the yellowed keys of his terminal.

"How much is first class?" Stella whispered into her ear.

"We will handle that later," Marlene said, handing her credit card to the agent who produced a one-way ticket from paradise.

"Thank you. I promise to pay you back as soon as I can."

"We've got a flight to catch. Let's go!" Marlene said as she began marching towards security. She strode with a proprietary air, her long limbs moving too rapidly for Stella to maintain the pace. Marlene possessed the crowded corridor like it was her catwalk, passersby scrunching their shoulders and angling inwards to make themselves smaller at her thunderous approach. Very quickly Stella found herself walking taller too.

They shimmied through the gate just in time for the aircraft door to slam shut behind them like a vault sealing Stella's fate.

As soon as the plane lifted off, Stella felt the gravity of her chaotic coup and began retching explosively into a too-tiny paper bag.

"I'm so sorry," she said, covering her mouth, her palate sickened and sour.

Marlene took pity and ushered her to the lavatory to clean up.

"Here, this will help." She handed Stella a little white pill.

"What is it?" The top notes of Marlene's floral perfume were comforting.

"Something to calm you down. We've got 14 hours of flying."

Within the hour, Stella slept like a baby, covered by Marlene in a fuzzy airline blanket in the oxford blue of her first class seat.

Stella eventually woke with a gasp, her mind in a Mayday tailspin. Notifications had piled up on her phone. Adam. Mom. Brother. Adam again. Ten missed calls, including elders from the Guam congregation. In an instant, the bubble of bliss inflating around her popped and in place of euphoria was dread.

Fuck! She didn't want to read the messages. She knew what they wanted from her—a return to her position as a selfless automaton in service of everyone but herself. She had anticipated it. But it wasn't like she Jerry Maguire'd her exit and made a scene. All the fish were still in their tanks. She hadn't insisted that Adam go with her. She slipped out the back door quietly, so why wouldn't they leave her alone? Why did they insist on using the force of family guilt and community obligation? Wasn't the fear of being destroyed by God enough?

Why? Because it fucking worked. All the messages were calculated to the same ratio of anxious vexation and guilt-tripping. Adam must've told his family she left because the messages graduated from the calm concern of her family to the hail and brimstone of her in-laws.

"Remember Jehovah sees evrything we do stella." Read a text from her semi-literate mother-in-law. "Turning your back on HIM leeds to no blessings. Hate what is bad. Do not make a fool of yourself as a pawn of the Devil in this system of things. You belong to him and to your hubsand."

The average education of Adam's family was 10th grade and the substitution of Bible reading for formal schooling did them no intellectual or linguistic favors. When the messages went unreplied for hours, they got nastier, the most savage of which came from Adam's brother and made Stella wonder if she was in real danger.

CHAPTER 4

Hollyweird

STELLA WAS WRECKED from the impromptu island exodus, the 24 hours of travel, and from guilt, but the sight of towering palms infused her with hope. It was her first time in Los Angeles. Of all her travels, the glitzy, throbbing metropolis had never been on her radar, but now it seemed like the Promised Land.

The American Dream, she thought as the taxi rolled down Sunset Boulevard. Hollywood, with all its pushers and pedophiles, had been maligned in the organization as the ultimate wasteland of sin. It was an easy target. But Stella was on a fact-finding odyssey now, sure there were many things she had been lied to about, such as the teaching that only Witnesses could be trusted or that "worldly people" only looked out for themselves. Marlene's strong grip, generously pulling her out of the rubble of her martyrdom, proved otherwise.

From what she could see on Instagram, Marlene lived quite normally, save for opulent nights at the opera or an occasional cliffside martini in Malibu, so when they pulled into a long driveway and up to a red-roofed Mediterranean villa—a mansion by all standards of wealth—Stella could not be sure if her jaw dropped literally or only in her mind.

She climbed out of the car like a wide-eyed Beverly Hillbilly. "Wow. Your house is gorgeous."

"I'll never get over the charm of this place. It's got those 1920s bones with that 2020 Botox!" said Marlene, unlocking an intricately carved mahogany door.

She ushered Stella into a cavernous room with grand ceilings. "You've had a wild ride, child. Just rest." She pointed to a hallway—one of several—forking off from the living area. "Your room is three doors down to the right."

* * * * *

"Stella, dear!" beckoned Marlene through the bedroom door the next morning. "Houseboy is serving espressos in the garden. You must join me and experience this effervescent day," she sang brightly.

"Yes, coming!" Stella yelled, struggling to disguise her scratchy throat. She washed her face, dotted concealer under her eyes, and scrambled outside to join Marlene.

The garden was a stone's throw past a brilliant blue pool. Stella hopped across the cold pavers to find Marlene perched elegantly atop a plush settee. Her hair was in loose red waves, a little messy from bed and she wore a sable fur coat over the thin film of a dusty rose negligee.

"It's a Byzantine dream, isn't it?" Marlene said, patting a pouf next to her and inviting Stella to sit.

"It's incredible."

The square garden was oriented around a trickling Moroccan tile fountain. Shimmering gold pots hung from a lattice which cast diamonds on Marlene's clean-scrubbed face.

Stella sat and shivered, attempting to rub warmth into her arms.

"Stella, where is your coat?"

"I fled from a tropical island with two suitcases, remember?"

Marlene leaned over to light a small clay hearth. "Yes, and no credit card. I believe you just might be a grifter. What a specimen that would have been to add to my collection of curious anecdotes. 'Let me tell you about the Christian con artist. I met her on an island, this cocktail of streetwise shrewdness, garnished with cult naivete.'" Marlene seemed to lean into the arc of Stella's swindle with the sweet salivation of a true raconteur. "What a con it would have been—straight up, with a twist."

"No, seriously. I will pay you back. Just give me your Venmo."

"I don't have Venmo."

"OK, PayPal?"

"No PayPal either. I'm positively analog. But don't you worry, I'll think of a way for you to pay me back." She tossed Stella a blanket. "Here, warm yourself up."

"This is so cozy." Stella's eyes wandered along the cascading ferns and colored glass of the lamps overhead.

"I just love the birds in the morning." Marlene pointed to a green-breasted hummingbird hovering over a pink hibiscus. "We are lucky to be alive. Life is such a gift," she said, clutching her chest. "I cry more often from gratitude than pain."

Stella's grief at the state of her health was temporarily paused as she examined the bird's iridescent breast. "Why do birds seem so cheerful? Surely it's just our humanization of them. Perhaps cheer is not their dominant emotion at all. Perhaps they are all quite serious despite their cute little bodies and chirpy songs. Maybe if they could talk, they'd all be George Costanzas or Anderson Coopers."

"You must be in a bit of a shock."

"I just hope I made the right decision," Stella said with a heavy sigh. "There's no going back now. And I'm dreading talking to my mom. She's probably devastated."

Marlene smiled empathetically. Then with the swiftness of a thespian changing masks, she grabbed a glass bell and rang it with such ferocity Stella thought it might shatter.

"Houseboy! Get your ass over here with our espressos *now!*"

The rattle of porcelain cups on metal announced his presence before he could exclaim something incoherent that resembled, "Yes, Mistress!" from near the house. Opera poured out from the speakers and, as if to signal that Nick had arrived at Gatsby's, in walked a man in a tuxedo.

"So, he lives with you?" Stella asked with a furrowed brow.

"Where is the anise and walnut biscotti? You only bought almond?" Marlene grabbed the metal O-ring on his leather collar and yanked him so hard he nearly dropped the silver tray he was holding.

"It's fine, Marlene. I can eat almond," Stella said, attempting to rescue the man from violent retribution.

Marlene silenced her with a raised finger. "No, he needs to learn," she said sternly, taking his cheeks between her fingers. "Look around. Observe how privileged you are. Now show it!"

"Yeth, Mithtreth," he mumbled through a ball gag, saliva dripping down the plastic sphere. With near-epileptic tremors, the pudgy thirtysomething placed two espresso cups on the table.

"My handmaiden Hope is so much better at this kind of elevated tray service. But maybe one day he'll learn." The insult was meant to land on Houseboy, who was still within earshot before he scuttled off like a cartoon mouse in the direction of the house.

Draining the last drop of her espresso, Marlene stood and beckoned Stella down the path. "The pool is heated. Let's swim."

Stella followed silently behind.

Marlene lowered herself into the steamy sapphire water. The silk slip clung to her chest and flowed out from her waist as she sliced through the water like a swan.

Stella slid onto a thickly padded lounge chair and remained motionless for several minutes, her gaze bordering on catatonic.

"You OK?" Marlene asked, twirling around to face the entranced woman.

"I think I *was* in a cult," Stella whispered absently, her eyes dilated in disbelief. She had been ruminating on Marlene's words for 48 hours now and the truth of it was as hard to bear as it was to refute.

"I know you were."

"I couldn't bring myself to call it that before, but where else could this violence come from?"

"Violence?"

"My brother-in-law texted the most awful things." Stella picked up her phone and squinted into the screen. "He called me a bitch, a cunt, a hag, and told me I will be destroyed at Armageddon."

"Report that shit," Marlene said in stoic seriousness.

Stella tried to shake off the tsunami of self-doubt shuddering through her body. "He meant to scare me, to play on all the fear the cult stokes in every sermon. So much for agapé love. What a hypocrite. Why can't they just leave me alone?"

"Yes, girl. Get it out. I'll say it with you, 'Leave me the fuck alone!'"

Stella smiled reticently.

"No, I mean it," Marlene implored her even more earnestly. "Say it out loud. Again and again until you've exorcized this demon."

Stella craned her neck toward the house to ascertain whether Houseboy was nearby.

"Don't worry about him!" Marlene snapped. "I'm so fucking angry! Leave me the fuck alone!" she chanted once more.

Stella cleared her throat. "Uh, OK… Leave me the fuck alone."

Marlene pounded her wet fists against the lip of the pool. "Louder! Leave me the fuck alone!"

Stella stood and tilted her head skyward like a crow, belting into the whooshing palms: "Leave me the *fuck* alone!"

Noticing Houseboy's frightened expression in her periphery, Stella collapsed into a ball of laughter on the chair.

"Houseboy, bring us martinis," Marlene said in an authoritative bidding, transforming abruptly once more into an unforgiving Dominatrix.

He jumped at the command, seemingly at near-collapse from the demands of service or was it the fear of punishment? He returned in a matter of minutes with two chilled glasses.

"Want anything else, dear? Cucumber water? Inflatable swan?" Marlene asked with sweet sarcasm.

"A tiger on a gold leash," Stella joked.

"Yes! Hedonists unite!" Marlene moved to the edge of the pool to clink glasses with Stella.

Stella sank deeper into the lounger and took a sip. "I've never had a martini." She smacked her lips comically. "Mmm. Good."

The glitter of the sun on the Moroccan pool tiles bounced off Marlene's glass like a beacon. "You know what I love about you, Stella?" she said, resting her chin on her hand adoringly.

"No. What?"

"You look so worldly, but you are so fresh off the boat, an ingénue, a freshman!"

"It's true," Stella chuckled. "And it's funny you use that word. 'Worldly' is one of those judgmental terms the Witnesses use to describe every person outside the religion. Quite the opposite of a compliment."

"Shake it off, darling! You've escaped the compound. You're a real-life Kimmy Schmidt!"

"Yep. Bunker days are behind me. I hope…" Stella's tone once again lost its confident timber.

"You hope?"

"I'm scared and excited and... so curious about this *slutler* situation," she said, not wanting to wade into discussions of self-doubt. "I can't believe you don't have sex with him and he is motivated to serve you like this." Stella leaned forward in unabashed awe.

Marlene welcomed all of Stella's innocent interrogatives, peeling off the layers of her peculiar life like gossamer stockings catching the light in a bawdy striptease. She laughed and increased the volume of the Puccini.

"Mustn't let him hear us and get a big head," Marlene said as she climbed out of the pool, her petite breasts glistening under the sheerness of the negligee. She rained down on Stella as she toweled off at her feet.

She turned away from Stella and removed the dress, revealing her callipygian back. She wore blush lace panties and no top. She lowered herself to a chair as delicately as if she were a fine masterpiece being placed on display in the Louvre.

"You don't mind?" Marlene asked, gesturing to her chest. "I loathe tan lines."

"Um, no." And Stella didn't. She had never seen a woman naked up close in her adult years. Marlene was ravishing. As lithe and muscular as Stella wished to be. Not a trace of cellulite, no wrinkles, and certainly no acne.

"Houseboy has been serving me for a year now. Oh, the tests I've put him through to earn this kind of intimate devotion. He's come a long way. He didn't even own a suit! I've smartened him up immeasurably."

"I still don't get it. What motivates him if not sex?" Stella asked, pretending not to let her eyes wander to the succulent rubber of Marlene's thick nipples.

"He has the heart of a sub. He lives for this. To serve in such a fabulous tableau, who wouldn't jump at the opportunity?" she said, raising her glass.

"And he's not like… your boyfriend?" Stella wanted so badly to suck Marlene's tits.

"God, no."

Marlene detailed how she had found Houseboy on a site called Fet Play. "Fet" like "fetish" she explained to her green new companion, this bewildered refugee from paradise.

The persona Houseboy presented to the world was one of *Leave It to Beaver* though he harbored the willing heart of a loyal whore. He craved humiliation and Marlene had earned his devotion with equal parts cruelty and care.

"If this is his fantasy, why isn't he paying you?" Stella asked. "Why isn't this your profession?"

"It's been my lifestyle, but it's clear that I'm on this path for a purpose; that you and I met for a reason. We have so much to teach one another."

"What could I teach you?"

"You're quite an accomplished filmmaker. I watched your documentary about Guam. Very well done. All your media is on point. And now you should be served. Imagine us living in a Domme chateau with our stable of submissives, cruising around in green Jags, and being milk-bathed on the nightly." Marlene had the most decadent way of painting a scene. With rich tones, she inked a fantastical canvas that inspired Stella's salivation.

"Aren't you already living the dream?"

"This is a villa, darling," Marlene corrected haughtily. "I'm talking a European chateau."

"But how could we—how could I—have any of that?"

"I can teach you."

Stella's eyes lit up. "Where does a Baby Domme start?"

"Self-exploration. Naming your desires and limits. Testing them," Marlene rattled off like a professor of perversion. One could envision the clipboard in her hand. The list of boxes to check. Her hair in a porno updo. White lab coat. Leather heels. Pushing up the specs on her nose.

"What kind of limits?"

"Sexual, spiritual, psychological. Continual examination is key. It's crucial that you spend the lion's share of your efforts identifying your own intersections."

It all sounded so heady, so lengthy a process. Stella impatiently craved a more immediate grab. "What if we started a domination business together? You're so good at it. Why stop at lifestyle domming? In fact, you could teach me to domme and I could help you go pro!" she exclaimed, her tone full of pitch and persuasion.

"I've been thinking about this very thing since we first met. How magnetized our constitutions, pushing into one another's shortcomings and drawing out one another's strengths."

Marlene related that she had quickly observed how Stella let shine her inner Miranda Priestly. Her penchant for spreadsheets and networking made it easy to envision her coiffed and taking calls in a corner office, a steaming latte on a glass table top with white orchids on the windowsill.

"I've built several brands," Stella bragged excitedly. "I could run the media, finances, basically be the back of house. You could focus on the clients. Not that you need the money. You're already doing so well, but Adam really took me for a ride at the end. I lost a lot of my savings."

"How much is left?"

"Um, not as much as you have obviously," she said, gesturing to the palatial surroundings. "I feel so behind. Wasted my life serving others."

Marlene lowered her sunglasses and kept her eyes locked on Stella.

"Oh, you want an exact number?" Stella replied under the laser focus of Marlene's stare. "I have enough to pay you some rent if that's what you're asking."

"No, no. I'm not asking for rent money. Nevermind," Marlene said, waving her hand dismissively. She seemed disappointed at the lack of precise glimpse into Stella's finances, but she did not press for more.

Her tone transforming to that of a giddy teenager, she sang: "Let's talk about this invitation I got for a clandestine sex party in the Hills..."

CHAPTER 5

Cupid Club

WHEN MARLENE FIRST SUGGESTED the costumed ball of an exclusive sex club for which one had to be approved, the discussion quickly led to the question of anonymity.

"Should we wear masks?" Stella queried as she uploaded full body sex-pot photos—directed by Marlene and the first she had ever taken—to her application.

"I probably will, though I doubt I'll fuck anyone," Marlene replied.

Since then, Stella had been swirling with anticipation. Now the night was finally here and the hours passed like a slow-motion drip from the kitchen faucet. The hair-trigger nerves of her excitement misfired into copious layers of eyeshadow shellacked beneath her brows. In her signature experimental spirit, Stella had attempted a kind of 11th-hour *trompe l'oeil* of cosmetology and created a mask using only makeup and face jewels.

"I look like a deranged drag queen," Stella said defeatedly, glancing up from a magnifying mirror as Marlene walked into her bedroom.

"This is what your makeup is supposed to look like *after* you fuck a bunch of strangers," Marlene jested. Stella whimper-laughed, not one to deny her companion the satisfaction of a good sex joke even at her expense.

"Aw, I'm only kidding. Let me see." Marlene leaned in close, taking in the gradation of glitter around Stella's eye like a sort of psychedelic sand painting. "It's alright. We'll fix it," she reassured. "Your hair looks amazing and so do your tits."

With the help of an expensive stylist, she had transformed her frizzy brown hair into a silky black bob with Bettie Page bangs, an alter ego she had been fantasizing about for years.

Stella had an itchy Amazon finger, as evidenced by the ensemble she wore—a feathered collar, a flirty black skirt, embellished fishnets, and the cascade of her luscious décolletage cradled by the underwire of a lacy D-cup bra. With the body of a Sicilian goddess, all olive skin and bronze, it didn't matter much what Stella wore. She could wear a burlap sack à la Monroe and still be ravishing. What she couldn't do was make a mask out of Maybelline.

"It's all the glitter under your eye. It's way too Mad Tea Party."

Stella thousand-mile stared into the mirror, overwhelmed by the task of schlepping the cross of obsessive beauty only to be crucified by the rusted nail of self-critique. It wasn't that she lacked aesthetic sensibility. It was her inexperience playing the sex card in any theatrical game that threw her off balance.

Her breasts were pushed up to full plumposity, defying as much gravity as possible. Her waist was snatched and accentuated against her wide hips and full thighs. This hourglass silhouette had been her presentation since puberty, though many an elder's wife had accused her of leading good men towards bad thoughts.

Marlene looked up to read the doubtful curve of Stella's back like a movie house marquee—*Now Playing: Lady Sings the Blues.*

"It's not that bad, and I'm probably not even going to wear my mask," she reassured. "Just wing this line and get rid of all this underneath." She thumbed a bit at the corner of Stella's eye and smiled. "We used to call glitter 'the herpes of the circus.' Everyone was covered and there wasn't any cure. But it's going to be dark, and with your feathers up on your shoulders—Yes! Fierce!" She snapped her fingers in machine gun punctuation.

With this bit of direction, Stella straightened her spine. *Fuck the elders' wives.* She pulled the bra down revealing an inch more of cleavage. *Fuck them all.*

Her predicament improved, Stella turned to take inventory of Marlene's editorial and admire her elongated figure.

"You look like you're heading to battle on the Death Star!" she praised.

Marlene was a warrior goddess, all ox bone and pelts of white fur, her skirt in car wash strips of calfskin. Stella's eyes lingered a beat longer at a leather bolero, cropped at the rib cage and hanging open at the chest. Marlene's abdomen was pulled taut as if by the ribbons of a corset. A cascade of auburn hair fountained from the top of her head through an embossed bracelet she fashioned as a crown.

"Going to battle with Gonorrhea!" she quipped through a burst of inelegant laughter.

"What about toys?" Stella asked, holding up a bullet vibrator.

"I might bring my strap-on."

"To fuck a man or a woman?"

"Either. Both. The point is that I'll likely be the only woman serving hard cock." Marlene held up a stiff silicone dildo.

Stella switched on the silver vibrator which buzzed pathetically. "It's too weak. I'm addicted to my Hitachi Magic Wand, thanks to you. I need an industrial-strength jackhammer to get off now. Imagine I bring a power strip to plug it in."

"And blow out the whole party!"

"Now that's a story. They'll never forget us. Dildo Domme and the Circuit Breaking Circus." Stella performed a little mouth trumpet of the Big Top theme.

With this, they launched another raucous tit for tat of punch lines. Was this real life—suiting up for a sexcapade? *If my mother only knew.*

All the while, Houseboy had been holding his post outside. The black BMW fired up as soon as the women pushed through the front door and into the shock of the chilly December air.

"Hello?" Stella said with a quizzical expression as Houseboy exited the car and dutifully zipped around to open the door. He wore a chauffeur's cap and pressed navy blazer. A bubblegum pink skirt punctuated the ensemble with a curious question mark. He kept a white rose clenched in his teeth and his knees sheepishly bent in futile attempts to lend imaginary inches to the backside-bearing skirt.

"Show us your little secret," Marlene commanded as soon as they were settled in the vehicle. Houseboy pulled up his skirt.

Stella grabbed the headrest to crane a closer look. "What is that on his dick?"

"It's a cock cage. I'm his keyholder," Marlene explained, holding up a small silver key. In her other hand, she held a bottle of Dom Perignon.

"Champagne?"

"Of course," Stella agreed, watching Marlene's leather stiletto bob. She snuck a lustful peek at her muscular calf, running her eyes up to Marlene's chest again, hoping to catch even a momentary glimpse of nipple.

She turned her attention back to Houseboy's curious accouterment. "And what is a cock cage exactly?"

"It keeps the little bitch in check. Reminds him he's in service to me."

Stella flinched at the abusive choice of words. "Does it hurt? Isn't he cold?"

"Oh, he enjoys the discomfort. Plus, it keeps him from getting too excited, if you know what I mean. Try. See if you can get him going."

Stella pushed her face up to Houseboy's ear and exhaled dramatically. "Do you like being locked up, little slut?"

"Yes, Mistress."

Houseboy's face betrayed none of the tremors within his cage. Stella turned to Marlene and crinkled her pinky to indicate the wee man was on the move.

She took a sip of champagne and cracked her window a few inches, resting her head on the door frame to let the cool night air blow the fringe of her bangs.

The car rolled down Sunset Boulevard past skyscraper palms, mid-century hotels, and larger-than-life billboards that made it a living museum. LA was like that—a never-ending homage to itself. Hollywood was *consumed* elsewhere but *cannibalized* by its own. It fed on the worship, a hungry hound of its own art, commerce, and flesh. It kept an eye to the past but a pelvis to the future.

Five or six sips of Dom and Stella was feeling tipsy. She was still a lightweight.

"Oh no. I don't want to get wasted," she said, refusing another pour from Marlene. "That hangover last weekend was rough."

"We will be drunk to the level of high-class effervescence and not a bubble beyond," said Marlene, sliding the bottle back into the bucket of ice.

"Not a bubble beyond." Stella nodded and pushed her glass towards Marlene.

As they neared the coordinates of the drop-off, both women grew more skeptical about their destination. Gravel crackled under the wheels like sizzling popcorn as they pulled around to face the dead end of a cul-de-sac. The buzz of street lamps cast a sullen glare on the innumerable derelict tents of LA's forgotten populace. Makeshift shanty towns lined the curbside in every direction like the set of some post-apocalyptic tale.

"This can't be it."

"This is it?"

They took turns wondering aloud.

"Should I call someone to check the address?" Houseboy offered.

His question went unanswered for several moments, as though the two were waiting for some portly, red-faced director to shout down the tube of his amplified bullhorn, "Cut! Cut! It's all wrong! Fire the props master! Cue the horse-drawn carriage!"

Marlene seemed to write it off as part of the adventure. Having chased good stories down the backroads of the world, she was never slow to add a page to the anthology. Neither of these women were strangers to that sweet spot of danger, coated thickly by the sour pucker of fear.

"Stop. This will do," Marlene instructed.

Their heels hit the pavement like hooves. Stella had taken the advice to wear her new thigh-high boots and in true *Pretty Woman* fashion, they were doing their diligence, these few miles from the Walk of Fame. There was no one in sight. Not even the residents of the encampment. Nothing but the rustling of tarp and the distant brutal hack of a smoker's cough to counter the percussive foley of their heels on the asphalt.

They spent 10 long minutes shivering on the sidewalk like undulating cups of tapioca before the shuttle rolled up to collect them. They gratefully piled into the first row to sit and wait as the shuttle filled with guests.

"Dear Yelp," Stella began, raising her fingers to type at an invisible keyboard and assume what Marlene referred to as "The Announcer Voice," a cadence and delivery of speech central to her sense of humor. "Of all the sex orgy shuttles I've had occasion to ride in, this was, by far, the most lacking in ambient décor."

Marlene perked up, a willing audience to Stella's impromptu sketch comedy routines. She had a true talent for smash-cut voiceover delivery, especially when it came to the absurdity of life.

"You know," began Marlene, smiling. "It's my personal mission to coax into the spotlight that inelegant clown you've had locked away as part of your programming in the cult."

"I love it. We're going to stay together, right?" Stella asked, contemplating just how a room full of sexy strangers might amplify their nascent attraction. "What if we get totally into it?" Her tone was a delicate soufflé of rabid curiosity and dramatic foreboding. "What if we fall down the rabbit hole and can't find each other?"

Marlene didn't answer immediately. Instead, she reached for one of Stella's feathers, pensively twisting the plume between the pads of her fingers, dragging a fingernail up Stella's neck. Pushing back a lock of Stella's hair, she whisper-sang into her ear: "One pill makes you larger and one pill makes you small."

A rush of warm exhilaration spread through Stella's abdomen. It was as though a tiny Wonderland tea cake slid sweetly down her throat. She could almost feel herself double in size.

Marlene spoke the final words directly into Stella's ear: "Go ask Alice, when she's 10 feet tall… Anyway, I didn't bring my strap-on, so I won't be fucking anyone." She winked at the driver, who had been eyeing them curiously in the large mirror. "But you, little one"—she crab-clawed at Stella's knee—"you've never been to something like this. You might end up spread-eagle from the chandelier!"

Stella laughed. At this point in her life, she was willing to entertain the very real possibility of sexual folly.

It was then that a burst of laughter came from some distance behind the van and, like a pulse of high femme sonar, the unmistakable sound of pumps on pavement echoed in both of their ears. Stella craned her neck around the sliding door to see two similarly clad figures. One of the women wore a powder pink fur coat and a thick cat collar with the word "Slut" bedazzled in rhinestones. Her long, straight black hair was parted down the middle in a "hey, batter" swing at the aesthetic of any number of Kardashians. The other, a pipsqueak of a girl, donned something more in the vein of Party City police whore, her breasts spilling out of a plunging, skin-tight "boys in blue" bodysuit. The nylon threads of her fishnets sliced into the toned flesh of her thighs.

Upon coming into focus of one another, an air of kindred immediacy imbued the exchange.

"Cupid Club?" Stella leaned across Marlene's lap, soliciting the approaching girls to quicken their pace.

"Cupid Club!" the two confirmed, clearly a few too many cocktails in, perhaps among other things.

"Oh my gawd, I love your feathers!" The pipsqueak clumsily reached to paw at Stella's collar. Marlene leaned back in reserved amusement, making space for the gesture to pass her without contact. The pipsqueak's breath was rank with tequila and an overabundance of unblended highlighter made virtual tire tracks across the bones of her cheeks.

"You girls are fire," Kitty Collar gleamed, far more composed than her friend.

Stella's pulse quickened at the wrist. So new was she to her sapphic explorations, such attention from the feminine kind raised her temperature a few hundred degrees.

As the pair sauntered down the aisle, the van filled with a saccharine cloud of bubble gum perfume. Stella felt Marlene's eye roll revving up as she brought the corner of her collar up to her face, deeply inhaling the scent of Egyptian lotus and myrrh that lingered in the downy white fur. In contrast to the building squall of Stella's excitement, the drawbridge of Marlene's libido began clicking closed. *Tic, tic, tic. Nothing today, thank you.*

With each hairpin turn up the steep hills, Stella's excitement intensified. Upon arrival at a great house, they were instructed to an entrance cloistered from street view. Tequila Caboose clopped noisily behind them until the party location revealed itself cinematically—a four-story Tudor mansion resembling a medieval castle, moat and all. It was a true Hollywood hyperbole.

"Alright, fallen woman. Follow me," Marlene said, taking Stella's hand and leading her into the house.

They stepped into a dim room and at the end of a long hallway glowed a giant pair of female eyes in red-light district neon; creepy and compelling;

nefarious and severe; a prelude marker to the great room. The home was cavernous and resplendent with no shortage of gothic décor. It was as though Kubrick himself had a hand in the dramaturgy. *Eyes Wide Shut* in final say.

"This is amazing," said Stella, spinning on her heels. "I feel like I'm on a movie set."

Wandering the halls of a house like that, it was hard to imagine anything other than orgies happening there. This sprawling estate at the foot of the Hollywood sign with its plush crimson carpets and spiraling stairs. If stone masonry could talk, perhaps it'd whisper of the occasional ritual sacrifice. Rumor had it Katy Perry shot a video there, with all the Illuminati fodder such things implied.

Stella and Marlene entered a sunken living area with an alcove to the left. In one of two Louis XVI chairs sat a man. A statuesque woman in lingerie reclined languid on the floor pressing her cheek to his knee. Another woman, naked, equally tanned and toned, rode his cock in reverse, her feet on the floor, her body bent forward. Her hard silicone breasts bounced as if programmed with a trick of CGI. The motion was animatronic in its expression. It was a staged scene, a planned vignette to get the party going. Three pairs of eyes trained on Stella and Marlene as they passed.

The DJ in the corner, looking every bit the West LA waif, could have been mistaken for any brunch-hour patron at the Chateau Marmont. Her flat-ironed hair, chopped just so, framed the jutting cheekbones of her face as she clutched a headphone to one ear and dropped another industrial track. The whole scene was *Texas Chainsaw* by way of King Arthur's Court.

Stella scanned the crowd. Most of the women were in revealing costumes or lingerie. Most of the men fully clothed in tuxedos.

"Hmm. Predictable aesthetics," Marlene appraised.

"You don't like it? I think it's fabulous."

"Heteronormative. Mostly white," Marlene deadpanned.

"But you can't deny the pulse of the room," Stella insisted.

Marlene nodded begrudgingly. "The guests are homogenous but not unattractive. Oh, well. This experience will be good theater for you. I'll enjoy being a voyeur while you quench your thirst for exhibition, my little Doberman. It's the perfect opportunity to watch this Pinscher run."

They climbed a spiral staircase to the second floor of the mezzanine. A wrought iron balcony wrapped around the room. For a moment they parted company. Stella moved to the opposite side, glancing often to Marlene through the aubergine light. They shared a smirk at the many limbs and lips, a lascivious chorus that chimed in unison, 'Only orgies happen here.'

"Is this what most sex parties are like?" asked Stella a few minutes later between sips of the fresh cocktail Marlene chose for them.

"Eh. Nutrients come from other meats, other fruits," Marlene gestured with an elitist air.

The ratio of silicone breasts to natural was a landslide in favor of surgeons from Malibu to Los Feliz; every zip code in between raking in the autopay installments of this superficial slice of LA's young and perverse.

"I would make it more intimate. More queer. Less swinger," Marlene continued.

"I get it. This is the Carnival Cruise of Cunnilingus. The Wal-Mart of Wet Dreams."

Marlene chuckled but they were soon rapt with attention at a scene unfolding across the room. The women sauntered over to take a front-row seat at a medieval cage. Marlene reclined in a chair while Stella perched on the armrest.

A woman was on all fours, her head protruding from the cage, her neck and limbs locked in place by riveted metal clamps. Her aesthetic was Harajuku Lite. Her hair was in pigtails, secured by elastic "Love in Tokyo's." Her white thigh-high stockings, gartered and clipped into pink lace panties, pushed to the side.

A young Asian man in full coat and tails went about fingering Harajuku from behind, teasing and testing her with the sting of a leather crop. Aside from the mask and his erect penis, jutting eagerly from his unzipped crotch like Pinocchio's nose, he appeared to be on his way to the opera. He was so stately and starched he could have been fresh off a private jet from Kyoto. Perhaps she traveled this way in the belly of the plane like his prized Pomeranian, freshly groomed in her kennel, panting for her treats.

From this angle, they could watch the man's fingers kneading the sticky folds of the caged woman's cunt. Stella exhaled deeply.

"You know my favorite sex position?" Marlene asked, breathing the question into Stella's feathers.

"What?" Stella turned to look at her, their faces inches apart. Her vulva throbbed. She hoped they would kiss, though she found Marlene as hard to read as a foreign manuscript.

"Calling shots from the corner in floor-length Givenchy," Marlene teased.

Harajuku's body arched to its limit within the confines of the cage, her face thrown back as far as the collar allowed, the red light overhead baking her cheeks tropical. Her lips parted with a sharp intake of breath and quivered as her body contracted. Her eyes shut tight and her furrowed brow broke with the glow of fresh sweat. Just as the wave of sensation crested, the man thrust his fingers farther inside her, sucking her back down into the trough and up again to crash into the tides of ecstasy.

He moved to stand before her and exert his ownership with violent thrusts of his cock into her mouth, instructing her to hold out her tongue. The man let out a guttural growl as she sucked each drop of his cum down her throat, her lips airtight as a wet vac hose.

"How I would turn the tables on him," said Marlene. "Fuck his face till that foolish mask slid off. Twist that bowtie enough to cut off a bit of air. I love to bring an alpha to submission. I'd love to see this one belly up and begging."

Marlene's macho sneer excited Stella, stirring up her feminist urge to do the same to a man one day.

Reaching into her satchel, Marlene retrieved a hank of rope. Taking Stella's hand, she ran the folded bite against Stella's palm. It was a welcome surprise.

Marlene smiled. "It's time to bring some femdom energy to this party. Care to join me?"

Stella pumped her eyebrows.

They moved from the alcove to the sunken living room. Marlene pulled up a chair and motioned for Stella to sit.

"Wait," said Stella, who began removing her feather collar, then her bustier. She sat in only her bra and skirt and shot Marlene a knowing smile.

Marlene circled her sensually, dipping her hips at each step. She traced her finger across Stella's cheek, along the curve of her shoulders, and across her abdomen. Stella shuddered.

The strum of an invisible Spanish guitar and the mounting beat of a leather drum appeared to ring through Marlene's heart. She pushed Stella's hair to one side, leaned in hungrily, then let the rope graze Stella's chest as she let out a long, slow breath. Unbeknownst to her, Marlene's breasts were exposed. Her nipples punctuated like little jarhead soldiers as the thick leather of her bolero betrayed her ever so slightly.

Hot, Stella thought. They were in a dance. Maestro and maven. No one else mattered.

Marlene pulled Stella's arms together and coiled the rope around her. She moved like a lynx, stoking the sexual squall in the room. A circle formed. The worldly watchers among them seemed to feel the *duende* rising.

Stella's shoulders sank. She was surprised how her body bent within Marlene's grip, the twisted jute, the pull of her gravity. Her mind was at ease, supple like butter at a blade's edge.

Marlene began moving faster and tying Stella's entire abdomen with greater confidence and flair. At each advance of the mercury, ticking ever upward, Marlene was a master of restraint. Push and pull. A little more. A little less. Stella felt the flame of their connection ricochet through her body and manifest as thousands of tiny bumps quivering on the hoarfrost of her arm. She could hear her own heartbeat in the time Marlene kept with her feet, her fingers holding phantom castanets that vibrated with each sweep of her arms. The rope dug pleasurably into Stella's nipples, the constricting hemp forcing the spillage of her breasts up and out.

Marlene finished the tie and presented her bound subject to the admiring audience. Stella looked up from Marlene to the crowd, making eye contact with a standout among them, a dashing man in a military blue cape.

"How do you feel, darling?" Marlene whispered into Stella's ear as she took a bow.

"You're so sexy. I love how you handle me," Stella flirted. "And I *love* being the center of attention."

"I suspected you would."

Marlene started loosing Stella from the rope. She redressed. The magic show was over. The girl sawed in half was whole again, the rabbit put back in the hat.

Stella checked the time. 11:33 p.m. Her pulse quickened. The rope dance had only intensified her desire to press Marlene's body against hers. The climax of midnight and the dawn of a new year seemed the perfect moment to seize on her longing.

However, the well-suited stranger was still watching them. His gaze was fixed. He took detailed inventory of Marlene, obviously trying to decipher the exact nature of relation to her raven-haired companion. Soon, gallant strides carried his elegant body in their direction, his wool cape billowing behind him as he wove between the threesomes and moresomes fucking all around. He stopped beside Marlene like a leading man hitting his mark. His nostrils flared in agreement with the oud undertones of her perfume. He let a few luscious moments pass before he spoke.

"I had not expected to witness such a cunning baile tonight," he said in a whisper, leaning close to her shoulder. His crisp English accent lent a raised pinky to his praise.

Marlene shot him a skeptical side-eye at first, shifting away from his sudden presence. However, her momentary suspicion seemed to dissipate at the sight of his warm visage. His countenance invited depth. There was certainly a beacon in his expression and in the airbrush of his flawless brown skin and the thick of his cherubic curls, blessings of his African-Italian heritage.

"This party was lacking soul. Modulation. So, I did something about it," she replied coolly.

"I agree." He smiled wider. "A full breath. Ceremony."

Stella relished the chance to watch Marlene readily engage. So rapt were they in their little cinema of intrigue, Stella moved closer to see what it was all about. The man was aristocratic from the brass of his buttons to the tip of his Roman nose. A throwback and a futurist. Quite the dapper dandy.

"This isn't my typical crowd," he volunteered, confirming Stella's intuitions. It was the ascot and the buttoned spats on his Sevillano leather shoes that screamed: This curious bird doesn't fly in a chevron with any old gray-plumed flock. He was a Lilac Breasted Roller if ever a feather fit a cap.

"Tell us something of your crowd," Marlene invited, taking a sip from her martini.

"It begs a proper introduction," the dapper dandy propounded, flourishing an upturned palm and dipping his head in a deferential bow. "Cyril James, and you?"

"Marlene," she introduced. "And this is Stella."

"You take no prisoners," he said, brushing a knuckle along the edge of Marlene's fur collar and praising her image with a wave of his hand. "Red Sonya has arrived, darling." He was so flamboyant.

"And this, Bella Donna..." he continued, giving Stella's feathers a flirtatious little blow.

She couldn't pinpoint his exact sexual orientation. He was every bit the Merchant Ivory gentleman—fey and witty and sugar-dusted as a fairy—but was he actually gay? Either way, Stella wanted to know him. He was her kind of gentle giant with limbs as long and lean as any Greek monolith in the Louvre.

"You two are carved of precious stone," he laid on. "And those shoes..." He gestured to Marlene's feet.

His flattery was genuine, if engorged on theatrics. His eccentricities pulsed in a pitch only certain ears could hear.

Marlene responded to his compliment by retrieving the speared olive from her martini and running the drip of the brine along the plump of Stella's cleavage. Stella took the cue and pulled the olive from the pick with her teeth. Marlene was quick to bring her mouth up to fetch it from Stella's lips. The moment further stirred her desire. Marlene brought the olive to the dandy's lips in a *Mad Men* version of suck and blow. With the tip of her tongue, she pushed it forward, passing it to his pucker while simultaneously slipping off her shoe.

"This little piggy would like to play," she said, pointing to her foot and wiggling her toes.

Cyril beamed. His rows of gleaming teeth still clenched the olive. He flung off his cape, pulled straight the lapels of his emerald green waistcoat and dropped, without hesitation, to his knee. It was as if they'd rehearsed it.

Marlene looked deep into Stella's eyes as the dapper dandy placed the olive between her toes. She held it there as he licked along her arch and swirled his tongue at her ankle. She ran her fingers down Stella's arm in a furtive gesture, presenting Stella's hand. He kissed each knuckle and then Stella caressed his clean-shaven jaw. She stroked his bottom lip with her thumb and pressed it into his mouth where it parted, wet and receptive. She pulsed her thumb in and out of his mouth slowly while he sucked. The gesture was Domme-lite, but the spark of it ran readily from the core of Stella's dormant instincts. She smirked into Marlene's eyes, sensing that she too felt the thrill of a conduit running through them.

Cyril looked up to them with delight. He was no stranger to this altar.

Marlene extended her hand. With equal heft, both the women pulled him to his feet. He straightened his lapels in a swift "job well done" gesture and swung his cape over his shoulder to close the curtain. As if drawing breath into the same set of lungs, all three of them sharply inhaled before Cyril broke the spell with a word.

"Would you believe I run a 19th-century immersive theater?" he offered, as though the digression of foot worship had been just another part of the conversation.

"Actually, I would." Marlene laughed.

"Very spooky stuff," he added. "How often do you make your way to Paris? If I had my magic carpet I would whisk you both away right now. Put you on the VIP list. Or better yet... the stage!"

Stella checked the time again. Her leg jittered to the throb of the music. 11:59 p.m.

As if conversing with Stella's inner time bomb, the DJ announced the hour over the sound system. The lights flashed.

A leggy woman in an embroidered kimono ran up and grabbed the dandy's hand. "Cyril, darling, you promised! They're waiting. It's almost time."

Cyril sighed and let slip the slightest roll of his eyes. He reached into his pocket and produced an embossed business card.

"Open invitation to you both. Paris Catacombs. Anytime." With that, the woman pulled him up the spiral stairs.

The lights flashed again. The countdown to midnight began.

5, 4, 3, 2, 1... The room exploded in a chorus of cheering and applause. From the ceiling rained silver and gold confetti, a celestial shower.

A tremor formed in Stella's lip. The entire scene was anathema to her old beliefs. New Year's was so very pagan. The celebration of earthly pleasures was one thing, but here she was on a date with a woman, watching sport fucking in the burrows of every corner. The hedonism suited her. The bacchanalia felt surprisingly unforeign.

"Kiss me," Stella said, slamming down her drink and sliding closer to Marlene.

Marlene narrowed her eyes and held Stella's gaze. Though Stella's hands trembled, the natural command was there.

In the unfamiliar terrain of feminine seduction, Stella experienced a new vulnerability to rejection. Had she miscalculated Marlene's attraction? *Why is she so still?*

But then Marlene moved closer, their bodies radiating proximal heat.

It's finally happening, Stella thought. She pulled their torsos flush, their knees kissing in a separate embrace. Marlene swirled her finger between Stella's breasts. Stella responded by sliding her palm along the moon of Marlene's thigh. She let it rest there, squeezing the leather-covered flesh. Marlene ran her tongue along Stella's earlobe, then whispered, "Imagine commanding this entire room. In fact, this entire party."

CHAPTER 6

Mardi Gras

"IT IS STRANGE how at home I felt at Cupid Club," said Stella, watching Marlene touch up her hair in a wall of mirrors. A breeze blew through the french doors of the great room, billowing the gauzy curtains like the chiffon skirts of ballerinas in flight.

"That's because you're a pervert. Probably always have been," Marlene replied.

They'd spent every day together since they'd met—two full months—so Stella had become accustomed to this sartorial ritual. Marlene dressed rather plainly for her business meetings some four or five days a week. Her hair was always slicked back, lips inked red, as she inched the same black pencil skirt down her slender thighs.

"I suspect you are some kind of assassin," Stella joked. "You're so secretive about these appointments."

"I assure you if I was taking out some criminal kingpin, I'd tell you. And you—have you been looking for work?"

"I've managed to maintain a few of my media clients in Guam. Even the hotel forgave my abrupt exodus and keeps sending me work, but the big news is that I booked a tourism shoot in New Orleans."

The film reel Stella had been building for years had garnered the attention of a puckish travel media start-up and she was just the kind of plucky female director they'd love to hire.

"Wonderful. I've been longing to go there myself," said Marlene.

“Come! We can meet up after my project wraps.”

“Give me the dates and I’ll have Hope book it. But do think about where you’ll go after New Orleans.”

Marlene had begun dropping not-so-subtle hints about Stella finding a place of her own. Their post-isle honeymoon had been glorious—both a fantastic foray into a new world and a soothing balm to Stella’s guilt-glutted heart—but it was time for Stella to get on her feet.

Within the week, she scored an elegant studio in Koreatown. The block was the prettiest in the neighborhood with its Spanish Colonial Revival and Art Deco towers stacked like tiers of wedding cake. Her building was a love child of the two and she wasted no time outfitting it. The spacious single, replete with a bank of windows on the Hollywood sign, became a benchmark in her quest for *La Vie Bohème* and soon everywhere the eye fell, there were blushed or burnished jewel tones and images of Edwardian women in repose. She set out to reach the apex of hyper-feminine motifs in the cinematic gem. It was her little dream house—*une petite palais*—in the sky.

* * * * *

It was raining when Stella landed in New Orleans. She surprised herself by saying a short prayer as the wheels hit the tarmac. The visibility had been a cause for concern to the pilot and the turbulence bore that fact. But when her taxi pulled up to Sweetwater Wonderland, Stella smiled. The sight of the veranda called to her in a slow drawl. The rocking chairs and white columns wrote poems of pecan pie and petticoats. It was the kind of house that had kept secrets for eons. A sign above the doorbell read, “Ring twice if you fancy to be free.”

Mavis, the owner of Sweetwater Wonderland was nearing 90, a paper crane of a woman in her nightgown. Stella felt terrible to have woken her, but there was something otherworldly in her eyes that suggested the woman never slept. Perhaps she adjourned to the belly of a grandfather clock and was only animate when some caller in the night fancied freedom and rang twice at the door.

"Well, you've brought this on yourself," Mavis said, making eyes at Stella's suitcases. "Ain't no bellhops at Sweetwater, sugar. You'll have to lug those on your lonesome."

Stella followed the fishhook of the old woman's spine from the creaking hallway of the foyer to the base of a fairly grand stair.

She handed Stella a curvy brass key and regarded her intently through the cataract cloud of her eye. "Your room is the first on the left. We serve breakfast in the courtyard from 7 to 10. Any trifling after hours wakes the dead of Lafayette. I'll pity your soul should they come for you." She laughed to herself on this, the ten-thousandth recitation of that quip.

"Aren't you a fuzzy peach, just so, with your figure? Lord, what I'd tell you of my day. Would you agree that youth is wasted on the young?" she said, pinching for Stella's cheek with the gnarled-up vines of her fingers.

Where's Houseboy when you need him? Stella thought, lamenting each step with the weight of her baggage in tow. Three trips and one broken wheel later, she slid the blade of the key into the bolt of the door marked "Seventh Heaven."

Stella's shoot for the New Orleans tourism board would take her to all the hot spots in the city, from Café du Monde to Jackson Square. She filmed sleepy swamps and sprightly gardens and sprawling city parks and practically every street in the French Quarter, and yet she did not truly know the city until the end of her week in Nola.

As soon as she wrapped her shoot and said goodbye to her crew, it was time to hit up some parades and wander in her vagabond style. Mardi Gras was just heating up and Marlene would soon join her. She had heard about a parade off the tourist strip, something for locals. They called it Chewbacchus.

Stella angled her way to the front of the crowd lining Elysian Fields as the sky graduated from candy floss pink to midnight blue. The streets were wild with reverie, everyone bopping to brass and donning some homage to a sci-fi hero. A larger-than-life iridescent Yoda rolled by, flanked by a squad of high-stepping Leias. "Yodamn Right" read the masthead of one float and, "Krewe of really awesome parodies" another.

Stella was showered with confetti from an exploding Death Star. She pressed record and rotated her camera to the sky, letting the shiny streamers fall on her lens. The *Star Wars* motif blasted triumphantly from a truck containing a jailed Darth Vader. A stormtrooper rolled by with a drink cart fashioned as the Millennium Falcon and handed her a red Solo cup with "Han" scrawled on it in black ink.

Stella's heart was wide open to receive all the impish treats on those ancient streets. She began strolling and passed a couple of bars, the sound of forgotten gypsy jazz chords pouring out of each of them until a different melody beckoned her. She yanked open the door, the sign overhead swinging and creaking. It read, "St. Roch Tavern, established 1930."

The bar was a blast from the past. A spirited blues band rocked out in front of clapboard paneled walls, while women in overalls and twee sweaters two-stepped cheek-to-cheek under Christmas lights.

Stella caught the eye of the lanky guitarist and he smiled. He was chic in all black—a slim-cut blazer, skinny jeans, and a huge tuft of afro bouncing like a bobblehead on his stovepipe torso as he wailed. The gritty soul crush of the song, and even his Fender guitar, reminded Stella of her father. Her youth was spent listening to him noodle at intricate chord patterns. She'd stretch out like a vampire in his guitar case while he riffed endlessly.

The moment the song ended, the towering rock god came bounding off the stage straight for Stella.

"Can I buy you a drink?" he asked, the gold glitter under his apple-green eyes sparkling. "I'm Isaiah."

"Stella. Um, sure," she replied, setting down her camera.

"First time here?" He motioned for the bartender.

"Yeah, how'd you know?"

"They got you," Isaiah said, unraveling a streamer from her hair with his long, elegant fingers.

"I had no idea Mardi Gras was this cool. I imagined something kind of gross actually."

"Well, Bourbon Street is gross. Just a bunch of tourist titties flopping for the beads. You gotta hit up the local krewes. Have you ever been to a spaceship wish machine?"

"What's that?"

"I'll show you." He popped out his elbow for her to take.

She took her drink to go, linked her arm through his, and embarked on a woozy traipse down the midnight streets. His skinny legs set a quick pace.

They wandered through the back alleys of Bywater, the roar of the crowd fading with each turn. As they strolled, they were beckoned into many a house party. Isaiah seemed to know everyone. He stopped at a large white Victorian house covered in giant paper mache roses to bum a cigarette from a friend and chat about the local politics of some performance he was organizing with the help of his "patroness." With one foot propped up on a porch stool, the backlight from a trio of candles transformed his afro into a halo. Stella snapped a sneaky portrait.

They walked on. Isaiah, in his smart black boots, was careful to guide Stella past the multitude of potholes. He began a solemn soliloquy about his father's death and his childhood in Nola, relating that his family had a grand ole steamboat of a home in the Lower 9th Ward, falling deeper into disrepair since Katrina. He spoke about his new experimental film score, and love and wanting and illusion.

"Am I talking too much? Sorry. You're just so beautiful." He tipped his head down and smiled, his long eyelashes fluttering innocently.

He wasn't, Stella reassured him. Something about his coyness clued her in to what would follow.

"So, are you married?" His eyes were aching with anticipation.

"Why do you ask it like that? Do I seem married?"

"Kinda."

"I kind of am. I left recently."

"Oh, watch out," he said, pulling her around a puddle. "I was married too. Very bad business."

Stella revealed to Isaiah details of her island exodus, her new life in LA, and her sexcapades under the tutelage of her Mama Domme. He was intrigued, pulling her tighter as they walked.

"Do people always tell you look like Jimi Hendrix?" she asked, admiring his sweet face, a constellation of freckles peppered across his cheekbones.

"All the time. I fucking hate Hendrix."

"So violent. Hendrix isn't the kind of artist you hate. Reserve such decided animosity for shitheads like Marilyn Manson."

"I'm a musician. We have violent opinions on such things," he said proudly before breaking into laughter. "I'm kidding. Who could hate Hendrix?"

"You seem so docile."

"I can be. Under the right hand," he said, the southern drawl of his baritone lending sultriness to the suggestion. "I probably deserve a good whooping."

"Let's see if you earn some funishment, Voodoo Child," she said with a flirtatious smile.

"I would never let anyone but you call me that."

Their banter had the immediacy of old lovers and the joviality of new ones. With the rat-a-tat of a taut percussion section, their repartee had a decisive rhythm. Stella was free to flex her wit in mildly insulting quips while Isaiah played the subby misanthrope who gladly accepted the humor-tinged barbs of her arrows straight to his melancholic heart. He reminded her of all the boys in high school she was forbidden to date—musicians and actors and art class sweethearts looking every bit the bad boys with their Pink Floyd T-shirts, baggy jeans, and ratty Chucks.

Soon they had arrived at a storefront littered with twentysomethings whose cigarette smoke wafted thick above their heads in the balm of the sodium lights.

Isaiah led Stella into a vintage clothing shop where they wound around to a boxy retro refrigerator. Ten dollars later, a doorman recited the rules for the "Spaceship Wish Machine."

"Watch your head. No pushing. Enjoy." The bouncer yanked on the long silver handle and frosty air poured out.

Stella climbed through the refrigerator into what looked like a pillow fort. She ducked into the makeshift labyrinth constructed from two-by-fours and blankets, Isaiah holding back the streamers dangling from above so she could follow.

The sound of a band echoed, but deep in the maze, Stella couldn't detect from where. They hit a dead end only to find two granola girls making out with such abandon that she and Isaiah were forced to awkwardly backtrack to the first turnoff. Stella looked down the dim, narrow chute and back at her platform heels calculating the exact amount of humiliation of a potential fall. Miraculously, she stuck the landing with Isaiah's body absorbing her impact like a bumper.

"Great success!" he said in a goofy accent.

Stella's face wore her confusion.

"Borat?"

"Haven't seen it. Cult kid, remember?"

The spaceship was far from the frigid icescape promised at the door. In fact, it was sweltering from the frenzied crowd. At the far wall, two men stood at boards and turntables pumping out a bouncy electronic soundtrack that had everyone pogoing.

As soon as Isaiah turned to greet some friends, Stella was beelined by a perky bird in black.

"Bonjour! I'm Yvette."

The woman stuck out her arm straight as an arrow for a handshake, a very American thing to do for someone with a French accent. She offered to pour Stella a drink from a frat house-style card table topped with half-empty liquor bottles.

"Do you like this band? They're French," said Yvette.

"Is this Polo & Pan? They're amazing. I can't believe they're playing here!"

Stella could not help but admire Yvette, who was petite with muscular arms and knobby knees. She had a heart-shaped face with wide-set blue-green eyes and thin lips under the shade of an imposing and fated Roman nose, twice broken. She wore a low-cut tank top, a tweed mini skirt, opaque tights, and heeled boots.

Seconds later, the two women were moving together on the dance floor. Yvette was an impressive dancer, swaying sensually to any song that played, her glossy brown hair wavy around her shoulders. The rainbow strobes splashed thick lines across her halcyon face. She was the life of the party—chirpy and bright, prepared to laugh at all the boys' jokes. With more jocularity than all of them combined, she could drink them under the table and had that fabled fucking *je ne sais quoi.*

"Is that your boyfriend?" Yvette asked, nodding in the direction of Isaiah.

"No, we just met!" Stella replied, leaning in close to her ear and yelling over the music.

"Ah, cool. Hey, I'm going to the bathroom. Do you want a bump?"

Stella nodded.

Her face full of radiance, Yvette grabbed Stella's hand as if they were school girls at play and pulled her through the crowd to a tiny bathroom.

"I've never done it!" Stella admitted as Yvette tapped a tiny vile of powder into the cup of her long fingernail.

"Like this," she said, inhaling deeply.

She reloaded her nail and held it up to Stella's nose.

Stella inhaled as quickly as possible then swallowed dramatically. "It tastes… metallic."

"Sniff again. Like this." She pressed a finger to each nostril. "The taste will go away."

Yvette moved closer and wiped some of the white stuff from Stella's nose. Stella had not noticed her breasts before, but as she looked down the shallow neck of Yvette's tank top, she became even more enraptured with this foreign creature.

Then something unexpected happened. Yvette shuffled her petite body just inches from Stella, past the invisible platonic line and Stella *knew*. A wave of anticipation washed over her.

"Can I kiss you?" Stella yelled as sensually as possible over the rising bass.

A smile fanned across Yvette's cherubic face. She nodded excitedly. Stella's hand moved to the small of her back and fit perfectly there like some starlet's handprint on that infamous Hollywood boulevard. Her touch was tentative at first. They kissed politely, no tongue, just wet, parted lips. Her mouth was small and fit entirely inside Stella's. Yvette pressed her bony hips into Stella, her ebullient chest greeting Stella's décolletage, and kissed her deeper. A flare ricocheted up Stella's spine like a pinball machine. *Ding, ding, ding.* All her sexual nerves triggered.

Stella locked the door then pressed Yvette noisily against it. Lust took over. Yvette's eyes went wild. Stella peeled back her neckline and kissed the tops of her breasts. She wanted to strip her in the bright light of the bathroom and ride her in the cold empty tub, pressing their warm bodies into one flesh. It was as instinctual as her desire for any man, only it felt forbidden and all the more irresistible.

A knock came on the door. "Hey! I need to take a shit!" screamed a drunk woman.

They burst into laughter, rearranged their clothes, and emerged from the bathroom electrified.

Isaiah had been watching from the periphery. He knew better than to interrupt a moment sooner. At half the height, Yvette was twice the man he was.

"You two are having more fun than anyone in the room." He leaned in tentatively on a single toe of his pointy boots. He, of course, wanted in.

Stella laughed. "It's true. We are."

She felt a thrill at excluding Isaiah. It harkened back to schoolyard days bratting boys, never letting them catch her no matter how obsessive her crush. Dancing with Yvette was a rush, not only because she was the sexiest woman in the room, but because her attention was so focused on Stella.

"Can I join?" Isaiah asked with pleading eyes.

Stella looked at Yvette who smiled big and shrugged her shoulders. It was clearly Stella's call. Yvette seemed to have a sense of the dynamic already.

Stella took Isaiah's chin between her fingers. "Do you think you've earned that privilege?"

His cheeks flushed and his tight pants bulged. "Uh, seems I have not," he admitted.

Marlene would be so proud, she thought. *Look at my command of this man… and this woman.* Stella pulled out her phone to send Marlene a text: "Hope you had a good flight. I'm having a domtastic time with a hot man and a very cool woman at a party in Bywater. Come join us!"

Yvette was beaming. Stella turned to her and cupped her hand around her ear. "What do you want to do with him?"

"I don't know. He's cute. Do you like him?" Yvette whispered back.

"I like him, but I like you better," she said and then kissed Yvette deeply.

"Isaiah, go get us a fresh round." Stella thrust two plastic cups at him.

As soon as he was out of earshot, the women let loose the wicked cackles boiling from within, but Stella realized she did not, in fact, know what to do with Isaiah. As natural as her inclination to take control, she didn't know how to follow through. She had the joystick in hand, but no idea where to land the plane. This was where Marlene's guidance was essential.

Her phone chimed. Marlene wanted to know many, many details before she would agree to party with strangers. Stella felt like she was negotiating with a curmudgeonly parent, so she relented, telling Marlene she'd see her at Sweetwater Wonderland later. She stuffed her phone back in her purse.

"You're really fun," Yvette said, resting her head on Stella's shoulder.

Multicolor fog wafted through the room like some *Casablanca* scene set up just to capture their invisible heat on film. To Stella, there was no one else in the room. She trained her attention on Yvette, feeling herself ebb closer to climax from the electricity they generated as they danced. The Frenchwoman was a vision. For several intense moments, all Stella could verbalize was "wow." Caffeinated on a cocktail of drugs and desire, she did not know if Yvette had extended an invitation for sex or was making calculated moves to make Stella boil over with passion.

"You're so graceful," Stella offered, fretting the dorkiness of such a compliment in the ribald context of the moment.

"I used to be a dancer." She sat Stella down in a chair and slid onto her lap. "Made a lot of money at the clubs in New York," she said, wrapping one arm around Stella's neck and reaching into her own pocket to grab a joint.

"Oh… You mean… um…?"

"Yeah, strip clubs," she confirmed, turning her head away from Stella to let a billow of smoke unfurl from her lips.

It was at that very second that Marlene appeared in the room as if she had been lowered down on a wire, the smoke lending a kind of cinematic grand entrance. Her hair was slicked back in the brutal bun of a ballerina and her lips graphic in deep Russian red. Her lithe body was poured into an all-black ensemble—a thin turtleneck, snug on the sculpted V of her rib cage and a miniskirt in fine Merino wool. Her vintage Gucci riding boots had tracked the slightest trail of water across the floor. Her ensemble was oddly similar to Yvette's, though in such a silhouette, she appeared capable of several back handsprings.

Stella rightly startled. "Oh, hey. I didn't think you were coming."

"You told me to, didn't you?" Marlene smarted, one hand on her hip.

Yvette smiled blithely and introduced herself without a care in the world. "Hiiii, I'm Yvette!" She took another drag then offered the joint to Marlene, who refused.

"Yvette, this is Marlene," Stella said, patting Yvette's thigh in a silent request for her to move off her lap.

Yvette greeted her again while Marlene grinned with thin-lipped disinterest.

"Want a drink?" Stella offered desperately.

"I don't know. Is this party any good?"

Stella's mind spun like some frightened toddler strapped into the mechanical nightmare of a Tilt-A-Whirl. Did Marlene feel some possession over Stella? She had told her to get tested before the trip, but their sexual burn had been so painfully slow. Two months living in the same house and nary a yard beyond first base. So curious was Stella to put her mouth on a woman, to know the taste of those intimate folds on the lick of her lips. She had been waiting. Hoping. Would she like it? Would she be any good?

"Do you know Polo & Pan? They're Parisian, like Yvette," Stella said, inching backwards into the throbbing mob.

The awkwardness of thc lovc triangle screeching like nails on a chalkboard, Stella kept moving to the center of the room and began dancing. Yvette leapt into the crowd with Stella while Marlene reluctantly danced just outside their circle, pretending to be lost in the music and refusing to make eye contact.

When it was obvious no amicable ground could be gained with Marlene, Stella exchanged numbers with Yvette, urging her to stay in touch, and said goodbye to Isaiah who had been chainsmoking in the alley with members of his band.

CHAPTER 7

Three's a Crowd

STELLA WOKE to an empty room, several rejected ensembles draped across Marlene's bed.

Stella donned a smart black and white jumpsuit, flat-ironed her bangs, winged liner around her eyes, and slid oversized, of-the-moment shades onto her face. Locking tight the door to Seventh Heaven, she made her way downstairs.

Marlene was halfway through her first cup of coffee, sitting in the garden, ready for her co-starring role as one of Two Fine Ladies Dressed for Breakfast. She wore a sandy blonde wig and was outfitted in a chic mumu in navy blue. Large tassels embellished the low-cut neck. The silhouette of her figure was visible in the light shining through.

"Those shoes!" Stella exclaimed as she took her seat like a fellow cockatiel clutching her claws around a branch.

"Morocco." Marlene pointed her toe to model the tapestry woven in intricate threads of gold like a crest in the shape of a compass. "I commissioned an artisan in Chefchaouen. That ensemble though!"

Stella looked like a doll come to life. Her jumpsuit coquettish and hugging her curves. Her hair piled high on her head. Marlene looked her up and down, clearly enamored.

"He texted." Stella leapt in, making eyes at Marlene over the rim of her sunnies. Her inner Doberman licked its chops. "I have to say, he seems totally down."

"Tell me about this Isaiah character. You met last night?" Marlene asked, spooning fresh fruit onto her plate.

"Yep. I told him I was exploring my dominance."

"Does he have any experience?" Marlene inquired clinically.

"He wanted to kiss my feet." Stella laughed, the memories of Isaiah in the Spaceship Wish Machine flashing like a film strip in the glint of her eye. "I think he would try anything I suggested."

What a labyrinth it was, this journey down the path Marlene lit, her own torch burning brightly. What an experiment!

"We shall see," Marlene replied with skepticism.

"You get off on foot worship though. Seems like a perfect match."

Marlene tore at the edge of Stella's croissant and shrugged. "We shall see. Now show me this Nola of yours..."

* * * * *

Outside an art gallery on Royal Street, a bruise of storm clouds gathered like an inkblot, a maelstrom in an otherwise azure sea. The sky glared with a swell of deluge as revelers in Carnival fever sought refuge to shake dry the mist and smack their lips with a bit of étouffée.

Huddling under the canopy, Marlene snapped open her umbrella and linked her elbow through Stella's free arm. They clutched one another like in-utero twins. However, minutes later the sun evaporated the rain clouds and the streets of New Orleans did not disappoint. In every direction, there were dogs dressed up for the Krewe de Barkus. Schnauzers and Shih Tzus, Labradors and pugs. A wagon tricked out like a tiny Fleetwood Bounder. The Chihuahua and Jack Russell inside were dressed up as Heisenberg and Pinkman, "Barking Bad" handwritten on the sign above their heads.

Stella led the way. A dance troupe of adolescent girls waved their pom poms in unison like a seafloor of anemones swept in the choreography of the tides. They stomped percussively on the pavement in matching glitter-dusted boots, the leather fringe bouncing like confetti. There was a potpourri of feathers and fans jutting from the crowd and music coming from every direction.

"I want a jazz funeral," said Stella, looking up through the bubbles blown from balconies. It was a cinematic moment. An 8mm memory for the deathbed final reel.

Under the shade of Marlene's Chinatown parasol, Stella gave lessons on how to Instagram. When it came to tech and media, she was the expert where Marlene was the novice. It was an area where the dynamic totally shifted, like a seesaw tipping en pointe to balance their weight. Then it was Stella the sage and Marlene the eager pupil. Stella wondered how Marlene had come so far in life without even rudimentary computer skills. She seemed so wise about so many other things. And so wealthy. How was it that she could suspend a 250-pound man from the ceiling yet she couldn't resize her browser window? It sent a wave of panic through Stella to think of the workload she'd take on if they went into business together, which they had been discussing with greater frequency. And yet, once she dismissed such worries, she was compelled towards it.

"Shall we beignet?" Marlene suggested outside a bustling café. She stalked a table by the window while Stella stood in line and scanned the scene. Nola culture was a thing of its own. Most prevalent among its inhabitants was Hipster Train-Hopping Gutter Skunk, identifiable by copious and irreverent stamp-like tattoos in a script of random glyphs all about the limbs. The flesh of their bodies akin to steamer trunks, hoisted through customs from Goa to Greece, swamp things they were, in embankment brown hues. A troop of tank tops. A cult of cut-offs. Perhaps a bandana jaunty on the neck, a septum piercing or gauged earlobes, but always—always—a hacksaw haircut like an orgy of several mullets akimbo the same scalp. It was a party, all business in the back above the party to the side beneath the crop of the front. The immersion blender special. Fresh off the bus from Brooklyn, banjo in hand, leaning hard into the conformity of their non-conformist flout. They sat in rows and sold poems for a dollar. They gathered on the stoops of flophouses plucking at the twang of their thirst for Southern lore.

Stella returned from the counter, toting cappuccinos with meringues of white foam.

"You're taking chances eating beignets in black," Marlene warned as a server slid a tray full of pastries onto their table, but Stella had a one-track mind.

"I don't know if Isaiah is a beta. He's not"—she searched for the word—"pathetic like Houseboy." She blew on her cappuccino to cool it, forcing a tiny crater into the foam.

"Pathetic?" Marlene recoiled.

"No, sorry. I meant, geeky. He's really hot, but like a sad little boy underneath."

It was clear Stella was a fast friend, not only to Marlene, but in general. She was a hummingbird, a hostess, a classic case of extroversion, with no shortage of #followers and an unquenchable thirst for connection. She was only beginning to flash little signs of elitism, spiking her otherwise hyper-inclusive way. It was obvious that for Marlene, Stella's tendency to offer blanket invitations was a source of mistrust. Her generosity of spirit called out Marlene's snobbish inclinations; her quick hand to draw the bridge of the tower in which she dwelled. Stella could see it challenged Marlene to occasionally lower the price of the toll, to see the redeemable, as Stella had practiced to rote degrees within the cult.

"I'll let you know what I think when I meet him tonight," Marlene replied, taking a too-hot bite of beignet.

"Yes! So, you'll go?"

"I'll go, but I don't really do pick-up play. I'll have to feel the vibe."

* * * * *

Back at Wonderland, a small bonfire party had gathered in the soppy grass of the garden, replete with harmonica wailing in herald to the evening.

Two stories above, Marlene leaned into a vanity mirror, painting lashes onto lids where there were few.

Stella popped her head around the corner. She then leapt into the doorway, her breasts hiked to the heavens in a colorful off-the-shoulder blouse and a second-skin pencil skirt. Her lips were red as punctured cherry.

"Love it," Marlene praised. "You're giving the children all the Carmen Miranda!"

Marlene wore her hair slicked tight in a bun à la Flamenquita. A gossamer shirt in snakeskin had several buttons undone and her black trousers were tucked into black suede boots. A golden charm, in the shape of a many-limbed tree, caught the light on her neck. Midnight in the garden, for those clued in. *Eve bit the fruit. The juice ran down her chin.*

"I brought my remote vibrator," Stella offered, perking at the thought of kinkcapades in the Quarter.

"Want to try it?" Marlene piqued. "That could be fun."

Marlene had encouraged Stella to bring toys. She too had a bag full of goodies. The flame had been lit.

"It's in," Stella said, handing the remote to Marlene, who set aside her makeup and began fidgeting with the buttons.

"Tell me what it's doing," Marlene invited.

Stella complied in full performance mode, pressing her thumb and index finger together as though threading an invisible needle. She jabbed when the vibrator pulsed weaker or stronger, mimicking the hum with raspberry breaths.

"Safeword?" Marlene asked.

"Domton Abbey." Stella never failed to invent a pun for all things domination.

"Clever."

"You've got the rope?"

Marlene opened her embossed leather satchel to confirm. "Got it."

"I can't wait to see the look on his face when we are both commanding him. I was so turned on by that moment with Cyril!"

"I'm not going to do anything too complex if it's his first time. Doesn't mean I can't tie you though," Marlene flirted, sliding the rope around Stella's waist and pulling her tight.

* * * * *

Outside the tavern, a busking artist petitioned portraits while a sexy sax wheezed from nearby. As Stella and Marlene traipsed through a wine and cheese shop to get to the inner courtyard, several patrons turned to watch them pass. Dialed down as they were, the city slicker neon still hissed above their heads.

Hipsters lingered at whiskey barrel tables and chairs made from old wooden crates. Guided by the hostess, they were seated a few feet from a small stage. A jaunty jazz quartet played. Tiki torches glowed while the fragrance of fire smoldered in the blue air. It was a European terrace scene, baptized in backwater mud.

They bopped to the impassioned brass and tinkling marimba while sipping wine and noshing from a colorful charcuterie board. They were giddy, Stella especially, at the prospect of co-domming.

It was then that a hand reached for her shoulder. She melted a bit when she turned to face Isaiah. His hands crept low on her back as they embraced.

Stella made introductions, stepping aside for everyone to meet. It was formal at best and she could tell Marlene was going to be reserved. She felt expansion where Marlene seemed to contract.

"You ladies look beautiful," Isaiah complimented, biting his plump bottom lip.

For three or four songs, Isaiah engaged only with Stella, which made her nervous. The night was young, but Marlene's lukewarm reaction seemed permanently inked. Isaiah perceived Marlene's distance and bristled, ordering several drinks on their tab.

When the band took five, Stella suggested they play pool. They moved inside to a small room ornamented with black and white portraits of jazz musicians on every wall. The billiard table filled nearly the whole space, glowing yellow from a single antique chandelier.

Stella shifted on her feet and squared her shot behind the cue ball. Her skirt rode up as she leaned forward to slide the stick back on the web of her fingers. Isaiah cleared his throat and adjusted his crotch. Stella drew back her elbow, ready to release. It was then that Marlene cranked up the vibrator.

Stella gasped, bowing her forehead to her arm and laughing into the crook. She looked up to Marlene, accepting the challenge. She rebalanced on her feet, licked her lips, and let it rip. Corner pocket. *Swoosh.* It was hot.

Stella could see that Marlene felt chemistry in this play, a kind of purity in their perversion. She motioned for Isaiah to come closer. She placed his hand on her skirt atop the vibrator and gave Marlene a nod. Marlene hit her again.

"Oh, that's hot. She's controlling you?" Isaiah beamed. "And you're going to dominate me? *Fuh-uck.*"

Swaggering over to Marlene, beer in hand, Isaiah propped his elongated torso against the pool table. He cocked his head close to Marlene's cheek, placing his hand on the table across the width of her body. Stella was pleased to see him flirting with Marlene. Perhaps they would have the chemistry for a *ménage à trois* after all. *Just relax into it,* Stella thought in her silent direction to Marlene.

Isaiah pushed his lips an inch from Marlene's ear and whispered, "I can't wait for you to tie me up."

With his back to Stella, she saw only the sudden grimace on Marlene's face. Stella registered Marlene's discomfort and invited her to the bathroom. Isaiah pinched Stella's ass on the way out.

"You should probably take this," Marlene strained a laugh, handing Stella the remote to her vibrator under the stall door.

"What? Why? You're leaving? We're just getting started." Stella's heart sank. She couldn't deny Isaiah was a little different than before. Gone was the sensitive artist and in his place a hungry hound. "He's being a little weird, but he's probably just nervous."

"You met him once. Maybe this is how he really is."

"Maybe, but he was subby with me before," Stella defended, her voice rising in panic as she hurried to finish peeing.

"The way you posture and preen for his attention is... *awkward.* You're not in your strength, you're at his mercy."

Stella knew Marlene never played second fiddle to anyone. And yes, maybe she had oversold Isaiah.

"I am in my strength. Don't you think he's hot?" She opened the stall door and searched Marlene's face for confirmation.

To Stella, Isaiah was a boy, nine years her junior. She felt confident to apply her newfound dominance to him, to turn the tables ever more in her favor. She needed a crash test dummy and he was just the type.

"Sure, but it's apparent you've not talked at much depth. He's a dilettante, the kind who samples dominance like an appetizer to suit his own taste. I've encountered many like him, stunted by the burdens of their programmed masculinity, the toxicity of entitlement, and the fetish to consume."

Stella was dumbfounded by the elaborate indictment. "You can't give him a chance?"

"Look Stella, this is just a schoolyard game of grab ass, which I don't feel inclined to referee."

"Why are you being such a buzzkill? You don't like any of my friends, do you? Did you want this trip to be just about you and me?" Stella asked. Perhaps Marlene's persnickety condemnation was a veneer for her jealousy.

"Not necessarily," Marlene replied coolly, looking into the mirror and powdering her nose from a silver compact. "It's just that generally I dismiss these kinds before the first date. I prefer more experienced submissives. This one hasn't earned my dominance."

Stella scoffed. "Oh OK, even though you just do this for fun."

"For fun?" Marlene retorted, clicking her compact closed.

"It's your lifestyle, not your profession, but you won't accept anyone else who's also doing it for fun? There are lots of things you are a novice at," she insulted, her pitch escalating. "Like how to use a computer!"

Marlene stood stone-faced then thrust the vibrator remote towards Stella once more. "You go have fun now."

"Fine. I will!" Stella barked as Marlene stomped out.

Gobsmacked, Stella retreated to the toilet stall for several long moments.

"You have to domme yourself first," Marlene would say, at times sending Stella into a tailspin of understandable rebuff. The last thing she wanted was to rein herself in. As a missionary, she broke her teeth on the bit of abnegation; broke the spine of her spirit under the heft of that load. How could the path to the temple of her dominant nature be so steep with these moments wherein she had to heel?

Fuck Marlene and her judgments! If I wanted that kind of bullshit in my life, I'd have stayed in the cult!

CHAPTER 8

Crossing the Rubicon

STELLA RESOLVED to prove Marlene wrong by domming Isaiah herself, so she retrieved him from the billiard room and announced that they were going back to his place. He eagerly obliged, practically sprinting down the kinetic streets, which were still popping and sizzling with the spirit of Mardi Gras.

Bursting with anticipation, Stella was disheartened to find that Isaiah's apartment was a cyclonic mess. Dirty dishes filled the kitchen sink and counters, and sheet music blanketed nearly every piece of furniture.

"Uh, sorry. I've been too busy to clean," he said, rushing to sweep a pile of wrinkled clothes off the bare mattress. It was an otherwise modern unit in the Magazine District. Had Isaiah not been a hoarder, the exposed brick studio would have been chic.

He attempted a meager straightening up of the bachelor pad while Stella dismissed herself to the bathroom.

Gazing into the water-stained mirror over the sink, she told herself very firmly that there was no reversing this flow. She was crossing the Rubicon, removing the mantles of Married Christian Woman, sewing the Scarlet Letter to her chest in proud stitches large enough for God to see.

She was using this man to get to the other side of the river, to force herself out of the reservation as a traitor. If she committed this "sin," there was no going back to Adam or Jehovah and the last thing she wanted was a breadcrumb trail home. She couldn't risk her newfound tinsel of courage being capsized by the waves of religious guilt and its time-honored companion, self-doubt.

Burn all bridges. Burn them bright. Burn them completely.

Adultery was the only way forward. She had been separated from Adam for months and had not slept with anyone. She needed to clear her sexual cache, to pop her post-marital cherry and it was obvious that wasn't going to happen with Marlene. How exciting to think it would happen with a submissive man! She threw back her shoulders and rejoined Isaiah.

"Finally, I've got you to myself," he said, wasting no time peeling off her clothes and latching onto her breasts with his pillow lips.

She throbbed with pleasure. "Ugh, I'm so wet," she said, clutching the back of his head and stroking his muscular shoulders.

"Not wet enough," he said, sliding his fingers between her inner thighs.

She sighed with pleasure. He hoisted her to the mattress and went about voraciously devouring her. She was woozy with sensation, her body languid and open as if the sockets of her joints had been unhinged and she had been flayed for inspection. Every movement he made felt as if performed in sensual slow motion. She twitched with delight. She waited for his tongue to grow tired, but his look of satisfaction told her he was in ecstasy at the taste of her.

He climbed on top and kissed her deeply. She had never savored from another's tongue the flavor of her own flesh. It was deviant and dirty. Briny and pungent. He moved higher on the bed, angling his erect penis at her mouth. She rolled to her side and kissed the tip, peering up at him with drunken doe eyes. His torso was long and chiseled, his skin smooth as silk. He looked like a god.

"I've never done this before," Stella confessed. She wasn't even sure the Bible forbade oral sex, however, she and Adam had always feared they would be smited for any southerly migration of their affection even in the bond of matrimony.

"Oh baby, that's so sexy," he said, moving his hips back and forth.

She slid her lips down his shaft and back up again. She salivated intensely. It was heavenly to have his thick flesh in her mouth. She loved sucking the bulbous head, rimming just underneath with the tip of her tongue. He was long and smooth and so hard. Adam was so old and wrinkled in comparison.

So, this is what sex would have been like with a man my age! she thought, her eyes closed tight in rapture. She thrilled at the control she felt over Isaiah, how he moaned and jolted ecstatically as if struck by pleasurable pings of lightning.

"Oh shit, I'm gonna come," he said, sliding out of her wet lips.

He pulled her up on her hands and knees. Slid inside her. She gasped. He was so much bigger than Adam, filling her entirely.

"Oh my God, you're so tight. Your pussy feels so good," he groaned, grabbing the thick flesh of her haunches. "And your ass!" he said, smacking her as he pulsed quicker.

Stella arched her back and whimpered. She was putty in his grip, gladly flopping like a ragdoll to the rhythm of his hips. With her flesh bouncing like gelatin, she felt a new sensation—the fuck-you pride of a wide-open whore.

"Use me, baby. Use me," she whined, her sweaty cheek pressed into the mattress.

"This tight fucking pussy!"

"It's yours. Take it. Take it!"

He fucked her harder and she begged for more until her hair was a damp tangle against her forehead and her whole body was perspired.

"Where do you want me to come?" he asked breathlessly.

"Come on my tits."

He flipped her over, groaning violently into the void as he stroked his pulsating cock over her. With a final throb, her breasts turned creamy with the rivulets of his pleasure.

* * * * *

Stella tiptoed into Seventh Heaven and undressed near the window. A half-moon hung low over the swampland. It was God-knows-what-hour and she just wanted to rest. Looking over at Marlene sleeping soundly, snoring ever so slightly, she wondered just how disappointed in her she would be.

When Stella woke the next morning, her makeup a skewed palette across her face, Marlene was already dressed. The air was thick with humidity. It was nearly 11 and their last day in town.

"Hey," Marlene greeted her.

Stella didn't answer right away. She flopped to her side and shoved her face into the pillow with a groan.

Marlene sat on the edge of the bed. She pulled her suitcase close and rifled for her cosmetics bag. She had already packed away her toys. "What happened?" she asked sympathetically.

"I don't want to talk about it," Stella grumbled, curling up in a chaos of covers.

Her energy was heavy as lead. She told Marlene to go sightseeing without her and that perhaps they'd meet up later.

For most of the day, she got stuck rehearsing a scorned lover's speech in her head should Isaiah contact her. By five, she had been stewing in it long enough, so she reluctantly picked up her phone to message Marlene.

"Come meet me for dinner at Adolfo's!" Marlene replied immediately. "Let's regroup. There isn't anything a few sinful cannolis can't cure."

It was clear that Marlene intended to make amends. It sounded like she even missed Stella. As much as Stella had enjoyed her time to wander untethered, this trip to Nola was an adventure she wholeheartedly wanted to share.

* * * * *

Stella smiled as she entered the restaurant, her leopard print coat clashing with the cliché of the red and white checkered tablecloths. Adolfo's was Italian bistro quintessence, replete with wax-covered Chianti bottles and waiters well into retirement age.

Marlene was perched on a bar stool, sipping a bourbon and watching a silver fox couple two-step on an otherwise empty dance floor.

"Hey, you look better. I got us a great table," Marlene said, gesturing to the corner of the room.

Over dinner, Stella confessed a bit of what happened with Isaiah.

"I ended up flipping in the ghetto on a dirty mattress," she said with a chuckle. "At first, it was really fun. He went down on me for like, an hour. He was even sweet when he was fucking me, but as soon as he came, he disappeared to the bathroom. He wouldn't even cuddle me. Something about another woman. Just snored himself to sleep on the couch."

"Post-nut clarity. That's the nature of a one-night stand," Marlene said, dipping a corner of bread into the steaming broth of a bowl of mussels.

"But I felt so connected, why didn't he? Am I not attractive enough? Is it my cellulite?" wondered Stella, pushing away a half-eaten dish of iceberg lettuce.

"Doubtful. You gave him an easy layup and he took it." Marlene stabbed her fork into a tomato in Stella's bowl.

"Ha! I see what you did there." Stella grinned.

The night was still young and Marlene admitted that Stella had roused herself quickly. Once again, like a toddler, she got right up after a fall. It was understandable, but like a child reaching for a flame, she did get burned.

Stella confirmed the feeling that Marlene had judged the situation too harshly but was also sweetly apologetic for pooping out on their last day. Stella could feel the warmth salving their spirits, but even as their laughter was returning, some doubt did survive in her mind like the ovule of a weed, dormant for a time and still destined to germinate. Would Marlene always be this uptight? Would they ever co-domme?

"Why is it so hard to domme and have good sex? I feel like I'm still a virgin," Stella pondered into the depths of her wine glass.

"Because you won't take the time to test them. This is the low-hanging fruit of casual sex, my dear. Most women are left unsatisfied."

"And this is why you don't fuck men? How can six seasons of *Sex and the City* be wrong?" Stella joked, throwing back a swig of cabernet.

"The fucking men bit is always complicated. That's why I rarely do it anymore. I did meet a gorgeous artist at a gallery around the corner," Marlene taunted, her eyes full of lust. "She pummeled me with questions. 'What brings you here? Who are you with? What do you do?' Such a sub! I can spot them a mile away."

Stella managed a laugh. Of course, Marlene had felt left out at the bar. Yes, Isaiah was a boob, but she still could have played along in the early hours of the night. And Stella didn't dare mention her lingering regret at not sleeping with Yvette.

They hacked into the rich chocolate ricotta of a crispy cannoli and then sauntered onto the street. Frenchman was rollicking. Several first line brass bands vied for the gathering crowds while each juke joint offered up some sorrow or some swing.

They sashayed with a group of drunken seniors on the sidewalk, an old cat with a cane teaching them to "Stanky Leg" as the glee of ragtime poured out from a nearby bar and spread through the marrow of their jumping bones. Dancing was good therapy and soon their tension had melted away.

The pair was like this—forever vacillating in a wealth of expressions. One moment like monarchs holding court or sparring philosophies on kink, turning swiftly in a breath to juggle hoops, a pair of jesters. So often this way, two little girls, in mother's pearls pantomiming high tea.

They pushed through revelers of all levels of inebriation, the night air drying their perspired brows. An imposing silhouette of the Christ with outstretched arms loomed over St. Anthony's Church like an omen. They paused for a moment to take it in, then rounded the corner to Orleans Street. How strange was this journey Stella was on. Romping through the pagan Catholicism of Mardi Gras with a Christian Dominatrix.

They turned onto Dauphine Street and Marlene began counting the house numbers. She stopped in front of the address on a pamphlet she had been consulting.

"The Sultan's Palace!" she exclaimed. Before them stood a large manor, stately and ornate. "This is the Gardette-LePretre Mansion!"

"The Sultan's Palace?" Stella piqued.

Shielding their eyes from the glare of the street lamps, they tilted their heads to regard the expansive three-story facade with its cast iron galleries and the blush of pink paint in contrast to the cold onyx of the metal.

"Apparently, this Turkish sultan bought it from a dentist or something. He brought in trunks of silks and opium and all his harem girls. There were rumors of wild parties, drug-fueled orgies. All that jazz…" Marlene's tone was that of a campfire storyteller.

"Sounds like the perfect dommune."

"Oh, don't think I haven't thought about starting a dommune! A house run entirely on sub labor. Imagine it."

"Domton Abbey. What are we waiting for?"

"Massacre." A voice from behind them punctured their conjecture like a needle pushing through the taut even weave of cross-stitch linen.

They swiveled around. There, standing on the landing of a house painted the yellow of a coal mine canary was a finch of a woman in monochromatic blues. Her light brown skin was aglow, her hair parted down the middle and bound over each shoulder in thick salt and pepper braids.

Both the travelers were startled. Front and center on her stairs, she was like a deity on high and they like two pilgrims at the foot of a temple. The tintinnabulation of wind chimes hanging from the eves seemed to signal the start of something mystical.

"That house was the site of a massacre," the woman continued, an Ankh amulet swinging over the crest of her pendulous breasts as she gestured towards the site. "One day the place was curiously silent. None of the usual echoes of laughter and debauchery. A milkman, out on his rounds, sees a pool of blood seeping from the threshold of the door. Murdered. All of them. Body parts everywhere. The sultan buried alive in the backyard."

They continued to stare. Such a lovely place. Such a grim history. A shiver ran across Stella's clavicles.

The woman read them up and down as though her eyes were her fingertips and the travelers before her a tome of braille.

"Would you like a reading?" she finally inquired, a smile spreading across her face slowly like molasses.

"A reading?" Stella asked.

The woman pointed insouciantly to an almost imperceptible sign in the front window that read: "Mademoiselle Marais, Clairvoyant Guide and Spiritual Advisor."

Without waiting for a reply, she pivoted on a sandaled foot and waved a beckoning hand. Stella and Marlene followed her up the paint-chipped porch. Stella felt the tremble of toeing a precipice, as if entering a realm not entirely of this world.

The interior of the house was filled with jewel tones and dark wood, a mask on the wall, of Guatemalan origin, presiding over the sitting room to which they were led. It was an orderly arboretum of robust and well-tended plants, a sanctuary smelling of calendula and rose.

"You're adventuring, that's clear," the woman called from the foyer.

Marlene smoothed her wavy hair, setting her coat on the arm of a divan.

"Call me Adivina," she introduced, a C-sharp gap in the center of the ivory keys of her teeth. She handed them a laminated card and opened the shutters to allow the moonlight to illuminate the room. The floorboards whined underfoot as she took her seat in a grandfatherly green chair. To her left rested a metronome.

"I am gifted in many disciplines, but tassology is my true calling. These are the fees." She gestured to the card in Stella's hand. "We should settle this before we begin."

It was essentially a spa menu with prices corresponding to the service. "Cash Only" appeared in bold.

"Well, I think we should go for your specialty," Stella concluded, looking sidelong to Marlene to see if she agreed.

Sixty dollars cash was placed, as instructed, into the sewing basket Adivina produced from the floor. She set the metronome in a tempo of semibreve and, without explanation, disappeared down the hall. Stella and Marlene locked eyes. Each tick of the pendulum added to their shared suspense.

"I would have been disfellowshipped for this," Stella confessed. How she thrilled at the rebellion of sitting in that salon. She welcomed the opportunity to commune with the "darkness." She had never truly accepted the existence of demons. Perhaps that was why she was so unafraid.

Adivina entered the room carrying a tray with two porcelain tea cups, once again assuming her place in the ancient chair.

"I'm going to speak the stories while you drink. Keep mindful as you listen. Be sure to leave your last sip. Do not finish the tea," she instructed, handing each of them a cup rimmed in gold with pomegranates painted on the sides.

Only the clicking of the metronome punctuated their first few sips of a toasty floral tea.

"Now regard the Ophrys," Adivina enjoined, directing their attention to a brilliant purple orchid at the other end of the room. She closed her eyes. "The bee orchid, the prostitute, the Magdalene of her species. Highly specified among her kind and masterful in deceit. Her evolution gifting her form and pheromone to dupe the mating urges of male bees. The narcotic of her perfume rewires his reality."

Half of the words she used were like a cipher, but both Stella and Marlene understood. The theatrics of the flower's allure functioned like a cunning mistress.

Adivina reached for the metronome to dial up the tempo. The women, fully enraptured, sipped slowly, careful as instructed not to drain the tea from their cups.

"The great blue agave," she continued. For the first time, her eyes flashed with a look of true concern. Adivina related a vision of a large maguey swirling over the women's shoulders, the rosette blooming with a wealth of thick, spiny leaves. "But the heart—the heart is filled with crown rot."

The women sat up straighter. Adivina paused again. Her eyes narrowed. "Yes, its lesions are filled with the eggs of an insect. The heart festers and decays. Be wary of drinking that spirit."

Adivina halted the metronome. Taking Stella's cup, she swirled counter-clockwise then studied the contents, tilting it closer and farther from view. She followed this ritual with Marlene's. She seemed to engage in some dialogue. Then she held them together. Returning Marlene's to the tray, she began with Stella.

"You have been bridled. You have been yoked. A caravan of shame you pulled behind you. The black bile of gossip, a guillotine of judgment."

A strong wind tangled the chimes outside against the center clapper. Stella felt her stomach drop to her boots and a rush of blood flush her chest as though an arrow had punctured her rib cage. She said nothing. The trembling of her lip said it all.

"A young girl wraps her body in swaths of linen. She makes a cocoon. It is a shell to the torrents of lust. She digests herself within. She must choose metamorphosis or mummification."

Stella inhaled sharply. Her large eyes filled with water in the moonlit room.

Adivina took Marlene's cup. Again, she seemed to converse with the remnants therein.

"You have never been bridled, though you were left to the wilderness. There is a child, crawling wet from the waves, turning to the wreckage. There is the capsized ship from which she swam. Her loved ones treading water do beckon like a symphony of sirens."

Marlene clutched tight her hands.

"Ease your grip on the reins. Lather your stallions. Kept in a stable, they will weaken and die."

So enthralled were they in the reading, neither Stella nor Marlene had seemed to notice the way they'd sunk into the center of the divan, the cushions dipping into the springs, their hips and shoulders melding like conjoined twins.

Adivina looked up to the women, holding their attention as though they were statues she'd carved, cold cheeks of alabaster now flush in the presence of truth.

"Some purpose between you is betrothed here," she continued. "There is a voyage. You are vessels. Great treasures in your bellies. You are Minervas meant to mirror one another, but do not nail the other to your bough."

With this, she replaced the cups to their saucers. The room seemed to exhale. Reality interrupted like a hiccup and a bashfulness crept in, as though the women were grabbing for their clothing, dropped into heaps on the floor.

Outside, the trumpet solo of a brass band sounded in time with the rusted hinges of wrought iron gates, pushed open by the wind. They were unlocked as if by the chalk-white hand of some ghost of the Confederacy, holding tight a key from Guinee. With an ear to the ground, one might mistake the metal wince for the blade of a bayonet, dragged sharply along the cobble of the street.

CHAPTER 9

Fake It Till You Make It

A FEW HOURS after their solemn reading, the women were scrambling to pack and get to the airport for a red eye. By early morning, they were back in LA.

In the bustling rideshare zone outside LAX, the air was thick with jet fuel and gasoline. Marlene stood tapping her foot and checking her phone with manic frequency while Stella was propped against a bench in a pleasant daze. Weary from travel but still high on Nola, she gazed past the swarms of international travelers at the Space Age structure of the airport. It resembled a UFO blinking and grounded in human terrain, its curvilinear steel trusses sprouting like giant spider legs defensively over the holodeck.

In the movie of her life, she was the alien landing on a foreign planet, forced to learn a new language and adapt to a completely different set of rules. The roller coaster of emotions she experienced with Marlene, the heartache of being rejected by Isaiah—she would take all the growing pains if they also yielded this kind of cinematic satisfaction.

A familiar black sedan rolled up to the curb and out flew Houseboy with a profusion of apologies to preempt Marlene's scorn.

"Why were you late?" Marlene growled, twisting his earlobe until he grimaced.

"Sorry, Mistress," he said, Marlene's luggage in midair as he hoisted it into the trunk. "I thought I'd be on time, but the 405 is all backed up from an accident."

Marlene slid into the backseat and appraised with approval the basketful of refreshments Houseboy had prepared as instructed. Stella enjoyed the poshness of it all, their naughty little secret, this man in their service with his dick locked tight, but she winced at Marlene's unnecessary cruelty.

As they sipped mimosas and nibbled on pastries, Houseboy gunned the car onto the freeway in response to Marlene's direction to "hurry the fuck up."

"God, that trip was fabulous," Stella said, sighing into the window.

"Tres fab, for sure," said Marlene distractedly, entranced with some business on her phone.

After traveling for an hour or so, Houseboy pulled the car to a stop in front of a squatty two-story apartment building. He glanced in the rearview mirror curiously.

"What are you doing? Did I tell you to stop here?" Marlene squawked, looking up from the daze of her phone.

He was puzzled speechless for a few seconds. "Mistress, your apartment."

"No, *her* apartment," Marlene huffed.

He dared not argue.

"You have an apartment *and* a house?" Stella asked, perking up and taking inventory of a building that resembled some motel in a bad '70s cop drama.

"This is my place," Marlene said with her arms folded tight as if it was obvious.

"So, you have two homes?" Stella asked, her heart panic fluttering at the apparent omission of facts.

"Never said I had a house."

"But..."

"You assumed."

"I spent two months in someone else's house? Who? Who lives there?" She leaned forward, attempting to lock eyes with Houseboy in the rearview for even a moment of confirmation that she was not indeed crazy. He looked away.

"What does it matter? I'm a woman of means even if those means aren't always monetary," said Marlene, her face contorting into a challenging scowl.

Stella sat back in her seat in stunned silence to fully assess whether she had gone mad. She wanted desperately for Marlene to fill the dead air with a confession, an apology, some admission of guilt. Any explanation that might justify this egregious misdirect.

"I swear you said many times it was *your* house, *your* design..." Stella insisted.

"All true. It was my house, my responsibility *at the time.* It was entrusted to me by dear friends. While I didn't design it, I did approve the design."

Marlene seemed satisfied in her defense despite its inane ludicrousy.

"Approve? You mean, in your head?"

"Stella, there are just so many things you don't know," Marlene said, her jaw beginning to twitch.

"Yes, like why you lied to me!"

"I saved you. You were half dead thinking you were cursed by God," Marlene said, her eyes traveling all over Stella in judgment.

"But what about going out of town? You said..."

"Also, true. LA is such a sprawl. Leaving the Hills for Silver Lake *is* going out of town."

"You can't be serious," Stella blinked as if she had just discovered herself plagued with cataracts.

"You gonna sit there and sulk or do you want to come in for a drink?"

"I'm gonna go home. I'll call an Uber," Stella said with intentional stubbornness to gain some kind of ground.

"Houseboy can take you."

"No! I'll get home on my own." Stella's face was awash with bewilderment at the blatant subterfuge. How had she not detected Marlene's lies sooner?

Houseboy unloaded Stella's bags and gave her a sympathetic shrug. Perhaps he wasn't such an unwitting henchman after all.

Marlene strutted up to a gate and flung it open. Without offering Stella a goodbye, she stomped across the walkway to what was apparently her real abode.

Stella collapsed defeatedly onto the curb to await her ride, which arrived within a few minutes.

In the backseat of the car, her head began to spin with fearful conjecture. What else had Marlene deceived her about?

She was oblivious when the driver announced they had reached her destination.

Finally upstairs, Stella rolled her suitcases inside her apartment, yanked the curtains shut, and flung herself onto the bed.

Her trust in Marlene was in tatters, but who else did she have? They'd crammed so much into these few months, talking every day in floods of textversation, even making plans to start a domination business together. The depth of connection she felt had drawn her into the immediacy of their romance, but now she felt herself reaching from the quicksand of cult trauma for some handful of reeds.

Ever since the fortune teller's reading, Stella suspected Marlene must have her own state secrets, wrapped and sealed in a stone grave. How had Adivina divined this?

Marlene texted some silly meme in an obvious attempt at reconciling without apologizing, but Stella could feel herself retrieving some of the eggs she'd placed in their basket.

In the same day, she received no less than three calls and texts from elders either reminding her of the upcoming Memorial of Christ's Death or encouraging her to "Draw close to Jehovah again" by scheduling a shepherding call with her local elders. The timing was bizarre. Stella felt the old religious panic revving up. The adage to trust no one outside the organization began playing like a broken record. The bric-a-brac of the cult was still in her. Insidious doctrines stubbornly clung like fiberglass in flesh. The old judgments were sewn into her tissue, silently praying not to be discovered and exorcized finally and forever.

CHAPTER 10

Ménage à Trois

STELLA'S HONDA barreled towards Utah like a runaway train. There were almost no cars on the highway at that hour. Only the hulk of a few Freightliners rocked with the weight of their cargo, pushing east into the high desert moon. The cool March wind ripped through her hair as though she was strapped into the front car of a county fair roller coaster.

Belting at the top of her lungs, she was barely able to hear the pitch of her own voice in time with the soprano of Tori Amos and the pounding piano chords conjuring the coyote cry up and out.

It shook the speakers and echoed out into the cosmos, carried on the wings of all the better angels heralding this prison escape so long overdue. Perhaps it was not a roller coaster she was riding, nor even the torque and oiled pistons of that dependable Japanese engineering, but rather the ash handle and crisped birch of a witch's broom.

She had been singing the feminist anthem since she was 14, never expecting it would become her theme song on this day of deliverance. Gone were the pangs of guilt that frothed up in her throat the first few months, as if some miracle cure of all that religious shame had been administered as easily as a spoonful of elixir.

"It's not my fault!" she cried into the air. "I was in a motherfucking cult!"

Her lungs were full of dynamite. This would not be her first banshee wail, for this road trip was her primal scream therapy.

The Utah state line was just a few miles away when she unzipped her pants, whipped out her new cordless Hitachi Magic Wand, and went to work on Operation O. The nascent exhibitionist in her wanted to be seen with her foot propped up on the dash, her legs spread wide as she tugged on her nipples.

The orgasm pulsed through her pelvis like the epicenter of a great quake, generating a seismic wave of satisfaction to the top of her head. She could only remember one time Adam made her come. Only a year ago, she donned a platinum wig and a skimpy bikini, oiled her tropically tanned skin, and made him chase her to the roof and fuck her on a lawn chair.

Four months post-escape and she rarely thought of Adam anymore. She had grieved so much during the marriage that there were no tears left to shed. Adam contacted her once to implore her to write an admission of adultery and send it to the elders so that he could be exonerated and regain "privileges" in the congregation. She refused. She told him their marriage didn't end because of another man. It ended because she realized she was in a cult with a helpless freeloader. A letter like that would result in her disfellowshipping and might kill her mother. Adam would have to figure his shit out alone. But the elders wouldn't let her off that easy. She'd been receiving texts and calls at increasing frequency. They said they just wanted to encourage her, but what they really wanted was for her to fall on her sword so Adam could be "scripturally free" of her. That cross was not hers to bear.

Will Ken make me come? she wondered as she shifted into third gear to hug tight the switchback curves. *Will just the sight of him be enough to excite me?*

The road steepened and narrowed to a single lane, the massive red buttes of Salt Lake City sparkling with fresh snow. She must've climbed a thousand feet before she pulled up to Ken's street, an even tighter jaunt into the mountains. There were no other houses around. Perched on the cliff in supervillain solitude was an ultra-modern chalet. The setting sun bounced off a bank of windows encasing the house and made the place glisten like the Taj Mahal.

Ken ran outside to greet her. They hugged tentatively. He looked her up and down, clearly taking inventory. She did the same. This was their first IRL meeting, though they'd talked on the phone. She'd been introduced to Ken through her travel client. He was an influencer with a million followers—just the kind of modelesque host they loved to see white water rafting or bouldering for some hip outdoor brand. Ken's texts and calls had quickly become flirtatious, but Stella had not stoked the flame, for every day had been spent at Marlene's side. When things went sour with Marlene, Stella packed up her car and hit the road for Utah like a woman on fire.

Here standing before her, Ken was even hotter. He looked like he had been freshly polished by a jeweler under a magnifying glass. His teeth were Colgate white. His bronzed skin had an airtight sheen. He was muscular and compact like a soccer player with a lustrous head of golden hair, twisted into a fashionable man bun.

"Need help with the bags?" he asked, leaning down tentatively. His accent was still thick with the surf of Bondi Beach.

"No, I've got it."

"Good, because I just got a manicure."

They laughed nervously.

"How very metro of you," Stella smarted.

When they stepped inside the grand gallery of his three-story house, Stella was instructed with haste to remove her shoes. It looked like a model home, immaculate and unlived in with of-the-moment boho elements like cowhide rugs, a black walnut tree stump for a coffee table, a plethora of plants, and even an indoor koi pond. It smelled of leather and pine, a Millennial outdoorsman's wet dream.

"Brand new Brazilian flooring, except Claude keeps scratching it up," Ken explained, rubbing the floor with his socked toes.

He swept up a wily orange tabby and scratched him under the chin. "Don'tchu, baby boy? Don'tchu?" he cooed to the cat, who executed a series of desperate escape maneuvers. "Claude! Come back. Daddy made you a star and you are so ungrateful. You know people think being a stage parent is easy. It's not."

"So, you're making this much money as a cat influencer?"

"It's a bit insulting to call me a *cat influencer*, Stella. C'mon. I'm an icon and so is Claude. And we are busier than ever. Claude went three rounds of callbacks for Fresh Step. If he wasn't such a little shit he might have booked the spot," he said, gritting his teeth. Claude paused and looked up, but soon went back to spit shining his anus. "Let me give you the tour."

He led her past the living room up the stairs, which wrapped around a massive boulder that spanned the height of the house.

"You're welcome to sleep with me, clothing optional." He gestured to a low California King in the master bedroom. "My friends sleep here all the time. It's cozy."

"OK, but you have another..."

"Bedroom, of course. Your choice."

Back downstairs, they sunk into the couch to get acquainted. Was he flirting? It seemed so, but he kept a middle school dance distance, clinging to his cat like a life raft in foreign seas.

The doorbell rang. "Ooh, who could that be?" Ken asked with the goofiness of a magician pulling a quarter out of her ear.

"Expecting company?"

"It's my man crush!" he squealed, his baby blue eyes flashing with anticipation.

Was he joking? His sexual orientation was harder than a hieroglyph to decipher.

The door swung open and in walked the most strapping mountain man Stella had ever seen. Less pretty than Ken, but almost a foot taller, this guy never had a manicure in his life.

"This is my mate Mason. He's so in love with me, he drove all the way from Provo."

Mason laughed, unfazed by Ken's advances. "Yeah, sure, man! It's only an hour." He locked his jungle green eyes onto Stella and smiled. He was boyish in the face with an upturned nose. *Can't be older than 25.* He looked like an Alpinist, a playboy who would be perched fireside at a Swiss lodge with a gaggle of busty blondes at his service.

"OK, you two, I gotta finish this Fancy Feast video. Mason, entertain Stella. It's her first time here."

Mason fixed his gaze on her and laid in with questions about her origin, her destination, and her work. The real question at the tip of his tongue seemed to be, "Who are you to him?"

Stella's mind raced. She did not want to spoil their chemistry with the mention of a cult or an ex-husband. *Too soon. Just relax. Enjoy yourself.*

"So, you're on a road trip? From where? How do you know Ken?"

She tried to contain her excitement at his interest.

"Pour me another whiskey and I'll tell you anything you want to know." She held out her glass. He laughed and slid in closer for the pour. She liked his mouth when he grinned, the way the apples of his cheeks were like polished ambrosia. His tawny hair had a dramatic, jaunty wave at the cowlick. He was brimming with life.

An hour or so later, Ken reappeared and plopped onto the couch in the slender space between them.

"Stella's never smoked. Can you believe it?" He held out a joint.

"She's a woman of mystery," Mason said, taking the hand-roll between his fingers.

"Stella, crikey. We have so many ways to corrupt you this weekend. You're like a kid!" Ken joked.

"Hand me that joint," she said, placing it between her index finger and thumb like she'd seen in the movies. She had tried to smoke with Marlene but abandoned the cause after a series of coughing spells.

She took a long drag and began hacking with all the grace of a coal miner.

"Water!" was all she could get out.

Ken rolled to the floor in cruel laughter while with lightning speed Mason fetched a glass of water.

Stella gulped it down embarrassingly. Mason moved closer to pat her back like a baby while she learned how to inhale and exhale again. Even in her state, she couldn't help noticing how broad his hands were, slightly roughened like a climber's would be.

Collapsing on the couch, Stella felt a wanting from both of them. They eyed her for consent. She wanted it too, but not just yet. She knew not why she was so confident with them, but there was no denying how preternatural a command she felt.

Why spoil all this delicious sexual tension now? she thought, excusing herself to the bathroom. Her head swirled. Gazing into the mirror, she took a long look at the glassy-eyed woman, cheering her towards the goal of climbing into bed with not one, but two gorgeous men. She tiptoed down the hall to find the boys on Ken's bed.

"Is this what I think it is?" she flirted.

"Get your mind out of the gutter, church lady," Ken joked. "I told you. All my friends sleep with me. Get in your bag. Practice for tomorrow."

Ken unzipped the sleeping bag that laid between him and Mason. Stella was thoroughly confused by the gesture. Ken seemed most definitely to be flirting with her. Was she so high she couldn't read the signs? Nothing made sense, but the bliss she felt was like a bear hug soothing her disembodied mind. She climbed into the bed and once the manic teenage glee subsided, she fell into slumber.

* * * * *

Stella awoke to Ken snoring and Mason beaming at her.

"Morning," he greeted with a groggy smile. He wiped the crust from his eyes and sat up. "We better get on the road." He reached across Stella's chest to smack Ken on the ass. "Wake up, bro! Time to hit the road if we want to get a good spot."

Ken awoke with a start and lunged towards Mason. Stella leapt out of her sleeping bag to avoid being tackled. The Ambiguously Gay Duo wrestled playfully until Mason pinned Ken under his beefy biceps, pulling at his hair, and ruffling it into a fabulous mess.

By 10 a.m. they were piled in the car, indignant puss and all. While Ken sat in the back and fussed with the cat, Stella learned that Mason was an engineer from a small town in Louisiana with the good manners to balance his Harry Connick Jr. drawl with enough city slicker liberality. He had moved to Utah to spend more time off-grid, camping, bouldering, alone in nature. He was more Muir than Thoreau. The natural world was his true love and Stella had always admired people who were at home in the elements. There must've been a good deal of evolutionary biology to support her attraction to him. Perhaps it was like Aristotle said, "Whosoever is delighted in solitude is either a wild beast or a god." She hoped he was both. She wanted to be devoured by such a man.

"Turn down the music! Claude hates Glass Animals." Ken's mood had shifted. The cat was slithering between the backseat and the trunk of Mason's Jeep. She could feel Ken burning a hole through the headrest. He noisily ripped through the wrapper of what must have been his fourth candy bar. Why was he so upset? Had he not engineered this whole love triangle?

As they climbed higher in elevation, a confection of snow began falling as if a benevolent baker in the sky was sifting powdered sugar. Stella could make out ski lodges dotted in miniature along the evergreen hills. She temporarily forgot about Ken's souring mood and pinched herself with gratitude. She was floating in a lust-dusted snow globe of hot, younger men. Life had suddenly become so good.

They pulled into the campground and emptied out of the car with haste to soak in the idyllic scene. Stella inhaled deeply the sharp, fresh air so disinfected from urban soot it almost singed her sinuses. For a moment, she parted company and strolled pensively along a babbling brook. The land was otherwise free of human sounds but boisterous with animal activity. Crepuscular creatures scampered through the bush, bedding down beyond the clearing of their dusty little camp. Over the dragon's tail of a ridge, thousands of dark spires made up a looming, caliginous forest.

Ken hooked Claude into a harness and tried to take him for a walk. The cat resisted with a guttural snarl, digging his claws in the dirt.

"Smoke and mirrors, my friend. Smoke and mirrors," said Mason, shaking his head.

"What is?" asked Ken defensively.

"This whole cat influencer thing. Your cat hates the outdoors. We've tried this before!"

"He loves it and so do I. Now hurry up and set up before dark. I've gotta work on this post."

Mason obliged and unloaded the gear from his Jeep.

"My girlfriend would never help me do this," he lamented as he laid out the tarp of a bright orange tent.

"I don't mind. I should learn since it's my first time camping," Stella replied.

"Well, she's my ex now," he said, locking two tent poles together. "We broke up... again."

Mason made a fire and Stella mock-congratulated him on being "so manly." They had developed a snarky backhanded banter as full of faux insults as it was of bona fide lust. She sat on a log and warmed her hands on the crackle and pop of the kindling, watching the sparks fly into the butter pink sky as the sun set and song birds bellowed their last melancholy melodies for the day. If ever there was a definition of romance, this was it. *Why isn't he trying to kiss me though?* She contemplated laying it all out. *I'll tell him that if we are going to make out, now is our chance.*

But it was too late. Ken came stomping through the crisp leaves carrying Claude and lamenting his lack of wifi. His stomach was in knots from his Butterfinger binge. Everything was wrong. Just wrong.

"Camp is all set up, let's get to the hot springs," Mason encouraged.

"Stella, take this chocolate. I can't eat anymore," Ken said, handing her a half-nibbled bar.

She broke off a square and put the whole thing in her mouth. "Ew, this is kinda gross."

"Here, give it back," Ken demanded. He was relentlessly moody for such a pleasant evening. The doldrums were in full swing like he was some eternally damned Tennessee Williams character. He could play the doomed diva like nobody she knew.

Mason ignored his mercurial friend and began trekking up a dusty hill. Stella slipped on a headlamp and scrambled up behind him, her quads tensing at the incline.

"I'll meet you later. Gotta find wifi!" Ken yelled from below. "Don't do anything I wouldn't do!"

Mason shook his head with a wry smile. "OK, man. Sure!"

They marched on until the top of the hill opened up to a scrubby plateau. Suddenly, there before them were dozens of glowing eyes. Dotted along the bushes, every creature froze. The air smelled of sage and pine with only the faint rustle of leaves in the wind of the new moon.

"Deer," Mason whispered.

"Incredible!"

"Look up."

They raised their eyes to the sapphire night sky, their torsos kissing as they twisted around to take in the panorama of silver studs blinking from the detached darkness. Mason reached up to turn off Stella's headlamp.

"This is the most stars I have ever seen in my life," he said in awe.

"Life is a treasure hunt, you know. I guess I still believe in God after all," she waxed in a hush. "Maybe he did create us to go on this epic search and discover exquisite places and moments like this. And look at how the animals watch us like we are the performers. Maybe we are. All the world's a stage..."

"Someone is high."

"No, just grateful. Well..." she said, rubbing her stomach. "Maybe a little drunk. I'm feeling something."

Mason shook the whiskey bottle. "You've barely had a drop." He extended his hand towards her head and she thought he would take her in his arms right there with the glowing eyes and the sagebrush and the stars, but no. He clicked on her headlamp and wrapped his wide hand around hers. "Let's go."

After a few twists and turns through narrower stretches of brush, they were good and lost. Stella didn't mind. She felt safe with the mountain man. Time stood still like it had the night before. She was both in the moment and far, far away, lost in a cozy cocktail of serenity and anticipation.

After backtracking through the dirt a few dozen feet, Mason had oriented them again. They trekked until the path opened up once more. There before them was another brilliant Easter egg—a deep, dark river shimmering like a million diamonds in the moonlight. Perched alongside it was a natural hot spring. The steam rose from the pool into the blackness of night and evaporated mist into the Milky Way.

If there is a God, he might very well be Nora Ephron, Stella thought.

Mason held tightly to her hand as they descended some 30 feet down the slick, uneven boulders to the pool. He then busied himself laying out towels, while Stella queued up a sexy playlist. Bass rumbled from the speaker as Sabrina Claudio's "Put On Repeat" began to play. Stella hurriedly disrobed down to her bra and underwear and lowered herself into the hot spring. The moss was slippery underfoot as she rotated around to catch a peek of Mason as he stripped down to his boxers. Her headlamp washed a beam of light over his taut abs. His shoulders were chiseled like an Adonis. Stella quickly switched off the light, pretending she wasn't transfixed by his figure.

He grinned knowingly.

"I don't know why I can't get warm," she said, her breath a steamy exhalation in the frigid night air.

Mason grabbed the whiskey and slid in next to her. "This'll warm you up."

She took a swig.

"I'd like a taste," said Mason.

She handed him the bottle, but he set it on the rocks. "No... a taste of you."

She smiled wider than the Grand Canyon. "I thought you'd never ask."

Mason wasted not a second before he pulled her in by the waist and pressed his lips into hers. She grabbed the back of his neck and, with a single motion, their slick bodies became flush. He reached up to unhook her bra and sent it floating across the water. She threw back her head in delight as he plied her breasts with his broad hands. He pushed her body skyward and at the moment he began sucking from her, they heard a voice...

"Hey, guys. You down there?"

Stella flapped across the pond like a befuddled goose to retrieve her bra, but it was nowhere to be found. Ken was already descending the stone staircase. Stella wrapped her hands around her breasts in a futile attempt to cover them.

"Stell-uh," Ken said with a playful lilt. "Party started without me?"

Ken stripped naked and jumped in the water.

Stella and Mason exchanged surprised glances.

"What?" Ken asked. "Isn't everyone skinny dipping?"

"I'm just dipping. Nothing skinny about it," Stella joked.

Ken swam closer to her. "You look perfect to me," he said, gently unwrapping her arms to reveal her naked torso.

She sank into the water. Her body pulsed with a strange sensation. Her head seemed to detach like a balloon and hover several feet in the air. Ken's face was distorted and alien as he moved in to kiss her neck.

She could see that Mason was startled. He splashed up behind and leaned her back onto his broad chest. Her breasts floated like lotus flowers, her nipples erect upon breaching the steamy water and meeting cold air. Ken pressed his chest against hers. She was sandwiched now with her head on Mason's shoulder. He kissed her lips while Ken planted soft kisses along her shoulder. Mason's face dripped like a Dali, while the music drifted through her bones with a baroque echo from far away. The rhythm of their bodies displaced the water and caused it to slosh against the rocks in time with the melody. The surrealistic beat began to hypnotize her. She opened her mouth to speak but was unable for several minutes… or was it hours?

Ken suckled her breasts, pleasurably nibbling on her nipples while he seemed to be caressing Mason. Were they lovers? Stella's haze of a brain tried unsuccessfully to make impossible calculations.

She twisted around like a wild-eyed sloth to face Mason in hopes of getting an answer to the question yet unspoken from her lips.

"Having fun?" he asked.

"Mmhm," she said, taking his face in her hands and staring into his colossal cadmium eyes. She pressed her lips into his and felt phantom hands moving all over her body, first on her back, then her ass, slipping off her panties, running down her thighs.

She smiled wide, drew both men to her, and whispered, "I feel like Beyoncé on her birthday."

Before she knew it, she was floating on her back, suspended like a magnificent bridge between the two men. She wrapped her legs around Mason's neck and he pressed his face into the eager flesh between her thighs. She had never felt anything like it. Sensation on top of sensation, she was overcome. She sighed from the deepest part of her diaphragm as Ken bent down to kiss her tenderly and Mason slipped his hungry tongue all over her sex. She twitched and whimpered for several pleasantly agonizing moments before, weightless and throbbing with ecstasy, she cried out to Cassiopeia all her delight.

Mason then grabbed her by the hips and slid inside. Ken's face lit up like a Christmas tree. When she reached for him under the water, she found he was as hard as one too. Mason pulsed in and out while she stroked Ken, who seemed utterly spellbound by the sight of his friend. Ken came closer in what she expected to be a kiss, but he reached for Mason, who escaped the advance by moving Stella towards the perimeter of the pool.

She braced herself against the rocks. It was just the two of them now moving rhythmically. Mason leaned close and whispered to her how fucking sexy she was, which sent her hips into wild rotations around his cock. He was full and thick inside her desperate, slick pussy.

They moved faster. She pushed against him with the grandness of her ass. He grabbed and smacked her wet flesh. Stella attempted to lock her arms in a sturdy brace, but she was too weak. Her thighs absorbed the shock from the rocks, but the pain was nothing compared to the euphoria. She and Mason were dewy and drunk and unbound by earthly law.

"I want to play with you all night," Mason said, reaching around her pelvis, his fingers in determined pursuit of her clit.

"Me too," she said breathlessly, pressing her wet cheek to his neck.

They slipped around the mossy pool with abandon, as if they were completely alone in the universe, until a train clattered loudly onto the tracks across the river. The headlights poured over them, illuminating the glistening flesh of their tangled torsos. Mason flipped Stella over to rest on his chest again and slipped his fingers inside her. Her body contracted. She cried out again, powerless against the explosion of a juicy burst of penultimate pleasure.

They sank heavy into the water as if two lovingly fused stones.

"This is surreal," said Stella melodiously.

"The best night of my life."

Ken was nowhere to be found. Stella and Mason had disappeared into a world of their own making, now locked at the lips for several intoxicated moments.

"I'm so tired," Stella said with a yawn that wouldn't cease.

"We can go." Mason climbed out and extended his hand to her.

"I'm too... cold," she said, teeth chattering. "I can't get out."

"I'll help you." He laid out her clothes near the edge of the pool and held up a towel.

She sprang out of the water squealing. He closed the towel around her, rubbing her vigorously. She felt childlike in his care.

"My hair! God, I'm so cold."

"Here." He took the towel from his waist and wrapped it around her head. He held her pants out, bending down for her to step into them. They had a hearty laugh as he mistakenly tried to fit her shirt over her towel head, but within minutes she was fully dressed and they were climbing up the rocks towards the trail.

"I need to lay down. I think I drank too much. My legs are so…" she stumbled as she attempted to climb the steep path.

"You really didn't drink that much," Mason said, steadying her.

They followed the trail back to the sagebrush plateau where he grabbed her and kissed her deeply. "I want to do that all over again on dry land."

"Mmhm. Must sleep first though," Stella replied drunkenly. She shuffled behind, holding tight to his hand to stay upright.

Back at the camp, they found Ken stewing in the car. "Oh look, it's Adam and Eve. The tent is all set up. Just waiting for the lovebirds to return."

Mason laughed nervously. "Let's just get some sleep. Sun will be up soon."

He guided Stella into the tent and laid her down on the sleeping bag in the middle.

"My hair is still wet," she said with an epileptic shiver.

"Yeah, and you smell like a skunk," Ken said, turning up his nose. "You sleep over there." He pushed her against the wall of the tent, rearranging the bags so she would be farthest from him.

Stella laid on the stiff, cold ground for an eternity, but when she couldn't take it anymore, she rolled over to make a plea to Mason. He was fast asleep or pretending to be. "Help!" she wanted to scream.

"Ken, I'm so cold, I can't sleep. Do you have an extra sleeping pad or a blanket?" He didn't respond for several long minutes as she sat shivering like a dirty dog. She jostled his shoulder. Claude hissed at her and raked the blades of his claws across her hand.

Desperate, she unzipped the tent and stumbled out towards the car. It was locked. *Jesus H. Christ!* How could the most erotic night of her life have devolved into this pneumonia-inducing nightmare?

Back to the tent she went, cursing and cold, tossing and turning all night.

By sunrise, all the sex had been sucked out of the air and Ken was still pissed and punitive. "Stella, you really need to take a shower," he said, waving the air. *"Pee-you!"* He scooted out of his sleeping bag in disgust.

"Well, let's just go then. I didn't sleep a wink." She looked to Mason for help, but he offered nothing.

"Yeah, edibles are sometimes like that," Ken said nonchalantly, stepping out of the tent.

"Edibles?" Stella asked, sitting up with a start.

"Yeah, you took an edible, remember? Maybe that's why you were such a slut."

"I didn't take an edible."

Ken held a straight face as long as he could before bursting into maniacal laughter.

"Ken!" Mason exclaimed, unzipping his sleeping bag.

"What?" Ken replied in mock innocence as he folded Claude's tiny sleeping bag onto a picnic table.

"The chocolate, Stella. You ate the chocolate, right?" Mason looked at her incredulously.

"Oh my God. You didn't tell me that was an edible!" Stella's heart began to beat like a drum. "How could you?!"

"I thought you knew," Ken lied. "You said you wanted to do edibles."

"Ken, you know she's not experienced," Mason said, moving towards him. "Dude, that's fucked up."

"Oh, who the fuck cares? That little piece was basically a microdose. You two had an *enormous* amount of fun. You're welcome!" Ken said, slamming the back door of the Jeep shut.

Stella remained paralyzed in the tent for several minutes. She couldn't trust Ken and didn't feel entirely confident she could rely on Mason either. Her body hollow and weak, she could smell the stench of stale minerals in her tangled hair. Her bladder ached and there was no bathroom within walking distance.

Ken hurried everyone along in clearing the campsite and Stella complied in frightful, stoned obedience.

The ride home was spent in icy silence more frigid than the snow-capped peaks all around them. An unspoken fear of Ken's continued retribution hung in the air and Stella and Mason dared not talk, much less flirt. Mason's solution was to turn up the music and stare into the horizon as if he was trying to concentrate on something very far away.

As soon as they got home, Ken could not be bothered to help empty the car and, like a petulant child, flew off to his bedroom, slamming the door with such force the entire metal staircase shook. Stella stood in the foyer, bags hanging off every arm, shoulders cramped into unforgiving knots. She was still stunned and confused. Mason sat forward on the couch and stared into his phone with the same avoidant intensity as in the car.

Stella dropped the bags to the floor. She sat down next to Mason, her fellow hostage in this emotional hijacking, and whisper-screamed into his ear. "Ken drugged me!"

"I know. Stella, I had no idea. You gotta believe me." The innocence of his eyes told her he was not guilty of the crime, rather an unwitting bystander in a sociopath's demented sexual game.

He ran his hand across her face. She was not immune to the stimulation of his touch even under these circumstances.

"I need to leave." Before the words were spoken, she heard the crackle of lightning and the rumble of thunder. She walked to the massive window overlooking the dense forest below.

"Thunder snow," Mason explained, joining her.

"I've never seen anything like it."

Heavy sheets of snow began filtering into the pines.

"It's going to make driving a bitch," Mason warned, jiggling the keys in his pocket nervously.

"I need to get out of here. Can I stay with you?" she pleaded, glancing at the stairwell.

Mason hesitated. "Um, yeah, but only for a day or two, OK? Until you get on your feet."

Ken tramped down the stairs in a huff, catching his towel as it tilted like a tower on his head. "Stella, it's been great, but I'm leaving tomorrow so you'll have to find a place to stay." He made an irritated sweeping motion towards the door.

"No problem." She rose to grab her coat. "Mason, let's go."

"Mason?" Ken questioned, hand on hip in injured astonishment.

"Yeah, I'm gonna head out. Talk to you soon, brother. Have a great trip."

Stella rolled her suitcase out the door. The snow was thick and heavy. She shielded her eyes from the downpour and sprinted to her car.

"OK, now be very careful going down this road," Mason yelled over the thunder, throwing her suitcase in the backseat of her Civic while she slid in.

Leaning on the doorframe, he cautioned her, "Follow me. Drive slow."

He did seem to care about her and despite the awkward drama, her wretched smell, and the unceremonious eviction from Ken's, she felt a thrill.

However, it didn't last.

She barely made it onto the highway when the snow began coming down so hard her windshield wipers could not function under the weight. Making an emergency stop at a gas station, she lost Mason altogether.

Moments later, she was back on the road going as fast as she could. *50, 60, 70…* It was dangerous to speed like this. As she gained momentum, her car slid across the slick pavement. She recovered with a few pumps to the brakes, careful not to lose control entirely. Thankfully, there was little traffic on the road.

Where is he? she fretted, speeding up and rifling through her purse for her phone.

Then *bam!* A black streak skidded across her windshield with a heart-stopping thud.

"Shit!"

She maneuvered the car onto the shoulder as quickly as possible.

Catching her breath, she reversed a few feet. Studying the rearview mirror, she saw a bird twitching and squawking behind her a foot into the road. She jerked the car into park and flew out. With a wild wave of her arms, she motioned several cars away from the creature.

Squatting down, she could see the crow had the same jet-black plumage as she with her chemically altered hair. A trickle of crimson blood seeped from its heaving breast as it fought for one last breath. What could she do… for the bird or for herself?

Her flight felt so similar. Had she not been so hasty in her escape that she had been metaphorically struck as well? Was God punishing her? Was she under the devil's control? Had the other shoe already dropped just like the Witnesses warned?

Sopping in snow, she returned to the car. Mason had texted. He was waiting for her at a rest stop a few miles ahead and had dropped a pin for her to navigate to. She adjusted the rearview mirror and commenced with a pep talk.

"Go get him, girl. You did not spend 25 years in a cult to go out after a few months!"

With that, she pressed defiantly on the gas.

A hair-raising hour later, she and Mason began settling into his modest two-bedroom apartment in Provo. He had just moved in, he explained somewhat apologetically, as he gave her a tour. They rounded the corner past his laundry room and he quickly closed the door on the messy space, bitching about his roommate's dirty little housekeeping quirks as young people do. Stella was grateful to be far past that stage of life, inhabiting her little palace solo.

He showed her to the bathroom and she could not wait to scrub off the filth of the camping debacle. She had been self-conscious about it all along, applying copious amounts of deodorant under the three layers of clothes she wore and smoothing fragrant Moroccan oil in her frizzy hair. Somehow, Mason seemed not to notice. He flirted with her just the same, taking every opportunity to touch her waist or her thigh as they got acquainted once again. There was a silent but clear dialogue between them that they would indeed finish what they started, this time on dry land.

Stella quickly hit the shower, raking her razor up every inch of her body and scrubbing her hair with ferocity. The oppressiveness of female beauty standards aside, this was the least she could do to not feel like some Yeti wandered in from the woods. She made a vow to herself to never go camping with a crush again.

Exiting the shower, she made a mess of her suitcase, fretting about just which outfit would both look sexy *and* keep her warm. She decided on black leggings, a thin long-sleeved shirt sheer enough for her nipples to show through, and a silky floral robe.

Grateful for Mason's kindness, she offered to make dinner. Examining the sparse contents of the bachelor's pantry, she found just enough ingredients to cook her mother's marinara.

She uncorked a bottle of cheap red wine and filled two tumblers—Mason had no wine glasses—while he sparked up a joint. He looked so cute leaning the bulk of his muscular body against the counter while she stirred at the stove. She splashed a bit of the wine into the pot, the garlic and onions sizzling with a fragrant nostalgia that tinged her sinuses and ached her heart. The pasta was a dish she had cooked often for Adam, an easy go-to when they arrived home from their ministry physically and emotionally spent.

The sauce simmering to perfection on the stove, she took the joint from Mason in exchange for a spoonful of marinara, which the lick of his lips and the shine of his green eyes confirmed was delicious. She scooped the steaming penne into two bowls and added the chunky sauce with a heap of Parmesan to top it off. They sat cross-legged on the couch and slurped to satisfaction. Not a moment after they finished, Mason playfully grabbed at her legs—she somewhat resisting—until he scooped her up into his arms and carried her up the stairs. She giggled, psyched and stoned all the way to the bed, where she was disrobed with urgency.

Mason, bent on bringing her to climax, sucked on the tenderly engorged folds of her lips with equal parts delicate and intense force until he could no longer resist the urge to mount her. She exhaled euphorically as he slid inside her. He leaned in to kiss her neck and lips while he pulsated and groaned. She kissed his massive biceps as he moved up and down like a hydraulic pump.

When they finished, he wrapped her in his arms and held her tight. His tenderness surprised and delighted her.

The next morning, he greeted her fully clothed with coffee.

"How'd you sleep?" he asked, glancing at his phone.

"Great, after you did what you did," she said, pressing her finger to his lips.

He chuckled halfheartedly. "Yeah, that was fun, but look, my girlfriend is coming, so you've got somewhere to go, right?"

"Girlfriend? You said you broke up." Stella sat up straight as a board, slamming the coffee mug down so hard it sloshed onto the nightstand.

"I said we were on a break, but if she finds out she will be pissed. So, you can head out today, right?"

All the warmth in Stella's throat drained. How had she so misunderstood Mason's intentions? Was the way he made love to her meaningless?

She rose quietly from the bed like a haunted woman and began packing.

"Stella, I'm sorry. I don't mean you have to leave right this second, but... sometime today."

"Yeah. OK."

"Let me help you." He picked up her discarded clothes from the night before and folded them into her suitcase. "Why don't you check out Moab next? It's not too far."

"Maybe. I dunno," she said, unable to hide her dejection. "I've gotta go to the bathroom," she said, scampering away. She waited by the door until she heard Mason gathering his keys.

"Stella, I'm going to work," he yelled from down the hall. "Text me when you leave. And take care! It was fun!"

She sucked back her tears and forced a genial goodbye through the bathroom door. But before the front door was locked, she burst into wet, broken sobs that couldn't be quelled.

The brilliant morning sun mocked her gray mood. She shuffled along freezing bathroom tiles, avoiding herself in the mirror. She plopped down on the toilet, but the throbs of her cheeks sent her back up squawking like a chicken on the chopping block.

She was now forced to face the train wreck in the mirror. Twisting around, she was confronted by a smattering of sallow green rosettes painted across her ass like leopard print, bruises from the hot springs.

When she lowered herself onto the porcelain again, she hovered, holding her breath and centering her weight to avoid reigniting the agony in her inflamed cheeks. Her stomach rumbled like thunder. Within her gut brewed a sour mash of pain and paranoia.

"What happened?" Stella whispered, prone to copious self-talk ever since leaving the cult.

A hazy montage of the previous day began playing in her mind. The dry crackle of the campfire in the cold. The boys exchanging knowing glances. The glow of eyes in the sagebrush. The bottle of whiskey they downed.

Her head was a ticker tape of regret. She picked up her phone and instinctively scrolled to her mother's name. A tear trickled down her face. She kept scrolling, hoping for a sympathetic name to pop up. *Marlene?* Yes, maybe.

Marlene answered right away.

"Stella, *dah-ling,*" she said jovially, as if no cavernous rift had split them weeks earlier.

"Hey, Marlene," she replied, her voice thin and helpless.

"How are you?"

"Fine, I guess. On a road trip. Kind of finding myself. I got into some... um... unexpected adventures." She sighed long and deep.

"What's going on?"

"I'm sorry," she said pitifully. "I didn't know who to call."

"What's wrong?"

"I think God is smiting me for leaving. What if I have... AIDS?" Stella sobbed.

"Why are you worried about AIDS?"

"I had unprotected sex. I feel sick."

"No, not that vase. Put the flowers in my Mikasa crystal!" Marlene's command was stern and direct. "I have Houseboy over," she explained. "I've been where you are now. Remind me to tell you about the Bedouin who fucked me sideways in a cave in Petra."

"I feel so gross. I'm sitting on the toilet constipated. My ass looks like it got caught in a Texas hailstorm."

"Drink lots of water," Marlene advised maternally. "Breathe. Drink. Breathe." She demonstrated with dramatic breaths.

"My head is kind of... in the ether. I can't remember how it all started exactly. I think I wanted it, but now I don't know..."

"No wonder you're freaking out. I have a clinic in West Hollywood. Very queer-friendly and clean. We're going to sort this all out. Get that battered peach home. I'll be waiting."

CHAPTER 11

The Dragulator

STELLA RANG the doorbell with a heart full of anticipation and heard the bombastic thumps of Marlene's footsteps coming towards the door. They greeted one another with the same level of enthusiasm as root canal patients but covered it up with faux kisses and dramatic accents and *all that jazz*. Stella had so few friends anywhere in the world; she needed someone. She needed Marlene.

Marlene was in yoga pants with her hair in a high ponytail. It was strange. Around the Hollywood Hills villa, she wore only the finest silk.

Stella tried to conceal the surprise creeping up her face as she stepped inside the apartment. The worn beige carpet and popcorn ceilings were far from opulent. She felt like she had just pulled back the curtain on the Great and Powerful Oz. Marlene put on such great airs that one would expect her to be carried around by 12 strong men, laid on a gold divan, and lulled to sleep by lutes.

Marlene, however, considered the place "a reflection of my talent for imbuing the mundane with luxury" and "a gallery of my extensive travels and bohemian tastes." She'd thrifted treasures in every flea market from Melrose to Mulholland, that much was true. While her decor was lovely, Stella had a less grandiose appraisal of the infinitesimal galley kitchen with its yellowing linoleum. For many weeks, they had convened only at Stella's apartment. Now she knew why. Marlene's place was a dimly lit walk-up with little of the charm she presently described with such *imagination*. There was no seating save for a wicker peacock chair and a few wooden stools at the kitchen counter. It was a strange way to live.

"Human furniture suffices!" Marlene cackled, flopping down on the floor to stretch like a cat. "I like it this way." She gestured to the living room. "More space for my theatre of the bizarre. My guests are more likely to be tied to a bench than lounging on a couch anyway."

She jumped up and busied herself making cocktails. "Gin or vodka?"

"Whatever you want," Stella called back.

A few minutes later, out came a round of gin martinis in chilled glasses with three olives at Stella's request.

"So, do you want to talk about Utah?" Marlene queried sympathetically. "Did you get tested?"

"Yeah, everything is fine. I don't know why I freaked out so much. Thanks, Nancy Reagan and cult fearmongering! I guess I'm just always waiting for the other shoe to drop when it comes to sex and drugs." But then Stella's throat flushed with warmth and her tone shifted. "Still, it was so hot, Marlene. The most erotic night of my life," she gushed. "Is that fucked up or what?"

"Maybe, or perhaps you're a masochist living out a bit of nihilism where you had none before."

"I think I am getting off on the 'wrongness' of things."

"You've never had the opportunity to be deviant or to consider if that word applies to things you like. Your lens has been so myopic."

"Nothing has felt wrong, just long overdue. Even though I was drugged."

"Which most definitely was wrong," Marlene interjected.

"Yes, but I would have fucked Ken sober. And I wanted Mason. And them worshiping me together… I was in heaven. The most fucked up part was how they treated me afterwards."

"Aftercare is so important."

"Well, this was just vanilla."

"It's vital no matter the interaction. Vanilla or kink. You're coming down from a high. There's a definite drop, especially when drugs are mixed in."

"Yeah, I've never had sex without cuddling…" Stella trailed off in sudden sadness.

She was loath to dwell on the loneliness that had been knocking more persistently at the door since her split with Adam. Her kink education under staunch feminist—almost fascist—Marlene forbade pining for a man, for such a thing would render her weak and stereotypical. No, Marlene had set her on the path of a higher calling. In almost monastic terms, Marlene prescribed a detachment from heteroromantic desire. She judged harshly any contradiction to the kink code. She had used the word "dickmatized" to describe Stella's dalliance with Isaiah. It was meant to cut, to make Stella feel inferior to her, with Marlene's lack of need for anything as basic and banal as a boyfriend.

The truth was that Stella's body ached to be big-spooned in bed. She had not considered the chemical withdrawals she might experience leaving her closest companion. She was forced to come face-to-face with a tense and twitchy feeling in her body as she bedded down at night and woke alone in the morning. No one to hold her in the crook of their arm and the apple of their eye. No one greeting her at dawn with coffee and affection. She had cut out tender parts of herself to get free.

There were times, Marlene related, that she felt she was surfing the waves of Stella's newfound freedom with her, gleaning bits of sea glass with Stella's tendency to swallow too much water, to be sucked into the undertow of fast fuck dating hookups, snared by the longline snood of some twentysomething fisherman with a row of pearly teeth and washboard abs.

"Be careful, Stella. I've done fucked up things too, but always have an escape if things go too far. Anyway, let me finish the tour."

"The tour?" Stella asked, inwardly judging. *What more could there be to see in this dump?*

"Welcome to the Dragulator," Marlene said proudly, bringing Stella into a room down the hallway.

It was an entire space dedicated to dress-up, her own personal boutique, and it was stunning. The small room brimmed with hats and gloves and headpieces, beaded clutches and corsetry. With its mahogany wardrobes, the sumptuous plush of velvet, everything fringed or tasseled like Satine's boudoir, Stella couldn't help but be impressed.

"Leather from Italy. Lace from Spain," Marlene said, running her hands over an embossed handbag and an eyelet blouse. "For me, costuming is a primary modality of expression and so many of my fetishes reflect the fact. What better place to lather a clotheshorse than a personal kink boutique?" When she was in full Marlene, she looked and sounded like a lesser-known Hepburn sister minus the transatlantic affectation, although the thespian in her could put one on.

The Dragulator was indeed splendid. It was the culmination of hundreds of vintage hauls from curio shops around the world. Turning a second bedroom into a personal closet was so egocentric. In this, Stella admired Marlene. The cult had programmed her never to think of self and many a time she had been counseled by the elders for peacocking her colorful ensembles to Sunday service. In Marlene, she saw a woman literally taking up space. And this is what drew her to such a questionable companion even in the aftermath of a deception as great as hers.

Marlene strutted over to a leather trunk and opened it slowly as if preparing to perform a magic trick. She ran her hands along the crocodile leather. "This is my boudoir box. It's like a goose with golden eggs," she enticed, swinging it open.

The inside was lined with red satin and in it hung an imaginarium of silver and steel, silicone, floggers, and rope. It jingled like a belly dancer's coin scarf as she wheeled it closer for Stella to take a wide-eyed look. Not only were there the expected adults-only accouterments but also a bevy of botanicals and vials. There were strange little powders and floral waters, a veritable apothecary, which Marlene did not allow Stella to touch.

Marlene spritzed a silk handkerchief and held it up to Stella's nose. "This is the scent I use to train Hope."

"It's lovely."

"Rose and nasturtium." Marlene took a deep inhalation then folded the fabric into a perfect square and set it back in the box.

"But what do you mean 'train' her?"

"Just what it sounds like. She's trained on my scent."

"Like a dog?"

"Like a deeply devoted submissive," Marlene corrected, continuing in her trademark haughty air. She snapped the boudoir box closed as if the magician realized she had revealed too much. "I told you I live well. Poor little rich girl, you know. Even the richest of the rich don't have what I have in the depth of love and adoration of my submissives."

"Speaking of wealth... What *do* you do?" Stella waded in cautiously to a subject she was sure would prickle Marlene.

"I'm a bartender at LA's swankiest cocktail lounge," Marlene said, more like a brag than a humble admission.

It made sense. She had an extensive knowledge of liquor and knew a veritable who's who of LA's elite.

"Why keep that from me?" Stella asked, sitting cross-legged on the floor, waiting for a full confession to tumble out of Marlene's mouth.

"Don't tell me you didn't love John and Rosyln's house!"

"Who?"

"My dearest guests every Thursday night for the last five years. They always have me housesit when they jetset."

Stella sat stunned. "Can I have another?" She pushed her glass in Marlene's direction. "I just don't understand why you're still bartending when you have such a talent for kink."

"For one, Stella, I'm not out yet."

Marlene returned with another round of martinis and sat across from Stella much the same way they had that fortuitous day in Guam. Marlene explained that she had been raised a born-again Christian and that she still carried so many of the red letters of that gospel into every aspect of her life. Though her sapphic orientation had been revealed as a teenager, she was still closeted as a Domme. What her mother would make of it she could only imagine. To this, of course, Stella could relate.

"Despite the cognitive dissonance most people assume is required to keep both bibles and butt plugs on heavy rotation in the Rolodex of one's frequent engagements, I have never denied my love of God," Marlene continued, sounding like an evangelical.

Stella was necessarily skeptical. "Do you have any idea what God says about the things you practice?" It wasn't that she retained those scriptural judgments, but she wondered if Marlene knew what kind of patriarchal bullshit she was condoning by calling herself a Christian.

"I know it's hard to understand from your perspective, but BDSM is full of religious undertones."

"I get that, but the worship is directed at you, not Jesus."

Marlene sighed. "God is my primary partner, what can I say? I know you remember that afternoon in Adivina's salon when my heart was read out like a scroll."

"Of course."

"The truth of the matter is..." Marlene seemed unsure of what she would say next, the corners of her mouth not nearly as taut as they usually were when she so proudly lauded her virtues. "Sometimes my visits home feel like a breaststroke back out into the dark. I come from a family of dysfunctional dropouts and they don't want any part of the shore."

Marlene related how she pictured the voyage of her family as the capsized ship of which Adivina spoke. She identified with treading water, the heaving of her lungs as she'd sopped and clawed her way through the riptide of infidelity and addiction. Looking all around only to realize she was alone, her kindred still bobbing out there in the inky black water. Her mother was bipolar and had abandoned the family multiple times during her youth. There were many nights slow-walking her mother's bicycle alongside her after Marlene retrieved her from bad men's dens.

Going home felt like pulling the trigger in a game of trauma roulette. There were visits she'd spent in near-total survival mode, skipping the trip wires of interpersonal conflict like a soldier ducking and tumbling through hostile terrain.

"Why didn't you tell me this?" A wave of empathy washed over her. "You know I come from an abusive family too," Stella implored, placing her hand upon Marlene's.

Marlene was quiet and the wattage of her hazel eyes dimmed for a moment. It was clear to Stella that she'd hidden these wounds from many people in her life, bending to the southern script never to let 'em see you sweat, but now here she was in the tungsten of a vintage lamp, opening up.

Stella sat quiet and calm and for the millionth time admired the beautiful bones of Marlene's face. Her greedy consumption of others, her over-the-top self-worship, and her pure vanity should have sent Stella packing, but she was endlessly drawn in. It wasn't the sex Marlene had that was taboo, it was her absolute conviction that she deserved everything she wanted. It bordered on idolatry and Stella, in her rejection of every Christian teaching that bound her against her nature, aspired to give zero fucks and thumb the nose at God himself like this "Christian" Dominatrix.

Because of Marlene, she was walking taller down the street. Standing up for herself with men. Drawing boundaries where before she only had regrets.

Marlene squeezed her hand and moved closer. Stella's pace quickened in anticipation of a kiss. Instead, Marlene reached around to grab a vintage beret off a shelf and place it on her head.

"I thought you'd look great in this. Come see," said Marlene, positioning her in front of an oak cheval mirror. She stood behind Stella, caressing her arms. "Let me dress you... then maybe *undress* you." She winked.

Stella nodded submissively. Marlene began unbuttoning Stella's blouse. Stella gazed back at her in the mirror, watching Marlene remove her bra. A rash of goosebumps spread across her chest. Marlene strapped Stella's trembling breasts into a latex halter then proceeded to oil them up like mounds of dough on her kitchen counter. Stella sighed and felt her body sink into familiar depths.

A wicked smile spread across Marlene's coral cheeks as she plied Stella's breasts like a baker. She spun Stella around, ripped off her pants, and slid her into a leather skirt. She then took a soft silicone dildo and worked it between Stella's slick tits.

Stella laughed. "You're such a perv."

"I know, but you love it because you are too."

"I've never worn latex. Does it look good?"

"You know you look hot. Now we just need somewhere to take these tits and show them off."

CHAPTER 12

Magic Mushrooms

STELLA PULLED OUT a built-in cutting board and hacked at a mound of magic mushrooms like she was prepping a feast of puttanesca. Her *I Love Lucy* kitchen was cramped but charming with its cream vintage stove and butter yellow tiles. Above the lavender sink hung a framed Oscar Wilde quote: "Our ambition should be to rule ourselves, the true kingdom for each one of us; and true progress is to know more, and be more, and to do more."

She had quickly and lavishly furnished the 600-square-foot studio with its large living/sleeping space, walled-off dining area, and highly coveted walk-in closet. It felt indulgent coming out of her ascetic missionary existence. Her version of a Parisian boudoir was all velvet furniture and dreamy 19th-century prints. They were her favorite artists from teenhood—Degas and Lautrec, O'Keefe and Alma-Tadema. Psychedelic landscapes and gauzy goddesses adorned her temple with its north-facing wall of windows overlooking Koreatown's cacophony of architectural styles.

It was Marlene's idea that they do mushrooms together as a healing balm to smooth over what she called their "misunderstanding" about her place of abode. It didn't take much to convince Stella, who was so famished for the kind of high-fashion hijinks Marlene offered, she might have said yes to heroin if they could shoot up in ball gowns.

"When's the last time you did mushrooms?" Stella inquired between chops.

"Last November, my handmaiden Hope prepared a lovely weekend at The Ritz Santa Barbara. She's perfect with such things. She was a devout Scientologist," Marlene said, sitting at the table peeling a tangerine.

"Interesting. So, you're collecting us for your cult." Stella paused her chopping to look Marlene in the eye.

"I could be a cult leader..." she snickered. "Hope and I have an intimate dynamic, full of laughter and consensual violence, true love and friendship," Marlene said, knowing full well Stella's yearning for such a thing. "She's so in love with me. Her devotion knows no bounds," Marlene bragged on.

"But you're not attracted to her?" Stella's real question was, Do you fuck her?

"Our dynamic hinges on her attraction, not mine. That's kind of the point. Sometimes I call her over to bathe me and finger fuck me like a little personal massager until I get my kicks. Then I dismiss her."

"The whole point is to torment her with unrequited desire?"

"She's profoundly grateful to feel the things she feels. Have you completed that BDSM checklist I sent you?"

"I *looked* at it," Stella admitted. "Honestly, I didn't understand some of the kinks. Hard to say whether I would enjoy being wrapped like a sushi roll, having my nipple hairs ripped out, all while being waterboarded," she mocked.

"My vanilla friends often have that reaction to my kinky life."

Was that an insult? Stella wondered, drawing in a sharp breath and holding it until her ego was dissuaded from self-defense. Marlene's airs did tread a thin line between observation and accusation.

"Well, I'm not really vanilla," Stella replied firmly. *And, are we just friends?*

"You are on your way. Do the checklist and we will see."

Stella felt a challenge, a bit of a glass ceiling with Marlene. They had not slid into the post-kiss bliss Stella had expected. Why was Marlene holding back when she had come on so strong?

Stella divided up the mushrooms evenly and laid them on the glass tabletop. She picked up a small piece and nibbled cautiously. Her mouth twisted downward in disgust. "Ick. Why do they taste so funky?"

"Try them with a tangerine," Marlene offered.

It was true. The tangerine helped. They laughed at the sight of the other chewing her cud, like a couple of brown-eyed bessies out on the grassland.

The excitement to share a trip together gathered in the faint crow's feet at the corners of their eyes. The golden hour lent their complexions a honey-dipped glow as the featureless busts of their shadows crawled up the wall. With each wave of digestive enzymes, time began to bend.

"The sunset! We have to go see it!" Stella said.

They grabbed their coats and ran to the door. Stella scooped up a portable speaker and queued up "Riders on the Storm."

"Look!" Marlene called out, pointing to the red paisley carpet in the hallway. "You see it?"

"It's *swirl-ing!*" Stella said, toe-stepping gingerly across the floor, gyrating to the keys of a groovy Fender Rhodes. "Quicksand!"

"Lava!"

"Blood!"

Stella dragged the tips of her fingers along the walls as if she was stirring bioluminescent waters. "The walls too! We are in the portal. We broke through to the other side!" she exclaimed, noticing how the walls skewed and sparkled iridescent. She stopped to examine herself in a large mirror at the end of the hallway. "I can feel the spirits heavy in my body. I am possessed. No chance of going back now."

"Are you a good witch or a bad witch?" Marlene asked in the exaggerated timber of a hag.

"Depends who you're asking!" Stella said, pressing the elevator button. "The Witnesses would say I'm very bad."

She was interrupted by a fear-inspiring vision as the elevator doors slid open. A wooly-bearded man of 70 regarded her silently from inside the car. His face looked like a grapefruit lit from within, venous and translucent, blue capillaries tracing a roadmap across his ruby cheeks. His nose was surfaced by oversized pores and from his flaring nostrils, wisps of white hair crept towards his beard like the twisted limbs of a haunted oak.

Marlene stepped into the elevator. "You coming?" she beckoned.

Stella breathed deep then crossed the threshold and took her place next to Marlene. "Look," she whispered through clenched teeth, elbowing Marlene in the ribs.

Marlene shot her a puzzled glance.

"He's a Witness."

Haunted Oak stepped forward as if to confirm Stella's paranoia. He swung a worn leather bag at the buttons, glancing back at Stella with a cold, disapproving countenance.

Marlene smiled at him politely then turned to regard her companion. Stella's face was pale, her pupils dilated.

"How do you know?" Marlene whispered.

"He heard me! He's watching us," she said, flattening herself against the wall in an attempt to hide behind Marlene.

The elevator stopped at the lobby. The man muttered something under his breath then exited.

Stella grabbed Marlene's arm, bracing herself woozily. She felt slothy and dense, as if a boulder had been lowered onto her shoulders incrementally. Her stomach churned. *The gears are changing,* she thought. *I'm assimilating.*

"I have the posture of a demon," Stella said, slumping her shoulders forward ape-like. "He felt my energy. That's why he sent us to the basement."

"I could have sworn we pressed the button for the roof."

The spore of paranoia was contagious.

"We did! He un-pressed it! How does one even cancel an elevator button? How? What kind of voodoo mama juju? Did you see his Bible? And his book bag? He heard. He *knows!*"

Marlene said nothing. She reached for Stella's hand and quietly hummed the theme to *The Twilight Zone* as they spilled out of the elevator and raced up the stairs to the roof.

A 360-degree view of Los Angeles spread out around them in high-def technicolor. The sky blazed every color of the rainbow and refracted like a prism in the setting sun. A familiar lullaby echoed from an ice cream truck on the street below as if Tim Burton directed the scene. The cityscape looked like a miniature set—the Hollywood sign off in the distance full of promise, both real and imagined. The expanse was paranormal in every direction.

Domme and Baby Domme's Excellent Adventure had commenced.

"This. Is. Incredible!" Marlene said, unleashed from her erect posture and restrained sentiment as she bounced around the barren white roof.

Stella smiled Cheshire-like. "I know. Amazing, right?" She had finally impressed Marlene.

Stella moved to the edge of the roof. "Look! A trapped princess lives there!" She pointed to the building across the street. The French Norman construction resembled a medieval castle. Tattered, sun-bleached curtains billowed out of a third-story window. Her imagination was running as fast as the psychedelics coursing through her blood. Portals of altered perception opened all around them like the beaks of famished baby birds, waiting for them to feed meaning into every particle in the air.

"I wonder what your neighbors would say if they looked in *your* window. Did you know your bathroom was visible from here?" Marlene pulled Stella close.

"I know what *I'd* say. Drop a tip in the jar!" Stella laughed. "I go full Bathsheba when I bathe."

"You saw her bathing on the roof. Her beauty and the moonlight overthrew you..." Marlene sang, piling her hair up onto her head and looking coyly over her shoulder.

Stella took the cue and began singing along. "She tied you to her kitchen chair. She broke your throne and she cut your hair. And from your lips she drew the Hallelujah!"

They sang the last line of the Jeff Buckley song together, smiling into the affirmation they found in the other's eyes. Like children reaching for building blocks, they were erecting a remarkable world.

"What if you *did* see me bathing? Would you take me to your castle and foul me like King David did?" Stella asked, slathering another layer of melodrama onto their vision. No allegory was spared in their dissection of each moment.

"Most definitely. But I'd tie you to *my* kitchen chair," Marlene said, a giddy cosmic grin spreading across her cheeks.

Inspired by the imagined plucking of an electric guitar, Stella began prancing around the starchy roof as if it was a ballroom.

Marlene looped her arm through Stella's and spun her around. The cool of the approaching night was chilly against their cheeks. They spun faster and faster in a bout of uncontrolled laughter.

Another wave of endorphins crested, flushing Stella's abdomen with warmth. On the frontier of her cerebral cortex, smashing through the tulips, the doors of perception opened and pulsated electro-pink.

"That sunset!" Stella pointed towards the burning ochre horizon. "I've never seen anything like it. Is it real? Is it the mushrooms? It just can't be." She raised her phone to take a photo.

"My God." Marlene sighed. "This is how I know He's real."

"God? I don't know anymore. It's so confusing. Once in a while, I'm filled with gratitude and I want to pray." Stella threw up her hands. "But I feel these terrors that if there is a god he will destroy me, or at the very least, torment me in this life. I felt that when I saw that man in the elevator. Like a shadow trailing me, waiting for me to fuck up."

"Well, we are tripping. You can't be sure that man was a Witness. But, if you want to pray, darling, pray! We could do it right now."

They clutched each other tight and Marlene thanked God for their senses, for the sunset, and the willing presence of one another.

However, their contemplative silence was broken by a blood-curdling scream. They looked once again to the window with the tattered curtains. Two silhouetted figures, a man and a woman, circled each other like angry bulls. Arms waved, voices raised so loud they could hear them across the street. Their shadows morphed and swelled like boogeymen run amok from under the bed.

On the street below, two officers exited a patrol car and approached the building. The blocking of their bodies played out in miniature as if the women watched the saga from box seats above.

"This is a routine fight. I can tell by their body language," Stella asserted, leaning over the railing. "This is how Adam and I fought."

The emotional violence of the spectacle sent her spiraling into memories of her marriage. She caught a glimpse of herself in one of the soiled panes of glass on a gazebo that sat unkempt in the corner of the roof. For a moment, her reflection seemed to warp into a familiar face, flushed with rage and seething in tumult. *Is this how I appeared to Adam? A monster tearing into the flesh of his self-esteem?* She pressed her forehead against the glass and felt a mainline shiver from her crown to her gut. A stout well of empathy choked through her esophagus. She watched the current run through her body like some astral belt against a soundless galaxy. It always seemed to come back—grief and pity and a tinge of regret, not for leaving but for staying well past the expiration date of their happiness, of her sanity. She recoiled at the thought of reawakening that angry dragon even though the call to domination rang so clearly. Would taking on the stern persona of a Dominatrix trigger the ugly bully in her?

"I can relate," Marlene confessed. As she spoke, her face adopted the same mirrored distortion in Stella's view of the glass. "I know that vortex well."

Another scream pierced their ears. Neighbors had gathered in doorways to consume the unfolding scene. More police cars arrived. Red and blue strobes set the block ablaze.

"I have lived in similar dysfunction."

"Honestly, I don't know if I could be a Domme," Stella said. "Putting people down, being cruel. This is what it leads to."

"No! That's not true. Not with examined communication and consent." Marlene's language was suddenly lucid. "The purely evil Domme is a porn fantasy. The truth is, there is so much nurturing involved."

Punctuating Marlene's monologue was the sight of the man being cuffed.

"I can't watch this anymore," Stella said, shivering. It was the cold and the drugs mixed with Haunted Oak and the Shakespearean lovers. There were tremors running through her nerves. The shackles of her brainwashing still laid ominously in the fringes of her druggy mind.

"Bathe for me, Bathsheba. Run a hot bath," Marlene suggested, sweeping Stella's bangs to one side and drying the cold sweat that had broken on her brow. Stella often felt mystified by the oscillation of Marlene's amorous affections, but in this moment, her eyes were a wellspring of soothing invitation.

"I need a new scene too," Marlene confirmed. "I'll watch you through the window."

Stella already felt warmer at the thought.

In fear of Haunted Oak, she passed the elevator and took the stairs while Marlene waited, like a hawk perched on a high wire, watching the final curtain fall on Shakespeare Out of Love.

Down on the seventh floor, Stella went to the bathroom to prepare what had become her ritual—a steamy bubble bath. She pushed the faucet to its hottest setting, poured in a stream of soap, and began arranging tea lights around the perimeter of the tub. She turned on a portable light that cast rainbow hues across the seafoam tile.

Turning to the window, she saw faintly Marlene's silhouette on the roof as the blinds went up on Bathsheba. She could feel her gaze as though her iris contained a whole proscenium, inside which Stella took center stage.

She removed her clothes in an inch-by-inch striptease and turned to light the candles with a long stem match. She sucked in her stomach, arched her back, and imagined the best angles of her body on display for her midnight stalker.

She dipped one toe in the bath then gathered a handful of suds and let them fall onto her breasts, the foam cascading down her nipples and along the half-moon curve of her belly. She climbed in and sunk deep into the bubbles. The scalding water stung the thin skin on her body while the exhibition of her flesh raised the hair on her limbs. The weft of Marlene's watching from the other side of the window imbued each movement with intention.

Marlene consumed Stella's intimate custom, one so fit for a creeper peeper king. Was that the cymbals of a tambourine trilling up from the citizens below? The laughter of harem girls carried over from some temple of sin?

Stella wondered if Marlene was enjoying the bathtime burlesque. At moments she felt silly and childlike in her motions, though she was trying to channel her inner Dita. She scooped up another handful of suds and hoped the discerning audience of one was fishing her pockets for tips.

"I would summon you to my palace in a heartbeat," Marlene said, appearing several minutes later in the bathroom doorway. An explosion of lavender announced Stella's sensual intentions. "Although I never listen to electronic music when I trip."

"I know what you like," Stella replied, pulling up Puccini on her phone. Marlene was her guest and she felt duty-bound to honor her greater dominance.

Marlene disrobed and revealed what could only be described as the apex of a dancer's body. Stella could not help but stare. She felt Marlene's desire for her to do so. The flash of Marlene's landing strip as she moved towards the tub excited her.

Marlene slid in next to her. Even with Stella's leg dangled over the edge, their slick bodies could barely be contained within the porcelain. Stella pushed the hot water from the faucet towards Marlene to warm her up. They were almost scissoring, like twins in a womb, stewing in the amniotic fluid of the human experience. There was a long silence before Marlene finally spoke.

"I see you," she said tenderly. "You really do care about people."

Stella's cheeks flushed. She looked into the crystalline prisms of Marlene's eyes and tried to steady the sentimental quiver of her bottom lip.

"Ever since you called me Baby Domme, I can't shake these thoughts about the lost realities of my nature. Like a prophecy scratched onto ancient scrolls," Stella said, thrusting her hands into the air as if conducting an orchestra and letting them fall dramatically to the thick of Marlene's calf, which she played like an instrument.

The music splashed paint on the infinite walls of her velvet interior. Stella had no doubt she was conducting an actual symphony, her companion's body the solo viola. She closed her eyes and watched the movie playing under her eyelids, a Tuscan kingdom with gilded chapels that went on forever. She was flying one minute and the next on a slalom rollicking through a fractal labyrinth. Morphing. Twisting. Turning. Radiating light.

Marlene now took a turn stroking Stella's legs.

"I am listening," she confirmed as she lay sinking into the abyss, taking in Stella's stream of conscious reporting.

"I am who I am seeking." Stella opened her eyes and tears came seeping out. "Oh my God. My first epiphany! I need subjects! Like yours. I want to live the way you do. I hear a voice saying, 'Stop hiding who you are and rule. It is written in your eyes, your hips, your lips, and your thighs. You were born a queen!'"

"Yes!" Marlene rejoiced for the draconian religious shackles that lay broken at Stella's feet.

She praised her glimmers of wisdom but cautioned that there was still much infancy in her monarchical musings. Stella's imagination, she said, was spiked on the promise of power, like an empirical heiress exploring the armoire of royal robes. She was admiring herself in the mirror, slipping her feet into oversized shoes, twirling in delight at her adult reflection. Her visions came easily because those garments were destined to one day suit her figure like tailored second skins.

"Even in the midst of salacious scenes, the queen is a specialized instrument of healing," Marlene interjected, her voice reflecting the same amalgamation of psychotropic spiritual download. "The queen is a catalyst…"

Marlene's voice became muffled as Stella slid down, dunking her head completely under the water. The sound of her racing heart in her ears was amplified by the pressure of being submerged.

"We are tripping, right?" she asked, emerging from the water, a bout of bubbles jetting up from below.

"We are most definitely tripping," Marlene granted with a stony smile.

Stella laid back in Marlene's arms, her head resting on the bones of her chest and her body between her legs. Marlene lifted her hands and let drip a trickle of water onto Stella's forehead.

Baptism into the Church of Her, Stella thought, her eyes closed tight as a kaleidoscope of stained glass tumbled through her acid-washed mind.

She opened her mouth and received the droplets on her tongue. She imagined herself Lazarus drinking from the hand of God and went limp in complete surrender to Marlene. Through tears of relief, she opened her eyes and watched the multi-color strobe slink across the walls in ecclesiastical rays of light. It was a rare and sublime moment of submission in her love. Everything was right in the world. The feminine divine had been made more real than anything terrestrial. She felt complete in a way that had eluded her for so many years in submission to man and church. The union was a big bang, a spiritual explosion of feminine revelation.

"How lovely you look in this light," Marlene said.

Stella reached for a hand mirror on her sink. Her hair was wet around the frame of her face, her bangs starting to curl. The water dripped down her face revealing faint eggplant shadows under her howling brown eyes. The cover of her foundation gave way to dozens of freckles on the angular bridge of her nose.

Marlene leaned over and kissed her tenderly. The flicker of the candles painted Marlene's cheekbones into a masterful chiaroscuro.

"I love you," said Marlene.

"You do?"

"I really do."

"Mmmm. I love you too," Stella replied drunkenly. As the opera crescendoed, she played her final note, tracing dozens of circles around Marlene's petite breasts and thick nipples.

Eventually, she tired from the furiousness of her conducting and rested her head on the corner of the cool tub.

A charred odor flooded the room.

"Do you smell something burning?" Marlene asked.

Stella sat up, sniffing the air like a truffle pig. "Shit! My hair."

She jerked her head off the tub. Clumps of her tresses sizzled in a tea light. She pawed frantically at her scalp. "Is it bad? Did I burn off much?" She swiveled around to let Marlene examine her. She pushed down paranoid thoughts of baldness, but the panic in her eyes betrayed her. *What an unexpected punishment this would be from you, God! Penance for my vanity, my excess, my egotism.* Had the man in the elevator been a reverse talisman? An indication that Stella was not out of the woods with the angry and exacting god she had been trained to fear for every insubordinate thought, and certainly for such a gross sin as this sex- and drug-fueled night?

Marlene pulled at the singed strands of hair. "Let's wash it and see."

She stood and tugged Stella by the hand into the small shower. She ran her fingers lovingly through Stella's thick hair, lathering it with shampoo. Stella put her arms around Marlene's waist like a sleepy child steadying herself on a parent, while Marlene slid her hands down the curve of Stella's back.

"Your hair is fine," Marlene reassured. "No big loss."

They stepped out of the shower, toweled off, and flopped onto the bed exhaustedly.

"I really do love you," Marlene said, lying against a pillow on her side. She pulled the comforter over Stella.

"I love you too," Stella murmured, half-conscious. "Do you think a man will ever love me again like Adam did?"

"Fuck these douchey LA guys. Swipe left, Stella. They're wasting your time," she said in reference to the furiousness with which Stella had been dating and the equal measure of disappointment after each empty escapade.

"You know my love for you will just continue to grow. I'm not going anywhere," Marlene promised.

Within minutes, the eldritch herb lost its hold and the women yielded to sleep.

* * * * *

At the sound of a kettle boiling the next morning, Stella woke and put on a silk robe. The new sun crested over the mountains and poured a prism of dusty light across the room.

"She's alive!" said Marlene with a smile. She sat at the table with a pen in hand.

"How long have you been up?" Stella asked, shuffling into the kitchen.

"Not long."

Stella frothed some soy milk and poured it over her espresso. She slid into a broad woven chair with an ornate flowered back—her throne.

"What are you writing?" Stella's eyes sparkled with anticipation.

Marlene held a note, her handwriting long and elegant like the fingers that penned it. She cleared her throat, and like a beat poet perched on a box began reading aloud.

"LA woman, Sunday afternoon psychedelics at a table beside a rear window. Ktown kitchen 4 p.m. light, she chops magic mushrooms, laments a bit for lost time with boys better left for dead, these Hamlets, these Horacios, these excellent adventures with Bill and Ted. There are always women, there are always rooftops. The day is not yet done. There was the sunset, the wind chimes, her tears, and our clutching. We should thank God always, always. Of course, the bath. Let me tell you another time about the Italian maestro and his luscious glistening breasts."

CHAPTER 13

The Penthouse

"DIDN'T YOU SAY the penthouse in your building is vacant?" Marlene asked as she pounded up the dusty hill of a Griffith Park trail.

Their steamy night in the bath had renewed their bond and fueled their resolve to go into business together. They were back to the test kitchen, several sauces simmering on the range, their hearts spice racks with all the lids undone from zealous use.

"Yeah, but there's no way I could afford it," Stella pushed back, nearly out of breath as she attempted to catch up. Propping her hands on her knees, she scanned the vista from nearly a thousand feet above the sprawling metropolis. It was one of those LA "pinch me" moments with all the mansions perched alongside the Hollywood sign, the patina green dome of Griffith Observatory, and the endless grid of the city stretching west to Santa Monica. "God, this is beautiful. I still can't believe I live here. Are we almost to the peak?"

"I thought you were a runner!" Marlene yelled from 20 feet up the trail, her ponytail swinging as she galloped up the uneven terrain. She seemed to care not that Stella couldn't keep her pace on Hogback trail, the most difficult in the whole park.

"I am a runner, but you hike this all the time, so… maybe you could slow down a little, Simone Biles."

"Hope is stellar at admin. I'll have her look into details on the penthouse," Marlene said, finally pausing to regard her winded friend.

She was a master of delegation when pressed to do business she considered heavy lifting. It worried Stella. Though Marlene could sprint her favorite trail like an Olympian, she was trapped in a rerun of outdated arts organizing that bowed to a decades-old past. Her business acumen was still wearing low-rise jeans and syncing its iPod. In terms of crafting a real business plan, Stella felt the weight of carrying the duo almost entirely herself. Then there was the issue of money.

"How are we going to fund a new lease?" Stella asked, leaning back into the alcove of a craggy rock wall to shade herself from the midday sun.

"Hope will foot part of the bill. That bitch is working overtime! She wants to buy me a house," Marlene said, barely moving out of the center of the path for a trio of red-faced hikers to pass.

"But she's a single parent," Stella protested.

"Who makes well over six figures." Marlene registered the doubt creeping into Stella's eyes. "Stella, you've simply never cultivated a D/s relationship. Maybe one day you will have a slave of your own and things will click for you."

"I'm trying, but you've dissuaded me from every potential sub I've met."

"Because they're sycophants not submissives."

At times it felt like Marlene willed against her success. Why else would she have presented such an unbroken series of Sisyphean challenges to ascertain Stella's supposed Domme-readiness?

"Let's say Hope does get involved," Stella posited. "How does footing the bill for our business benefit her? How do we know she'll stick around? If the lease is in my name, I'm going to be liable."

"She would love nothing more than to be in a 24/7 dynamic with me. Think of it as sub capital!" She knew Stella hadn't been calculating "Acts of Service" into the bottom line, much less financial domination. "Besides, wouldn't it be so meta to have kink dynamics built right into the blueprint of our brand?"

The fact that Stella had not realized her filmmaking goals made Marlene's persuasion almost overpowering. After several months of shooting for tourism boards, she felt throttled by the punishing hours, the shitty, demanding producers, and the obnoxious social media influencers she was forced to film.

"Alright, I'll call my landlord," Stella said, plopping down on a bench to unlock her phone.

She smiled wide as a video from Yvette popped up. She lounged poolside at some glamorous locale, relating plans to move to LA for a new job. Yvette's beautiful cleavage bounced gleefully as she shared the news. She concluded with an urgent desire to reunite with Stella the moment she arrived.

Butterflies fluttered up Stella's esophagus in anticipation of seeing the Frenchwoman again.

Marlene huffed impatiently, pretending not to peer over Stella's shoulder as the video played.

"Yvette's moving here," Stella announced in a daze.

Marlene frowned, tightening her already taut ponytail. "That girl from Nola?"

"Yeah." Stella began distractedly filling her water bottle from a fountain until it overflowed.

"When?" Marlene asked, looking down at her nails.

Stella took a long gulp of water, withholding an immediate reply. Squinting into the distance, she admired the snow-capped peaks of the San Gabriel mountains. *The American Dream.*

"Soon."

* * * * *

When Stella learned that the penthouse was a mere $2,400, she seized the opportunity to move on up to the deluxe apartment in the sky. She was nervous about taking on two leases, but Marlene convinced her to keep her studio as a living space and devote all 1,000 square feet of the penthouse to their domination business.

The bones of the apartment were stunning. It had the same vintage faux fireplace as Stella's studio but with 270-degree views of Los Angeles. Two sides of the unit provided vistas of downtown and the Hollywood sign, while the bedroom had a west-facing view to soak up the sunset. The vaulted ceilings were a good 20 feet and Marlene eyed the Tudor beams like a cowboy sizing up a ribeye. The lust in her eyes said it all. She couldn't wait to "rope a slab of beef and suspend him from those heights."

The two envisioned a more intimate space than the typical stark dungeon. Something of a parlor, a bohemian drawing room fit for the sort of quaint and meticulous modulation Marlene manifested in her brand of kink. She created a small version of the Dragulator in the massive walk-in closet, replete with a built-in vanity and now a wide selection of leather and latex. She brought wigs and all the cosmetics for sissification.

When it came to naming the business, Stella's knack for branding came on full blast. She suggested they call it "Domicile." It wasn't the first in her long lexicon of puns that would come to fill the glossary of their shorthand.

With the name decided and the space secured, accouterments took precedence as the next acquisition. They would have to improvise and it was here that Marlene's thrift shopping prowess was put to the test.

* * * * *

Seeing the pair on a fine Sunday morning sifting through the treasures of the Rose Bowl Flea Market, one might have assumed they were just two vintage betties, new to the city and outfitting their home on a dime. Who would have guessed that plush footstool towed behind them in their granny-goes-for-groceries cart was destined to be riveted, bolted, and fit for shackles?

Stella had spent every day of the previous two weeks furiously at work on the branding and website. Most days when Marlene woke at noon, she had an inbox full of Stella's work for her approval and a flurry of text messages to follow.

"I'm the Hunchback of Notre Domme!" Stella joked, drawing Marlene's attention to the knots in her back. "Seriously, I'm in a codependent relationship with my MacBook."

Marlene pawed through a pile of classic movies as the pair strolled through the market. "Look! *Working Girl.* I wore this one out. Should we get a VCR for the penthouse? For shits and giggles, we play bad porn through the crackle of VHS?"

Stella tried to smile through her yawn. Marlene's affinity for VHS did nothing to minimize Stella's image of her as some retro imitation of a modern-day businesswoman, all shoulder pads and padlocked attaché. She was Melanie Griffith, strutting down Fifth Avenue in her hightops, black pumps in tow. Sure, she made a scene, but could she navigate a spreadsheet? Or was she a glorified secretary, posing in someone else's Choos?

"I have a head for business and a bod for sin. Is there anything wrong with that?" Marlene whispered in the husk of a movie star. She clipped along the market as if operating on a wind-up clock.

Stella shrugged and hurried to keep up.

"Why are you so tired?" Marlene asked, taking inventory of Stella's eyes, which bore the colorless signs of insomnia. "You're such a grandma sometimes, I swear."

"Uh, well, I wanted to finalize the logo with your changes. And we have to figure out how to file the business license. It's hard to know exactly how to categorize this enterprise," Stella said. "Did you talk to that Domme friend of yours? And did you fix the issue with the bank so you can transfer money into our account?"

"No, but I will this week."

"Marlene, you said that last week." Stella sighed. As hot as her blood boiled, she was afraid to ruffle Marlene's feathers with anything resembling a correction.

"OK, DMVenus. I'm going to do it."

Marlene had started calling her "DMVenus" every time Stella pushed back incomplete paperwork or enforced a fleeting deadline.

"I needed it done yesterday. I'm putting in a lot of work here. You know we will be in the red in about a month if we don't get our first client?" Stella said, tiptoeing into a conversation she feared Marlene would evade. "That's why I sent you a budget."

"I found the carpenter on Fet! Not to mention the value of Hope's work. And Houseboy."

The one thing they agreed on had been Stella's hire, Marco. He was a gentle brute of a man and a perfect bodyguard. Marlene approved Marco, less in deference for Stella's judgment than a need for expediency, as Stella was hurrying the process along much like a pernicious child who has seized upon a parent's weakness to be granted some favor.

Marco was a new acquaintance, a zen gangster she met at a coffee shop. He was six and a half feet in height, a thick cut of bacon at 250 pounds. He spoke in the only accent acceptable for the role, a Big Apple brogue parked halfway between Brooklyn and Palermo. He blustered with anecdotes and aphorisms reflecting a hard-knock life lived with gratitude and a well-worn copy of *The Taoist I Ching*. He was street smart, quite plausibly an ex-con. Stella didn't dare ask.

*****

An afternoon at PetSmart was all Stella and Marlene needed to procure puppy play equipment—a large dog kennel, leashes, and bones. As they shopped the aisles, panning the rivers of their twisted imaginations for triple X gold, Stella couldn't resist tossing a few squeak toys into the cart. When she attempted to add a choke chain collar to the mix, Marlene removed it like a parent snatching sugar cereal out of her five-year-old's sticky fingers.

"I'm gonna put you in it," she threatened playfully.

"Are you ladies finding everything okay?" A voice from the end of the aisle startled them just as Marlene had secured the collar in place.

A stocky redhead had heard the conversation from the adjacent aisle. She came around the corner like a Hobbit schoolmarm fresh off the Shire, her round cheeks ruddy with the smart of rosacea. Her name tag read "Deb" and she was clearly not amused.

"Are you going to buy that?" she questioned, much like a highway trooper asking for proof of insurance.

"We are now," Marlene acquiesced, loosening the collar from Stella's neck.

"Yes!" Stella exclaimed in victory.

"We are *not* using it on subs," Marlene insisted under her breath.

"We might. What if we are Domme and *Dahmer?"* Stella suggested as the two pushed their cart and disappeared into the endless offerings of kibble. "Get it? Jeffrey Dahmer?"

Deb eyed them suspiciously from the top of the aisle, her thick fingers planted firmly on her hips. She might as well have been a linebacker, for her build and stance signaled that she would not be easily disobeyed.

Stella cleared her throat dramatically.

"Oh shit, the Shire is not having it today," Marlene said, finally noticing Deb's increasingly vehement death stare.

Stella was powerless against the sharp burst of laughter that bubbled up through her esophagus and was expelled like a naughty fart. She slapped her palms over her mouth to contain any secondary chuckles. Marlene was helpless against her own amusement and braced herself on the cart as if she had been assassinated by a faraway bullet. A punctuated snort rang through the store like an insubordinate exclamation point.

"Oh, no. She's coming back," Stella whispered.

Marlene straightened up to greet the unimpressed manager.

Deb's expression changed from irritated to fake polite. "You ladies shopping for a pet?"

Why does she care if we fuck off in PetSmart? Stella wondered.

"We—" Marlene started in a flat tone Stella feared would invite an even messier confrontation.

"No, ma'am," Stella interceded, hoping to avoid a conflict. "I think we've found what we need. Thanks for your help."

As the pair exited the store, Stella took the receipt from Marlene's hand and snapped a photo. *Is this money well spent?*

Marlene held the dog collar up to Stella's throat. "See, Baby Domme? Where there's a will, there's a way."

"Wait. That's not on the receipt."

Marlene snickered wickedly. "No, it's not."

"Marlene!" Stella cried, lowering Marlene's hand from her neck and twisting around to see if the store manager was watching them. "What if we got caught? Dude, we could go to jail! Did you see that woman? She was ready to attack."

"Dude, I outsmarted her." Marlene wore a look of smug self-satisfaction.

"How often do you shoplift?"

"It's corporate fucking America. Those bastards aren't hurting over one collar, believe me."

Stella contemplated her culpability. Even in her rejection of Bible principles, this was going too far.

"Security cameras, Marlene! Think before you do something like that again, especially with me. Not trying to get arrested my first year out of spiritual prison."

"You're so worried about money all the time. It's my way to show you I've got things covered. This ain't my first rodeo."

"So, this is how you're a 'poor little rich girl?'"

"Stella, don't be so sanctimonious," she said with the indignant pomp of a dethroned duchess. "You've been in the bunker too long, girl."

"You didn't answer me."

"I only ever lift little things. A tiny bottle of essential oil from Erewhon or you know, labeling my organic quinoa as non-organic... No big deal! I'm not a thief, I'm just *thrifty.*"

CHAPTER 14

Debbie Dommer

THERE IS NO WAY to elegantly dislodge a wedgie from latex. Stella's twisted panties were like a climber buried under the rubble of her bubble, worked deeper and deeper into the martyred crevasse of her ass crack.

"Do you ever get wedgies in your latex?" Stella inquired as Marlene sat touching up her eyebrows at the vanity.

"Stella, you don't wear panties with latex! Major fashion faux pas."

"Oh no. I have to start over? It's like a baby seal convention in here."

"Latex is meant to be tight. You don't want it flapping around like chicken wings."

Stella began peeling off the catsuit like a diver returned from the deep. She threw her panties in a ball on the floor. "I thought we were supposed to be torturing our slaves, not ourselves," she joked, trying to stuff down her self-consciousness as Marlene helped her roll the black rubber up the width of her thighs a second time.

"Thanks, '90s heroin chic, for the lifetime supply of body dysmorphia!" she said, looking down at the bulge of flesh cascading over the fold of the suit. "It's stuck. You sure this isn't too small?"

"Trust me," Marlene replied, clocking the anxiety in Stella's eyes. "This is just how you have to work it. One inch at a time." Marlene loosened the laces that ran up the sides, then pulled the latex over Stella's waist with relief.

Zipping up the front to the blossom of her breasts, Stella turned to look in the mirror. The grommet lace looped over her hips like a roller coaster track. Marlene began oiling her up as if waxing the bumper of a shiny Buick Riviera.

"Unzip this a bit…" She tugged at the zipper between Stella's cleavage, playfully revealing more. She rubbed circles across her nipples.

Stella laughed, a ping of pleasure sparking between her legs. "OK, yeah, this is hot." The python curves of the lace accentuated her hourglass figure to riotous degrees. "Fuck Kate Moss. I'll never give up fettuccine Alfredo again."

"Girl, you look like a supervillain. The only thing missing is a utility belt with a quality selection of lubes."

Stella grabbed an imaginary gun at her waist and aimed at the mirror. "Hands up, misogynist. You're going down."

Marlene joined her in the mirror to clown. She wore latex separates in a go-to '40s silhouette—a puffy-sleeved "Yes, Mistress" blouse with ruffles at the neck and a black pencil skirt that squeezed her Vargas Girl legs into the sharpened point of an arrow.

Yes, hot.

* * * * *

As Stella and Marlene sat hip to hip in the back seat, there was an audible squawk each time the car cornered an intersection, like a baby bird screeching "S.O.S." from the folds of their rubber-clad lady havens.

"Should I be sweating this much? There's a swimming pool in my crotch," Stella complained, still suffering under the weight of her sex appeal. "And why does every kink party take place in a creepy mansion or some Skid Row dungeon?" Stella's ruminations colored her expression as she peered through the window at the cinder block warehouse to which they were presently being deposited.

Houseboy zipped around to open the door and, like two prizes from a toy capsule vending machine, they spilled out onto the sidewalk. Stella couldn't help but giggle. *The poor pantless man in his cock cage.* He did not look her in the eye, but her amusement lit him up and she noticed an insubordinate chuckle upon his lips, cracking the serious facade of his servitude.

"Corn starch!" Marlene commanded and Houseboy sprang into action. Reaching into the glove box, he produced a small sachet that puffed a subtle white dust cloud.

Marlene took it from his hands and offered Stella a final warning. "You're not going to be able to use your phone while wearing these."

She fished for Stella's little digits as they squirmed into place inside the short latex gloves. "You're going to be sort of challenged, but it does tie the whole look together."

Stella pumped her hands open and closed, getting a feel for the tight grip of the rubber and pressing it firmly into the web of her fingers. "It's like a hand condom," she praised.

"If you only knew." Marlene winked. She smoothed over her ensemble and slid a Lucite clutch under her arm before turning to Houseboy to make one final demand. "Check in every hour with the pictures I've instructed you to send." She reached up and savagely twisted his bottom lip, bringing her mouth several inches from his and making a long, exaggerated kissing sound.

Marlene had given him a number of strange and humiliating tasks to perform throughout the night as he waited to chauffeur them home. She was rewarding him with something of a scavenger hunt to keep him stimulated and engaged.

A lanky man dressed head to toe as a sissy nurse met the women at the gate. At his prompt, Marlene offered up the password for entry.

"Rubber baby buggy bumpers."

She could hardly keep a straight face. "Please don't," she begged Stella who was already straight lipped to suppress her laughter. Marlene squeezed Stella's forearm as her face flushed with the pressure of an imprisoned bloom of fresh giggles. They were basically two teenage girls hiding their Sunday service jokes behind the shield of a heavy book of hymnals.

Sissy Nurse pressed the red button on his side of the wall and the automatic gate slid open at an awkwardly sluggish pace. A woman with gauged earlobes handed each of them a clipboard. She wore a harness that exposed her gigantic breasts, inked with tattoos of cobwebs that spun from her nipples to her collarbone. With her black coffin nails filed to razor points, her aesthetic was Lee Press-On Pagan.

"Please read, sign, and indicate which color wristband you'd prefer." Her pentagram earrings caught the light like little strobes—a perfect match to the sterling studs pierced through her dimples.

"Wristband? Does that mean we get unlimited access to all the rides?" Stella's joke was received with a tepid smile. It ricocheted from the marrow of all adjacent funny bones and slid like a cracked egg down the side of the warehouse wall. Everyone winced. Stella smoothed her hair.

"The color indicates the level of involvement you wish to have. Green is, 'Please approach me. I want to play.' Yellow is, 'Open to being approached,' and red is, 'Just here to observe.'"

The bright green of Stella's wristband gave her supervillain aesthetic a little kick of comic book color. Marlene fidgeted the waxen yellow paper of her own and lamented its earnest attempts to cheapen the antique opal ring she wore.

They made their way down a hallway lit up by purple strobes. As they rounded the corner towards coat check, more of the partygoers came into focus. The first room, where many of the guests were mingling, looked like the free clinic fishbowl of candy-colored condoms. They were tasting the rainbow like Skittles, all glossy and freshly shined. There were so many facekinis and gas masks, so many patent leather platforms.

The space was sprawling and industrial with cement walls and exposed pipes, a total cliché setting for a fetish party. In one room, several people lounged in line for the vacuum bed.

"Splash Mountain after all," Marlene whispered into Stella's ear.

"Rides unlimited. Green means go," Stella cracked in retort, holding up her bracelet.

Someone hit the valve and the bed steadily shrinkwrapped the next willing victim. Each curve of the gimp's body was revealed, encased like fresh beef jerky in the cellophane of some roadside truck stop.

"Let's check the scene upstairs," Marlene suggested. They slinked up the staircase like Siamese cats.

Rounding the corner at the top of the stairs, they came into a more intimate playroom. As usual, their entrance garnered several piqued expressions.

Stella scanned the room as she pressed the tines of a handheld miniature spur up and down her neck.

"Is that? No, it can't be! Is that *Deb?*" Stella nodded in the direction of their pet store nemesis. The feisty fortysomething was in head-to-toe purple latex flogging a man tied ass out to a Saint Andrew's Cross.

"Deb? *From the Shire?*"

The women laughed nervously, both instantly reminded that Deb may have dirt on them from that fateful day in her domain.

"Well, well, well. Deb is a fucking Domme!" Stella exclaimed as if she had pulled the mask off a *Scooby Doo* villain. They stood transfixed by the Dance of Deborah for several moments.

"She has great technique," Marlene observed.

"Yeah, her backhand is aces," Stella quipped sarcastically.

"No, I mean it. Florentine flogging takes skill. Deb is experienced."

Deb finished with the submissive and handed one of her floggers to a blonde with helium-filled lady jugs who leaned in and kissed her wet on the mouth, stroking her spiky, cropped hair dyed imperial grape to match her catsuit.

"Woah, get it, Deb!" Stella cheered from afar. "That bitch is kicking ass and taking names. I think we need to meet Debbie Dommer."

Deb emerged from her bombshell smooch to a gaggle of admirers gathered in a horseshoe. She appeared to have celebrity status among the kinksters, like a Le Mans winner at the finish line. All that was missing was the flashing of bulbs to signal her victory.

"Let's go meet her," Marlene suggested.

Deb seemed to recognize the women on their approach. Stella slowed down, while Marlene kept her strident pace and pushed forcefully through Deb's fans.

"Well, hello," greeted Deb cautiously.

Stella smiled. Marlene spoke. "I wanted to tell you I admire your technique."

"Yeah? Thank you."

"We met at PetSmart," said Stella.

"I know and I'm not entirely surprised to see you here," Deb said with a gentle smirk. "I suspected you had similar interests." She cracked a flogger against her thick purple thigh.

Marlene laughed.

Finally, Stella thought, *some levity!*

"Well, I had no idea about you," Stella said, wading into the waters of reverence. "How long have you been at it?"

"Domination? Got into the LA scene about 15 years ago."

Marlene continued, "Are you pro?"

"I trained in a dungeon, but I find it hard to monetize my services full-time."

Stella's heart leapt. Dollar signs flashed in her eyes. She had heard these words many times in her life. It was a clarion call for her to intervene, to offer her business savvy to the less fortunate. She had the immediate urge to invite Deb into their operation *(Domme, Dommer, and Dommest?),* but she knew she should consult Marlene first. The more Deb spoke, the more Stella wanted her. She was bright but humble. Wise and grounded. There was an immediacy and candor to the *Tao of Deb* that put everyone at ease. There was something in the readiness of her unapologetic awkwardness that suggested this woman had truly come into her own. She was here. She was queer. *You'd better get used to it.*

After some small talk, Stella made a polite excuse and then led Marlene through the eddies of partygoers, pausing to do a double take at a ghastly scene along the way. A sissified man of sixty in a veritable pageant of taffeta laid prostrate under the dangling foot of a Dominatrix. She spat insults as he received into his eager mouth the shavings of her ashy soles.

Stella's face twisted up in disgust. "Parmesan callous crust is a kink?"

"You must've missed the double dong action over there." Marlene pointed to two naked men on all fours. They seesawed, cheek-to-cheek, a long pink dildo between their hairy asses.

"Oh, no! She's going to make them suck it?" Stella reacted in horror as the officiating Domme removed the toy from their crevices and shoved the chalky ends into the men's mortified mouths.

"Carnival of the bizarre," Marlene deadpanned.

"Doot-doot-doot-doo-doo-doo," Stella launched into the Big Top motif. "Step right up, folks, to the Grossest Show on Earth!" she continued. "Holy Uranus, look at that double dong action! This pair of dueling dildo-ers is really *plugged* into the scene, wouldn't ya say?"

"Well, Dorothy, you're not in Kansas anymore. How do you like the circus freak tent?"

"Are you into that? Would you do that? Have you?"

"Probably not."

"I'm not sure I'm into this whole dungeon scene."

"Relatable, but I wanted to expose you to it. Sure, there are far too many bad pleather boots and Hot Topic hauls, but the community is important," Marlene critiqued.

"Yeah, it just doesn't feel like your aesthetic or mine. Like, it's just not very sexy or sophisticated."

"It does smack of the awkward late bloom of the Dungeons and Dragons set."

"Is this why you never trained in a dungeon?"

"I've been fortunate enough to have a natural knack and not need a mentor. Plus, most dungeons require you begin as a sub."

"I cannot imagine you doing that. Anyway, I have a brilliant idea," Stella said, pulling Marlene towards the bar. "What if we hire Deb as an advisor-cum-all-around-badass? Her dungeon experience adds street cred." Stella's eyes twinkled with possibility. "I'd like to see us with 10 clients by the end of the quarter. Deb could help us network, find clients, buy whips and chains…" Stella said, transitioning to a more jovial tone to warm Marlene's heart and gain her approval.

Marlene snickered. Stella often spoke like the CEO of a startup. She was a bit of a cult leader in her own right. "Hmm. I could see her value. But you know how I am about thoroughly vetting people."

"I know," she agreed. "We will absolutely do a background check. I do it on fuckboys all the time."

"Alright. Let's see what she says."

Back at the Le Mans rally, Deb was still holding court, though some of her admirers had dispersed.

"Do you prefer Deb or Deborah?" Marlene asked, shifting focus back to operation "All Things Deb."

"Debbie is the only version I don't answer to," she replied. "There's something to it that just doesn't fit."

"Never Debbie," Marlene confirmed, swiping her hands together as though crumpling an imaginary piece of paper. She flicked the phantom scrap into the ether with the tips of her fingers.

Marlene smiled across the group to Stella who wasn't missing a beat. She flashed that toothy grin like Veruca Salt polishing golden eggs and being gifted the world, the whole world. *Give it to me.*

That was it. This little conference was all Marlene needed. A week later, Deb reported to the penthouse for duty.

Deb blushed even Marco's cheeks. She wasn't traditionally attractive, of course, but she radiated such good humor and maternal safety that Marco couldn't help but be charmed. His gentle giantry (he towered 18 inches over her) and Deb's compact feistiness made them an odd little power couple, as much as Stella and Marlene. So, it was no surprise that upon meeting her, Marco smiled, took Deb's hand in his oversized paw, and kissed it tenderly. *One big, happy family.*

CHAPTER 15

House of Cards

"DID YOU SECURE the hand mirrors for *The Vagina Monologues?*" Marlene joked as she stepped through the front door of the penthouse with Houseboy humbly in tow. The jacarandas were in full bloom and a few of the lilac flowers that littered the hallway flew into the apartment. Marlene curtly instructed Houseboy to clean them up.

Stella launched in without missing a beat. "On this episode of 'Getting to Know Your Noni' we'll explore the floral elegance of our sexual core," she jested. "Spelunk the cavern of your sexual health with a closer look at your vulva."

"Headlamps on! Okay, now closer. Yes, much closer… Now touch your O'Keefe. Touch it! Touch it!" Marlene joined in.

They snort-laughed in unison.

Stella broke the fever of foolishness and busied herself arranging wardrobe options for Marlene. She was surprised Marlene had agreed to host a party. Stella knew how exclusive she could be, joking that she expected the oracles of *The NeverEnding Story* to be standing at the doorway, laser melting anyone who tried to pass with less than the purest heart.

"Did the shoes arrive?" Stella asked.

"Lewdy Vuitton," a submissive man whom Marlene had been long-distance domming for some weeks, was instructed to purchase and post for delivery four pairs of couture shoes. Marlene provided the sizes and list of acceptable designers. It was part of a hair-brained scheme to flip the shoes for cash and funnel the funds into their start-up.

"The shoes are exquisite," Marlene confirmed. "It's going to be hard to let them go."

"For the business!" Stella declared, pounding a playful fist on an oversized pillow. "This is a good plan. I was worried."

"Worried about what?"

"Where you'd get the money to contribute to our expenses," Stella said hesitantly.

"Who needs money when you're rich with devotion?"

Stella forced herself to keep quiet. This was no time to get into a debate.

Through the meticulous journaling practice she enforced, Marlene had learned of Lewdy's fetish for fine leather. The glossed lambskin of Hermès gloves or the shank of a cruel black Jimmy Choo may as well have been his robust and reclining Titian nudes. She had crafted each journal prompt to siphon the wellspring of his memories and expose his sweetbreads.

On his next business trip to LA, she instructed him to reserve a day for her use. It would be an evening of cards and cold martinis, slinky '50s housewives, and an experience rich with nods to his adolescence. She would vice his imagination in the grip of those cashmere-lined gloves. His heart pumped through her fingers, throbbing like the udder of a cash cow she was eager to milk.

Marlene began zipping around, prepping the space, and instructing Houseboy on the placement of seating.

"Are we gambling dildos?" Stella laughed as Marlene laid out a pile of toys.

"Kind of," she confirmed.

The doorbell rang.

"You two are so similar. Your vibe... everything," said Deb as she strutted through the front door.

"I think of us as Endora," Stella said, turning to Marlene.

"From *Bewitched?* You've said that before. You're hot for Endora."

"She reminds me of my grandmother. She was ahead of her time, trying to pull Samantha out of servitude to her husband and into her own divinity. Plus, she had great style," Stella said wistfully.

As soon as Hope arrived, the pre-game salon commenced. It was a chance to pamper and bring the team into the dugout before the big match. Houseboy began serving the women from a bottle of bubbly and a bounty of charcuterie. Turkish apricots, Marcona almonds, artisanal cheeses—it was a feast.

As for the dress code, Stella was a picture-perfect pinup. The theme of the evening was one for which her closet offered a bounty. Her hair was teased big Texas and her curves poured into a high-waisted nautical romper which drained the sand from the center of her hourglass and built castles into her cleavage and derrière. You could have easily posed her in the porthole of some postcard wishing you were here. Her feet were adorned with strappy gold Gucci stilettos.

Marlene went full-blown Italian Riviera in a leopard print pencil dress. Half a bottle of stronghold gel shellacked her hair into faux short curls, setting off the thick gold hoops on her ears. For her, of course, it was a pair of wicked black Louboutins.

Deb had coiffed her newly dyed cherry red hair into a stately updo and wore an emerald green A-line wrap dress with a pressed collar and a strand of pearls. The look was spot on with the demure Ferragamos Lewdy purchased in her size.

Hope had spun the most kink aesthetic into her ensemble with a girlish latex halter dress accented with a thick belt in cherry red PVC. It was a pair of patent leather Valentino platforms for her.

"Shall we get *The Vagina Monologues* started?" Stella asked.

"Lezzz do," Marlene championed. "The best sex is orchestral, not only strings," she began, sitting up straight in a peacock chair hauled from her apartment. "That's the problem with hookup culture." She fluffed at the scarf around her neck. "It's so genital-focused. I want it full body! Full heart! Full mind! Give me woodwinds! Give me brass! Lick my feet!" she exclaimed, popping a date into her mouth. She held up a red book entitled, *The Boudoir Bible,* and presented it to Stella with a question mark.

"Yes, I started reading Betony Vernon," Stella confirmed, draining the last bit of champagne from her glass. "And *The History and Arts of the Dominatrix*. We should have a podcast. Weekly installments of our most intimate diatribes and musings. We could call it, 'Domversations!'"

The women cackled, as giddy on the champagne as they were at the chance to be at the foot of the preacher's pulpit. Stella and Hope exchanged clandestine smiles as she topped off Stella's champagne. They were both smitten by the feminist spirit flowing so freely from Marlene's robes. She had kept them separate for some six months.

"You know, Hope has a particular fantasy about this room. Don't you?" Marlene said, caressing the sheepish woman's hip with one hand while gesturing to the group with the other.

"Yes, Marlene. I do." Her dimpled cheeks flushed at the admission. She was sexier than Marlene had described. Her dirty blonde hair was parted in the middle and hung in messy tresses down to her curvy waist. She was fresh-faced except for a rich coat of red lipstick, no doubt applied by Marlene to soften her androgynous bent. Her skin was pale, nearly translucent, and her nails were unpainted.

"Oooh, what is it?" Deb cooed, leaning forward in her chair.

"Well, she's been enjoying this double Domme energy from a distance and wants to feel it up close," Marlene said, standing and leading Hope to the middle of the living room. "Don't you, Hope?"

"Yes, Marlene. I want to be a good girl for your friends," she said, kneeling.

"Position two," Marlene called out. Hope's body snapped onto all fours. "Positions training and protocol are indispensable; submissives must learn these fundamentals."

Marlene produced a silver bowl from the boudoir box and balanced it on the small of Hope's back.

"Ladies, a benefaction from your glass?" Marlene led the group, pouring a polite amount of bubbles from her champagne flute into the bowl.

The liquid sloshed a bit as Hope trembled but attempted to hold steady. As each of the women followed suit, Marlene spoke a private utterance into Hope's right ear.

Hope replied, "I am."

Marlene whispered again into Hope's left ear.

This time Hope's response was, "You are."

It was clear from the tremor of her tone that she was aroused. With each step in the curious ritual, she appeared to sink deeper into subspace. Stella was rapt to witness it to this degree. The overwhelming desire to one day be its cause roiled at the base of her spine. In witnessing these moments of humble servitude, her thoughts turned to her ex-husband. How could their dynamic have been different with the language of communication and consent? Could she learn to elicit devotion as expertly as Marlene?

Marlene produced a vial from the boudoir box. Stella recognized it as the container that Marlene had not permitted her to touch. It was some sort of powder that she dabbed on her lips then leaned forward to brush onto Hope's mouth. Hope whimpered and smiled before licking it off. Stella sensed the private dialogue taking place. There was an entire conversation in those gestures.

Marlene now invited Stella to engage. Stella's tribade senses were firing on all cylinders. As if receiving an invisible scepter, she moved quickly into command. She had been waiting.

"Position one," said Stella with a confidence that surprised her. Remnants of champagne bubbles fluttered up through her chest.

Hope sat back on her heels. "Yes, Mistress Stella."

Stella took Hope's chin between two fingers and spoke into the woman's pleading irises. "Put your right hand on the part of your body that longs most to be touched."

Hope shot a quick glance to Marlene, who nodded ever so slightly with approval. Hope slid her hand down the center of her body to land on the round of her pubis.

"Now, put your left hand on the part of your body you least want touched."

Hope's left hand remained still.

"My kind of girl," Deb agreed like a parishioner nodding in time with the message of salvation. Stella now felt the weight of those heavy priestess robes upon her shoulders.

She grabbed a flat leather paddle and slipped it between Hope's legs, spreading them wider. She used the thin edge of the leather to push Hope's fingers into the slit of her labia and move them around. Hope smiled. The tops of her creamy white breasts jiggled. How Stella longed to give her an "all hands on deck" massage with the other ladies. It was something she personally enjoyed, having recently discovered the joys of group sex. And yet, it felt too possessive. Hope was not hers to inhabit. That kind of intimacy could be interpreted as a takeover and she knew Marlene would not tolerate such a thing.

"Continue massaging those wet lips," Stella instructed, releasing the paddle from its work. "Position two! Ladies, come closer and hold her dress up for me. She deserves some funishment."

Stella lifted her arm dramatically and let the paddle land squarely on the rubbery middle of Hope's peach. Hope clenched her teeth. Only a tiny utterance escaped her lips. As she stained Hope's porcelain flesh carnation red, excitement rushed through her lungs. Though she felt Hope's body begging for more, she stepped back and handed the paddle to Marlene with an imperious little bow. A flood of questions about her performance flushed her mind. Was Marlene pleased with her violence, her restraint, her deference? Had it earned her the opportunity to do the same to the mysterious Lewdy?

Suddenly the moment had arrived. It was time for the main event. Houseboy had disappeared and then re-entered the apartment quietly. With Marlene's direction, he stepped up to present Lewdy Vuitton, who was blindfolded like a prisoner before the high court. Marlene introduced the women to her specimen, but what truly piqued the moment was when she placed a lampshade over Houseboy's head and ordered him to the corner of the room.

"You're my lamp now," she said, tugging hard on his ear as though it was a pull chain. "I turn you on. I turn you off." She twisted his nipple through his shirt before pivoting back to Lewdy. Still blindfolded, he didn't even know how many people were in the room.

As a child, Lewdy watched from the lower level den of his parents' picket-fenced home as his mother and her friends played afternoon bridge. In his journals to Marlene, he wrote of the arousal he felt at the voyeuristic view of their legs below the table, his erector sets pushed aside in favor of the erection-inducing peek at their shins and shining shoes. The blindfold would soon be removed and Lewdy would find himself in a similar scene.

The women were lined up in the living room. They looked like a page ripped from the *Ladies' Home Journal.*

Nothing to see here, just a casual '50s card night. Just a few birds chirping while their blokes down at the bar do play.

"Time for inspection," Marlene said. With this, Lewdy spread his arms and legs wide, maintaining a statuesque pose for examination of his physique.

He was an attractive man, very Don Draper. His thick brown hair would have gone so well with a letterman jacket. He was a former athlete and with the workout routine Marlene instituted, he was quite a bit leaner and more cut than before.

Marlene circled him, taking inventory of his body. Just as she instructed, the fresh bark scent of sandalwood rose from his collar. She took his hand to ensure his nails were manicured. She held his wrist to the light to check the cufflinks.

"Good boy," she praised. "You followed every instruction." He parted his lips as if to speak but she silenced him. "You don't speak!" she commanded loudly, and then softly into his ear, "You don't exist unless I tell you to."

Watching this, Stella was reminded of all the times that Marlene had played with that energy in her ear. To some degree, she could empathize with being on the receiving end of Marlene's honed intention.

Though she was smaller, Marlene seemed to loom over Lewdy. She was a giantess scooping up by the handful the citizens of his Chi. Stella marveled at the way he expanded and deflated with each of her actions. From behind, Marlene reached around his torso and pawed at the pearls of his buttons, undoing the first few before Deb called out, "Oh, yes! I think that little slut is wearing way too many clothes."

Marlene agreed. "Let's strip this little bitch so I can cage him!"

As Marlene moved around to finish with the buttons, she drew the room's attention to his hard-on, thick as a bratwurst, so the girls could have a laugh.

She invited the women to remove articles of his clothing. Stella took a long turn at his torso, caressing his broad chest and attentive nipples while Deb worked his pants off in an equally languid striptease. Stella then grabbed the crown of his hair and yanked his head back aggressively. He could not suppress a deep moan.

When he was completely naked, still blindfolded in a room full of strangers, his erection was at max capacity. Not ideal for caging.

Marlene slipped off his blindfold and invited the women to follow her into the bathroom. There, she doused him with ice-cold water from the handheld showerhead as though it was the height of summer and the head was a squirt gun. It was like watching a girl at the fair shoot fish in a barrel.

Once his boner bit the dust, Marlene gave a short presentation about how to properly cage a man, showing various devices as though they were Tupperware. Even her vocal inflection fit the role. Like Lucy spooning "Vitameatavegamin" with gusto and a smile.

"Just add water," she laughed, punctuating the show. If there had been a compact handy, she would have stopped to powder her nose.

After caging him, Marlene made Lewdy crawl into the dining room where she instructed him to avoid direct eye contact unless explicitly invited. With Lewdy's eyes obediently averted, she clipped a leash to one of the rings of his cage. His dick was almost purple, swelling through the slats in the metal.

"How I love restricting an erection," she said with an evil smile. Clearly, he loved it too. "Position one," she commanded, tying the leash to one of the bolts on the bench. "Stay till I come get you."

"Freshen our drinks and bring them in," she told Hope.

Hope serviced their drinks and when she arrived at Stella, they again exchanged knowing looks. Stella felt Hope's desire scandalously buoyed to hers. She knew that Hope's obsession with Marlene partly stemmed from the withholding of certain pleasures. In many ways, it seemed unethical, but Stella dared not challenge her mentor. She knew she was a novice and that Marlene had a short fuse when it came to defending her dommeliness. But what did this flirtation with Hope mean?

Marlene ushered Lewdy under the table. There were several things she whispered to him that Stella couldn't make out. Curiosity almost got the best of her but she didn't ask. Aroused by the display of strict control, she scribbled notes on the steno pad in her mind like a cone bra-clad secretary taking dictation. She longed to unpack this strange lifestyle like one of the myriad hat boxes on the Dragulator shelves. What veils, what plumes, what stunning feat of millinery did this journey have yet to reveal?

With a single finger to the crown of his head, Marlene forced Houseboy to his knees beside the table. He held the tray of sex toys. A smile spread across Deb's face. She took a long sip from her glass and winked at Marlene. Lewdy wasn't visible under the table, but it was clear from the breath Stella felt on her knees that he was in a state of rapture.

As the game continued, each of the women enjoyed a four-hand massage. A blindfolded Houseboy at work on the trapezius as Lewdy performed reflexology below. He was now sitting in a small pile of vintage handkerchiefs dampened with the righteous Amrita of their pleasures. He didn't know it yet, but Marlene planned to let him keep a few.

The rest of their time was spent gambling orgasms in a game of strip poker. Like a royal flush version of truth or dare. Some kisses swapped. Some panties dropped. The smell of sex in the air.

CHAPTER 16

Yvette, My Coquette

YVETTE WAS A PARTY GIRL adventuring round the world. She had spent the last year embroiled in a plan to land a job with a French beauty company as it expanded to Los Angeles. Since their sexy meeting in New Orleans, she and Stella had been exchanging flirty texts that escalated to racy videos after Yvette announced she was moving to LA.

The day finally arrived and Stella invited the Domicile crew to her place for a welcome party. After introductions all around, Stella and Yvette absconded to the kitchen to make cocktails and catch up.

"It's so good to see you again," Yvette sang like a Francophone songbird. She was bent at the waist, her head bobbing towards Stella as if she were a wind-up figurine on a cuckoo clock. Instead of announcing the time, she was requesting a kiss.

Stella wanted to kiss her badly, but it wouldn't do for her guests to see her locked in a lusty embrace in the kitchen, especially Marlene, whose neck seemed to stiffen at the sight of Yvette bouncing around the room with such guileless glee. To avoid her entirely, Marlene planted herself in a chair with proprietary hauteur and feigned a depth of conversational interest with Marco so intense that she appeared not to blink for several minutes. Marco took the rare opportunity of possessing Marlene's undivided attention to explain in rhapsodic detail the finer points of Krav Maga, to which Deb added salacious anecdotes. Neither seemed to mind Marlene's counterfeit cool.

"Back in Pocatello, you know, as I was prepping for the police academy, I was well on my way to earning a brown belt," Deb said, clenching her fists and delivering a swift roundhouse kick to an imaginary opponent. "Damn asthma held me back," she continued, squinting with a regretful gaze at the illumination of city lights outside. "Yep. It was pretty, pretty severe," she finished solemnly with a pat to Marco's broad shoulder.

Stella, keen to avoid offending Marlene, grabbed Yvette by the hand and led her through the living room and down the hallway. They snickered like bandits all the way to the bathroom where they could pick up where they left off in Nola.

But they were soon interrupted by a knock.

"Stella, I know you're doing *whatever* it is you're doing, but you have guests here," Marlene reprimanded through the door.

Stella and Yvette froze and suppressed their burgeoning giggles with hands to their mouths.

"Uh, yes. Do you need me right this second?" Stella shot back, wrapping her hands around Yvette's waist.

"Don't take all night in there. We're leaving," Marlene chastised, her heels clomping loudly away from the door.

"What's her problem? Is she jealous?" Yvette asked, kissing Stella on her bare shoulder.

"She's just so fucking uptight sometimes!" Stella scream-whispered.

"Party favor?" Yvette held up a small vial of white powder.

Stella smiled. "Sure, but I want it here," she said, pressing her finger to Yvette's jubilant breast.

Yvette spread the powder across her chest, but when Stella lowered her face to the line, it trickled down Yvette's cleavage. Yvette threw her head back and cackled in her wicked way as Stella dug her nose between her breasts like a drug-sniffing dog.

"Lick it," Yvette instructed with a devilish glint in her eye.

With the tip of her tongue, Stella gladly obliged, keeping her eyes fixed on Yvette's. She went in for a ravenous kiss, pulling Yvette tight against her breast. She was ecstatic with conjecture about what it would be like to fully consume her. Her fantasies were like Matryoshka dolls, each figurine concealing another, a new part of her sexual identity unlocked with each interaction.

After feasting for a few minutes more, they rejoined the crew and jumped into an Uber for drinks and a show at Black Rabbit Rose.

Yvette sat atop Stella's lap in the backseat of a Suburban that wreaked with the overcompensation of Febreze. She cooed kisses into the apple of Stella's cheek and, always the life of the party, instructed the driver to turn up the volume on "Bohemian Rhapsody." Everyone but Marlene launched into a raucous singalong. Marco pantomimed a fierce air guitar, then sparked up a joint and passed it around while Deb impassionately wailed soprano on the solos until spirited head-banging broke out among them all. It was bliss.

But it was an ugly love triangle. Marlene was not happy and, from the front seat, took to giving the poor driver point-by-point directions "off these busy main streets and onto these less traveled side streets you should know."

Arriving outside the club, they hit the kinetic streets, with Deb clucking like a mother hen ushering her waddling chicks up the path.

"Alright, alright. Everyone got their phones? Let's have a good—and safe—time, everybody." She seemed to be addressing Stella and Yvette in particular, having noticed the crystalline powder precipitating like frost on the fur of Stella's coat.

Inside the club, Yvette plopped herself down on Stella's lap like an old cat, wrapping her arms around her neck and drunkenly kissing her. Their tongues met greedily in the sticky darkness of the room while a local funk band played a gritty little soundtrack to their desire.

Marlene excused herself from the table and never returned. It was understandable. She hadn't once joined in on any of Stella's spontaneous play. *Who's the church lady now?* Stella thought.

Stella had been anticipating the moment she could be alone with Yvette since they first met in the "Spaceship Wish Machine." Though her attraction to women had only surfaced recently, it behaved with the insistence of a lifelong passion. It begged to be uncovered, pleaded to be fulfilled just as her attraction to men had as a virginal bride.

So, after a good hour or so, she said goodbye to Deb and Marco, and put herself and Yvette back in an Uber towards downtown.

The elevator ride to Yvette's 17th-floor studio in the sky was ripe with delicious sexual tension. Stella was still woozy from the edibles they had taken at the Hollywood speakeasy. Her core had been tingling with the subtlety of hot peppermint all evening.

As soon as they walked in, Yvette busied herself in the kitchen preparing Stella her go-to whiskey on the rocks.

Stella glanced around at the studio apartment, which came adequately if predictably furnished for a corporate rental. Everything was white and modern and generic, far from the vintage sheen of Paris. But the view could not be argued with. A million city lights danced outside the floor-to-ceiling windows.

Yvette handed Stella her glass then smiled and stood as still as a statue, patiently allowing Stella to admire her. This was their dance. The pursuer and the pursued. She had learned that Yvette would sooner telegraph her desires through her almond eyes than verbalize them in some plain, inelegant American way. Stella loved reading the storybook of Yvette's libido in the flutter of her lashes.

Yvette suggested they play some music and, after sitting Stella on the bed, bent over from behind and shot back a million-dollar smile. She ran her hands along her legs up to her ass and slapped it. She stood tall and confident and teased her top off, giving her hair a disco queen tousle. She unzipped her skirt and inched it in triple slow motion over her hips in time with the sultry R&B song. She wore a diaphanous bra and panty set. Black lace, of course, which Stella wanted to rip into with primal lust.

Yvette kept moving to the music, sashaying closer and closer. She flipped around and slid her ass across Stella's leather skirt and along the naked flesh of her thighs. Stella ran her nails along Yvette's hips and up her abdomen, curling her fingers around her navel possessively. Yvette leaned back, cheek to cheek, and writhed harder in time with the thick electro beat. Her long tresses tickled Stella's collarbone. She inhaled deeply, letting Yvette's heady bergamot perfume enshroud her.

Stella's glance became fixed on an oversized neon sign dominating a building in the near distance. It silently proselytized like the foreboding eyes of Doctor T. J. Eckleburg. Groaning and flickering in all red caps, it read: *Jesus Saves*. Stella felt a flush of wetness between her legs.

She grabbed Yvette's arms in a forceful restraint, pressing her chest into Yvette's back as she nibbled on her neck. Yvette exhaled with pleasure. Gripping her arms tighter, she lifted Yvette and placed her atop the bed.

Looking her intently in the eye, Stella kneeled and slowly removed Yvette's boots. She peeled off Yvette's socks, then set about the intimate act of kissing each of her elegant toes just as men had worshiped Stella's before. Flipping the gender script filled her with a wholly new sexual carbonation.

Yvette had lovely high arches and her feet were long and narrow—larger than Stella's, though she was far more petite. Her nails were painted blood maroon. Stella enjoyed studying them, drawing out the anticipation, making Yvette squeal when she ran her tongue between her toes. She pulsed her tongue in and out like it was the hollow between her legs. Penetrating her. Wet and deep.

Stella laid down and pressed her thigh against Yvette's as a haunting French song by La Femme played and a husky female voice started to coo. "Tell me what he's saying."

Yvette grabbed Stella's hand as she translated the French lyrics. The vocalist sang beat poetry over a reverberating slide guitar and layers of synthy voices that echoed in a bubble of stereophonic bliss.

She moved onto her knees, straddling Yvette's lower half. Her inner thighs had just enough trembling, ample flesh for Stella to rub her cheek across. *God, her skin is soft!*

Her inclination to top Yvette was as instinctual as lying prostrate on her back for a man. It was time to do what she had been longing to do for months. Stella moved the thin strip of panty to the side to reveal the pretty pink petals of Yvette's labia. Stella spread the folds of her flesh to expose the glistening interior bud. She leaned down to touch the tip of her tongue to Yvette's clit. Her first taste of a woman. How curious she had been for so long. She did it again, saturating her palate with Yvette's sweet, salty flavor. The more she feasted, the more passionate her appetite became. Yvette squirmed as Stella continued plying her tongue, experimenting with different techniques until she felt Yvette jolt as if she had been shot by a sniper. She exhaled dramatically, grabbing Stella's head and pressing it against her thigh. Stella smiled and rested upon her druggily for a few moments. Yvette squeezed her hand tightly and smiled.

Stella continued her oral migration north across Yvette's corseted waist and kissed the inked curve of her abdomen. She had that beautiful longitudinal line of muscle from her sternum to her belly button. Her tattoo was fitting—a colorful dragon whose tail pointed at her navel and whose tongue hissed at her breast.

Yvette reclined languidly on her pillow, moaning with each caress, giving Stella the audible encouragement to continue her sensual journey to the splendid spillage of her breasts, the touch and taste of which Stella had been craving since that romp in the bathroom. Peeling off Yvette's bra, Stella was flooded with equal parts desire and insecurity. At 28, Yvette was still so perky. Her teardrop breasts laid elegantly atop the narrow bridge of her ribs, floating to her sides so naturally. They were more beautiful than Stella had imagined dozens of times in her fantasies of this exact erotic moment. *Can these be real?*

Her breasts were chalk-outlined in the shape of a skimpy triangle bikini, the tops caramelized in butterscotch by the Mediterranean sun, the undersides a creamy vanilla which made them appear more spherical and ripe. The rosy saucers of her areolas were large and soft. Stella worked the juices inside her mouth to coat her lips and suck on her hardening nipples. She savored the sweetness of Yvette's flesh like a sommelier taking in a full-bodied wine.

Yvette basked in the glory of Stella's sexual revolution, opening herself fully like a swimmer floating on her back, resisting nothing, being carried on the waves of their exploration into the depths of her eroticism. At first, Stella chalked up her own desire as a kind of douchebag male lust. But as she lay in the dark with Yvette, she felt something deeper.

Yvette pawed at Stella's clothes until they were free of any barrier to the union of their impatient flesh. She then climbed on top. Their inner thighs glistened as they writhed in V formation. Her nipples wide awake and erect, Yvette wore a mix of pain and pleasure on her blushed cheek.

"Take it all, baby. It's yours," Stella growled as Yvette slid along her slick flesh. Stella was intoxicated with the hourglass curve of her hips, the dragon which seemed to breathe more fire as she moved, and the rapturous sight of Yvette's perfect bouncing tits.

Yvette responded by pressing herself deeper into Stella. They tumbled over and Stella mounted her. She gripped Yvette's calf against her perspired face, her entire body covered in a dewy coat.

As Stella rocked against her, it became impossible to prolong the insistent climax. It came knocking at the door unrelentingly. The kettle went off in the form of a protracted moan, Stella expelling the proof of her pleasure which could not be prolonged a moment longer. She whirled open into a chamber of infinite white bliss, clutched Yvette's knee ferociously against her breast, and shivered until she collapsed into a ragged slump at her side, exhaling the breath held for minutes, maybe years. Squeezing the birdlike bones of her hand, she smiled with satisfaction.

* * * * *

Stella did not know what to do the morning after in the bright sober light of their post-coital haze. Yvette rose from bed first and busied herself on her laptop while Stella drifted between real and pretend sleep. She was nervous about how she looked all mussed from the messiness of sleep. Was there drool crusted to the corners of her mouth? Frizzy hair that could not be tamed sans the Saharan heat of an iron?

Stella snuck into the bathroom without making eye contact and got to work on Operation Morning Breath. A bit of spackling of the troublesome chin pimple, removal of the inner eye barnacles, a swab of deodorant, and 10 minutes later she pretended to emerge as if she had just rolled out of bed. *Isn't all seduction some form of half-truth?*

Yvette was beautiful even under the conditions of bedhead and almost no makeup. She woke up just as tan and lithe as before. Her smudged eyeliner looked *tres chic.* Stella wanted to pose her in the dramatic light of the giant window with a newspaper and a cup of coffee, take her picture, and send it to *Vogue*. She was *that* girl.

They smiled and greeted one another tentatively. Stella was clumsy in her affections and Yvette didn't exactly go to bed with a woman every night. Stella climbed back under the sheets and Yvette followed, sliding naturally into the crook of Stella's shoulder where she held her there until it was apparent Yvette was lobbying for round two. Much to Stella's relief, sober sex unleashed the hounds in both of them. Yvette came loud and hard against the grind of Stella's groin, and as the day progressed, their awkwardness morphed into a sweet, friendly affection.

They spent the afternoon sharing a lounge chair by the pool, Yvette's happy, wet cleavage keeping Stella entertained for hours. They had a giggle about both being sore "down there," and then Yvette took a dip while Stella lit a joint and ruminated under the afternoon sun.

Being with a woman felt deeper than just the public flirtations that so adrenalized her with Yvette. It felt like a stance for womanhood, for the divine feminine. A political statement even in private. A middle finger to the patriarchy. Some holy communion. It felt like making love to herself. It taught her who she was as a woman.

She had first experienced it with Marlene in the bath, but they had left it there. However, there were no red lights with Yvette, so they sped ahead. She felt her prowess swell when Yvette was around; her confidence buoyed. There was nothing they couldn't do together.

CHAPTER 17

Strike a Pose

THE WINDOWS WERE OPEN and a cool evening breeze carried the scent of orange blossoms from the trees. Soft, rose-colored light accented the racks of costumes and jewelry Marlene had arranged along the perimeter of the penthouse living room.

United in their mutual love of film noir, Stella and Marlene unfolded the concept for a short film and photo series for the Domicile website. Marlene sent a flurry of images, from the Thierry Mugler runway in his heyday to a scratchy 1930s Marlene Dietrich film about a showgirl turned Domme. Stella didn't bristle at the challenge to turn the penthouse into what looked like a million-dollar set. She craved the creative exchange, lapping up the references like a hungry kitten at a rare saucerful of milk.

The Domicile site would display only the most cinematic imagery. It would be smart, cultured, and cunning. It would appeal to a discerning clientele.

Stella lined up her arsenal of equipment with the precision of a surgeon sanitizing her scalpel. She busied herself with lights and camera, briefing Marlene on the set and equipment—oh, how she loved the nerdspeak of film, going on passionately about her new colored gels or the dreamy slow shutter she would use. But even after years of shooting, Stella had a stomach full of nerves. She did not know if it was imposter syndrome that swirled like rancid waters in her gut or good old-fashioned pre-work jitters.

Marlene dropped her robe and pawed her way onto a tufted chaise lounge. She wore a black bodysuit, French cut at the hips, and patent leather heels with large gold buckles. Her legs looked the better stretch of seven solid miles and her lips were painted the deep red of 1940's victory parades.

She stretched onto all fours, feline Fancy Feast, dipping and writhing as Stella feverishly snapped away. The lights warmed Marlene's skin as an imposing, playful charge filled the air like a big game cat had jumped up on the hood of the Jeep right at the start of the safari.

Sliding around on the floor, Stella became even more childlike, twisting and turning her crystals, inverting her perception and snatching it up with the net of her shutter. She was a huntress in this way.

Marlene slid a strap-on harness over her hips. She raised one leg to straddle Stella and ran her fingertips over the head. The dildo buoyed with her movement a few inches from Stella's face. The growl of Betty Davis' belting nearly drowned in the pitch of their laughter as Marlene gyrated the rubber between her legs. Stella snapped away, finding all the best angles to make Marlene look like a giantess.

When they finished shooting, Marlene changed into yoga pants while Stella started editing. As they sat and poured over the photos, Marlene seemed to be riding a wave of panic.

"I've always been so private and now here I am with my dick out," she grumbled, her voice rising an octave.

"Then why are you wearing it? Do you not want me to use these photos at all?" Stella's leg began to jitter.

It was clear Marlene made herself vulnerable to Stella in ways she rarely had, but was she on board with starting the business or wasn't she? There was always some impediment to progress.

Thankfully, Deb was on her way. Stella hoped she'd be the tiebreaker needed. Marlene appeared to respect Deb and be less adversarial in her presence.

Within the hour, the three women were gobbling up pad see ew in the living room. Stella was distracted and crunching numbers on her laptop for the millionth time.

"Marlene, I'm nervous that if we don't publish the website soon, I'm going to run out of money."

"Money isn't everything," Marlene replied, stabbing a square of fried tofu as she sat in her peacock chair, the grandest seat in the place. She had moved so much into the penthouse, Stella wondered if anything remained in her Silver Lake abode.

"Tell that to Deb when it's payday," Stella shot back.

Deb set down her Thai tea with a look of embarrassment. "I think what Marlene is trying to say is that you have to build relationships in order to have regular clients."

Marlene smiled. "Yes, thank you, Deb. And we will pay you, of course."

There were many times Stella was so stymied by Marlene's lack of accountability that she knew not what to say. But she wouldn't be defeated, not after chewing off her leg to get loose from the Watchtower trap.

"I know what to do!" Stella announced, looking up from her keyboard, the yellow curry on her plate curdling at the edges. A light bulb had gone off. "It's all about SEO and ad spends. We just need a larger share of market voice. Then we can make our goals. I'm going to rewrite our business plan so we can get in the green by month three."

"Profitability by month three is pretty ambitious, no?" Deb queried, sliding onto the couch next to Stella as if they were bankers assembling at a Wall Street bar. Deb peered onto the screen where Stella was at work on a spreadsheet. "Usually takes new businesses years to realize profit."

"I'm going to launch the site this week and then do a huge ad campaign. This can work!" Stella exclaimed, finally taking a bite of greasy noodles, the pepper flakes pleasantly torching her tongue. A swell of hope rushed through her.

"No. We aren't ready," Marlene objected.

"But you approved the last round of changes!" Stella said, slurping back a broad noodle. She cringed at how high-ranking Marlene considered herself in this part of the business she knew virtually nothing about. Stella didn't want to kowtow anymore. She wondered if Marlene was using the perfectionist standard as a way not to advance the business plan. Was fear holding her back or did she not know what the hell she was doing?

"I'm not ready to go public," Marlene protested. "Look, I brought in Lewdy my way. I can do it again."

"This is such an inefficient way of finding clients. We need to be online—website, Fet, social…" Stella argued, pushing her plate away once again. They were constantly getting their stubborn claws caught in the delicate weave of their business ideals.

"I don't know how yet, but I'm sure something will work out. Always does. I'm so blessed. I thank God every day." Marlene clasped her hands and gazed upwards.

"Marlene, you can't just wish and pray."

"You're clearly getting triggered... and a little tossed," Marlene accused, pointing to Stella's glass of whiskey.

"I've had a few sips! But yes, I am getting triggered." Stella sighed and closed her laptop. "I have invested too much. We have to make this work." She tapped at her phone screen furiously. "There, it's done." She jumped up and went to top off her glass from the bar cart in the dining room.

"What did you do?" asked Marlene accusingly as she got up to follow her.

"I transferred some more money. Domicile is now $5,000 richer," Stella said without looking at Marlene. "Deb, you'll be paid Friday, as will Marco. This will cover rent next month, which otherwise would have been impossible. Marlene, I really need you to match my contribution or get it from your subs. *Something.*"

"Look, I'm not comfortable with that kind of decision-making while you're in this state," Marlene objected.

"And what's your solution?" Stella finished her pour and returned the decanter to the cart.

"Stella, this is supposed to be fun!" Marlene exclaimed with her hands in the air.

"This is a business! That's what we agreed to. I don't have years' worth of savings. Do you? It's do or die," Stella said, throwing back a swig of bourbon.

Deb clamored to their sides before Marlene was forced to answer Stella's query. "Look, there's no reason to give into despair at such an early juncture," she encouraged. "This team was not meant to fail. Sex work may be a battlefield but goddamit, I believe in this platoon."

"The pantaloon platoon," cracked Stella unexpectedly.

"You cannot resist a good pun. Doesn't matter how angry you are." Marlene wrapped her arms around Stella. "That's what I love about you. And Deb is right. Be patient! We are just getting started. It takes weeks, sometimes months, of skillful domination to cultivate a lasting dynamic."

Marlene's phone chimed. "I've gotta go," she said, grabbing her bags from the foyer.

Stella followed her out the front door dejectedly. Marlene took her gently in her arms. "Stop worrying so much."

Stella shrugged. "Sure."

Marlene beckoned Stella towards the elevator. "Walk with me. We'll figure this out."

Stella sighed as the elevator descended to the lobby. "OK, OK. You're right. But let me do the big marketing campaign we need to attract clients."

Arriving in the lobby, they pushed through the front door to see Hope pop out of her Subaru and rush to open the car door. She looked smart in a chauffeur's cap, navy blazer, black skinny jeans, and leather driving gloves.

Stella knew the stirrings of Hope's heart, that she pined for more intimacy, more pleasure, more pain. Marlene left her wanting and so Hope laid down at her master's feet all that she had. Marlene loved to brag that Hope had given her the PIN to her debit card, the keys to her car, and the assurance of continued financial devotion. They were even house shopping.

"Good evening, Mistress. How was your night?" Hope asked cheerfully, shooting Stella a quick smile. Stella began trodding sullenly up the front stoop. She paused a moment before going back inside.

"Is this my rent check?" Marlene said, sliding into the car and holding up an envelope placed on the backseat.

"Yes, and a little extra for utilities. I know you've been using your A/C more this summer."

"Wonderful. You are proving to be more valuable than I expected."

"I hope so. Your well-being is my priority. If there's anything else I can do..." Hope said, closing the door and hurrying around to the driver's seat.

* * * * *

Stella needed moral support, so she called Yvette who arrived at the crest of blue hour.

"I love it," Yvette said, pointing a long red nail to the shiny silver pole front and center in Stella's studio.

"I installed it for you. All for you." Stella said, tapping on the metal and admiring her handiwork.

Yvette peeled off her cropped leather jacket. "Shall I dance for you?"

She removed her high-heeled boots and slid out of her tiny leather skirt. Her cleavage erupted from the top of a shimmering silver bodysuit. It was high cut on the legs revealing the embossment of a swarthy tan across her hips. Stella swooned like a schoolgirl at the sight of her.

Yvette sauntered around the pole a few times, dipping her hips with each pointed step. She wrapped her hands around the pole and then quickly inverted herself. Her ankles hit the metal with a clank.

"I'm rusty," Yvette apologized, laughing good-naturedly. She never seemed phased at any misstep.

"Baby, if that's rusty then I'm not even going to even try."

Yvette arched back, popped out her chest, and flashed a sexy smile. When her buoyant breasts threatened to escape the hatch of her neckline, Stella felt a surge of wetness. She had been longing for another performance by Yvette. To be the audience, to step into the male gaze and be dazzled by an overwhelm of feminine seduction thrilled her. The power inversion suited her voracious appetite for dominant experiences.

Yvette wrapped her coltish legs around the pole, spinning a couple of full rotations before she landed in the splits. She slid her body across the hardwood floor seductively. She kissed Stella's leg, first at the ankle and then in paced, provocative increments upwards, arrived between her thighs. She looked up at Stella for a cue to continue. Stella took her hand and led her to the bed. Yvette began peeling off Stella's pants.

"I've never gone down on a woman," she confessed sheepishly, her mouth an inch from Stella's pussy.

Stella ran her fingers through Yvette's silky hair, dragging her nails at the temples. Yvette pressed her lips to the folds of Stella's vulva, a tender kiss. Stella guided her, stroking her buttery skin, holding Yvette's jaw as her tongue explored new terrain. Stella laid back on a pillow and they both seemed to be lost, floating in the clouds, for she did not know how much time had passed when Yvette finally crawled up her body and straddled her.

Stella felt a spiritual connection to Yvette during sex—a free-spiritedness. They had erected a sort of church where their ecclesiastic spirits could soar. There were no limits. The ether that filled their chamber was a sweet incense, a possession, a full incantation they summoned effortlessly.

After a sweaty romp, they adjourned to the bath, sitting opposite, with their knees jutting out in the center like the descending dragon of Hạ Long Bay. They passed a smoldering joint and took the smoke and the bathwater's rich scent of eucalyptus deep into their lungs. Despite the thrill of imbibing every molecule of Yvette's essence, Stella could not help thinking of her business woes with Marlene.

"She's got this rigid Catholic nunitude about her." Stella took the joint from Yvette. "And yet she says I'm the one who's too serious."

"I know, I can feel it. And I don't think she likes me," Yvette said, running her hands through her long chestnut hair and twirling it into a bun, her delicate gold necklace sudsy on her chest. "I know you can be successful. Why do you even need her?"

"Well, I'm not a Domme. I'm what she calls a 'Baby Domme.'"

"Still? Haven't you been learning for like, six months?"

"Yes, but…"

"And aren't you running the finances and marketing?" Yvette insisted, laying out her case. "You have to dive in and try it. You'll learn as you go. I did. I had clients in New York pay me for all kinds of things—dinner, shows, sex, whatever."

Stella admired how much of a Holly Golightly Yvette was. At 28, she seemed to have lived lifetimes. She had an armor about her with men but maintained such a succulent core for Stella. She never failed to cheerlead any and all sexual pursuits, unlike the oppositional Marlene.

"You're right. I'm a quick study. I wanted to launch the website ages ago. We need to book sessions. I'm paying rent on two apartments!"

"Do it, baby," Yvette said, the joint between her lovely long fingers in one hand as she took Stella's face in the other and kissed her deeply.

"Fuck it!" Stella said, suddenly rising, suds clinging to her slick flesh. Yvette looked her up and down lustily.

Stella grabbed her laptop and returned to sit naked on the toilet seat. She'd spent hours tinkering with fonts and formats, realizing she'd already been domming in the digital for years—another type of web spun from allure. She took a long puff and held it in her throat. Seized with a seismic aversion to failure, she exhaled and pressed "publish" on the Domicile website. That's it. No more consultation with Marlene, whose promise that Hope would contribute to business expenses had not materialized in more than a month of rent and a few items from PetSmart.

"She's lost her right to veto," Stella said. "I'm footing the bills; I make the fucking decisions."

CHAPTER 18

Meeting Mr. X

WITHIN WEEKS, client inquiries filled the Domicile inbox on multiple platforms. Stella's media blitz was bearing more than modest fruit. The avatar of her social media could Tango Ocho a dance of well-honed tease and denial. After all, an imagination captivated is the purist submissive in the world.

Stella had still not revealed to Marlene that the site was live and certainly not that she was interviewing clients on her own. Her plan was to secure a client first then dazzle her with a great big catch.

Unfortunately, her interviews read like the script to a bad romcom. There was a shifty 27-year-old Bostonian with a tickle porn addiction who sped-talked his way through an excruciating coffee date. Several just wanted facesitting. And many more lamely offered for Stella to "do whatever you want with me," as if that was payment enough. Stella soon realized that the youngbloods had no money and she tired of their attempts to justify a lack of tribute. "Brains will get you halfway there," she'd say. "Bills will take you the rest of the way."

Considering Marlene's sapiosexual bent, Stella decided to take a closer look at a man who called himself only "X." He was among the first 100 followers on Instagram and was immediately hooked by a photo of Marlene sipping mezcal from a cordial glass with several hanks of rope at her feet. Stella had expertly peppered their social media with lifestyle photos, elevating them above the typical dungeon Domme aesthetic.

Mr. X's messages were thoughtful and his inquiries caramel-coated with a razor-sharp brand of Chamuyo. He was good-looking by every traditional Western standard. He was rich, intelligent, and very fortunately, a filthy pig.

Stella replied to his DMs with instructions to complete the application on the website. She also sent along a thorough BDSM checklist she built in Google Docs, which was sure would impress Marlene. She had followed her lead precisely in so many processes.

It was now time to investigate in person. Stella walked swiftly down the palm-lined streets to her destination, The Prince, a Koreatown staple. To the click of her heels on the pavement, she silently rehearsed her line of questioning, adrenalized by the prospect of reeling in this big fish on her own.

She chose a booth in the back facing the entrance. She soon saw the shadow of a man approaching the front door. She straightened her torso, forcing the tanned arches of her shoulders back like the Doberman Marlene believed her to be.

The man's eyes seemed to enter the room before the rest of his body and immediately zeroed in on Stella. How could they not? Her midnight black hair shone like the chrome of a Cadillac. She would have been perfectly cast as a *Blade Runner* fembot fatale in her all-black ensemble that included a semi-sheer top over a push-up bra and her signature leather pencil skirt.

She leaned back in the red vinyl booth and smiled ever so slightly. *Do not smile, do not smile,* Stella corrected herself. Her vision of herself in full dommeliness did not include smiling.

Mr. X approached and she stood to greet him. She was taken aback by how attractive he was, further chipping away at her suspicion that all submissive men were pasty doughboys begging for the pegging.

Even with her heels, he loomed half a foot above her. His mane was thick and black. His tan was a bit too tan and his shirt a bit too starched. If one were to see him looking over the rim of his Warby Parkers, taking inventory of the morning paper, they might think him a stock broker. Then there was the question of the lack of wedding ring. Maybe that ping on his phone was a text from a lawyer with the latest alimony news.

Mr. X had presence. He took up space in a way that made Stella want to double hers. She read in his face both desire and control. *Is this the stature of a truly submissive man?* she wondered. Marlene had, of course, apprised her of the value of an alpha submissive, but Stella never failed to be skeptical, always pressing her for proof of genuine submission in such a specimen. And so here she was, pressing for proof from Mr. X himself.

"Have a seat," she instructed, gesturing to the booth. She felt Marlene in the room like a Cyrano as she parroted her pitch and posture.

"As you wish," he said, a lilt of an accent slipping out. "This place is quite unique." He gestured to the medieval-cum-Korean decor. The walls were brocade in crimson and adorned with ornately framed New American oil paintings (a portrait of George Washington; a pastoral landscape in flaxen tones). Several suits of armor stood in all their battered metal glory in pockets of the room. Pure Ktown kitsch.

"Let's start with a drink," Stella said, studying the menu.

"You made an excellent choice with this bar. The mezcal selection is impressive."

"Choose something for us then, Mr. *Xxxpert,*" she said with a trill of her tongue.

"Gladly." He smiled, revealing the dental caps of his Clorox white teeth. A trained eye clocked the subtle injections of Botox to his forehead. "If you will, let us try the flight. I want to know what your palate prefers," he offered, his Argentinian accent lending a Telenovela star quality.

Stella had to admit it was sexy. "And what will *you* drink?" she asked with a flirtatious smile.

"Well, whatever you tell me, of course, but as a distiller myself, I have plenty of opportunity."

The drinks arrived and Mr. X explained the variety. She took a tiny sip, careful to pause between glasses. Mr. X sampled each of the agave spirits, remarking on the tone and timber of the flight in an impressive demonstration of his knowledge. He was charming, but not to a fault. Stella sensed a warm-blooded creature under his boardroom bravado and before she knew it, she had sunk ever so slightly under his spell. But she'd been too nervous to eat dinner and now she could feel the mezcal dulling her focus. *I'm not going down like this,* she told herself, then beelined for the bathroom.

Closing the stall door, she began typing furiously into her phone. "I'm interviewing a very promising client." She longed to text Marlene and revel in her victory, but the timing was premature. She needed an approach that would guarantee Marlene wouldn't derail all her work out of spite. She messaged Yvette instead who cheered her on as maternally as a soccer mom sending a beloved child onto the playing field.

Stella returned to the table determined.

"How would you earn my dominance?" she abruptly pushed in.

"Earn? Well, I hadn't thought of it that way," he replied.

"That's obvious," Stella replied in the flat tone she had developed for this role. It wasn't a caricature of a Domme, exactly. It was Stella allowing herself to cut the sweetness. *Add less sugar to the pie,* she told herself. *Do not apologize. Command.*

They discussed kinks, of course, but Stella was more interested in the real man behind the deviant desires. Mr. X admitted to being in a 12-step program, dangling his struggle with addiction like a pocket watch at the end of a gold chain. Stella swam deeper, inquiring about the minutiae of his upbringing. He lowered his shoulders, leaned closer, and spoke more softly when discussing his childhood. But when he talked of his sexcapades, his voice was slathered with seduction. He loved to ride the razor's edge, like the pulse of an artery throbbing at the point of a switchblade. His accent became hypnotic in its melody. So, Stella did what she always did on vanilla dates—she flirted.

"What is your impression of me?" she asked, suspecting it would be flattering. She could see the lust in the bedrock of his broad shoulders, inching closer to hers with each confession.

"First impression: I was stunned by your beauty, your smile, your cleavage, and the energy that you possess. You are sensual yet strong."

"And what is your impression now that we are two hours deep?" Stella milked him for more. She wanted the goods. She wanted him to pour his poetry all over her.

"Shall I reveal all my secrets just yet?"

Stella was becoming drunk on her desire for worship. Catching herself, she snapped to attention.

"This meeting is now adjourned," she said, stiffening her back against the booth. "I will be in touch."

"It is my privilege to have met you." Mr. X stood to kiss her hand and she allowed it. When his lips lingered too long on her knuckles, the wingbeats of her heart went wild in a flutter of sex and spirits. She quickly pulled away, sashaying out the door slowly to allow him to take in the fullness of her hips. Reaching the street corner, she paused to catch her breath and calm her heart. A text popped up on her phone.

It was him.

"Final impression. By the time you left, I was floating, like a leaf that fell from a tree and never touched ground, suspended for that moment, confused by the dream that said eternity but you were already gone with your skin and your Sicilian nose and that prose written all over your body…"

God, he is good.

* * * * *

Stella wondered what kind of day it would be with Marlene. At times, their relationship smoked like a car with one stiletto on the gas and one stiletto on the brake; one hand on the wheel and one hand up a skirt.

Mr. X was more than ready to book a session and Stella didn't want to lose his interest by delaying a moment longer.

As she sat at her vanity, she rehearsed lines, trying to articulate the precise words to persuade Marlene to trust her judgment.

Marlene rang. The intercom was on the fritz again. Stella sped down to the lobby.

"You should just give me a key," Marlene began as soon as Stella opened the door. She handed Stella a roller bag. "Hang on. There's more in the car."

The gunpowder soufflé of a neighbor's dinner wafted down the hallway as they pushed through the elevator door to the ninth floor.

"What's all this stuff? You moving in?" Stella joked.

"I'm outfitting the penthouse. I know what I need. Tools of the trade."

As soon as they were inside, Marlene tramped off to the walk-in closet, her platform sandals clopping loudly on the hardwood floors. She began hanging a dozen or more dresses, skirts, and jackets. She lined the floor with myriad pairs of boots and heels.

Stella handed her a martini.

"Are we day drinking?" Marlene asked.

"Just want to show you that I'm learning."

Marlene took a cautious sip. "Not bad. You went a bit overboard on the Vermouth though."

"Want me to make you another one?" Stella was eager to please. It was the only way she had a chance of sticking the landing of her news without a fracas.

"I'll drink this. Aren't *you* hospitable today?" Marlene said as she carefully clipped a pair of silk pants on a hanger.

A knot tightened like a vice grip in Stella's right shoulder. She threw back the martini with record speed.

"I'm feeling very optimistic about the business," she said, turning on a small Tiffany lamp and switching off the overhead light. "Here, I know you prefer this light."

"So much better," Marlene praised. "And I'm glad to hear that."

"So... I, um... found a promising client. I really think you're going to love him."

"How did *you* find a client? I thought we were leaving that to me." Marlene zipped up her suitcase and turned to look at Stella squarely.

"Well, I wanted to contribute. I'm paying rent on the penthouse and at my place. I'm investing a lot. I know how to run a small business. I've done it for years."

"This is totally different from your filmmaking business. This is personal. And you have a partner."

"Yes, yes, I know, but just—can you hear me out? Let's sit down." Her heart thumped like the wings of a trapped bird.

Marlene followed her into the living room and reclined on a velvet chaise. Stella propped herself up on a floor pillow with her back against the ornate faux fireplace. She did not enjoy this position below Marlene, but what other chance did she have at winning her favor?

"Please just look at him," Stella said, pushing her phone towards Marlene.

She saw a glimmer of hope, a smile in the corners of Marlene's scrutinizing eyes.

"Surprisingly impressive," Marlene had to admit.

The photos were well-curated and compelling, a showcase of bareback horse riding, standing amid sprawling agave fields, dangling from boulders harness-free, or glistening in the saltwater spray of a jet ski.

"I do like his hands," Marlene confessed. They were manicured yet masculine, strong and symmetrical. Thick, long fingers and wide-set thumbs.

"I knew it! I knew you would!"

"And he's well-traveled. Sophisticated. I'm getting Helmut Newton vibes in this set of photos from the bar. Looks like Barcelona."

"Right? He's perfect for you. For us. For the business!"

"Well, who knows? Might be a catfish."

"He's not."

"Can't be sure until I test him."

"I'm positive." Stella paused then let forth the admission like a Catholic schoolgirl at a confessional. "I launched the website. I met him."

"Without my consent? Are you fucking with me, Stella?"

"No! Look, I thought about it and I made an executive decision and I was right. You see? I was right! I have a big fish on the line, someone you *know* you like. Admit it. He's a good one. Rich. Experienced. This is the exact kind of client you say you want!"

Marlene's eyes bulged with the ferocity of a racehorse pounding onerously down the track. "Pull up the website. Now!"

Stella scrambled to her feet to retrieve her laptop.

"You approved everything. I only edited a few things, added the intake form..." she rambled nervously.

Marlene held out her hand impatiently, snatched the computer from Stella with unnecessary force, then sat motionless save for the rapid movement of her eyes across the screen.

"Obviously the site looks good, but you seriously crossed a boundary of privacy and consent by publishing it."

"What were you waiting for? You agreed to this business. You pushed me to rent this penthouse, we've talked endlessly—*endlessly*—about the kind of clients you want. We did the Lewdy thing. I was patient. What more can I do while you decide if you want a website published? Why are you holding us back? Are you afraid?"

"I hear you," Marlene interrupted. She stood up and began pacing. "He'd have to journal first, of course."

"Of course." Stella's pulse quickened with anticipation. Hope again.

"And tell me about this meeting. What did you say?"

Much to her relief and surprise, waves of understanding came in like a welcome tide to cool the fiery tension. Stella could see the nervous excitement in Marlene's eyes as she told her about the mezcal and the accent and all the delicious potential of Mr. X.

"Our relationship is like being in a room with infinity mirrors. We are so meta," Marlene said, abstractly twirling her hair as the sun set and cast golden light through the bank of windows. "I don't know where I end and our art begins."

She was calmer now, as if the idea of Stella taking the lead was no longer her worst nightmare realized.

"You cause me to shine the light on places within that I didn't know to examine," replied Stella. "And we are stronger together. Concave to convex. Your words, remember?"

The polarity of their natures did vex them. At the joint of Stella's wanton impatience and Marlene's too-precious restraint cramped a muscle that ached to be stretched, to be strengthened. They pawed painfully at the fascia and flesh of its sinewy mass. When they clicked though, the connection sparked a fire in each of them like no other had before.

CHAPTER 19

Maneater

STELLA AND MARLENE SAT on the distressed leather couch of Le Chat Noir, the Silver Lake bar that served as an ever-ready backdrop to Marlene's many evenings of heightened, semi-public erotica. For a few years now, it had been a frequent meeting place for her dommely dating antics. If the walls of those washrooms could talk, they'd have sold her up the river for a dime. Stella called it her "Lair de Maneater."

Along with its tropical gothic decor, it had good lighting and single-stall bathrooms. It was an LA institution in which to see and be seen. Any given Sunday on the terrace was a postcard of hipster Aperol spritz, all nose rings, mini sundresses, and thin-script tattoos up emaciated ribs towards the undulation of just enough side boob.

Marlene had always preferred to work alone, not only because she was savant, near autistic at times in her particulars, but also because she had a hard time tolerating her environment being out of her control. Stella convinced her otherwise, promising to be the perfect little Vanna White to her Pat Sajak—quiet and obedient, helpful and observing. She could tell Marlene dared not refuse her the opportunity after Stella's show of force when it came to executive decision-making.

Stella admired Marlene as she crossed her legs in her skin-tight Versace pencil skirt and tissue paper blouse, low cut and sheer. The gunmetal of Marlene's five-inch heel was a nod to *La Femme Nikita.* She never wore her hair down when first meeting a sub. She left flirtatious distractions at the door. She said she liked the feeling of calculation in these meetings. With each sip from her glass, one could almost hear the click of an attaché case and picture the billowing curtains of a Parisian hotel room. A woman in black nylons screws the silencer onto the barrel of a Ruger 22. Through the window, she sees her mark. Sets her sights. She squints and narrows her vision. *Goodnight, Senator, goodnight.*

That was how Marlene looked on the sofa in the corner, swirling her drink.

Stella's praise of the potential fat cat intrigued Marlene, but she still required two full weeks of journaling. Mr. X's journal entries read like Dan Brown erotica. Born and raised in Buenos Aires, he possessed the smug European superiority befitting his Puerto Madero address. There was the business with the Catholic school nuns beating him, his shameful arousal, the hint of a pearl-clutching crucifixion fantasy. A beautiful and imposing family friend who seduced him as a teenager. Their six-month affair. His grief when it ended. There was scandal and secrecy in all his sexual fantasies. Vanilla dating was child's play and by age 21, he had learned he wanted none of it. He was a hedonist with a refined palate for dopamine, a thrill-seeking adrenaline fiend, sharing needles beneath the bridge of an otherwise mainstream facade. With wealth, came opportunity. He had seen Dommes all over the world. Men and women. Some were good, but none, he said, piqued his interest to the heights Marlene did.

Marlene said she knew better than to be taken completely by his flattery, but she was impressed with his candor and wit, his boldness and bravery. He wrote to her like a 20th-century novelist, earnest like Ernest. Manly and unapologetic. Curt but wistful. A highly desirable twisted imagination. With Mr. X, few things were off the table and soon he was sent instructions for a first encounter.

A tribute for the initial meeting was paid promptly. Soon after, Marlene sent him the following email:

We will meet at Le Chat Noir on Sunset Blvd.

You will arrive at 6:45 p.m. You will bring a small bouquet of fresh lavender with a single peacock feather and a handwritten note in the sentiment of your choosing.

You DO NOT have permission to come at any point during this time. I would like your balls to be swollen as fuck when I meet you. I want your ass plugged. Be warned, I will confirm.

Err on the side of overdressing. Meticulous grooming is a must. With you, I don't suspect any issues.

Send a text from outside when you arrive and wait for a text from me, inviting you in.

Enter through the door off Sunset and take a seat at the bar to your right. There will be a drink in place. Keep your eyes on the floor until seated. Make no survey of the room. I will text you further instructions from there.

Stella was humming with anticipation as she fought the urge to drain her cocktail of every last drop. Outside the bar, the tallest palms all swayed in the gust of a favonian wind. Several dried jacaranda blooms sailed in through an open door and cruised across the marble floor like pairs of waltzing couples. It was then that he entered, just as instructed, and took his place across the room.

"Taller than I imagined," remarked Marlene.

Mr. X moved with the confident stealth of a shark, his fin slicing the water of the gathering Saturday crowd. Several people turned as he passed and the way he flipped the breast of his suit coat behind him as he sat sent a tiny pang of lust through Stella's pelvis. Just a few weeks in the business and look at this big, fat fish on their line.

"Hello there," Marlene texted from her vantage point behind him while Stella watched over her shoulder on pins and needles at the drama to unfold.

"La Bella," he texted in reply. A smile spread across Marlene's face, her flesh glowing like a polished pearl in the candlelight.

Stella could see the peacock feather jutting out from the purple cones of the bouquet of Spanish lavender he placed on the bar.

"Compliance with even the most frivolous whim smacks with the honey of actual longing. It's the creased origami of these little details that fucking turns me on," Marlene narrated to her eager companion.

"It's an Old Fashioned with Chichicapa from Del Maguey," Marlene texted, referring to the drink she had waiting for him at the empty seat. "I heard you're a connoisseur. I suspect you will like it."

Through the green leaves of a dracaena that partially obscured her view, Marlene studied him like a jaguar fixing its gaze on the plumes of a scarlet macaw.

"He is hotter than I expected," she admitted.

Stella nodded and smiled smugly, admiring his precision-tailored linen suit. It was the finest royal blue. Her bet was paying off. Mama Domme was impressed.

Marlene built the tension over text. She commented on his appearance and sunk into the voyeuristic charge of surveying him from behind. Stella could feel Marlene's predatory energy swell in the small space between them on the sofa.

Suddenly, Marlene rose and approached him, stalking from the side. Leaning in menacingly, she dug her nails into the back of his neck as if they were spurs piercing the rippled hindquarters of a gaucho's steed.

"Eyes forward," she whispered, taking an unabashed inhale of the scent of his scalp.

Goose flesh flushed his skin beneath her palm.

"Take your ass and my offerings to the couch."

She took a sip from his cocktail like she was lifting her leg on a fire hydrant. She pivoted on her heel and motioned for Stella to join her. Stella quickly followed her to the bathroom, disappearing from the eager X.

In the stall, the leopard print lining of Marlene's skirt bunched at her thighs as she hovered over the delicate lip of a Collins glass and let flow a stream of warm urine. She cradled it gently in her hand and, finishing, handed it to the wide-eyed Stella who guarded it like a precious lab specimen while Marlene washed her hands.

Marlene quickly cut back through the room, Stella in tow. She touched her knee to his as Stella set the glass before him.

Mr. X kept his eyes trained on the floor. He was obedient, for sure. Marlene slid closer to him and crossed her legs in his direction. She stared for a long while. Was he a snake? A shark? Perhaps a wolf? A coyote with a crown of cactus thorns?

They watched him savor the piss like it was a fine Reposado. He was such a pervert. He was raw, black and blue as a bone-in strip sizzling from La Plancha. Maybe he was a bull who would charge their muleta and garner a spear to the shoulder. Neither of the women knew in which habitat to place him.

Marlene sent him to the restroom. She told him to text when he was good and hard. Sauntering past a few people in line, Marlene rapped at the door of the largest stall and he let the women in. Stella watched in amused disbelief as Marlene pushed him to the wall by his throat and held him there. Her stance was wide, and the unforgiving cut of her skirt pulled on every curve like the orgiastic grasp of several hands.

He kept his eyes averted. It was not this bronco's first ride. A rush of blood surged to the base of his already upright penis. It dipped and pulsed like a dowsing rod between them. A captive bead ring PA pierced through the glans of his cock in solid 24-karat gold.

Still holding his neck to the wall, Marlene reached down and pulled the crotch of his unzipped slacks farther apart. She pursed her lips and let fall a long trail of saliva. He exhaled straight from his abdomen when it hit the tip. She did it again and took a tighter hold of his jugular.

Stella silently rubbed her thighs together as a squall of moisture soaked her panties.

"Jerk off," Marlene instructed, releasing her grip on his throat and reaching possessively over his hips to the horseflesh of his ass. At the crevice, she felt for the flat of the anal plug. She tapped the glass with her nails like an impatient diner waiting on her dish of sorbet. He smiled. His abdomen contracted with another sharp exhale.

"Your cunt is mine, *puta madre*," she hissed, levying insults as he worked himself to a frenzied edge. All she'd learned from his journals transmuted to automatic fire ammunition. She was a swift assassin when allowed the freedom to operate in this mode. Verbal degradation was a kink they mutually shared. Stella longed to let loose her own fatal barbs in the same expert fashion.

Marlene made him eat his cum with his back to the wall and in doing so, she finally let him look her in the eye. His expression sparkled with depraved appreciation as he lapped the semen off his thumb.

"Look at you," she said, holding his gaze, shaking her head slowly with a wince of disgust. "Filthy fucking pig."

She stepped closer. The heady scent of lotus oil rose from her neck like an Egyptian garden in bloom. She ran the back of her hand along the side of his cheek slowly, across the dew of the sweat that had gathered at his collarbone. Swiveling her wrist, she slid her palm under his dress shirt and pressed it firmly to his chest. She regarded the percussion of his heart like a Motown producer mixing the track of a triple-platinum single. She held it there and constricted her larynx, making the sound of her breath loud and steady. After several moments, when his breathing finally mirrored hers, she rapid-fire spat in his face.

"Puppet man," she taunted in a whisper. "You dance so well on the end of my string."

Oh, he is nasty. Stella smiled to herself. *Just like Mama likes 'em.*

X booked his next session the following day.

CHAPTER 20

Domton Abbey

"I'D LIKE TO JOIN YOU," Stella blurted out, wading into a discussion she feared would send them into another stalemate. She sat in a chair behind Marlene at the penthouse vanity and waited.

"I'm not sure that's a good idea," Marlene pushed back, looking up from her magnifying mirror, pencil in hand. "And remember, *you* met him without *me.*"

"Why is that not a good idea?" Stella asked flatly.

"This one is advanced. He's *very* experienced."

"I know. And now I have some experience too."

"Yes, you have *some* experience. But there are just some things you don't yet know."

"Such as?"

"Well, Mr. X has been journaling to me for a reason. It informs what I do in the session."

"But we are running this business together." Stella could feel her pulse quicken. "And we co-dommed Lewdy. I thought we were doing sessions together now. You agreed to mentor me."

Marlene sighed, pushing the mirror away irritatedly. "He's going to be here any minute now. You should have brought this up much earlier. I have been preparing for days. There's no time to get you up to speed now."

Without a reply, Stella stomped off towards the living room enraged. *Think of the business,* she told herself. *No, no, no.* She wouldn't be bullied.

Before she could formulate a retort, she heard the elevator ding and, pressing her face to the door, watched through the peephole the figure of a man growing larger. She swung open the door and greeted Mr. X stoically as if he had not held her kinky heart in the grip of his hands for hours at The Prince.

Marco, standing at her side, infinitely briefed about his duties, asked the man if he could inspect his person. It was Stella's idea, more for intimidation than out of any real threat that he'd be packing. Mr. X removed his tailored gray flannel suit coat. Marco ran his thick fingers down the man's torso and trousers and nodded to Stella.

"Come this way," she instructed.

Palo santo was the first scent to fill Stella's nostrils as X followed the candy apple of her ass down the hall. She wore a red latex pencil skirt that turned her bottom into a kind of chew toy for adults. She feared she might simply burst through the skin of the skirt like a tomato punctured by a knife. Her cleavage was doing what it always did at this suspension bridge angle—screaming for a poke. She was all gelatin on pistons from the moon of her cheerful breasts to the broad crest of her thighs. Her hair was as shiny as a midday lake.

In his hand, X held a bouquet of fresh white roses. He knocked three times on the door as instructed.

The circus was seconds from beginning, only this time Marlene was not a showgirl, she was the main event. Stella knew she was accustomed to private sessions and that she squirmed at the thought of an audience. In Marlene's approximation, this was her stallion to saddle. She seemed positively giddy at the notion of holding him captive for a few hours. She liked him, she said, though some part of her disliked how much she liked him.

He was a filthy whore, a moistened crevice for the famished tongue of insatiable lust, a fuck hole of wanton desire. He was dark in a way that Marlene admitted unnerved her. He was a rock that she obviously wanted upturned. The belly of a beast she had some instinct to disembowel. In his journals, he often shocked her. Not easily done. In the center of that shock sparked the asphaltum of a dynamite fuse. He was a pain slut with experience in rope. He fucked men, but only for sport, and he loved the swell of her testosterone.

"Eyes downward," Marlene reminded him as she opened the door.

With the expression of a naughty child, Stella squeezed through behind him. Marlene's face wore a kind of irritation that she would have to quickly conceal and they both knew it. With a silly curtsy, Stella moved deferentially to a velvet divan and took her seat. She lacked only an overflowing bag of popcorn for the big show.

Marlene was getting a bit thrown from her game. Here, in the context of shared equilibrium, all the moving parts of this debut production winced at the hinges as they played.

Twilight poured through the large windows, casting long shadows on the wall, and with the lilt of "Éthiopiques" playing in the background, Marlene regained her composure. The Ethiopian jazz was a collection X had mentioned in a journal entry and coincidentally one of Marlene's favorites.

"Position three." Her voice rode the crest of the wailing horn like a big wave surfer in some Zen communion with a pipeline of Lituya Bay.

Mr. X dropped to his knees.

"Greet me," she instructed.

He obliged from his pose on the floor. "I am a whore at your disposal. I am grateful to be used. Please command me."

She approached his upturned palms and stood straddling the roses on the floor. He had studied at least the first three submissive positions.

"Did you stretch?" she asked, nudging the roses with the toe of her glossy red heels.

"Yes, Mistress," he answered.

Slipping out of her shoes, she placed the balls of her feet onto his palms, pinning his hands with her weight. His thumbs curled with a tinge of audacity.

"No," she reprimanded in a flat, cool tone. "You make no choices here."

Of course, there was choice. At any moment, he could end the session with the utterance of a safeword and just like that, a heavy velvet curtain could fall, mid-act, on the freak show. However, he knew where to find the building's ledge. He was addicted to the rush, licking at its lips like a sloppy teenage kiss.

Marlene lifted her feet from his palms, slipping them back into her heels.

"Crawl behind me as I walk," she commanded. "As you crawl, breathe deeply from your abdomen through your chest. I want to hear it. Inhale as we progress. When I stop, I want an audible exhale."

She instructed him to stand facing a mirror.

"Look at yourself," she said as she positioned her body behind him. "Tell me what you see."

Mr. X raised his eyes to his reflection. The muscles of his jaw clenched as he mugged. Marlene placed her hand firmly on the back of his neck.

"I see your whore," he said, but his answer displeased her. It smacked of performance and invited a deep roll of her eyes.

"Your greeting's been spoken," she reminded. Her tone grew stern. "I want presence, not rote regurgitation. Give me what I want. *What… do… you… see?*"

There was a stretch of silence. "My hard-on," he finally answered.

"I don't give a shit about your cock."

Marlene deprived his vision with a blindfold. He jumped a bit when he felt her hands forcing his balls up into his inguinal canal, working swiftly in an attempt to preempt the rushing blood flow as a result of the genital stimulation. Reaching between his legs, she pulled his softened penis into the crack of his ass, tucking him tight as a drag queen and securing it with a generous application of duct tape.

It was clearly a sensation he had never felt. She yanked at him, strapping him so securely he wouldn't pop it even if he got too aroused. Next came the slow unbuttoning of his shirt and the searing pain of both his nipples being clamped. Marlene tugged at the metal chain between them and gave one of his areolas a playful lick.

"Position one," she instructed, dragging a chair behind her. Like a dancer setting the stage for a striptease, she placed it directly in front of him.

He dropped to his knees, sat back on his heels, each hand resting on his thighs, palms upward, spine straight, chest out.

"Stella, would you please?" Marlene asked, pointing to the small caboodle of makeup sitting atop the vanity. Stella quickly obliged. As much as she itched for more, Stella was dutiful in these small expressions. After the work she'd put in to come this far, she counted this session as just one more yellow brick in the road as she and Marlene skipped towards the Emerald City.

Marlene selected a tube of peach-hued lipstick from the box. She told X to remove her right shoe, cackling as she placed the tube of lipstick between her toes. She sat back in the chair to achieve the perfect angle from which to apply it to his lips with her foot. For a man with so many wilder fantasies, good old-fashioned foot fetish still took the cake. The corners of his mouth curled up in delight.

Thus followed a lengthy session of foot worship. The lipstick he wore smeared with each nuzzle and suck. He broke a sweat. He popped his tuck twice. There was laughter and punishment.

At one point, he had the audacity to suggest she liked it as much as him. What a bold remark. Her nostrils flared. He called her out. Challenged her a bit. She clearly questioned her grip on the reins. Stella thrilled at seeing Marlene in this kind of heightened play.

He'd put his foot in his mouth and Marlene made that literal. She put him in a swift three-rope gote and suspended him in the center of the room. She built a running cuff from his ankle through the lip of an added carabiner and hoisted his leg, pulling up until his big toe touched his chin.

Stella thought to herself how much she still had to learn. Marlene had questioned her dedication often, citing her lack of shibari skills as evidence against her.

"What happens when you open your mouth too wide?" Marlene growled, shoving the first three of his toes past his lips. His tongue was pushed out of place and glistened as a stream of saliva leaked to the floor. He looked crunched and ridiculous. Peach lipstick skid across his cheek like the tire marks of a Malibu Barbie car wreck. It was perverse. The humiliation was real. She slid the mirror over for him to have a view. *Does he really enjoy this?* Stella wondered. *Is something deeply wrong with him?*

The jute creaked under the stress of his weight. Marlene spun him slowly around in one controlled circle like a child on a tire swing. She chastised him for his brazen suggestion.

Before they knew it, two hours had elapsed. With one swift motion, Marlene threw her shoulders back. She untied him and carefully lowered him down. As quickly as she'd raised the curtain, as quickly as the train rushed in, the coach of deviant audacity zipped away like a subway car into a darkened tube.

As he descended to the ground, he held her gaze unflinchingly. There was both challenge and warmth in his eyes. There was palpable chemistry, real energy play. She shuddered, clearly still coming down from the rush. Loosening him tenderly, she rubbed the blushed flesh of his biceps around which the rope had burned just slightly.

"Permission to address you, Queen."

"You may address me but call me Mistress. This has been discussed," Marlene replied tersely.

"Yes, Mistress. I wanted to know if you had ever suspended a man of my size."

"Of course," she said haughtily.

"You tied me rather... coarsely."

"Well, does anything hurt? I was checking in as I went. You didn't speak up," she glanced nervously at Stella.

"It hurt, but I bore it. I don't mind if it brings you pleasure."

Oh, he is laying it on thick, thought Stella.

"Would you like a drink?" Without waiting for an answer, Marlene picked up a small bell and swung it quite unnecessarily in Stella's direction.

"You rang?" she said in a ghoulish baritone, rising from the divan. She couldn't resist the opportunity to do a Lurch impression.

"Make two Naked and Famous, will ya?"

The darting of Stella's eyes told Marlene all that she needed to know. "Oh, I forgot, you don't know anything. Ugh. Just bring me a tray with all the contents you can gather from the bar. Quickly."

Stella nodded. Who was Marlene, butlering her around like this? It didn't matter. The interests of the client must be served. Though it wasn't anything they'd rehearsed, she hurried to fulfill Marlene's request like a dutiful servant of their beloved Domton Abbey.

Stella rolled in the bar cart and, as Marlene began pouring the mezcal, her hand trembled over the glass. Mr. X moved up behind her.

"I should be doing that," he said in a hushed tone. "Serving you."

She turned and smiled. "Well, are you an accomplished bartender? I'm very particular."

"I know my spirits. But you are a professional, aren't you?"

"I am. How did you know?"

"I can tell by your technique that you tend bar."

Was he lying? It unnerved Stella to think he did a background check. Or did he see Marlene at Lounge 21? Stella knew Marlene did not want her vanilla career and her kinky one to overlap. At least not yet.

"How is your arm?" Marlene asked.

His bulky tanned bicep was still smarting from the rope. She handed him the cocktail then whipped out a bit of aloe vera, taking his arm in her hands to apply it.

"Please, may I?" He gestured to the small velvet divan where Stella sat.

"You may," Marlene said, motioning furiously behind his back for Stella to move.

Stella awkwardly relocated to a chair in the opposite corner of the room.

X tried to extend his body fully upon the divan but he was too long, so his legs flopped comically over the tufted arm. He motioned for Marlene to sit down, raising his head to make room. She sat and he laid his head on her lap.

"Now you can apply the salve. I want to be in the comfort of your bosom while you do so." He looked up at her tenderly. "Is that allowed?"

"I'll allow it. You did take a beating," she coldly conceded.

He gazed up to her breasts and let his eyes linger.

"I'd love to be suckling you right now," he half whispered. "Cozy and warm in your embrace like a child."

Stella was taken aback and she knew Marlene was too. Under vanilla circumstances, perhaps Marlene would have invited the advances of such a charming, attractive man, but this was not dinner and a movie.

"I think that's enough for tonight. You'll journal to me this week," she said, standing so suddenly his head flopped with a thump on the cushion.

* * * * *

When X left, Stella drew a steaming bath for Marlene so they could debrief. Stella sat on the toilet, lighting joint after joint for Marlene, the embers of their roaches dirtying the suds like flecks of pepper. Marlene's mind seemed to be infinitely looped on Mr. X.

"Did he think sex was for purchase like some impulse pack of gum at the checkout?" she wondered aloud to Stella.

"I don't know," Stella said, squeezing the tense arches of Marlene's shoulders as if they were Rocky and Mickey recalibrating after a brutal boxing match.

"Fuck!" Marlene blurted.

"What?" Stella released her grip. "Did I hurt you?"

"No, it's just that he has a kind of madness. It's like he's pressing his sternum into the pistol and daring the trigger, gambling himself into the quick draw of an empty chamber," she pontificated to the air, her stony eyes glazed. She reached for her phone, turning up the volume on an Al Green song in futile attempts to change the channel of her mind.

It was clear to Stella that Mr. X's fearlessness soaked Marlene. It licked up her spine and rimmed her like a beast. She was excited every time he journaled, bragging about the most lascivious bits to Stella. Marlene couldn't wait to read his take on their session. There was challenge in him, a fearlessness that toed the line of her limitations. It looked her in the eye, balled its fists, and thumbed the side of its nose.

Stella could see that some part of Marlene wanted to spin the cylinder with that single bullet inside. She knew how rare it was for her to encounter such chemistry. Perhaps he was the promised subsiah, after all.

CHAPTER 21

The Queen Mary

STELLA EMERGED from the penthouse closet as if stepping onto the red carpet. She was serving full Bianca Jagger in a perfectly tailored three-piece suit. It was a monochromatic creamsicle dream of fine ivory wool with a vest that plunged down to her navel. The gold chain of a vintage monocle dangled from the side pocket.

"Wow, you look like... *me,*" Marlene said, sizing her up.

"What? Really?" Stella glanced in the mirror of the boudoir and adjusted the rose pinned to her lapel in the same dark shade of red as her strappy heels.

"Where are you off to, *Single White Female?*" Marlene asked as she packed accouterments from her session into a leather satchel.

"The Queen Mary." She smiled wickedly. Rather than a crop, she carried a cane. Admiring herself in the mirror, she twirled it dramatically. "How was the session?"

"The dark prince? Stella, I told you. X is sketchy. I feel like I am riding a bronco every time we session. It *is* alluring. But that man is broken bones six seconds in. He's not stable."

"But you love the thrill of it. Don't you want your boundaries pushed? Don't you want a challenge?"

"Boundaries, yes. Limits, no. He's trying to mind fuck me. I feel him studying me, my fetishes for language, fashion, travel. Now he wants religious play."

"Bonsoir!" called a voice from the hallway as the front door creaked open.

"In here!" Stella replied, looking nervously to Marlene to gauge her reception.

Yvette appeared in the doorframe of the dressing room as if she too were gliding down a catwalk at Fashion Week. The scalloped neckline of her black velvet dress draped off her shoulders like the rushing wind of romance novels. A long slit up the side revealed the freshly shaved glow of her legs. A pair of emerald green earrings shined like the turrets of Oz on the lobes of her ears.

"Fucking hell, you're gorgeous," Stella exhaled excitedly, wrapping her arms around Yvette's waist from behind with a swell of pride at how glamorous they looked together. Stella brushed an errant hair from Yvette's ear and kissed her on the cheek.

Yvette sang a greeting to Marlene who nodded curtly as she changed into civilian clothes.

Trying to warm the icy air, Yvette addressed Marlene again. "How was your session?"

Marlene looked up somewhat surprised. She and Yvette had only a few conversations in the many months Yvette had been living in LA.

"I've pretty much perfected my Hikyaku Tsuri," Marlene began with a nonchalant insouciance Stella was well accustomed to.

"Oh, that's good," Yvette replied without further inquiry.

Stella hoped she knew better than to indulge Marlene's need for superiority through loquacious language.

"It's great you've got such a good client so quickly," Yvette praised.

"Yes and no."

Stella sighed. She knew that a few weeks prior, serious doubts about Mr. X began to itch in Marlene's mind, like a rash on the tender flesh of a hypochondriac. As he continued to book time with Marlene, the signs of his *Do Me* submission were glaring like hissing neon writing on the wall.

"I can't decipher what animal he is," Marlene continued. "Perhaps he's a skilled and prideful hunter, suited up in his camouflage, sights trained on big game. Just how many puma pelts hang on his wall?"

"He's exactly who you've been *saying* you're seeking!" Stella argued.

"But who is he, Stella? We don't know his real name or how he's acquired such great wealth. We aren't on a level playing field."

"But we've seen his Instagram. He looks legit," Stella argued.

"And he pays well, right?" Yvette chimed in.

"Money isn't everything. I see the flicker of overconfidence in your eyes every time we talk about this," Marlene said, pointing a finger at Stella like a chastising parent. "You know I have hard limits on religious play."

"What kind of religious play?" Yvette inquired.

"He wants a crucifixion," Marlene replied, zipping up her bag emphatically as if signaling the finale of some Shakespearean tragedy, a bloodbath of revenge served, a sea of corpses on the floor.

"But *I* don't." Stella said, propping herself up on her cane. Adorning the top was a dragon's head clenching a crystal orb between the fangs of its snarling mouth. She was thrilled at the heresy of a crucifixion. "And Marlene, seriously, are you really playing the Christian card?"

"Just because you're agnostic now doesn't mean my faith isn't real. You only experienced Christianity through the lens of a cult. I know it to be something much more nuanced," Marlene said, with the flick of her wrist.

"And just because I was in a cult, doesn't mean I'm not familiar with other religions. Quite the contrary. You know, I must've knocked on 20,000 doors. Talked with people of nearly every religion. Even in my brainwashing, I was something of an anthropologist." Stella replied. "And have you actually read the Bible? The patriarchal doctrine on which your entire faith is based? You think a fake crucifixion is your biggest crime against Jesus?"

"Is this about me reading the Bible or is this about money?"

"This is business! I don't want to see all my efforts—and money—wasted because of one little scene we could easily do."

"Yeah, sometimes with client requests, you just have to think of it that way—a job," Yvette added.

Marlene sighed. Her cheeks dropped to a kind of low-altitude deadness that let Stella know what was coming next could not possibly be good.

"You two are something else. What is your experience in professional domination, Yvette?"

"Hey!" Stella interjected defensively. "Yvette has been doing sex work longer than you or me. And she's fucking good at it."

"And so are you, baby," Yvette said, squeezing Stella's hand. "Would be nice if it was more appreciated."

"Huh," Marlene chortled. "Well, you two lovebirds have fun!" she said, stomping off towards the door, which she let slam with an angry thud.

"Jesus fucking Christ," Stella said, slumping defeatedly into the chair at the vanity.

"What is her deal?" Yvette began lovingly running a brush through Stella's hair. "You missed a spot. Let me fix it," she said, switching on Stella's flat iron.

As often as Marlene flared her temper to scorching levels, Yvette never failed to cool her back into a state of ecstatic calm.

*****

Arriving in Long Beach an hour later, Stella parked the car, took a swig of whiskey from her rose gold flask, then sped around to open Yvette's door like the fey gentlemen she imagined herself to be in that three-piece suit. Neither of the women had made Thanksgiving plans, for Yvette had never observed the holiday and Stella had long chalked it up as patriotic paganism. With that, they searched for only the most decadent dinner they could find—five rich courses on the famed Queen Mary.

Stella had added a dusting of gold bronzer to Yvette's collarbone and as she stepped from the car, it refracted the light as though it were the sunset off the coast of Saint-Tropez. Stella held out her arm for Yvette and they strode towards the iconic ship like Mr. and Mrs. Smith off to heist the Crown Jewels from some opulent ball.

A luscious pink sky of marshmallow cumuli billowed over a trio of red funnels jutting out from the long black and white ocean liner ahead.

Not a single guest could avoid staring as they transformed the Art Deco promenade into their impromptu catwalk. It delighted them to be the objects of such starry-eyed awe and they strutted with more dramatic flair through the grand lobby to the bar where they waited for their table reservation.

Finally arriving at the dining room, Stella was dismayed at the lack of grandeur. This was the noble Sir Winston's Restaurant & Lounge? No design detail of the aging and thoroughly unaristocratic vessel lived up to her titanic expectations. It mattered not, because she was sailing into a state of euphoria at the sight of her beautiful companion and the kinetic connection that could not be dulled by even the shabbiest surrounds.

They were seated by a genuinely befuddled host amid a smattering of couples well into their AARP years. Stella and Yvette welcomed with exuberant insubordination the curious glances of white-haired ladies and the libidinous ogles of their male counterparts.

"Please, no iceberg," Stella joked as she perused the salad menu. Dad jokes aside, Yvette was all smiles.

After a first course of creamy pumpkin bisque and an intermezzo of pear sorbet, they absconded to the bathroom. They passed a string quartet playing in the lobby, supplying the pair with all the additional shipwreck joke ammunition they needed, especially several cocktails and a bottle of cabernet deep.

Inside a tiny stall, Stella pressed her mouth to Yvette's, sliding her fingers up Yvette's slit in pursuit of the warmth between her legs where she wasn't wearing any panties. Yvette slipped her hands under Stella's vest and squeezed her fevered breasts. Their bodies pleasantly crushed against the metal wall, their passion began to make a racket. They froze when they heard the door lock on the adjacent stall. Yvette attempted to suppress that wild cackle Stella loved so much. Stella then squatted and propped Yvette's leg up on the toilet seat. She looked up at her for a moment, then began flicking her tongue between the slick folds of her pussy. Yvette sighed deeply as the soundtrack from both their mouths surely became an obvious indication of the randiness at play. Feeling Yvette's pleasure swell, Stella stood and covered Yvette's mouth with one hand while she pumped two wet fingers inside of her. Faster and faster, until Yvette's body contracted with a thunderous spasm and her head flopped raggedly into the crook of Stella's neck. Stella squeezed her tight and they held each other as if there was no one else in the world.

"I love you," Yvette blurted out, taking Stella's face in hers.

"I love you too," Stella replied with a soft kiss. There was always such a tenderness between them. The new sensation of feminine touch thrilled Stella to no end.

"Oh no," Stella said, popping their tiny bubble of wonder. She released her little bird and looked down at her own hand.

"Oh shit!" Yvette exclaimed at the sight of Stella's missing acrylic nail as if a finger itself had been severed.

Stella's cheeks flushed in embarrassment. "I'm so sorry. It must've come off… inside."

Yvette laughed reassuringly. "Don't worry. I will find it." She reached into her cavity and, as if rummaging around for lost keys in a purse, retrieved an almond-shaped piece of red plastic.

Stella took the nail from Yvette and shook her head. "What a bad lesbian," she joked.

"Ha! But still my favorite one."

They returned to their table ravenous from their romp. Stella admired the sexy post-coital mess of Yvette's waves atop her head and ordered another bottle of wine. They gobbled every last piece of sausage and sage apple stuffing, giblet gravy, and truffle mashed potatoes, along with the sacrificial bird of the silly American celebration.

Following dinner, they snapped a dozen drunken, blurry photos on the observation deck.

Back at Stella's studio, they could not resist another sweaty romp, after which they climbed in the shower and took turns lathering one another between impassioned kisses.

They had spent nearly half the year trying to recreate the spiritual perfection of their first time together, but it proved—like all gifts of unsolicited magic—to be rare and doggedly elusive. And perhaps that was best, for it allowed them to preserve that nirvana in a safe place that could never be erased from the velvety burrows of memory, like some snowy red and white wonderland under the shelter of domed glass.

CHAPTER 22

Going Out of Business

"I LOVE our weird little posse," Stella said, leaning against the wall of the boudoir as Marlene curled her long hair into Veronica Lake waves. "Deb and Marco are so damn cute together."

Stella found Marlene to be so lovely as she sat erect as a sphinx pressing false lashes onto her lids. Her chinoiserie-painted silk robe was open at the hip. Her smooth, muscular thigh crossed over the other, offering a flash of garter belt.

Stella was in a wistful mood, reflecting on how far she'd come from the confines of a cult to this rebel yell of a life.

"They're not together-together, right?" Marlene asked, pushing her face deep into a magnifying mirror to inspect an errant eyelash.

"No. I let her in for a special session with *Ronnie* last night."

"Ronnie?"

"This guy she dommes. I think he's a cop!"

"Do we want an officer of the law in our little whore house?"

"Deb says he's one of the good ones and we have no reason not to trust her." Stella sighed with contentment. "Reflecting on where I was a couple years ago is a trip! My entire community was repressed door-knocking evangelists. Now I'm running a dungeon with this motley crew."

"Hey, be careful who you're calling motley," Marlene jested.

"Be careful who you're calling a whore," Stella teased back.

"Well, if the shoe fits…"

"I know, I know," Stella said, thinking of her date with yet another six-pack of sun-kissed abs the night before. "But I'm learning myself sexually. You had your whole adolescence for that."

"True. If your mother could only see you now." Marlene wrapped a silky strand around the large barrel of the iron. It steamed. She paused and smiled warmly. "Hey, I'm proud of us. We did it. We're running this circus."

"We are. I should take your picture," Stella said, admiring the scene. A vase of roses in the corner had started to wilt and the burnished red of their slow and elegant death accented the brocade emerald sheen of Marlene's robe.

"I love this frame." Stella squared her fingers like a camera, winking one eye as if it were her shutter. "We need this pic for BTS on our IG."

"I always think you're referring to IBS when you say that. What's BTS again?"

"Behind the scenes. What's that phrase you always use?"

"JOI?" Marlene replied.

"Yeah, what's JOI again?" Stella squinted, attempting to recall the semi-familiar phrase.

"Jerk off instructions."

"Let's hope the ROI of your JOI is green."

"Wait, what's ROI again?"

Stella laughed. "Return on investment."

"We shall see tonight with this new client."

"Has he followed instructions?"

"He has. I'm enjoying this one immensely," said Marlene.

"Even more than Mr. X?"

"Stella, you know how I feel about him..." Marlene warned.

A previously flared tension cartwheeled into the room like a unitard-clad creep à la Cirque du Soleil, replete with a mug of clown makeup so ghoulish it traipsed into the macabre. Both women bristled at its cue while it stood there juggling the beanbags of all their tricky discord.

"Look, I know you don't want to talk about his request, but why don't you guide me through the crucifixion? Maybe with Deb?" Stella asked, as if trying to reverse course on the Titanic before it met that fateful iceberg.

"How is that any less of a boundary for me? So, I'd just be Pontius Pilate adjacent? No way! It's *why* he wants it that bothers me. At some point, his switch switch switched and a slow but steady boil has taken over his veins."

"We could have protocol. Are you thinking of the profit we're making on Mr. X alone? He's keeping our doors open," Stella argued.

"I know and he's acting like it."

"This is business, not pleasure. We are providing a service. He is a client." Stella felt her stomach drop and a surge of heat flush through her sternum.

"And like any business, I reserve the right to refuse service! He wants a fucking crucifixion! With blood! That is not on my menu, Stella. I'm convinced that he wouldn't even want it if it weren't a hard limit for me. That's the fucking point!"

"You're being paranoid," Stella's voice escalated to a thin shrillness like a piece of wire being stripped and stretched.

Marlene winced, her face sharp like a deadly diamond. "God, it's fucking sweltering in here. Did you turn off the air?"

Her curling iron sizzled against the plastic handle of her hairbrush. A noxious odor suddenly overwhelmed the windowless room.

"You need to seriously consider that this is not just your business but mine!" Stella exploded. "I've labored to make this work. My talents and ability have turned your hobby into a professional enterprise."

"There it is, Stella! Right there!" Marlene yelled. "That disrespect for anything that isn't flipping a coin in your direction. A hobby?! Ask my subs if they think it's a hobby!" Marlene slammed down her hairspray, looking Stella straight in the eye. "Who taught you? Who is the actual Domme here? You should watch your tone with me," she said, her voice hunting unsuccessfully for a maternal tenor.

"I think you know you'd still be stuck without me," Stella said, her accusing tone a knife puncturing the vulnerable tendon of their bond.

"You know, I don't have to do this with you." Marlene stood up. The leg of her chair made a foul squawk across the floor and nearly toppled over. Stella noticed a tattoo of blood on the embroidered cushion and an inkblot on Marlene's precious robe, right at her thigh, fresh and crimson. Her hair was undone, her lips pale and thin.

Marlene looked down at her soiled robe, clearly realizing the menstrual churn activated like a violent washing machine in her gut. "Fuck! Listen. What X is asking is vile. You do this with him—inexperienced as you are—and do not be surprised how the power dynamic will shift."

"Who cares about silly religious role play?" Stella flung her hands in the air.

"My reputation is on the line. As your business partner, I could be ruined in the community because of your actions!" she growled.

"You don't even participate in the community. You look down on everyone. And you have dangled the carrot of co-domming for months. I see what's happening. You're trying to keep me in your grips. If you share too much with me, I won't need you. You're afraid I will graduate."

"Nothing to be afraid of there!" Marlene smarted. "There's a lot more to domming than spreadsheets and fishnets. Are you so delusional to think you deserve to be valedictorian of Domme U on the merit of peering over shoulders for test answers?"

Words boiled up in Stella that were too abusive to utter. She felt like a sharpshooter sitting on a roof waiting for her target to appear in the crosshairs. Everything was coming into focus, the whole messy truth of disappointed affections. Marlene was studied in the art of feminine seduction, but Stella knew she puzzled and eluded her. The typical charms and traps were not working. Marlene had been so often cold and calculated. It let the wind out of Stella's sexual sails.

"Are you jealous?"

"Of what?" Marlene folded her arms squarely.

"I don't know. My progress. My relationships."

Marlene laughed condescendingly. "Not at all. I find your erotic frequency extremely juvenile. Perhaps if we'd met several years later instead of this freshman era of your freedom, I would have felt more attracted to you. I've more than shown you that I cherish the gray area we occupy, but when it comes to the 'Whole New World' of riding each other's magic carpets, I'm not too compelled."

"You know what? I'm gonna do my own thing now," Stella said sourly. "You don't want to be confronted. You can't stand a challenge to your righteousness. I defer to you so often, Marlene. I coddle you because you need to be dominant like you need the air. I don't see it as a strength. I am much more comfortable in my dominance. I don't always have to remind everyone I'm on top."

"Of course not! You're the queen of the humblebrag. You hide behind that passive-aggressive decorum, but you're plenty thirsty!"

"OK, fine. Well… I quit!" Stella snapped back.

"Fine!"

And with that, the final nail was hammered in the coffin.

Stella gathered her belongings with an obnoxious clamor, each motion more violent than the last.

Just then a thud came at the front door.

"Are we expecting anyone?" Marlene asked, looking down the hallway. "It's too early for Deb and Marco to be here."

The pounding came louder and with a quickening cadence.

Suddenly Stella's attention was fixed on a bag full of white powder in the corner of the room. She bent down and tweezed it between her fingers in disbelief. "Is this yours?"

"No, and we should go."

"Fuck, you don't think it's the—"

"Police? Yes! That fucking neighborhood association."

"We have to get out of here. I'm pretty sure this is cocaine." She moved towards Marlene across the invisible line erected in their feud and slapped the eight ball into her palm.

A man's voice sounded through the thick metal door, echoing down the hallway like a foreboding specter. "Police! Open the door!"

"This does look like coke. What is it doing here? Where did you find it?"

Stella slung her bag on her shoulder. "Let's go!"

"And run from the police?"

"Yeah, unless you want to be booked for drug possession and prostitution."

"Oh my God." Marlene was shocked into action. She grabbed her bag and, with newfound fury, began stuffing it with wigs and stockings. She threw off her bloodied robe, slid on a wool skirt, snatched a leather jacket, and strapped on her mile-high stilettos.

"Grab as much as you can," Stella commanded, yanking open a drawer and scooping up an oversized pile of sex toys.

The sound of scraping rang through the hall.

"Those bastards are going to bust the door down!" Marlene yelled, grabbing Stella's hand and yanking her towards the hallway. They tiptoed past the front door to the kitchen where a small door led to the fire escape. As soon as a duo of boys in blue busted through the front door, the women lowered themselves down the terrifying heights of the fire escape and flew out into the alley with an Olympic fury.

"Oh, shit!" Stella screamed out as she was boomeranged in her tracks. "Shit! Shit! Shit!"

Marlene turned to regard her frantic Baby Domme. In their panicked flight, Stella scooped up everything two arms could hold, including that infamous choke chain collar now cruelly hooked to the branch of a shrub.

"Hurry!"

"I can't get it loose!" Stella said, yanking the chain links violently.

Marlene clopped furiously back to help, her stilettos forcing her into a comical bow-legged stoop. Her movements recalled André the Giant with a dash of *Tootsie*. Marlene's auburn hair, loose on the side, blew back into her face, blinding her and catching in her mouth like cotton. They looked like cartoon robbers tramping down the pock-marked alley. It was a positively Chaplin-esque heist scene.

"Fuuuuck!" Marlene exclaimed as her toe caught tragically on a rock, thrusting her forward.

Stella looked on with horror as Marlene flew through the air and landed on her chest. Stella abandoned the dog collar, emptied her arms of a half-dozen rainbow-colored dildos, and ran to the downed Domme.

"Oh my God. Are you OK?"

Marlene let out a defeated whimper, blowing her wild hair out of her face. "What the hell are we doing?" She groaned, blood running down her hands. The gravel in her knees and palms looked like walnuts pressed into raw cookie dough.

"C'mon, we got this," Stella said, extending her hands to pull Marlene up.

Stella's hands now bloodied, she decided to abandon the pile of toys at the scene.

"Wait, you're going to leave everything?" Marlene asked.

"We have to. They're coming!" Stella said plaintively.

"This is crazy. Those toys cost us a small fortune." Marlene pointed to a large vibrator that had rolled pitifully into a pothole as if it were a time capsule of this morose trajectory of their lives.

They heard the climactic thud of a metal door ring through the alley.

Stella grabbed Marlene's wrist and pulled her down behind a pickle-green dumpster. The women squatted silently, hand in hand communicating their unholy terror through their eyes. They both tried not to breathe the sickening and sour air.

Heavy footsteps sounded closer and closer.

"They are going to find us. Can we fit back there?" Marlene mouthed to Stella.

Stella eyed the crack behind the dumpster. It was less than a foot wide. She shook her head. They were too far from the street to make a run for it. Their pursuers were closing in and a strobe of red and blue lights pulsed from the end of the alley like a disco gone so, so wrong.

"We have to get *in,*" Stella whispered.

Marlene closed her eyes as if praying to any god who might rescue her from the fate of climbing in the trash. She expelled a stiff puff of air then nodded in agreement.

Stella slid open the dumpster door. She took one last lungful of fresh air and raised her foot, her tiny leather skirt preventing her from fully extending her leg.

"Fuck!" She violently unsnapped three silver buttons and let the skirt drop to her ankles, revealing her leopard print bikini underwear. She was an alley cat climbing into the trash. There was no time for vanity or even self-respect.

Marlene unhooked her beloved pumps, hiked up her pencil skirt, and climbed in next to Stella, giving her the most defeated look Stella had ever seen on her pretty face. It was an entirely new expression, making a sad and revelatory debut this Saturday afternoon, deeply impressing upon Stella the gravity of Marlene's disappointment. There was no denying they had hit rock bottom.

No sooner had Marlene slid the dumpster door shut when a shallow knock could be heard upon it. The women startled, shooting one another whiplashed expressions of fresh panic. Marlene put her finger to her lips. Stella stopped breathing again.

"Hey, guys!" a muffled voice rang through the tin tomb. "It's Deb!"

Stella slid the door open. "What are you doing here? They're going to see you. Get in!"

"No, no. I've got the getaway car. Let's go!" Deb gestured furiously while she kept one eye on the alley.

She was every bit the mercenary, rescuing her outnumbered and outwitted guerrillas in this concrete jungle. Despite the absolutely fucktabulous danger they were in, Stella couldn't help but feel her heart melt at the sight of the woman they had secretly *Mean Girl*'d at PetSmart. She would always be Deb from the Shire with her adorable rosacea and her undeniable stoutness, but she was also their fairy godmother, not only in this high-wire rescue but in these months she had worked for them. Deborah had proven to be more than a mall cop, she was a friend.

CHAPTER 23

Damage Control

"NEVER DEBBIE" DOMMER lived in a third-floor apartment in a sprawling complex in Eagle Rock. "La Piedra del Sol" read the sign on the side of the stucco building.

Stella and Marlene stood with their backs pressed to opposite sides of the elevator, their makeup smeared from sweat, and Marlene's hands blistered like pomegranates with the coagulate of dried blood. Deb stood on her wide gait like an unwitting referee between them. She was completely unaware of the row that had just unraveled, but she was keen to learn what their little flight from the cops had cost them. These pigeons needed guidance, so she insisted they come to her home for triage.

"So, you don't sell them?" Stella asked, gesturing towards the collection of weaponry lining the better part of the dining room wall.

She and Marlene were now settled on Deb's sofa. Marlene looked undead, her pallor dancing some wicked little waltz with French courtesan vampires. She applied pressure to the gauze wrapped around her palm where a broken bottle had sliced into the ball of her thumb. The gossamer threads blossomed with her hemorrhage like her dressing robe had bloomed the red rose of her menses.

"Nah. Never. I enjoy collecting," Deb answered, taking a sip of her IPA and looking wistfully across the soffit of her cabinets. In the kitchen, a row of lanterns, salvaged and restored from WWII, sat like winning ponies lined up in a stable.

Stella hurried to the shower. In the light of the parking garage, they had discovered a used condom matted up in the back of her hair. What appeared to be nothing but a clump of mangled tresses birthed the crusted, yet still slimy hatchling of some stranger's better judgment. As much from pure anxiety as disgust, Stella dry wretched after Deb pulled it free with a pair of pliers from her glove box. As horrified as they all were, at least it wasn't some hypodermic needle lodged in one of their ankles. It's the kind of thing they would have laughed about under other circumstances, but really, what other circumstances would have yielded that level of train wreck? Their little bambino had miscarried and Stella could feel the trauma of it swelling. Hope for its survival seeped out of her like lukewarm faith in the face of an unanswered prayer.

Stella closed the bathroom door behind her. A rubber gas mask hung on a hook over the door and the glass of the goggles clanked with a racket against the wood. A towel and washcloth sat on the edge of a small wicker table. The little embroidered roses on the lining of the bath linens were a stark contrast to the well-worn pages of *Guns and Ammo* resting beside them.

She ratcheted up the hot water slowly at first, then full blast. She needed the sting of pain on her back as a distraction from the imminent depression setting in. She felt like a trapped animal while still in Marlene's presence. She wanted nothing more than to crawl into her own bath and get high. While she was in the cult, she never had the option to escape into a chemical bliss. Back then, her angst simmered in the imposed full sobriety of the Bible. *What I wouldn't give for a fucking joint right now,* she thought. *Something to take the edge off.*

She was furious with Marlene over her arrogance and impudence. She was also embarrassed to have failed to prevent whatever legal infraction they clearly made, and now an overwhelming feeling of religious shame crept up like some specter stalking her from the bushes, waiting to seize on any personal failure and pin her to the ground with screaming accusation. "See! You *are* a dog returning to its vomit. You *are* a dirty whore who will die alone in the streets!" Like the water trickling down her scalp and rushing down her legs, each emotion carried her woefully to the next in an inexhaustible supply.

She hated thinking that the cult might be right. Maybe she *was* doomed to failure outside the caged safety of the religion. Maybe God *had* smited her for disobedience. Maybe she *was* in the devil's hands.

Her thoughts turned to her poor mother, all the way in Texas. What kind of sorrow was she experiencing at the hyper-religious judgment of her only daughter? She had been advised to cut Stella off, though her maternal instinct screamed wildly against such abandonment.

However, Stella was living life too loudly online. Her newfound self-possession and confidence had surely been the topic of many an elders' meeting and now it was time to dismantle the threat. The JWs couldn't risk Stella's success exposing their lies. But Stella's mother was already burdened with so much—her failing health and feeble age, her narcissistic husband, and the fracture of her small family. Why wouldn't they just fucking leave her alone?

Stella's tears became indistinguishable from the stream of water soaking her face, but her sobs were audible. She couldn't hold them back. The separation from her mother was her deepest pain. Though she knew her life must be lived as her own, she felt guilty. If she had just stuffed down her sadness, she could have remained in good standing with the organization and retained the connection to her mother.

Stella had been in the watery abyss for nearly an hour when she finally gathered the courage to face Deb and Marlene again. She reluctantly turned off the shower and towel-dried her hair, staring unflinchingly into the mirror. Her eyes were bloodshot with purple hollows underneath. A new pimple had bubbled up between her eyes and was all too metaphorical for the toxic shit that had erupted this deplorable day. She pressed a single finger to the glass. "Thank you, Deb," she scrawled into the steam.

She emerged from the bathroom red-cheeked and wrapped in a towel. Deb handed her an oversized T-shirt emblazoned with "Jumbo's Clown Room" across the front. Turns out Deb had a penchant for a rowdy night at the strip club.

Marlene rose from the sofa for her turn to shower and brushed past Stella at the end of the small corridor. Through the fog of their anger and mistrust, they could feel one another's pain radiant like the heat of a sunburn rising from tender, overexposed flesh. The proximity of their bodies so briefly in that narrow hallway seemed to drag the spiteful swiftness of their movement to a slower motion, as though some magnet still pulled them towards one another. They both resisted.

When Marlene returned from the shower, she rejoined Stella on the couch, pulling at the hem of her "Machos Tacos" T-shirt. It was Deb's favorite food truck to hit up after a long night. With only one hand, Marlene couldn't quite fix the bandage.

"Deb, would you give me a hand?" she beseeched, holding up the clump of gauze, crookedly taped to her palm.

Stella felt a sting of sadness, but also relief that Marlene was asking Deb for help.

"You got it," Deb said, snapping into action, inviting Marlene to take a seat. Deb moved with the calm and sure demeanor of an EMT, scrubbing all her digits like a doctor before removing Marlene's shoddy one-handed work.

"Thank you, Deb," Marlene offered, looking up to her for the first time. "I don't know what we would have done if you hadn't arrived."

A well of tears gathered at the corners of Stella's eyes—the other half of the reservoir in Marlene's as they all sat in the living room. Little did the women know that like a seasoned sleuth, Deb had clocked the patrol car as she pulled up to the building in her souped-up camouflage Jeep. When Deb saw the women fleeing from the building—Stella's arms full of collars and silicone—she tailed them discreetly so as not to attract more attention.

As Deb related, she had thrown her car into *Night Rider* reverse and bounded down the alley. She cocked her ear towards the static coming from the police scanner on her dashboard. Ronnie had hooked her up on the down low. One could almost see the flutter of a cape in the shadow she cast on the ground. She was another hero's complex come to save the day of two fallen Avengers. It was her duty as far as she was concerned. She would *not* leave a soldier behind.

Stella had a flashback to Adivina's salon as she sat with Marlene and listened to Deb relate her story. This time, however, there was no moment of Siamese hip bones, only the severed flesh of their savage separation.

"Alright," Deb began, still holding her beer bottle and taking that authoritative stance like the honorary captain of Stella and Marlene's sinking ship. "Now that we've got you both cleaned up, we need to talk about damage control. This is going to require complete transparency."

The women sat wide-eyed and rapt. Deb's voice had changed, taking on the booming acoustic of a sergeant addressing the crew of some deep-down submarine. Deb was domming them and they were both more than willing to fall in line.

"Do either of you have prior criminal records or convictions? I'm talking about anything from back taxes to bodies in the basement. Stella?"

"No," Stella answered, sitting at attention when she heard the syllables of her name.

"Marlene?"

"Nothing."

"Aww, girls. C'mon. You haven't lived!" Deb teased, before clearing her throat and, with an awkward laugh, snapping back into her commander voice.

"OK, that's good. That's very good because you're both looking down the cold barrel at potential 2800s. I promise you the last thing we need is a 10-29f."

Deb took a decisive swig from her beer and sucked hard at one of her front teeth. She was swinging that big fat penal code from one side of the room to the other and it was *the* spectacle to behold.

"We can only assume a potential 647(b) PC," Deb ruminated, almost to herself at this point. "Marlene, my phone." Deb gestured to the armrest. "There's only one man to call."

What the fuck was happening? Deb had gone full-savant *Rain Man,* counting cards as some cosmic dealer peeled the women's fate from the very bottom of the deck. Their day had started with chai lattes and pedicures; Stella never imagined it would end with bloody thumbs and crusted dumpster condoms. But Deb operated like *RoboCop* as she pounded into the face of her phone—that short, thick finger of hers pulling at the golden threads of an untapped saving grace. There was a long silence before someone picked up.

"Hey, my man, I got a nighthawk, bright red. I'm calling one in," Deb's tone took on another layer of severity with this mystery person on the other end of the line. "Yeah, my brother, I know you do. You always do. I got two pigeons on the wire, Ron. Downy feathers, the whole nine."

As Deb spoke, it was clear to Stella that the most important thing they should have grabbed from the penthouse was their leather-bound glossary of Debisms. Alas, no such tome existed. They would just have to wait, anchoring opposite sides of the sofa, swimming in their oversized T-shirts, drowning in the disquieting din of their pounding hearts.

Deb continued her clandestine code talk with her chest puffed up like a cockatiel. Were her pupils glowing red? Was Deb an android? Was Deb a *Terminator?*

"I've got what I think was a knock 'n talk. I'm wondering if you might gander that for me when you can."

Stella and Marlene shot confused looks at one another with matching shrugs at the crests of their shoulders. The agreement they offered smacked of uncertainty. The whole evening had surged like a tsunami up the shores of their once-frolicking seaside escape. It buried all the revelers of their chic charade in raging mud waves of destruction.

"Oh Ron, you cat." Deb laughed heartily at some quip from Ronnie before continuing the arc of her one-woman *CSI* show. "Really? And when did that request come in?"

Deb's questions and reactions flipped like wishing well coins into an expansive abyss of mystery. The women hung on every word, but they had no clue what type of hook they were hanging from.

"Has anything been filed? No, of course. Standard protocol. Roger that. Well, okay Ronnie, you are the man... Well, I, um, I'm not alone in the room..."

Deb's demeanor changed once again. Her shoulders softened and a tender lilt sugar-coated her voice like a buttercream frosting slabbed thick over angel food cake.

"You are *always* my good boy," she muttered, covering up the phone with one hand. It was an awkward attempt to cloak this last bit of the conversation in some thin veil of privacy. She turned her body completely and, for once, it wasn't the rosacea that blushed her cheeks, but rather some blossoming of love.

Deb ended the call and both the women's spines jolted to full erection.

"Knock 'n talk, just as I suspected. There's no charge yet. The officers were there to gather intel. It seems there was an anonymous call to the precinct. Someone set the hounds out for a sniff."

How could what had just transpired sort itself into any assemblage of linear rationale? The bell of the trading floor was sounding out like the trumpet of the apocalypse, and at its call all the credit lines of their little operation were bankrupt. Their inner accountant thrashed into the room in a flurry of paperwork, shouting of audits and repossessions. Stella and Marlene were overdrawn. Their checks were all bounced and their sullen mug shots would soon hang on the wall of every precinct from Palos Verdes to Ventura: FRENEMIES OF THE STATE. WANTED FOR SNOBBERY, GRIFTING, AND SCROTAL ABUSE.

CHAPTER 24

Casta Diva

"I'VE GOT MY FEET pressed into the face of a ruddy Russian wrapped in plastic," Stella typed into the chat window on her laptop. Deb had texted to check on her.

"You sound like Marlene," Deb replied. "You should give her a call. No reason you two can't work this out."

The mention of *her* name punctured the balloon ballasting Stella as she scrolled through the latest Honey Birdette bondage collection and took inventory of the chrysalis of a boy tucked under her desk. Her feet slipped with sweat across his red beard. She wiggled her toes against his nose as hard as she could. He looked up at her with glassy eyes filled with gratitude. This was fun. Everything about her dealings with Marlene lately had been the opposite.

"I'm flying solo," she finished her thought in the text thread. "I can't see how Marlene adds any value to this business. I'm getting clients on my own. I tried in every possible way to please and appease her ego and it was never enough. She's self-sabotaging with her purity, if you ask me. And tell her to return the keys to the penthouse. She won't answer my calls!"

Stella turned up the volume and danced into the boy's face to the sounds of Alison Goldfrapp's sultry voice cooing over thick slabs of razor-sharp synth and heart-shaking bass.

She had rebranded the entire Domicile website and social media, replacing every picture of Marlene with one of herself. It had been a major overhaul. She'd spent long days and nights taking self-portraits with a tripod and a remote.

The one thing Stella didn't have to worry about was client inquiries. She was fresh meat in a market full of wolves. The hottest new Domme on the block. Within days of her media revamp, Yohan—the man currently enjoying the perspiration from her feet all over his face—had booked a three-hour session.

She hated to admit that she was beginning to understand why Marlene called herself a Christian Domme, however hypocritical she was. Many elements of domination harkened to and benefited from Stella's missionary work—the careful communication, the motherly concern for safety, the duty of delivering playtime in a satiating way. None of it had been overtly sexual yet. She certainly wasn't getting a lady boner from wrapping a fat man in a roll of cellophane. She did, however, get a giggle. The queerness of the scene and its clandestine nature tickled her. She was even getting off on the violence, though dear dumb "Yoyo," as she called him, had requested she break his nose.

"This isn't fucking *Fight Club,* Yoyo. No way."

He offered her $300 more to stomp harder.

"It's not about the money. It's about you rolling out of here with a bloody face. Imagine my neighbors seeing you laid out on a stretcher."

"Yes, Mistress, but can I ask you something? Can we end the session early and just talk? You seem so wise. I think it would be a better use of my money than this. I want to get married, Miss, but I'm afraid I'm too far gone. What if I can't be with a normal girl? What if I always want this?"

His little confession pulled at her heartstrings, so she cut him from his plastic cocoon and sat him at her kitchen table like they were a couple of normies; she slurping from a big bowl of ramen and he unfurling what she would learn was a common theme—the submissive's fear of reaching the point of no return.

If any casual watcher happened upon the golden glow of her window then, rather than an hour earlier, they would have counted the occupants as just another slightly odd couple at the dinner table. *Nothing strange to see here, folks.*

"Look, Yohan. Just accept that you're a weird little man with eccentric but perfectly harmless kinks. We all have them. It's a matter of whether we are honest about those desires that burrow deep in our sexual psychology. Accept yourself and find a woman who loves you for you. This isn't about monogamy or tradition, this is about self-acceptance and freedom of thought. Don't be shackled by the limitations imposed by your family, your religion, or your community. You can run, but you can't hide. The reality of your nature will pound on the door like a debtor whatever you do."

He smiled, his burnt orange beard still glistening with sweat from his embalming. "Really? You think so?"

"Yeah, you're a sweet kid with a good heart. You'll find someone."

"You know, you're like a big sister to me."

"Ha!" Stella exclaimed inelegantly, her mouth stuffed with an oversized floret of broccoli. "I thought you were gonna say MILF."

"No, you're like the sister I never had. Anyway, I know it's been over three hours, so I'll go."

"It's OK, Yohan. I don't mind. Glad I could help."

He dropped $300 in cash on the table and thanked her. It was a generous tip, netting her $1,200 from the session.

As soon as Yohan left, she stripped off the impaling boned corset and unforgiving pencil skirt she vowed to never wear in combination again, and slipped into sweatpants and Deb's Jumbo's T-shirt, which she had been meaning to return. As she sat cross-legged on the couch, stuffing her face with noodles, she checked her email to see if Elisha had met his journaling deadline.

She called him "Harvard." He was an Ivy League grad living in his parents' Beverly Hills home while he crafted his first screenplay—his big, bright arrow aimed with hope at the heart of Hollywood. Stella took to him immediately and he had not hesitated to send her $800, far more than the 50% deposit required to book a session. This eager beaver did not want to wait.

She required that he journal to her by hand, which pained him to no end, but she'd read his latest entry countless times, admiring his quick wit and vulnerability. The journal entry was entitled "Mad-About-You-Libs" and detailed Harvard's desire to be pegged. He left gaps in the story for Stella to fill in her preferences, from her favorite insults to the amorous gestures she would allow him to make. It was terribly endearing. Wordsmiths fucking turned her on.

He ended the five-page story with a soft plea to be cradled in Stella's arms like a baby; to have his body and emotions wielded like mere possessions. She was both comforted and intimidated by his years of experience as a submissive. He had seen some of the city's most established Dommes.

At 7:00 p.m. sharp the next day, Harvard rang her intercom.

Stella sat at her vanity. She dusted the hair off her sheer burgundy Catherine D'Lish robe. She knew she looked good, from the cinched waist that accentuated her bust to the peak of décolletage over her favorite lace bustier. But was the ensemble too sweet and not severe enough? *Latex or leather would have been more theme-appropriate,* she thought. Every choice she made that evening now became an anxious and insistent question for which there were a thousand additional queries but no hard and fast answers.

She swung open the door and Harvard thrust a bouquet of red roses towards her like he was presenting a passport at customs. She grabbed the flowers, thrashed them to the ground, thrust him face-first against the wall, and slid a satin blindfold over his head.

"Spread 'em!" she yelled, smacking his ass.

He quickly widened his gait. She ran her hands along his thighs as if searching for a Glock. She crouched down to grab at his bulge unnecessarily. She stood. Flipped him around and ripped off his eye mask.

God, this is fun. She couldn't keep the corners of her mouth from curling up in delight.

"Why hello, darling," she said as if telling an inside joke. She knew the drama was heightened. She had raised the velvet curtain for her audience of one in this immersive sex theatre.

Harvard smiled, eyes big as melons, his body an inch or two shorter than it would have been if he could muster the courage to pull it erect. "Hello. You look amazing."

"Dominating is like looking over the shoulder of your submissive while remaining two steps ahead," Marlene would often say. "You must anticipate but stay present." Stella took her words of wisdom to heart. They were embossed like scripture, sealed with a signet ring even though the acrimony between them remained.

Stella instructed Harvard to remove his shoes and follow her into her studio. She sat him in a chair and loomed over him like a tower.

He cocked his head up at her, but just inside his periphery was a trio of coarse, gray hairs on his tweed jacket. Stella clocked his embarrassment. She knew his "Lil Daisy" was sick and he had been cradling the dying dog in his arms for three weeks straight while studying for the LSAT and managing a neurotic Jewish mother who mined him mercilessly for data about how he was doing on those new meds. "You're already so skinny, I hope they don't turn you into a waif!" she would whine.

The tweed was too much. It was sartorially so anachronistic, hot and very itchy, but he had always wished to be older, wiser, less frivolous. Unlike his peers, he longed to be weighed down with much more important work than keeping his childhood bedroom clean and tending to the old mutt whose life was slipping away in tandem with his spirit. Harvard was an old soul in a boy's body, and Stella couldn't help but be excited by the contradiction. Her affinity for men 10 years her junior was surely some mourning of the loss of her younger brother who had blocked her number as soon as she left the cult. In Harvard, she found a way to rekindle a familiar dynamic.

"You listed mixologist as one of your skills. Come in the kitchen and make me a cocktail."

"Yes, of course. It is. I am. I will." Harvard shook his head shamefully. He clearly hated himself for the profuseness of words. He was sweating like mad. The sopping warmth turned acrid under his arms, forcing him to stand stiff.

He told Stella that he felt himself disappearing into her from the start. He even called himself "Harvard" now, forgetting his own name in the thrill of Stella's adoption and rechristening of him. Who was Elisha? Didn't matter. He was ready to kill that tiny old fool and be reborn as Stella's plaything. He couldn't wait for her to penetrate him greedily, to conquer and capture his village, to burn down the rows of stale and static houses in his mind, the old dwelling places of mothful sexual desire—they were practically graves anyway. He had felt himself dying with each vanilla encounter with a woman. He was tired of topping, pretending to enjoy some antiquated masculine role that had forever been foreign to him.

He wanted to be resurrected into the hand of this new feminine spirit in his life. He handed himself over fully and, in that surrender, imagined he would experience a shattering release, some ascension to the divine. And perhaps through this carnal exchange, he might channel his inner Joyce or Conrad or McCarthy and write The Great American Novel after all.

Harvard mixed two cocktails and they sunk into the couch.

"You look incredible. That robe is so glamorous," he complimented.

"Would you like to touch it?"

He would. He did. He remarked on its softness. Compared it to her skin. And then he took this as an invitation for greater intimacy.

"What are you doing?" Stella snapped as he inched closer.

"Oh, sorry," he slid back to his side of the sofa in haste.

"Enjoy your drink, Harvard. You came here as my manservant and our cocktail hour is almost over. Are you ready for the games to begin?"

"*The Hunger Games?*" he retorted.

He was sassing but she liked his sharp wit. "No, Harvard." She smiled devilishly. "The Pegging Games."

After discussing safewords and the color system Stella would use to check in, she stood, the copious folds of her gown cascading to the floor. She floated out of the room, the organza billowing around her in a slow-motion dance like a company of whirling dervishes. Harvard's hungry eyes followed her out of the room.

Stella disappeared for some 10 minutes. She wanted to keep him squirming. She already had her utensils laid out on the vanity: a leather crop, a studded dog collar, and some silly handcuffs lined with fur. She stared long and hard at the cock cage. Of course, that was Marlene's influence on her, but she was mortified of malpractice. She struggled to imagine herself securing it successfully, and if she couldn't guarantee the swift grace of a sexual Houdini, it seemed too risky. *The ring goes around the balls, the cage around the penis, but how do you lock it? What if I pinch him?* Absent the experience or expertise, she decided it was best to leave the cock cage for another Domme, another day.

She could hear Harvard fidgeting in the other room, the couch creaking under his shifting torso, ice cubes pinging against glass as he swirled his drink nervously.

It was time to make an entrance. Stella had the scene written in her mind as if on the worn pages of a dog-eared script. She opened the door and paused, lifting her arm above her head and resting it dramatically on the door frame in a way that crazy-whispered: "Alright, Mr. DeMille, I'm ready for my close-up."

"Come here, puppy," she commanded in her most stern voice, mustering an entire octave lower than normal.

"Yes, Mistress." He dusted off his jacket and made his way to her.

She could smell him, a cocktail of perspiration and cologne, something fresh like the outdoors. He was tangy but not unpleasant to imbibe. A mouth can lie, but who can stop the excretions of the skin? Who can argue with the expression of the body as it cools itself down from a fever state? He smelled nervous. All the glorious underpinnings of his mind were revealed to Stella through his body odor. She was a Doberman sniffing her way to a catch.

She could feel the stir of his flustered breath as she studied him. She used the silence like an electrician, slowly dialing up the voltage of their interaction with the absence, rather than the profundity, of words.

She stepped forward and smacked him, painting his cheeks red with the brushstroke of her fingers. He stood motionless for a moment and then leaned in with his oversized head inviting her to do it again.

"I really want you to dominate me," he whispered, drugged from the impact. "I surrender completely to you."

"Take off your clothes. Now!" She threw a pair of pink lace panties at him. "Put these on!"

He stripped and threw his clothes messily to the corner of the room.

"Dumb little doggy." Her first insult! It came so naturally. Was it too much? "Fold the clothes and put them on the table!"

He hopped to it as if his life depended on it.

She grabbed his shoulders and spun him around. She hooked the collar in place, running her sharp nails along the gooseflesh of his neck. He shuddered.

"Stand in the middle of the carpet. The exact center. It's time to learn your positions."

His face flushed with excitement.

"Position one: Sit on your ass with your chin down. Make no eye contact." Marlene's voice sounded in her head as if she were receiving downloads from the mothership.

"OK, now position two. Get on all fours!" She pushed on the back of his head. He sank lower.

"Not quite." She adjusted his shoulders, pressing her hand against his abdomen to flatten him. She then placed her half-full glass in the flat of his back, careful to balance it. "This is the Martini Test. I better not see it slip."

She walked slowly around him, slapping her crop on her hand as if processing an important decision.

"Yes, Mistress."

"I don't understand you," she said, removing her glass from his flesh where it left a ring of moisture. "You look like a dog, but you're speaking like a man. Speak like a dog!" She snapped the crop decisively on the tissue of his ass.

"Ruff. Ruff."

"Where's your tongue? Pant like a dog."

He let his tongue drip stupidly from his mouth, drawing in sharp breaths as if he was panting.

She wound up dramatically, like a Major League pitcher on the mound, and cropped him even harder.

He moaned long and loud.

"Now remember, Harvard, doggies need to communicate with their masters. Is doggy having a good time?"

"Doggy is having a great time."

"Doggy needs to learn to walk on his leash."

She attached a leash to the collar and yanked it ferociously. He lurched forward by the neck. His newly heavy and foreign "paws" followed.

Stella positioned him at her feet and leaned down to exhale a macabre breath along the ridge of his neck. She then led him to the window.

"Do you trust me?"

He assured her he did. With every stern command, she watched his dick bob like a marionette.

She opened the window and, with her hands secure on the collar, dangled his head through the frame just a few inches. She knew he wanted to be pushed to the edge and she intended to make that as literal as possible, though he wasn't in any actual danger.

The blustery night air washed over his cheeks. The restricted flesh of his scepter swelled against the plaster wall.

She pressed her palm against his chest to clock the ticking of his pulse upward as she tugged him in and out of the perilous void of velveteen sky.

"Where are you?" she whispered into his ear.

"Green, Mistress. So happy and green," he said, squeezing his eyes shut in satisfaction.

After a few more thrilling moments, she pulled him back in and let rip a series of stings to his face. His eyes went wild with adrenaline. Slapping turned Stella on to no end. It simulated that bitchy boss mother in her. This was her maternal clock and it was a revelation.

She commanded Harvard to position two and turned up the operatic soprano of Maria Callas. The premier notes of "Casta Diva" billowed symphonically from her speakers. She marveled at the way Callas meticulously kept the climax from unraveling. Of course, she could leap and trill with expert agility, but she held the notes in as if her mouth was a mother hen's breast guarding a tender sparrow not ready for release into the world. Stella aspired to this kind of power and restraint herself.

Stella strapped into a new leather harness and stood over the prostrate man, her cock dangling near his nose. She commanded him to kiss it, then thrust it deeper into his mouth. He smiled and salivated profusely, sliding his eager tongue all around the flesh-colored silicone. She poured lube into his palm and instructed him to give her a hand job.

"Position three!"

He pressed his forehead to the carpet, palms out, his body bent in half like a pennant worshiper in prayer. Throwing her gown to the sides, she mounted him. She rapped at the skin of his back with his bouquet of roses, softly at first in a sweeping motion in time with every lovely verse.

And as Maria Callas ruminated on the penultimate note in her throat like the swill of red wine bouncing off the curves of a glass, Stella raised her arms higher and let forth that eternal torrent of beautiful rage held hostage throughout her childhood, her marriage, and in her worship of everything but herself. The scarlet petals scattered across Harvard's back like water rushing open-mouthed over a boulder, while the thorns stippled tiny dots of blood like a Seurat.

She grabbed a thrush of his thick brown hair and pulled his head back. "Position two!"

He rose to all fours. She had never penetrated a man before, but Harvard had earned it. She slid the cock inside him and his eyes popped open like an exorcism. She pulsed slowly and he closed them again, smiling as if a paisley swirl of heroin coursed through his veins. He pressed back into her, moaning in ecstasy.

She turned up the music and thrust with greater force. The vigor in her limbs was like some buried tongue on Pentecost that sprang into existence by the hand of God. Like a flame dancing above her head loud and hot, she was speaking a language hidden inside of her. And out it came, as if her insides would incinerate without the release.

In a final thrashing, she released the entire bouquet of stems, like a maestro setting free the last note with her baton. She felt Harvard jolt, then his neck go limp in satisfaction.

The room was silent save for the last few seconds of analog static on the recording. Wisps of marabou from her gown floated in the air, as if part of the ceremonial offering. Her lip trembled and a tear slid from her eyes in pious catharsis.

CHAPTER 25

Deb's Five Steps to Domination

STELLA SHUFFLED down the stairs of her apartment building, smarting from a hangover. She and Yvette had painted the town red the night before and all her pleasure was now pained with a punishing headache.

There wasn't anyone Yvette couldn't charm—even the men of Boys Town. Their raucous night involved a spirited makeout session with a very gay and somewhat famous Brazilian soccer player. No one could resist her. Yvette was cool and graceful and wore a black leather jacket and platform boots most of the nights they hit the streets. She walked with her shoulders back, taking long strides in time with the drag of her cigarette as if she were still on the avenues of Paris. She smoked and drank too much and always had blow. Like a dutiful boyfriend, Stella held back her hair when she puked in gutters outside the most notorious clubs in WeHo.

Stella now slogged through the garage of her building, grumbling as she lifted a dangerously overstuffed trash bag into the tall dumpster. It was a precarious move. As the lid slammed shut, a Subaru rolled into the parking space next to hers—the spot reserved for the penthouse. She watched with unflinching attention as the car door swung open. It was Hope, dressed smartly in jeans, a white blouse, and a loose tie à la Annie Hall. The pageant-sized bouquet of peonies she carried bounced under its heft as she pounded across the garage. As she came closer, they exchanged the kind of sinister glances usually reserved for spaghetti western duels. One could almost hear the iconic trill of a whistle and the metallic jangle of spurs. Would pistols be drawn?

Stella's heart pounded, first with fright then with outrage. What business did Marlene have being in the penthouse? The nerve to have her slave deliver flowers right before Stella's eyes after ignoring her calls for weeks!

However, as Hope came within inches of Stella, her countenance and demeanor flashed a sad vulnerability that softened Stella. Her vengeance surpassed by compassion, Stella whispered almost imperceptibly to her: "Get out."

Hope averted her eyes and sped towards the door. Her obsequious devotion to Scientology had been easily converted to another kind of worship under Marlene's meditated hand. It was obvious Hope counted Marlene no small deity.

Pity for Hope aside, this was war. With her mind racing, Stella shot up to the ninth floor. *My apartment! My name on the lease! My money paying the rent!*

She pounded on the door, panting and out of breath. No answer. Just the muffle of voices. The peephole went black. She was being watched.

"Marlene, I know you're in there. Open the door. I want my keys back."

The occupants attempted to be undetectable. They were hiding.

Stella tramped back to her seventh-floor studio in a fury. She grabbed her phone and dialed Marlene. No answer.

"Fuck!"

She rang up her landlord. "Hi, Todd. How are you?" She did not wait for him to reply. "I have a situation in unit 900. There's a squatter. Uh, a former friend of mine who just won't leave. She's got my keys."

Todd was a snarky, passive-aggressive man of 50 who veered into laissez-faire territory when it came to matters in the building.

"If you gave her the keys, that's something you need to work out with her. But if you want a second set of keys, I have to charge you $50. I can get them to you Tuesday."

"It takes five days? I need them now."

"If you had called me before 5 p.m. on a holiday weekend, I could have helped you. Office is officially closed until Tuesday."

"But she doesn't live here! Can't you evict her?"

"If she won't vacate after 30 days, we can get the court involved, but that can be a drawn-out process. No guarantees the court order will be delivered to the authorities before 90 days. Evictions are a bitch."

"Ninety days! That can't be right."

"Believe me. I can't have her removed unless she's committed a crime."

But she is a criminal, Stella wanted to shout. *If you only knew.*

"I'd like to terminate my lease then."

"You know I'd have to keep your deposit, right? Why not talk to your friend? Work it out between you two. You've been a good tenant, Stella. No reason to default and have a negative rental history here."

Stella thanked the landlord and ended the call.

"Jesus. Fucking. Christ!" she screamed into the void. She needed air.

As soon as she stepped foot on the roof, she saw a familiar outline. Tailored suit. Broad shoulders. Thick, waxy hair. As he turned, a billow of smoke escaped from the man's lips. Ten stories below, the city roared with rush hour agitation. Was he Bruce Wayne surveying his kingdom or perhaps Two-Face planning a coup?

With a gut soup of nerves, Stella approached him.

"Your friend, she's minor leagues," the tall man said, turning slowly towards her as if on cue from a film noir director. He took another devilish drag from his cigarette.

Stella attempted to flatten her flyaway bangs. "What makes you say that?"

"You know *what.* I bet you would do it if the price was right."

"Money isn't everything." *Keep the tension, keep the tension,* she told herself. She ran her hands through her hair again nervously. *God, I must look a mess.*

"Money is power and you know that. And it's no issue for me. Name your price." He flicked the cigarette butt off the roof.

"The crucifixion? Indeed, that would cost you."

Mr. X reached into his pocket. "Here's an advance."

Stella looked down at the thick stack of one-hundred dollar bills as they flapped in a gust of wind. She took the cash from his handsome hands, not daring enough to count it in front of him. She wanted to flee. If she was going to dominate him, she didn't want him seeing her like this. And she had many, many questions. Her head swirled with paranoia.

"I'll be in touch," she said, strutting off towards the exit.

* * * * *

Stella spent the next few days in a rotation of obsessive-compulsive rituals that included, but were not limited to, spying on Marlene with binoculars, attempting to eavesdrop into the penthouse from the roof, fantasizing about a *Mission Impossible*-style entry through the window, and finally, the financial benefits and moral consequences of nailing X to a cross.

She needed Deb, who arrived with the heroic speed of a caped crusader, albeit one who stopped for chicharrónes.

"Why is he here? Did he call the police on us? Did he plant the blow? Why is she living in my fucking apartment?!" Stella rattled off, pacing like a madwoman in front of the large picture windows of her studio.

"Woah, woah, woah. Slow down, Woody Allen." Deb rose from the couch and began applying pressure to Stella's aching shoulders. "One thing at a time."

"Deb, wow. That feels amazing. Is there anything you can't do?"

"I told you I was having trouble sticking the landing of my triple salchow, right?"

"What?"

"Yeah, my damn sacral trunk. That's what a lifetime of pegging will do, you know? But I persist! And you must to! Don't let Marlene be your Tonya Harding. You want this, you gotta go after it."

"She's a fucking squatter. What can I do?"

"I'll put a call in to Ronnie about her squatting. Geez, I thought you too could hug this out. Can't say I'm totally surprised though. Two dominant women trying to co-run a business, everything getting more tangled than a room full of kittens with twine…" Deb scratched her head—her cropped hair in color-of-the-month hot pink—as if she was calculating the terminal velocity of the next implosion. "But what was that about blow?"

"The bag of cocaine that sent us flying out the back door."

"That coke was a prop from my session with Ronnie," Deb said with a far-off gaze. "It's baking soda. He loves when I turn the tables and punish him as the perp."

"Oh my God. I'm so stupid. I thought we were gonna get busted for drug possession. But, fuck, I need my penthouse back. We should break in."

"You'd be guaranteed a conflict if you did that."

"She's a thief!" Stella shouted.

"Well, she's entitled, I'll admit that."

"Deb, she shoplifted from PetSmart."

Deb's eyes went sideways. She moved closer to Stella. *Is she going to smack me?* Stella wondered.

"Come again?" Deb wanted answers. *Pronto.*

Stella flopped onto the couch. "That day we came into the store, she lifted a dog collar. I confronted her and she admitted she does this kind of thing all the time. Some 'Corporate America is bullshit' excuse."

"She lied to my face!" And that was all the convincing Deb needed. No, not on her watch was anyone going to burglar the pet store she so proudly managed. "I can't believe that happened right under my nose... Alright, Stella. Here's what you gotta do. Domme the hell outta this town. I believe in you. Gotta admit, I was skeptical at first."

"You were?"

"Yeah, I mean, you were all over the map, child. It was your freshman year. Understandable. Your two hemispheres don't connect. You were an 18-year-old trapped in the body of a 38-year-old. Your choices in men reflect the fact."

Stella bore the insult. She knew she deserved it. "I've wondered if I should stop hanging out with people whose wisdom teeth are still coming in."

"Something to consider. But, Stella, I've seen you grow. You work hard. And you're a helluva media wiz. I can help you this next leg of the journey."

"And I can help you. Whatever you want, Deb."

"Well, that's the problem. You're too eager to help everyone else. I get it. That old missionary spirit. But you need to focus on yourself for once. Stop hiding behind other dominant women."

"You think that's what I'm doing?"

"You're growing out of it. And there's only upside if you can shake off the rubble from this disaster with Marlene. I have no more excuses for a woman like this. Too bad. She has the raw talent, but not the integrity. She doesn't walk the talk and it's a shame because her talk is actually on the money most of the time."

"I've learned everything from her. She positioned herself as a guru and I took it all to heart."

"Well, those who can't do, teach. That's why she played Mohammed on the mountain."

"What should we do?"

"My first instinct is to bust that damn door down, but my roughhousing days are behind me. Let's get the law on our side, cadet."

"What do I do with this?" Stella picked up the stack of bills.

Deb shook her head. "I wouldn't touch that with a 10-foot pole."

"I think Marlene exaggerated X's danger. I think it makes her feel like more of a lion tamer to label him a dangerous beast." Stella wagged her head. "Or maybe she got dickmatized."

"I don't know, Stella. What if his greatest fetish is inverting dominant women? Taking their big D energy and shoving it back down their throats?" Deb asked with an aggressive stabbing motion towards Stella.

She had a way of talking that sent shivers down Stella's spine. It was as if Vincent Price was presenting some macabre goblin who ate babies for breakfast.

"Just be careful your buck fever doesn't lead you out of the blinds," Deb continued, pacing the length of the room as if she were preparing for a battle. "Check your safety at all times. Remember, big game can smell you before you can see it. I'm not going to try to talk you out of it, but you need a plan. You need…" She paused and spun on her heels. "Deb's Five Steps to Domination."

Stella's face lit up. She loved how Deb spoke of herself in third person. Her marketing lingo oozed appeal. She was speaking Stella's language.

"Tell me," Stella said, propping her chin on her fists in rapture.

Deb cleared her throat and rolled her shoulders back as if preparing to deliver a State of the Union address. She sparked up a doobie and paced for several pregnant moments.

"You're putting on a show," she said, pushing her body off the side of a chair and leaning in just inches from Stella's face. "A show needs a good arc. A story that both keeps him guessing and thrusts him deeper into the odyssey!"

If Deb's Five Steps were a stage show, the word "odyssey" would have been reverberated throughout the theatre. She was a natural Shatner.

"Number one: Start with confusion when he enters. 'Where am I? What is this?'" Deb pivoted her body wildly while she spoke.

Stella nodded, reaching for her laptop. "I'm taking notes."

"You should be. This is honed wisdom, my child. Bring him into a world! Establish the rules. Let the fantasy be totally encompassing—the room, your outfit, the decor, your voice, all of it," Deb instructed with a breathy intonation.

Deb scanned Stella's face to see if her advice had registered.

"Oh, this is good," Stella whispered, taking the joint from Deb.

"Alright. Number two. This is absolutely key. The inciting incident! You need to draw him in with a question that he can't answer. A thought that won't resolve until the finale." Deb's voice had that razzle dazzle emcee quality about it again.

"What would the question be?"

"Spend time on the question! That is the very thing that motivates him."

Stella was suddenly overwhelmed with self-doubt. She had imagined the session far less psychologically scripted.

"He is now working towards the goal using the rules you established. Then he reaches the tough part, some degrading task you give him."

"Like?"

"This is where you have to use your imagination! You've got to tailor the scene according to your desires, his kinks, both your limits... I can't tell you exactly what to do. It's not my scene."

Again, the flush of ineptitude. Stella doubted herself more with each bullet point in the creative brief. She puffed on the half-toked joint then held it out the window. A breeze caught the falling ash and blew it across the bokeh of city lights.

"Okay, I'll figure it out," Stella said with a resolve to "fake it till you make it." It wouldn't do for Deb to doubt her too.

"This is the submissive's low point, the worst he will feel throughout the session. He may even wonder if it's all worth it. And that's why for number three you must dangle the goal in front of him again. Show him the treasure chest. He knows he wants it. It's so close now…" Deb pumped her squared-off fists in unison like some popstar belting out a ballad.

"Number four: This is the car chase scene. But you've set up obstacles. He's going to be physically challenged to get to you and he's gonna fuckin' love that," Deb said, grinning ear to ear. The richness of her five-stepped genius clearly delighted her. "Make him lift an SUV. Save a baby from a burning building. Push this bastard. Like I said, take your time designing the scene. You don't want it to come off as amateur hour in the dungeon."

"Yes, yes. I can do that."

"Alright, number five," Deb continued solemnly. "He completes the initial challenge. He's conquered several obstacles. The prize is in sight. Show it to him again. Tease him. Make him beg for it and then…" Deb seized up all the air in her lungs and suspended her breath for dramatic effect. "The release! The boom bada boom! The big O!"

"You're my hero," Stella said, grabbing Deb's wide shoulders for a hug.

"I'm passing the baton to you, Stella. Don't fuck this up," Deb said, as she closed the front door behind her.

The moment Deb was gone, Stella's heart sank. Deb and her confident catechism had temporarily buoyed her, but now she felt adrift. The looming presence of Marlene two floors above cast a pall over her operation. It cloaked her spirit thicker than LA smog.

CHAPTER 26

The Crucifixion

"YOU ARE A PIMP," Marco stated, pulling a protracted drag from a hand-rolled cigarette. They stood on Stella's rooftop under a cobalt sky. "Look at you!" Marco pointed at Stella's fuzzy oversized leopard coat and laughed in the deep, raspy timber so characteristic of his geographic heritage. She loved his Brooklynese.

"I know. Is it wrong to pimp out Yvette if she consents to it?" She glanced down, pressing the stub of her joint into the plaster of a low wall.

"You think there's anything Yvette *doesn't* consent to?" Marco chuckled. "I'll install the cross like you asked, but this sounds crazy to me. A crucifixion, really?"

"I bottomed for Jesus for 25 years. Talk about crazy."

"Well then, your wish is my command, Mistress Stella," he said, pantomiming a formal bow.

By some bestowal of grace by the kink gods, Marco finished the installation just after midnight on Christmas Eve. He had fastened a metal crossbar to her pole and added hooks for rope so she could tie the sinful Mr. X in what would be her first official session with him.

Yvette arrived the next day, full of excitement.

"Mr. X wants to be crucified." Stella scanned Yvette's face for a reaction as she sat across from her on the bed. What were her limits? Had she any?

"Cool. Let's do it," Yvette replied with the nonchalance of a housewife agreeing to some new item in the shopping cart.

"You sure? It's Christmas and I'm sure Marlene would count this as a double offense against Jesus."

"I'm Jewish so I don't care," Yvette cheerfully confirmed a second time.

Relieved to have Yvette as moral support and eye candy, she pushed her anxiety deep down to keep Yvette from seeing just how nervous she was.

Against Marlene's warning, Stella read Mr. X's journals, for she had access to the business email to which he sent them. She knew him as thoroughly as she could, giving his pages a journalistic dissection.

When the day came, Stella suited up like a sci-fi superhero. In her tailored latex trench coat and gold-spiked heels, she looked as if she could defeat any number of *Matrix* villains with a swift scorpion kick. Underneath, she wore a PVC bodysuit with an ultra-high V cut on her Rubenesque hips, her breasts pressed against the smoky black film with only thin vertical seams to feign coverage of her nipples.

She outfitted Yvette in a sweeter ensemble—a second-skin lace mini dress with garters that clipped into her sheer black stockings. She wore crocodile stiletto booties to punk it up a bit.

Stella tidied and re-tidied the room, sighing into the mirror as she checked her makeup for the millionth time. Yvette tried to lighten her mood by turning up the music and tiptoeing around the pole, but she had been pouring her own drinks and before Stella knew it, she was tipsy. That's when the doorbell rang.

Stella opened the door. Mr. X was crisp in a tuxedo. Starched like a cadet. As though he had been steam-pressed into the suit by a launderer and hermetically sealed for delivery. Not a single wrinkle on the front of his slacks where a crease should have been from sitting in the car. Or did he paraglide in? His blue-black hair was plastered without a single errant wisp to muss the Ken doll coiffe. This presentation was part of both his servitude and a display of his machismo. Wasn't he a pretty peacock?

He stepped two feet into her studio and the stiff wall of his cologne—tobacco leaf and appropriated grit—thrust itself into her sinuses. His suit was too slick. His posture too pitched. His eyes too bright. His smirk too smug. *God, that cologne.* It was clobbering and delicious. She hated him for it. Stella couldn't remember if she had applied any deodorant. She could already feel the perspiration under her arms making her latex slick.

Regret filled the narrowing cavity of her throat. Her mind raced. Why had she not required Marco to chaperone the affair? She knew why. She feared she would be clumsy and inexperienced and she didn't want the watchful eyes of the beloved Brooklyn hulk turning scrutinizing and sad at her ineptitude.

She wanted to operate without oversight. Perhaps it was *she* who was seeking X and not the other way around. Maybe she was looking for *her* match, some kind of do-over to right the injustices of the beer-stained youth under her stepfather's regime. Had she subconsciously designed this whole battleground to assert some lost control and inflict vengeance on every pervert who stared too long, who swaggered too smugly, who touched without permission?

Mr. X opened the butterscotch square of his jaw to speak and Stella felt all his atoms in opposition to hers.

"Position two!" she barked, pointing an angry finger to the floor. His height advantage would be dissipated in doggy style.

He dropped to his knees without hesitation, placing the wides of his mansome palms on the floor. Even in his prostration, he was far too erect. His right angles were perfectly perpendicular. His immaculate geometry would have pleased her had the spiritual Geiger counter within not screamed into its trembling dial: *Danger, danger. Abort!*

"Don't you look pretty in your suit tonight?" she whined insultingly, sauntering slow circles around him. She wanted to vacuum-seal his spirit and deprive it of air; watch it choke behind the breathless glass of her body.

As Stella paced, she rehearsed the timeline of events in her mind. Deb's Five Steps to Domination could be followed only if X was truly subdued.

Alright, number one: Bring him into a world.

"Do you know why you're here?" Stella asked scoldingly. She wanted to probe him like a gumshoe with the blinding light of an interrogation room—*What was your business with Marlene? Did you call the cops? Who the hell are you?*—but she refrained.

She stood wide-legged, inches away from his face so his neck was forced either into a sharp angle upward or a limp repose towards the floor. He looked up at his inquiring mistress. Marlene would not have allowed the eye contact. This much Stella knew.

"I'm here to serve... and to be sacrificed on the cross."

Pat answer. No surprises there. *He's giving nothing away,* Stella thought.

"That is correct. But don't think you won't have to walk through the valley of death to get to your Golgotha. Your high priestess is not the only one who decides on your fate."

All the mythological metaphors were mixing like some strange green juice smoothie. She kept up the verbal charade for several long minutes before her ego let it drop in an obvious admission that it was inane.

With Mr. X subdued on all fours, Stella finally felt free to glance over at Yvette, who had been sitting quietly on the sofa. They locked eyes and shared a knowing smile. Stella once again felt the confidence her companion supplied. Yvette, even in her wild ways, grounded Stella. Her devotion was permanently inked. Yvette took her cue and catwalked over to Stella, planting herself in a Siamese power stance over X.

"This is Duchess," Stella said, recalling Yvette's stripper name. "She is capable of bestowing the most sensual gifts." She ran her finger along Yvette's bombastic breasts.

The women sashayed to the sofa and sat down hip to hip. Stella gave Yvette a slow, deep kiss, then instructed X to crawl to them.

"You have requested quite a ceremony. I read your journals. Catholic school was not kind to you. However, you must prepare the altar. These candles won't light themselves."

Stella had placed a ring of stout ivory candles around the pole in a "burn the witch" fashion. Perhaps she would let the flames lick his incorrigible toes just a little, but first, she must subdue his mind.

"Alright, altar boy. I want you to light this up... without using your hands."

For the first time, X could not conceal his surprise. His eyes dilated briefly and his jaw clenched. He scooted forward, the knees of his $3,000 suit dusty with the soot of a floor Stella had intentionally left a little dirty.

She placed a burning matchstick between his teeth. The flame rose nearly to his nose as he hurried to spark the first candle. Each time he dipped his head, the flame shot higher, threatening to melt his flesh. Stella felt the pride of victory.

On the flip side, the dead resignation X wore in his once-shiny eyes said it all. He hated this. Crawling around like an animal, soiling his St. Laurent, these two chirpy birds standing gleefully over him, erupting in excruciating giggles at his every defeat.

He persisted and rounded the bend to the twelfth and final candle. At this point, Stella produced one more candle and Mr. X let rip a smirk. It was the first moment of levity that night. Stella placed a fresh match in his mouth and the clever devil lit the candle as fast as he could.

During the brief exchange, Yvette had crept into the kitchen to refill her drink.

"Duchess, are you pleased with this dog so far?" Stella asked, taking Yvette's half-empty glass of vodka and Red Bull from her hand.

Yvette confirmed that the charade delighted her. Even in the bawdiness of her own decade of bacchanalia, she had not experienced the theatrics of the worlds Stella invented.

"You have shown yourself proficient with your mouth, now let's see what else it can do. First, let's get these hands out of the way. Position one!"

Mr. X, still on the floor, extended his wrists towards Stella like a caught criminal, smiling ever so slightly. Wisps of his hair had escaped from the Aqua Net helmet and bounced loose upon his perspiring brow. She noticed for the first time tiny shaven hairs along the rims of his ears. *He must work hard to be this manscaped,* Stella thought. His suit was rumpled and gray, and only now did Stella feel her body drawn to his. The pretty boy had been disheveled down to human levels. He looked like a real man instead of a mannequin.

Stella bent down and locked him in a pair of handcuffs.

Number three, number four... It was time to dangle the prize in front of him once again lest he give up. Stella would shine the spotlight at her trophy. Yvette had taken Stella's silent prompt and dimmed the lights, queued the music, and walked out of the room.

Stella pressed play on a sultry R&B number. Yvette strutted in slowly from the doorway through the coterie of candles. She placed one hand on the pole then spun gracefully around it.

Oh God, we didn't rehearse this with candles, Stella thought in a panic.

Yvette was unafraid. She inverted herself with ease, clutching the top of the pole with her ankles then extending one leg out with a pointed toe. Her long hair dangled dangerously near to the hungry flames, which seemed to bother her not.

The trap was set.

"Duchess, I cannot tell what our slave is thinking. Let's get that big brain out in the open."

Yvette dismounted the pole, knocking over a single candle but quickly recovering it with a "whoops!" and a smile as was her custom.

"Get up!" Stella commanded X.

He stood. She grabbed his belt violently, and in one swift movement, slid it off and struck his ass with the stiff leather. His entire body seized as if a single muscle. His eyes, squeezed tightly, indicated he was in pain, but a bulge from within knocked loudly on the door of his zipper. Stella motioned to Yvette to unzip his trousers. She and Yvette shared a cackle as it was revealed he was sans underwear. Private Benjamin had reported for duty with a full salute, manscaped, of course.

"You naughty little altar boy!" Stella sang.

She pointed at his erect member and Yvette knew what to do. She spit from high above, letting a long stream of saliva wet his eager cock. He clenched his jaw, threw back his head, and groaned with satisfaction.

"Stroke it!" Stella commanded him.

The scepter in his hand swelled like a balloon. Stella handed a leather crop to her lovely assistant. She bent him over and Yvette began smacking his smooth cheeks. His tanned glutes tensed as she increased the force.

Within seconds Stella's latex was interminably wet. She threw off her trench coat and guided Yvette's fingers between her legs. Yvette's face lit up like Rockefeller Center.

While Yvette kneaded her nimble fingers into her latex crotch, Stella grabbed X's disheveled crown and yanked his head back. Squeezing his throat, she smacked him across the face. He was stunned. They all were.

Yvette wore a very familiar look in her eyes—the desire to coat her victim with the sticky sweetness of her sex. Mr. X salivated. These two wanted to feast on one another. A pang of terror ran through Stella's body. This was not what she planned. This act was designed as the slow roast of pig flesh over a spit. Yvette, however, was not accustomed to protracted sexual tension. She never chose it over lower-hanging fruit. But this was Stella's charade, not some vanilla romp in the hay. *This is Deb's Five Steps to Domination, dammit!* She needed to regain control.

"You love this, don't you?" she growled.

He nodded. "Let's up the ante," he said with her hands still around his neck.

Stella eased her grip. "Go on."

"I would very much like to see you take a blood sacrifice from the lovely Duchess."

Yvette took a step back and Stella could read the alarm on her face.

"Why do you want this?" Stella asked.

"I didn't know how much I would enjoy seeing you interact with this *Goddess.* A thousand more should buy me that, shouldn't it, High Priestess?" His tone was full and commanding.

X stood and seemed to be 10 feet tall. Like her stepfather did when she was a child, Mr. X used his superior size to intimidate her, leaning slightly forward on the balls of his bare feet. He clearly sought her out, not to humbly serve a queen, but to feed on the carrion of a fallen monarch.

Stella's eyes surely betrayed her fear. She wanted to telegraph a silent warning to the unsuspecting Yvette. It would have required a dog whistle pitched at some heavenly frequency above X's ears or sonar for seeing in the long darkness cast by the span of this gargoyle's wings.

"So, the crucifixion was a ruse?" Stella asked.

"No, that once interested me, but I think Marlene would have been much better suited," he insulted. "Too bad she wasn't up for the execution. However..." A grotesque smile spread across his face as he glanced over his shoulder at the Frenchwoman. "I think Duchess would look divine tied to that pole and taking a scourging from you. I bet she has plenty of sins to atone for."

"And you think by insulting me you will tempt me into this game?"

"No, but I suspect tripling your wage will," he smarted.

Stella's mind was spinning with suspicion. Had he been planning to outwit her from their first meeting? Had he failed to coil his serpentine tail around Marlene and now set his sights on easier prey?

"What is your offer, altar boy?"

"Let's round it up to $3,000."

"I don't act alone. Go sit down." She swept Yvette by the hand and rounded the corner out of earshot of her emergent nemesis.

"$3,000!" Yvette exclaimed. "That's a lot of money. Let's go. I can do it no problem." She spoke rapid-fire, reading the hesitation on Stella's worried brow.

"Babe, I don't trust him. You see how he's laid the trap? It's a bait and switch."

"But I trust you! What can he do if you're tying me up? Plus, I love how you handle me." Yvette wrapped her hands around Stella's waist and pecked her on the lips, her breath heavy with vodka and nicotine.

"It *is* a lot of money..." Stella admitted.

"I know! We could go to Paris, book the penthouse suite at my favorite hotel. It's so decadent. They serve you chocolate and gold-dusted strawberries in the bath. It overlooks the Seine... Then we'll cruise the Riviera. I made friends in Monaco last summer..." As Yvette painted the al fresco watercolor of an enchanted lovers' getaway, Stella's mind wandered.

Her goal had been to dangle the Girl with the Dragon Tattoo over the dragon's mouth, catch Mr. X, make him wriggle and writhe, and ultimately satisfy his desire in some deviant manner. She had brought him this far with seeming success, but now she felt the clear inversion of power.

She wished she could fire up the Bat-Signal and conjure Marlene. Her desire for a conference with her estranged friend surprised her, but who else knew X as intimately and expertly as she? Not even Deb.

Stella returned to the living room with Yvette.

"Here are the rules," she said sternly. "I will perform this ceremony as you requested, but you will not participate. You will observe. That's it."

"I am your patron, so it's possible I will inject some small request here and there. Nothing unreasonable."

Stella hated him. He had her cornered for cash. He could surmise her net worth from the details she so willingly proffered—her small studio and her obvious fracture with Marlene. Of course, she needed the money. Like a sportsman mapping the backcountry trail of an untagged Merriam's elk, he had charted her path. He had tracked her migration. Soon enough, he gambled, her antlers would be mounted on his wall.

"You may request anything." Stella stepped closer and leaned in menacingly. "But I have the final say."

"Then it's only fair that I pay in full at the end of our session, but here is a generous deposit. Reach into my coat pocket, you'll find my wallet. Take the cash."

Stella opened the wallet and took the money from it. From her periphery, she could see Yvette beaming.

Stella was sweating profusely and needed to gather her wits, so she whispered to Yvette to hold down the fort while she galloped down the hallway. She closed the bathroom door behind her.

The face looking back at her in the mirror was weary. She wiped the perspiration from her upper lip then slumped onto the toilet, massaging the knot forming in her neck.

She finished and, opening the bathroom door, could hear a soundtrack on her captive's lips describing with horrifying precision the scene in the next room. The clanking of Yvette's rings against the metal piercing on his cock said it all.

Stella entered the room to find Yvette straddled across X. Their bodies were so entwined that neither of them could see her. She paused to watch the scene unfold. Mr. X, handcuffed in the chair, kissed Yvette tenderly along her neck. She responded with a giggle. He arrived at her breasts, then ran the stubble of his cheek along her cleavage. She inched forward and his face disappeared in her bosom.

Stella was cut by the betrayal. She did not know whom to hold accountable. Yvette was drunk; X was the devil. Who was taking advantage of whom?

The room was suddenly heavy. She felt the throb of a needle between her eyes blurring her vision.

She clopped loudly across the floor, stopping just behind Yvette. Stella and X locked into the dead stare of rival beasts.

"All the world's a stage, isn't it?" he said with a twisted smile.

"Yes, and all the men and women merely players. They have their exits and their entrances." *Don't try to upstage me with Shakespeare. I will Hamlet your ass back to hell.*

His face expanded with surprise at her literary prowess.

"Ah, baby, you're so smart," Yvette cooed in a half-lid stammer.

"Come here, my love." Stella took Yvette's hand and led her to the pole. They danced a few revolutions around it, Stella removing Yvette's stockings in a striptease.

However, Stella could hardly feign an ounce of passion. All the blood had drained out of her pretty face. Preoccupying her thoughts was the difficulty of tying Yvette for the "crucifixion." She had rehearsed the tie with Marco standing in for X, but the crossbar was much too high for the petite mademoiselle. With Yvette's wrists tied, she would not touch the floor. Stella paced the apartment looking for something on which she could stand. All she could find was a stiff shoe box. The whole charade was becoming more like an execution every minute.

Yvette was light enough so Stella tied her and began tracing her body with the tassels of a leather flogger. She gently struck her thighs and Yvette squirmed with delight.

"Ah, so much pleasure, but where is the pain? You obviously know how to use that thing," taunted Mr. X as he sat courtside.

Stella shot him a mean grimace. She was on his leash now. They both knew it.

"All in good time." Stella struck Yvette harder against the widest part of her thigh where she would feel the least amount of pain.

Yvette gasped. Stella searched her face for the safeword, but instead received a green light.

"Harder!" Mr. X yelled as if in the front row of the Colosseum, eager to feel the spray of some slave's blood across his sadistic cheeks. "This is a crucifixion, is it not?"

"That's hard enough," Stella shot back.

"Well, that is not at all what we agreed upon. This is child's play. Perhaps I should take over."

Now into his forties, he'd played every dungeon role from Los Angeles to Tokyo. He'd been the whore and the gimp and the daddy. He'd tapped every well, tried every position, slurped every oyster, and sabered every bottle of champagne. He was compulsive in his indulgence, pathological in his acquisition. He was a conquistador who'd made quite a life of colonizing every experience. In his submission, he was really only there to consume. Even on his knees he wasn't serving. He was taking and taking it all.

Mr. X stood, gesturing at the flogger in Stella's hand.

"No. Sit down!" Stella reprimanded sternly.

He obeyed and Stella reared the flogger higher, flinging it forcefully against Yvette's legs. Yvette slipped further into a stupor. Her head flopped like a ragdoll, her Star of David necklace bobbing between her breasts like a bad omen.

Stella traced a circle around the pole and began kissing the tops of Yvette's feet all the way up to her face.

"Baby, you OK?" Stella whispered.

"Yeah, yeah. I'm, *fiiine,*" she slurred.

"I'd like to see your little pet pay even more for her sins"—he put his handcuffed palms over his chest—"She's putty in your hands. Why not test the limits of your dominance over her?"

"She's not my submissive."

"Oh, but she is. You must know that."

Stella inhaled sharply.

"Oh, you *didn't* know that? How interesting." He wrangled his hands near his thigh and produced a pocket knife. "How about a bit of blood as penance? I'd like something to remember her by." X stood and moved swiftly towards Yvette. He nudged Stella to the side with his broad shoulders then raised his arms over Yvette's head. She looked up confused.

"What are you doing?" Stella asked, unable to conceal the terror rattling in her throat.

He smiled wickedly then sliced into the flesh of his thumb with the knife and let drop a flow of blood. It plopped onto Yvette's forehead between her eyes then ran down her nose to her open lips. She screamed.

"Fuck this." Stella stomped around to unlock his handcuffs, quickly to avoid any chance he might stab her with the open blade.

X had brought Stella to the very razor's edge she had designed for him. He loved to watch her betray herself. He loved to watch her plummet to the depths. He didn't feel beholden to consent. His soul was on some kind of fire and he enjoyed watching the flesh bubble up after someone got burned. It was precisely the double cross that thrilled him. In the end, it was his knuckles turning white around the throat of she who thought she'd come to choke him. What a sadist he truly was.

"Get the hell out of here," Stella snarled, grabbing his pants from the bed and lobbing them at him.

"Are you kidding? You know what this means, don't you?"

"Go now! Get the fuck out!"

He lurched towards her. "You're a very stupid woman." He waved the knife frightfully near her nose. In that moment, she wondered whether he might not kill them both. How stupid she had been. How hubristic.

"Don't think this is the last you'll hear from me!" he threatened, moving towards the door.

"If you don't leave right now, I'm calling the police!"

"As if I don't have them in my pocket too." He picked up his coat. "No need to embarrass yourself. I'm going."

She slammed the door behind him, locking it quickly. He pounded like a madman and shouted, "This isn't over!"

Stella ran to untie Yvette, removing her from the cross like a beloved sacrificial lamb on this day of the Christ.

"Babe, are you OK?" Stella asked, lowering her limp lover onto the bed.

Yvette wiped the blood off her face with the back of her hand, then began wildly scratching her body. Stella's eyes followed the violent stripes up and down her legs, now streaky with blood.

"Fuck. So scary," Yvette slurred, her eyes heavy. She retracted her arms and legs into the fetal position and with that, seemed to black out.

What have I done? A tear traced a path down Stella's cheek. She wanted to anoint the body of her belladonna with oil and wrap her in linen. She took her pulse and, convinced Yvette was just sleeping, climbed into bed, moving Yvette's head to a pillow and covering her with the blanket.

The whole place looked like a crime scene. With the curtains open, the street lights cast stippled shadows on the pole, which now stood as an ominous reminder of the penalty for excess. Like a phallic pagan altar, it mocked her until a deluge of exhaustion overtook her heavy mind and forced her to sleep.

But Stella soon awoke violently, bolting from her pillow like a Frankenstein. All the muscles in her calf were electrified into a monstrous, inextinguishable spasm. She grabbed her leg with both hands and attempted to soothe the anxious muscle but felt only the tightening of needles. Panting like a dog, she tried to quiet the triggered nerves.

Yvette startled. "What's wrong?"

"Charlie horse!" Even in her anguish, Stella was embarrassed to be seen in such a state.

Suddenly released from the vice grip of her cramp, Stella fell back on her pillow like an epileptic. Her body like lead. Her mind glutted with guilt. How had she arrived here? Perhaps everyone was right about her after all.

The cult: *You're a whore.*

Marlene: *You're a poser.*

Marco: *You're a pimp.*

X: *You're an amateur.*

And what must Yvette think of me? Stella wondered. *Will she ever forgive me for this?*

Stella had become the thing they had all warned against: "A dog returning to its vomit."

*****

Stella flopped over to find the bed space next to her empty. How had she not heard Yvette leave? Yvette's pillow was stained with blood and she had dropped her cigarettes on the way out. Stella held up her phone expectantly. No texts. She rang Yvette, but there was no answer.

Sitting up, she was confronted by a studio strewn with reminders of the previous night's debacle. She felt as though she had been dropped to the bottom of the ocean with a millstone around her neck. The deep regret in the pit of her stomach told her none of it was worth it. The sun doesn't shine the morning after a crucifixion. She half expected the earth to shake this dark day.

With her insides contorting like a balloon animal, she forced herself out of bed and to the toilet. Her stomach rumbled and her bowels let loose a putrid soup. She filled the bathtub and took a soak so long that her fingers and toes turned to raisins.

Her head in a fog, she stepped out of the tub and toweled off. And just for a moment, she swore she saw in the steam of the mirror the grimacing face of Mr. X.

CHAPTER 27

Ground Zero

"SHIT, STELLA. You look... awful."

"Thanks Marco," she said, closing the front door behind him.

"No, I didn't mean it that way. Just guessing the session didn't go so well." He glanced around the disheveled room. Candle wax and dried blood stained the floor, the pole was greasy with fingerprints, and on Stella's nightstand, the cash bore the distasteful truth of the crucifixion crucible.

"Disaster, as everyone predicted. But I need help with something else. We're paid up for the week, right?"

"Yeah, I got the deposit. But look, I can't break into the penthouse like you asked. I got priors. Can't risk it," Marco said, removing his Dodgers cap and smoothing the thin wisps of his dark brown hair.

"But it's my apartment."

"If I bust through the door and she's in there, then what?"

"Throw her out the window like Jezebel." Stella laughed. Marco did not. "OK, OK, I'm kidding."

"Not sure you are. You two are really at war, aren't you? And where's your girl Yvette?" Marco scanned the room for evidence of her presence.

"She kinda took off without saying goodbye," Stella said with a sigh.

"I hope you don't mind me saying, Stella, but you sure have a type."

"Are you comparing Yvette to Marlene?"

"Think about it." Marco moved to the couch and patted the cushion next to him.

Stella sat as Marco directed, but her head throbbed. Her bowels were still nasty. She couldn't focus.

"What you call dominance, I call narcissism. Believe me, I've been around the block. Been with a lot of women... You can't seem to get enough of the femme fatale."

From the lips of another man, this speech would smack of arrogance, but as she sat bare-faced, raccoon-eyed, and soulless, she sensed the brotherly concern in Marco's tone. He was right and she knew it in her gut. Marlene suffered from a grandiosity that bordered on sociopathy though it was the very thing that attracted her.

"Yvette has been a friend though... more than a friend."

"Stella, it's like she walked into a casting call to read for the part of the narcissist." Marco pantomimed holding up a script. "That's why she's gone. There's nothing left for her here. She took all she could. Same with Marlene, though she's more determined than most."

Stella's head sloshed with the weight of Marco's revelations. Were they true? Yvette was indeed an avatar of desire. Her fine art was in her creation of a mirage. She was a master of reflection, a blank page. She begged to be written on with fine ink. She splayed the white parchment of her empty pages so willingly that Stella couldn't refuse the offer.

"I haven't heard from Yvette *yet,* but I'm sure we will work it out."

"That's just it. These women don't want confrontation. They don't want to be exposed. That's why they both slipped out the back door."

"But I'm the one who fucked up last night."

"Yeah, and friends are there for each other when they fuck up."

Stella felt defensive. She didn't want to think of Yvette as a creature as vile as Marlene.

"I didn't even pay her! Don't you think she'll come back for that?"

"Count the cash, Stella. That doesn't look like three large." Marco nodded to the stack of bills on the table.

"Yvette is not a thief."

Stella's pulse quickened to a surprising pace as she thumbed through the hundred-dollar bills. She didn't have to say another word. Marco knew.

"How much is missing?"

"A thousand," Stella admitted dejectedly. "But maybe X took it."

"You want my advice, Stella?" Marco stood and paced for a moment, looking intently at the pole.

"Burn some sage or, hell, just burn it down." The softness of his brow communicated both his pity and concern. "And start fresh. You're a strong woman. You left a cult..."

"But it's like I got sucked into a new one."

"I wasn't going to put it that way."

"You don't have to. It's true," she sighed.

Marco spent the morning removing the pole and helping Stella clean up, and while he couldn't get involved in her scheme to break into the penthouse, just as soon as he left, she noticed a small leather pouch on the table next to the front door. She opened it to find a set of squiggly metal picks, some pliers, and a vice.

Several YouTube tutorials later, she was ready for Operation Overthrow.

She first surveyed the garage to make sure Marlene's car was not there. Then she crept up to the ninth floor to perform what would be her first instance of breaking and entering... *her own damn apartment.*

Her stomach had migrated high to her chest as she cautiously ascended to the top-floor landing. She figured she'd have better luck picking the lock of the fire door near the kitchen than the front door. It was the very passage through which she and Marlene had narrowly escaped the cops a few months earlier.

She pressed her ear to the old wood. Silence. Her hands trembled, making the handling of the tools precarious, but to her surprise, she successfully picked the lock within a few suspenseful minutes.

She shut the door quietly behind her and froze like a statue, measuring the relative stillness of the room. Was that a trash truck or someone stirring in the bathroom? Why was she so terrified of a confrontation? *It's my apartment, dammit. I have every right to be here!*

Within seconds, the pungent scent of Marlene's perfume swelled in her sinuses. She wondered if she too had been trained on those seductive tones. It both unsettled and enticed her.

Everything in the penthouse had been artfully arranged, as was Marlene's custom. Not a single piece of plastic in sight. She preferred old things layered in the patina chi of their previous incarnations. She considered shopping at the mall an unforgivable crime. She said it reeked of baby diapers, Cinnabon, and doom.

Stella tiptoed through the living room to find it outfitted with Marlene's boudoir box and several collectibles from her Asia travels. Despite Marlene's insistence on owning only things her fingers first touched, these were the kind of tchotchkes every hippie crystal chick in LA possessed, from a singing bowl to a gold-embossed gong. There were fresh flowers on every table, bestowals of gratitude from Hope and Houseboy and God knows whom else.

By the time Stella got to the bedroom, her mood was interminably busted. Marlene's queen-sized bed filled the room. There were more flowers. Her dinosaur of a laptop sat open and vulnerable on the nightstand, like a lone soldier abandoned by his troop. Stella hastily clacked at the keyboard.

"Dammit!" It was password-protected. She tried every smug combination of phrases she could recall Marlene uttering until, frustrated and boiling with anger, she smashed over the keyboard with the phrase: "Stupid fucking bitch."

Her last mission was to locate the house keys. She rifled through every drawer and closet, but they were nowhere to be found. Marlene's extensive collection of vintage dresses, shoes, and accessories filled every inch of the closets. Stella stopped to admire a '50s lucite clutch she had always coveted.

She hadn't much of a plan other than to assert her ownership of the penthouse in some forceful way and, if she did run into Marlene, she had an entire speech prepared. It was an oration of Gettysburg proportions. Or so she thought, for no longer than 15 minutes into her inspection did she hear the turn of a key in the lock and instead of assuredness, she was overcome with dread.

Unfortunately, there was no crawl space under the bed. With Marlene stomping down the hall, the only place to hide was behind a curtain like some silly villain in a heist movie.

Marlene plopped onto the bed and the intensity of her perfume filled Stella's nostrils once again. Would she notice that the laptop had been moved?

Stella heard the buzz of Marlene's phone.

"Yes, I got them. Delivered today. You did well. Mmhm. But I want that ass plugged when you pick me up."

Marlene ended the call and left the room. Stella could hear the faucet go on and the shower door close. This was her chance to escape.

She tiptoed past the bathroom, hoping Marlene wouldn't see her through the translucent door. She slid through the hallway like a stealth ninja and made it to the safety of the foyer. Marlene's purse sat open on the entryway table. She rummaged through it madly and found the house keys.

"What is this?" She pulled out a silver packet of pills labeled by day, a week of which were missing. Why would Marlene be on birth control? She had always made such a fuss of the gravity of "fluid bonding," insisting she hadn't consented to it in years.

Just as Stella was turning to leave, she noticed a small, white card tucked into the floral bouquet sitting pretty on the table. She opened it to find a neatly handwritten note.

I may not be your Messiah but you're my Aphrodite - XOXO X

Stella's chest tightened and her mouth went dry. *The birth control. The flowers. The card.* Marlene was fucking someone. All signs pointed to it. Was the last X in "XOXO X" a name? *The* name? Mr. X?!

Stella dug through Marlene's cavernous bag for clues and drew out a black felt box. She opened it to find a purple drawstring bag labeled, "Betony Vernon," Marlene's favorite jewelry designer. Inside, a gold bracelet and ring set glittered brightly. She had spoken often about Vernon's one-of-a-kind erotic jewelry. These pieces were luxury items and far out of reach on a bartender's budget.

Back in her apartment, all the muscles in Stella's neck twitched. She poured a small glass of mezcal on ice and squeezed in a dash of lime.

She pulled up Betony Vernon's website and boldly displayed across the top of the page was the bracelet. Out of production and now considered rare, the piece was being sold for $15,000. The gift had to be from Mr. X! There was no other explanation. How had she been so stupid? The bare threads of her ex-cult naivete had shown through like a bad toupée. She had somehow played right into the hands of a duo of diabolical masterminds.

Oddly, at that moment, she wanted her mom. She needed to hear a friendly voice and the impartial nurturing that only her mother could provide.

It was unlikely her mother would pick up. Stella's exodus from the cult guaranteed that her mom would feel a tremendous sense of guilt taking the call.

Stella dialed anyway. "Mom, I'm just going to leave a message because..." She could barely get the words out for the sadness welling up in her throat. "I miss you. You know I had to leave, but I'm still your daughter and you're still my mom." She ended the call before the dam burst uncontrollably and she felt a ripple of disappointment erupt through her entire body.

But then her mother texted. "Stella, I miss you too, but the elders don't think your influence on me is good. We aren't supposed to talk. I wish it wasn't this way. I will always love you. Please quit this sinful life and return to Jehovah."

Stella flopped down on the floor under a wave of grief like a tsunami. Burying her head in her arms, she wailed like a sick animal. Her face smeared with snot and mascara, her hair matted to her cheeks and soaked through with tears, she laid prostrate on the floor until she choked out the last gasp of plaintive pain.

Her mother was dead to her and she to her mother. Perhaps her mother had started grieving the moment Stella hopped on that plane to LA.

She wept not just for the loss of her mother from her life, but for the fact that her mother was still trapped in the confines of a cult. She hadn't been able to save her from any of the abusive systems Stella herself had escaped. She cried for the entirety of her mother's lost life. She wailed for the sadness she saw in her eyes for many decades. She grieved for her grandmother's pain, the kind of suffering she must've experienced in her abuse of her only daughter. A well of transgenerational shame sloshed through Stella with such force she felt motion sick from it all.

She could not throw her mother a line and certainly not her dead and gone grandmother.

But she had saved herself.

And with that thought, a barbiturate calm overtook her. She closed her eyes and felt herself floating above her body.

The room was silent save for the sounds of a neighbor's hissing water pipe and the faint caw of a crow. Dusk crept up the walls in a grim timelapse while an aching chill permeated her legs and spine. She remained paralyzed until her bladder threatened to burst.

Stella dragged herself to the toilet. Perching down on the porcelain, she became fixated on the chipped red polish on her big toe. She slid onto the chilled tile floor. Full of self-pity, she drew her knees into her arms and began rocking like a child. But then the "otherness" came over her again like a cloak. She seemed to leave her body again. Her arms and legs felt foreign.

I am who I am seeking.

She could hear the refrain in her head.

I am who I am seeking.

I am who I am seeking.

I am who I am seeking.

It wouldn't stop. She gasped for air as if she had been baptized in the deep. With a Pentecostal exhalation, she screamed.

"Fuck you, God! Fuck you, motherfucking fuck!"

The air rushed through her lungs again. "*I am* who I am seeking!"

The coagulation of grief and pain overtook her like an exorcism. She rocked in the safety and embrace of her own arms, squeezing tighter. *I have me. I have me. It's been me all along!*

It was a deeply reassuring thought. She could scoop heaping mounds of strength from her internal well of solace whenever she needed. She had no need for Jehovah anymore! Certainly not as a moralistic executioner. She was her own Shiva, a warrior of a child fending off the violence of a grown man, steadying herself against the twin threats of family dysfunction and teenage temptation. She had been a straight-A student, an anxious overachiever, but mostly a warrior. Always doing some kind of battle. Always prevailing in the end.

Her spiritual awakening as an atheist was complete. Reborn from the depths of imposed cultic monotheism was a woman in possession of the strength she had known all her life. Christianity had forced the stout muscles of her intuitive power to atrophy, but it was in her nature all along. She *was* an alpha. She could be a successful Domme.

* * * * *

Stella charged upstairs. "Marlene, come out!" She banged on the penthouse door. "I'm not asking anymore. I'm telling you."

The flesh on her inner arm stung. She ran her fingers along the inflamed skin above her wrist. Her first tattoo had been inked on a whim just an hour earlier. Finely scripted in cursive, it read: "I am who I am seeking."

"Marlene!" She struck the door again.

She slid her key into the lock and entered. Her eyes flashed about restlessly. She rushed to the bedroom. Marlene's laptop was gone, but in its place was a card from Mr. X. It was filled with cash. She counted it. *100, 200, 300...* She shoved $1,000 into her pocket.

She flew into the dressing room. She grabbed a pair of scissors and hacked into Marlene's precious stockings. Then her lingerie. She went at it with the fury of Edward Scissorhands, possessed by a vengeful terror that grew with each snap of the blades.

She moved swiftly to the living room and swung open the windows. She grabbed Marlene's yoga mat and tossed it out the window. And then her pillows. *Hell, why stop there?* She had given Marlene every chance to do right by her.

Her hands were anointed with fresh madness at the disposal of each of a dozen idiotic tchotchkes. A blinding flash of white passion filled her cantankerous limbs as she bound around the room on a determined path of war. She stopped when her eyes landed on Marlene's beloved boudoir box. Her conscience cautioned her, but was it the old cult dogma being stirred or a more contemporary need to heel?

"Stella! What the fuck?" A voice screamed from the street below.

Stella's heart galloped like a racehorse all the way up to her throat. It was *her.*

She pushed her back against the wall and peeked out the window surreptitiously. Why was she suddenly so afraid?

Marlene stomped along the sidewalk retrieving her precious possessions. A discarded dildo had landed comically suctioned to the window of a Ford Probe, its accompanying strap-on harness strewn across the hood like an unhooked bra.

"You fucking bitch!" Marlene screamed, looking up.

Swelling with adrenaline, Stella raced downstairs to the lobby. Through the glass of the front door, vaguely distorted in the warp of the antique window, Marlene looked like a different person. In this new excoriating light, Stella found her to be such a strange creature, a specter, some cult of personality that seemed so exaggerated as to be a figment of her imagination. She felt the anger seething out of Marlene's pores like the stench of a carcass.

"Go ahead," Stella challenged. "Step one foot inside here and those keys are mine. The police will be notified of a thief and a trespasser."

Marlene paused, her jaw squared haughtily and her nostrils flaring with egotism. Both their countenances went tense and twitching, all their inner gaskets blaring like car alarms after an earthquake. The strained silence now hanging between them screamed into both their skulls the gravity of this standoff.

Stella pumped her eyebrows with victory. "You're finished. Now get back to your shitty popcorn ceilings where you belong."

"Who do you think you are?" Marlene grumbled, sliding her key in the lock defiantly.

Stella looked on with disbelief as Marlene tried to pull open the door.

"No!" Stella clenched the door handle with all her strength, leaning back on her heels.

"Get out of my way!" Marlene ordered as she wrapped her arm through the door handle. "Fucking Baby Domme syndrome rearing its ugly head!"

"*Baby Domme?* You think you're some kind of high priestess worthy of worship? You're the most childish, unethical, narcissistic Domme I've ever met! You cheat and lie and swindle everyone in your life."

"Oh, go to hell, Stella. You're so naive. Good luck learning how the world works."

"And good luck finding another Domme to do the work you're too lazy to do."

"Just give me my stuff. I've been done with you for ages."

"Your shit will be on the curb tomorrow. Now leave those keys and get the hell out of here before I call the cops."

CHAPTER 28

La Serenissima

"THERE'S NOTHING more traumatic than being born and here you've done it two times in a year," Deb said, reaching across the passenger's seat to hand Stella her bag. An airport traffic officer waved at her furiously to move her Jeep forward. "OK, OK. Geez. Give a girl a minute. She's off to conquer the motherfucking world!"

"Deb, you're the best," Stella said. She could not help tearing up as she swung her leather backpack onto her shoulder. "I don't know what I would've done without you and Marco these past few months. I feel like such a fuck up."

"Aw, kid. You're not a fuck up. The way you stood up to Marlene. Pow bang!" Deb punched the air dramatically. "And she just left?"

"Yeah, I think the bitch is finally gone for good. Such a fucking dramanatrix."

Deb chuckled. "The puns never stop. That's what I love about you. Always picking yourself up. You're a woman on fire! Take Venice by the balls. Enjoy the party. Reel in some new clients. And eat a bunch of cannolis for me, would ya?"

Stella tried to smile but felt her face crumpling like a raisin.

"Don't make me cry. Keep your chin up!" Deb yelled from the car as she inched away.

"Love you! Call you when I land," Stella yelled back.

What Deb said was true. Death was an exhale and a release from struggle, but with birth comes a set of tiny, new lungs that must learn how to expand or cease to exist.

Call it escapism but traveling to a foreign land had helped Stella to reset many times in the past two decades of her tumultuous life. Every emotional rupture had a geographic answer. Breakup? Jamaica. Breakdown? Land Down Under. Divorce? New start in New Orleans.

* * * * *

Venice was a cacophony. It was Carnival, after all. With Stella's Sicilian roots, it was a strange omission that she had never been to Italy. She had sailed down a river in Borneo to see wild orangutans, but she had not stepped foot on the Motherland. Her mother would have been proud had she not been there for a pagan holiday so steeped in hedonism it was a wonder the Catholic church ever sanctioned it.

Venice became her Mecca when she learned that Madame Veronica's next international shibari party would be staged there. Veronica was a wunderkind of rope bondage—trained in Kyoto, globe-trotting to all ends of the Earth—and a personal icon of Stella's imagination. She was everything Marlene claimed to be but was not—a shibari master, a performer, and a community organizer.

Deb pointed her in the direction of a new mentor much like a mother steers a toddler across several lanes of traffic onto the safety of a sidewalk. "Go to Venice. See Veronica perform. This is who I think you've been looking for."

Veronica's intimate rope performances were held in the most opulent salons and palazzos everywhere from Paris to Vienna, but she exhibited most often in Italy. Her "Carnival Bacchanalia" was one of her signature events and it promised to be kinktastic.

However, Stella was still days from the promised glamour and was instead schlepping a 52-pound bag over bridge after ancient bridge. She had packed too much and slept too little, but the promise of a plush canal-view room spurred her on towards the finish line.

She opened the door to her hotel suite and sighed. The walls were brocade in scarlet and gold and every mirror frame, sconce, and piece of furniture was curvilinear and gilded to the gills. It reminded Stella of her grandmother's Sicilian salon.

The suite had the perfect balcony on which to perch and people-watch. The Ponte delle Guglie bridge stretched across the Cannaregio Canal some 50 feet away. She was in the thick of it, the surrounds noisy with the honking of boat horns and the chatter of tourists. She swung open a set of french doors two stories above the bustle of the street. She sat and studied a bee sucking nectar from the daisies in planters along the rail. It reminded her of Marlene and, she was sad to say, so many things did. The bee drew long gulps of the sweetness of the flower with its proboscis, so expert at extracting the gold. Had Marlene not been the same in her methods of mining human souls?

There was nothing left of Stella's rage after her final confrontation with Marlene. She expected to feel victorious, but as she walked through the nearly empty penthouse, she felt gutted, as if a tumor had been extracted from her flesh and she was still hazy from the anesthesia. The throb of a phantom limb stuck with her still.

Exhausted but hungry, Stella hit the streets. She turned into a narrow passage and imagined what it must have been like traversing these pathways in the Venetian heyday. It was called "La Serenissima" after all. The pastel buildings were weathered and imperfect, truly ancient, like a dollhouse cobbled from scraps.

A mustachioed man blew a nasty puff of cigarette smoke in her face as he brushed by her. Venice was a symphony of smells. The fishy brine. The odor of diesel. And food. Always food. The bakeries were the most pungent of all. Yeast and chocolate and sugar wafting up from the brick ovens to the heavens. An inexorable bliss.

She wandered through St. Mark's Square where couples in elaborate Carnival costumes strolled hand in hand, smiling at themselves, soaking up all the adoration from tourists who whipped out their phones to take hurried videos as if these mythical creatures would soon vanish from the mortal plane.

Stella settled into an iconic café with its stained-glass storefront and hand-painted panels of exotic figures from the 1700s. Taking a thick pinch of bread in hand, she sopped up oil and balsamic and piled it high with fresh tuna tartare. The aromatic basil hit her tongue first, while the silk of the oil commingled with the sugary vinegar. It was divine. As she twisted the spaghetti alle vongole onto her fork, she was reminded of her childhood where fresh clams were substituted for canned ones in the absence of greater wealth to buy such a luxury.

She pulled out a postcard and contemplated how to address her mother. Stella knew that her mother's only daughter giving herself over to the "dark side" could very well be some final straw in her swollen case file that the battle of Armageddon was nigh. Of all the whores coming in on the beast of Babylon, there was her precious baby, in full Hi-ho Silver, dressed in scarlet from head to toe. But Stella missed her anyway.

As she slurped the noodles, the lemony broth splattered pleasantly on her lips and made things seem right in the world, so she made the note short and sweet: "I've finally made it to the Motherland and my mother should know how much I love her. Unconditionally. Wish you were here."

The unfolding night beckoned her. She languished on the bustling streets, watching the old Italians greet one another and chat endlessly. She loved how they would burst into melody, increasing their volume through the Venetian alleys, using the acoustic chambers to amplify their screeds and songs. Even the Italian children were commanding with their husky tones, seemingly designed for much larger bodies than their shaggy bobbleheads held. The most vivid expressions of her divaness grayed out by the cult, she was drawn to the anarchical racket of the Italians.

The next morning, Stella stood with a dozen locals and tourists at a walk-up patisserie and ate what would become her daily breakfast—a Venetian frittelle, a chewy ball of fried dough dusted with crunchy sugar.

At precisely three o'clock, she arrived at Veronica's apartment. Veronica greeted her at the door with a tepid smile. She had perfected that devil-may-care nonchalance so fashionable among the French in the '90s in her oversized fur coat, black turtleneck, velvet trousers, and black combat boots similar to the ones Stella wore. Veronica spoke less than three words as she led her up a flight of stairs. Were they both nervous? Why did she not welcome Stella more warmly?

They entered an apartment bathed in light so sensuous it would have made Rembrandt swoon. They sat down on the couch and Veronica said nothing. Stella studied her entrancing face. She wore thick winged eyeliner, red lips, and had the even cocoa skin of a Gauguin. She had a thin tattoo that curled like ivy from somewhere on her back up to her ear. Her bobbed poker straight hair was shaved at the neck and rendered her a fembot Louise Brooks. When standing near Stella, one could almost hear the shotgun blast set forth the Battle of the Bettie Page Bangs.

Stella filled the awkward silence with a bit of self-deprecation. "I'm a total rope novice. Please start from the beginning."

A blonde in a colorful robe glided into the room as if her tippy toes were high heels. "Hello. Would you like me nude or clothed?"

"This is Barbie," Veronica introduced. "Barbie, Stella."

"Oh, nude if you're offering," Stella replied.

"Yes, soooo much better to make contact with the skin," said Barbie with the lilting, sugary voice of a tween.

Barbie dropped her robe and shrugged her bare shoulders sweetly. She was adorable, petite, and pale, her straw blonde hair styled in spongy vintage waves. The puncture of her raspberry lips made for the perfect little pinup.

As Veronica began to twist her rope around the nubile woman—her quick work sending jute in the air like fallen ash—Barbie giggled and tipped her head down, eyeing Veronica seductively.

"Are you trying to turn me on?" Veronica smiled wickedly.

"Maybe," Barbie replied with a flutter of her eyelashes.

The intimacy—the three of them in that romantic private room, the charming naked woman, the supple female hands that would touch her everywhere—initially suffered a bit under the weight of its immediacy, but the ice was melting.

Barbie was so eager to be taken. They were clearly not partners, but had they made love? All of Veronica's online imagery was of half-nude women in sorcerous salons, manicured gardens, and tufted beds. It was all so homoerotic, but was it real?

Veronica began the lesson by coiling Barbie's calves with rope and soon she was splayed like a frog, her legs bound, and her fleshy petals open and illuminated by a sheath of afternoon sun. Stella stroked Barbie's silken hair and waited her turn to tie the other leg. Veronica dragged the rope sensually across Barbie's strawberry blonde bush then grabbed a Carnival hat and began tickling her with the feather plume. Barbie giggled and writhed in the bounds of her tied wrists, her arms pressed against her full breasts, flattened like saucers of milk against the narrow slats of her rib cage.

Veronica instructed Stella on how to tie Barbie in a futomomo, inspecting it with praise. "You're a natural."

Stella smiled inwardly.

"Now pull it over her breasts. Wrap it. Go under," said Veronica, grazing Barbie's nipples and handing Stella the rope again. Barbie's senses were wide open to pleasure; her spine lengthening an inch at the sensation. It sent a charge through Stella's core.

Veronica then attached the rope to the ottoman at all four corners. She dragged the jute across her model's body and up and over her neck. Veronica pressed her closed fist deep into Barbie's pubic bone and the bound woman's head bent in submission. Another groan. Louder. She pulled the rope tighter around her victim's neck. Her sensual constriction lasted but a few seconds, however, when she released her, the muse gasped heavenward and did seem to go there, her body jolting with a spasm of ecstasy. A quick release sent her back down to earth and with a sigh, she smiled and proclaimed, "That was just like being on acid."

"Subspace," Veronica replied knowingly.

God, she is fierce.

Veronica loosened the ropes around the bench, pulled Barbie up by her leash, and pressed her knee to Barbie's hip.

"I love to use my body in impact play," she said as Barbie's torso slid with ease into an upright position. Veronica had an androgynous quality in the muscles of her neck, hands, and thighs. The way she moved with such grace and confidence drew Stella to her.

"More commanding."

"And more sensual."

Are we finally connecting? Stella wondered with hope.

"I bet you're a fun Domme," Barbie flirted as she reluctantly stood and donned her robe.

"Yes, I try to be," Stella replied modestly in deference to Veronica.

The lesson was complete, and the awkwardness between her and Veronica had faded only in the moments when they tied together. Soon the other two women were gabbing about boys and crushes and it seemed very vanilla given the heady kink into which they had just waded. Veronica walked Stella out, flicking open her lighter for a cigarette. She propped herself against the door frame in a one-word farewell as aloof as the welcome.

It was not until she rounded the corner out of Veronica's sight that Stella was moved to poetry by the event. The aftertaste of the eroticism hit her suddenly and stayed with her all afternoon. Barbie's wide open legs. Her thirst to be touched by the women. Her alabaster skin. That light!

* * * * *

Stella adjusted her pasties, admiring herself in a floor-length mirror. She wore her favorite evening gown, a balloon-sleeved black crepe that hugged her curves and draped low on her back. It was witchy. Her nipples were bedazzled in heart-shaped sequins with black tassels that swung with the switch of her hips, should they peek out from the deep V neckline. She snapped closed Marlene's lucite clutch lifted from the penthouse. *Just desserts,* she thought.

The toll of bells haunted the air as she traipsed starkly alone down the streets. The width of her dramatic boat-shaped hat scraped the walls of narrow alleys. She hoisted the hem of her Morticia dress around bends and over bridges, her teal silk cape flapping behind her.

From somewhere up ahead, the insistence of bongos mingled with the sound of her heels on the cobblestone. She followed the beat until she arrived in a square.

Silhouettes danced on the facade of a patina building, light cast from below illuminating the revelry of partygoers in a drum circle. It reminded her of Mardi Gras, where street musicians magnetized crowds in unsuspecting corners of the city. A brightness surged through her. This was the Carnival she had hoped for. It wasn't some external event or feeling that would grab her. It was there inside her waiting to be awakened. Her new life was more and more rife with moments of pure joy such as this.

She filmed the cinematic circle and let the spirit of Carnival wash over her before continuing her journey. Flying right by, Stella retreated a few steps to a nondescript wood door with red fog seeping ominously out. She pushed on it tentatively. *This must be it.*

She entered to find three large rooms with crumbling stone walls nearly empty save for a DJ booth. Stella sashayed past the makeshift bar, her dress quickly turning chalk white from the dusty floor. The industrial aesthetic was far from the opulent palazzo she had imagined.

She perched in a corner and scanned the crowd of twentysomethings in Carnival-cum-kink creations. Just as that little devil on her shoulder went full sartorial critic, an arresting trill of operatic sounds echoed through the room. A beautiful black woman in a fishtail gown floated in. A short Italian man sawed passionately on a violin behind her. The room fell silent.

Veronica sauntered towards a large metal ring dangling from a rope in the center of the room. From another corner, a waifish blonde in Rococo bustles moved towards her as if drawn by an invisible force. The beat of a haunting chant rocked the room under the rising soprano.

The audience formed a circle. Veronica took the model's shoulders in her hands and presented her as if she were a prized pet. She removed the blonde's feathered hat and pearl choker, dragging it sensually across her breast. Stella's desire to assist pinged like a bell as she saw Veronica place the accessories awkwardly on the floor. Where was the manservant to collect such things?

Veronica took the strings of her model's corset in her hands as if they were reins. In slow motion, she removed the corset to reveal a pair of rock-hard breasts sealed like metal bolts onto her willowy frame. She stood nude save for the delicate lace of her panties and the plume of a blush-colored feather in her hair. Veronica whispered into the model's ear and she nodded. Stella felt kindred with Veronica in that consent-seeking moment.

Veronica removed the woman's mask and began tying her wrists. The violin strings became an ominous strike against the red glow of the room. The music was choreographed in time with the rapid movements of her rope, building in a hypnotic crescendo until the lilting soprano burst forth in a climactic top note and Veronica swiftly hoisted the model into the air. The lungs of the room gasped. Veronica swung her around coyly, teasing her for quite a while before beginning to unloose her.

"Where are you from?" a tall man in a tux asked, approaching Stella from the back.

"Los Angeles," Stella replied, taking in the length of his lanky frame from his curly black crown to his shiny shoes.

"You came all this way just for the party?"

"And for Carnival. And where are you from?"

He handed her a flute of prosecco. "I come from Milano."

Stella entertained him. He was chatty and looked like a young John Turturro. Not particularly attractive, but a man needn't be for her to want to grip his neck with one hand and bend him over her knee with the other.

The free flow of alcohol greatly improved the conviviality of the crowd, for soon Veronica consorted giddily with her guests. A sort of conga line formed behind her as she motioned for everyone to follow her outside. John Turturro Jr. fell in line by Stella's side and, in an instant, she sensed his desire to serve.

By the hour of 11, the streets were noisy and crowded and Veronica's procession was as rowdy as a college rugby team. As the cool night air blew against her cheek, three Napoleons skirted by, billowing Stella's cape wildly. Captivated by the buoyancy of her breasts as they threatened to escape the safety of her gown, the last of the trio retreated to flash a million-watt smile and introduce himself.

"Enchanté. French?" The handsome boy took Stella's hand in his and leaned down to kiss it but paused with his lips just inches from her knuckles. His big brown eyes beseeched her consent.

"Sicilian. American," Stella replied with a smile.

He was adorable. Korean, perhaps of mixed heritage. His thick black hair was parted in the middle like some '90s heartthrob. He had a broad smile and bone-white teeth. Baby soft skin shaved close. She nodded and let his lips do what was natural—worship.

"Ah, Sicilian. Then I feel I must keep you close, you know, that saying about enemies and all."

"And what makes you think we might be enemies?"

"I wouldn't want to cross you."

"Napoleon was not known for his loyalty." She gestured to his attire, a French military costume, and rang like chimes the fringe of his gold epaulets. "There are three of you, so I must watch my back."

"I suspect you could handle more."

"Then you already have a strong sense of me."

"I'd like to have a stronger one."

"Come with us."

Stella smiled and took the man's arm as they climbed a narrow staircase. It opened into an opulent 17th-century drawing room. Here was the promised palazzo. Countless tapestried rooms branched off like arteries. They moved towards the great room where a 16-seat dining table stretched out underneath a pastel-painted ceiling. A chandelier cast diamonds of light on Barbie's translucent skin as she reclined on the table like a Christmas feast. She was naked—the tuft of her bush peeking out from her crossed legs—save for a red satin mask and matching peep-toe heels. The guests jockeyed for a view and soon all the seats were taken as if a game of musical chairs had silently commenced.

Veronica stepped onto the table and lifted Barbie to her feet. Barbie beamed. She was a candy cane, all sticky and sweet, the perfect foil to Veronica's cool, dark dominance. Veronica pulled her rope across every inch of Barbie's effervescent flesh, stopping to tease her pert nipples and smize into the crowd. As she took in the scene, Stella flushed with delight at the Rococo fresco above their heads, the dream of living inside a Sofia Coppola film, all these nubile Antoinettes, and by her side several doting Napoleons.

"Tell me your name," Stella directed the first boy.

"Bae. It means 'inspiration' in Korean." He pulled his two friends closer. They had been waiting with anticipation. "This is Emmanuel and Allistair."

"Aren't you all prestigious with these names and this regalia? A trio of conquering lovers set loose to capture a few fair maidens."

Emmanuel, with his prematurely receding hairline and pleading heather eyes, spoke up nervously. "None of these maidens hold a candle. I just want to know how to capture you."

Stella pinched the stubble of his pink cheek. He was twee, sad, and wanting. "So, you're looking for someone to hold your candle, eh?"

They all burst into laughter. Turturro, who had been watching in the wings, moved into the circle and introduced himself. No one bothered to catalog his name.

"So, how do you boys know one another?"

"University," Emmanuel answered. "London."

"An international brat pack. How fun this could be." She scanned the four hungry faces.

"Brat pack?" Bae's confusion made bare the fact that they were all too young to get the reference.

"I'm old enough to be your mother, you know," Stella said, internally acknowledging that was a brazen way to fish for compliments, of which they proffered more in haste.

Bae smiled wide, moving a few inches closer. He looked like the captain of the lacrosse team. In her basest vanilla desires, he was the clear victor should it come down to an old-fashioned romp in the hay.

"You're all doing so well controlling your desperate little fingers. You want to touch, don't you?" she continued.

They nodded eagerly, their springboard necks like puppy tails. Stella was in such familiar territory with these young bucks. She had to admit she had not outgrown such guilty pleasures yet. In fact, she was growing into the maternal urge to guide them. For such a tried-and-true taboo, she was shocked at how playing the cougar, the MILF, the mommy came so unconsciously, like a language she had known all along.

Veronica too had clearly honed her mommy dominance at a young age. Two delightfully fey boys showing out in full gowns and heels orbited around her affectionately, a mother hen and her chicks.

"What do you want to do to us?" Allistair inquired, the most desperate of the puppies for play. He would not likely have the self-control to endure her tease and denial. However, Emmanuel's quiet appetite and Bae's sweet zeal enticed her. She had no particular feelings towards Turturro. He was less attractive than the others and, she suspected, a bit dark on the underside. Yet, he stayed and waited, as if for scraps from her table and for that she respected him.

Emmanuel regarded her quietly, but his silent aspiration needed no words. She knew he wanted to be taken.

"You look older than the rest."

"Really? I'm 25," Emmanuel replied with a thick Francophone accent.

"It's the smoking."

"How did you know?"

She took his chin between her fingers. "I can just tell. Why are you sad? It's a party. It's Carnival."

"I've never really known why. Maybe it's the culture. Mustn't disappoint my fellow countrymen." He tapped his chest where a bank of faux medals hung. He seemed to have a persistent malaise, a dogged smidgen of depression to keep him as predictably fatalistic as his French brethren.

Stella instructed the boys to line up on a grand sofa. "Are you ready for training?" She leaned over with an accusing finger, her back exposed and muscular in the wide-open dress which hugged the top of her ass.

"Yes, Mistress!" Bae brimmed with enthusiasm, so proud of himself for the formality of his address.

"Good boy. Now to learn communication and consent. Lord knows every man needs it." She could not help slipping first into her role as an headmistress before indulging in any sexual games.

She clapped her hands. "Communication. I ask a question, you reply. More importantly, you ask for permission for everything." She clapped again. *"Everything.* Do you understand?"

The boys replied in unison: "Yes, Mistress."

"If I want to slap you, which I very much want to do, I must seek consent."

Allistair raised his hand. "I give you permission. Please slap me."

"And there's the consent." She let fly a percussive slap across his cheek. He opened his eyes in pleasant shock, his mouth gaping with a mix of pleasure and pain.

"Who's next?"

They all raised their hands. From left to right, she stung each of their cheeks with the palm of her hand. They percolated with glee. She felt a current course through them, these four birds on her wire.

Stella had not noticed the audience forming around her until Veronica came closer.

"I'm so intrigued. What is happening here?" Veronica asked with a twinkle in her eye.

"Oh, would you like a go?" Stella stood and gestured towards the boys. "Someone just dropped off this entire litter of puppies and they need house training."

"I've got another performance, but carry on with your training. And boys, pay attention. This is a masterclass!" Veronica said before she strutted away.

Turturro stood up. "Mistress, with all due respect, I'm not comfortable being on camera." He gestured to a woman surreptitiously recording them with her phone.

"Yes, I understand," Stella said shooting the woman a disapproving glance. "We need a private space."

"My uncle has a boat," Emmanuel offered. "I can call him. We can go to his villa."

Within minutes, the Napoleons were carrying Stella through the streets of Venice like an Egyptian queen. It was glorious—the battered soles of her feet relieved, the firm hands of four strong men hoisting her in the air as if she were weightless. She rested her head on Bae's shoulder as they inched up the arch of a stone bridge. He was handsome in the glow of evening, his black hair shimmering silver in the moonlight and gold in the tungsten of the street lamps. She pecked him on the lips. He nearly stumbled. She rolled her head to the right to peer into Emmanuel's angsty eyes and tenderly kissed him. Before he could react, the boys were lowering her to the ground, inches from a speedboat idling in the viridian waters.

Emmanuel climbed in first, introducing everyone to his comically Italian uncle Guiseppe. He was almost a caricature, as if gondoliering lusty regiments through the post-midnight canals was his entire vocation.

They sped away into the dark, with Guiseppe rounding corners so tightly they were doused with water like it was Splash Mountain. The motor buzzed in their ears, the propellers painting a phosphorescent trail through the canal. Guiseppe slowed to orate with great pride the history of significant buildings and monuments as if any of his passengers were lucid enough to appreciate such details. The boys cuddled up to Stella to keep her warm in the drafty boat, draping her with a long fur coat. Her thrill at commanding a caboodle had been stoked to its highest degree.

Guiseppe eased the vessel up to a landing and the boys lifted their queen into the invisible divan of their arms, off the boat, and deposited her, not at the front door of the spacious marble villa, but inside on the plush top of a king-sized bed.

Stella laid back on the abundance of pillows and allowed herself a moment of rest from the fever pitch of their journey. Above her head hung a Bouguereau in a heavy gold frame. The Madonna and Child with skin as translucent as papyrus, both rung with halos, sitting on a stone bench with white lilies all around. The rest of the room was decorated in the same neoclassical style and, like Marlene would have, Stella appreciated the lack of modernity.

With her eyes closed, she sensed the boys watching her from the perimeter of the room, like performers waiting for their stage cues from the director. Her mind was a flood with motifs for the tableau. *Incest, religion, the Last Supper, but no, no—not a crucifixion.*

She rattled off a list of items for the boys to procure then turned to Turturro. She was embarrassed to have forgotten his name and curious as to why he wanted to play with these rapscallions. He was not an acquaintance of theirs.

"Who are you? Why are you here?" she asked.

"Mistress, I am here to serve you. My name is Gabriele."

Now that she reconsidered him, he was indeed more attractive than John Turturro.

"You are experienced, aren't you?"

He confirmed what she already knew.

"I was hoping to please you in some way. That's why I'm here. You are a great beauty, of course, but also elegant and wise. I found you more interesting than anyone at the party," he admitted. "I feel I could learn from you as well. I hope that is not too much."

"I will tell you if you're being verbose. So far, I sense openness, sincerity, submission. All good things, Gabriele. You are older than these boys, I suspect."

"Yes, I am 31."

Emmanuel and Bae returned with great clamor and produced all the household items Stella had requested with news that Allistair had blacked out in another room. The wheels were coming off the puppy wagon.

"Alright, boys, listen up! We are going to play a game. There will be winners and there will be losers, but one thing stays the same: I am your queen. If you fail to obey me, you're out. If you perform well, you get a reward. Do you understand?"

The last three Napoleons standing nodded in agreement.

She turned to Gabriele warmly. "Wash my feet, good slave."

Gabriele took her foot in his hand and wiped it with a washcloth, tenderly drying it and then kissing her toes one by one.

"Yes," Stella exhaled. "Emmanuel, get over here. Do exactly as Gabriele does with my other foot. Bae, pour some wine, then rub my neck."

The boys worked like Cinderella's mice, decompressing her from the ball. It was a fairytale in reverse and just the kind of gender role inversion she relished.

Bae's soft fingers kneading her neck, he leaned in for another kiss.

"You haven't earned that yet," she reprimanded him.

"Emmanuel, play some music. Show me your good French taste in a striptease."

She did not expect his eyes to beam with such luminance. He was an exhibitionist in hiding. She loved coaxing out concealed longings. He selected a slinky electro lounge track by Sébastien Tellier called, "A Ballet," and began unraveling the white ruffle of his blouse.

Stella orbited him, dragging a wooden spoon through his curly walnut hair and across his face. "Yes, slowly, seductively, in time with the music."

He was a natural tease and his hands moved with ease at the unfurling of his garments. He was fitter than she had surmised and delicious to watch. Stella encouraged him with slaps of her spoon to his thighs.

"And so?" Emmanuel pointed to his last remaining piece of clothing, his underwear.

She took his bicep in her hand, ran the long nails of her other hand through his hair, yanked his head to the side, and slid the tip of her tongue from his shoulder to his ear. He went limp in her hands.

"Bae, the rope. Take his arms behind his back. Hold him like a prisoner." Bae did as he was told. Stella stretched the rope across Emmanuel's burgeoning erection. It was barely concealed beneath the thin cotton. She moved the rope back and forth, up and down, teasing until he had a full hard-on.

"Gabriele, man the rope. This prisoner must face punishment for his insubordinate cock!" She handed Gabriele the bundle of jute. "Remember, communication and consent."

"May I touch you?" Gabriele asked, clearly wishing to advance to the head of the class. He was the most obedient but in a perfunctory manner Stella wished to train out of him.

Emmanuel could not conceal the devilish grin spreading across his face. Although Stella had intuited that he would be the one most likely to play with the other boys, she had not been completely certain until this moment. Gabriele dragged the taut rope across Emmanuel's underwear.

"Bae, keep him restrained and grab the back of his head."

Bae tugged at a tuft of Emmanuel's hair. Stella's hand flew swiftly across his cheek. Emmanuel yowled with satisfaction.

"How do you feel, prisoner?"

"Wonderful."

"Let's see." Stella clipped her fingers under his waistband. "You look quite happy. Is it time to free willy?"

"Yes, Mistress," Emmanuel replied.

"Bae, you do the honors of stripping this prisoner. Do not rush. Show me how sensual you can be."

Bae obeyed and with Emmanuel fully nude, Stella offered him a reward.

"Emmanuel, darling, you've been a good little slut and have earned a treat." She took a sip of wine, curled it under her tongue, then pressed her mouth to his. She slowly released the warm liquid while grazing the tip of his erection with the cold glass. He swallowed and grinned as if he had just received a hit of opium.

Soon all the little sluts had stripped and Stella had coaxed out their erections like a snake charmer with the irresistible trill of a flute.

She lined them up on all fours and blindfolded them with scarves. After spanking each of their bottoms with her wooden spoon, she commanded them to gather in a circle around her.

"Gabriele, unbutton my dress." His fingers groped blindly for the back of her neck.

"Bae, remove my left arm. Emmanuel, my right." Her gown fell to her ankles along with one of her pasties, which she swiftly reapplied.

The radial heat from their bodies, the anticipation of every breath, and the pelvic proof of their pleasure filled Stella with satisfaction. She ran her hands along each of their hard, rippled abdomens then reached behind to pull them closer to her.

"Kiss my neck. Gently," she whispered.

Gabriele, at her back, took to sucking each line of vertebrae while Emmanuel breathed heavy into the crook of her neck and Bae planted tiny kisses under her chin.

"Now rotate to your right."

Their erect members tickled her waist as they moved, a virtual car wash of carnal sensation.

"Kiss me from my neck to my feet and keep moving. Feel one another and move in unison. I am the barber's pole, you are the stripes." Stella reached for the wine glass, threw back the last swig, and closed her eyes. She was Venus awash in the breeze, hovering atop her ethereal shell.

The boys moved harmoniously, oscillating rhythmically, she suspected, with a mutual desire for one another.

"I want to *feel* your worship. No hands. Only mouths, lips, tongues," she cooed as Bae and Gabriele arrived at her tasseled breasts.

Bae slid his tongue under the sticky sequin in an attempt to loosen it. Stella giggled with delight. A blush of wetness and warmth bloomed between her thighs. She began rotating the opposite direction, disorienting the boys, turning faster and faster until their hungry tongues could not keep up.

With wet streaks across her body, she guided each of them to the bed, reclining them just so, blindfolds and all.

They were beautiful in their own ways. Bae was lean with very little body hair. The hourglass of his muscular shoulders gave way to a cinched waist and meaty calves. He was the only one of the international bunch circumcised, and the prettiest of the men, smooth and unspotted as if his skin had never once been scorched by the sun.

Gabriele was long and lithe like a basketball player, with a dick to match, and manscaped to the same crop as his short beard.

Emmanuel was right in the middle stature-wise, as if she were Goldilocks trying them all on for size. He was compact but stocky with pecs and an ass you could bounce a quarter off. He had the golden skin of a tourist on the Riviera, with shoulders freckled and buttocks stark white. You could have placed him in any Hemingway novel as the young lover not yet scorned.

Stella moved to the middle of the bed, wrapping herself with the fur coat taken from the boat. She was every bit the Lady Godiva.

"Now, who will earn the pleasure of tasting the nectar of my flower?" she began rhetorically. "It will be decided with a kiss. Emmanuel, you are first."

He kissed her gently, allowing the abundance of his lips to feel every millimeter of hers. He tasted largely of wine and slightly of cigarettes.

"Very nice," she praised. "Let's see if your fellow slaves agree."

Stella guided Emmanuel towards Bae. He reached for his face. "May I kiss you?"

"Uh, Mistress, I don't know. I don't usually kiss guys," Bae objected.

"You don't have to do anything you don't want to but let me remind you this is a safe space where you may stretch your limits and pursue your desires as slowly as you like."

"I'm fine being touched. Kissing just feels so... so, intimate."

"Then Emmanuel will not kiss you, but you are missing out," she teased.

Emmanuel moved towards Gabriele, touching him tentatively on the knee. Without a word, Gabriele pulled him into a lusty kiss.

"Fuck. You boys are making me even wetter," Stella said, rubbing her fingers along the slickness of her pussy. "Taste." She pressed her wet fingers into the mouths of each of the boys and watched their cocks expand desperately.

"OK, I'm ready!" exclaimed Bae, who clearly had a competitive streak.

"No, you missed your turn. You will have to wait until I am ready. Gabriele, kiss me." She ran her tongue along the top of his mouth. He nibbled at her lip. The sweet flush of arousal soaked her already moist wetlands.

"We have a winner." She opened her coat and pushed Gabriele's head towards her pelvis. "Take off my panties with only your teeth."

"Mistress, when do we get to remove the blindfolds?" asked Bae just as Allistair stumbled into the room.

"Woah. What is going on?" Allistair inquired, gripping the door frame woozily.

"You are missing out on the fun," replied Stella.

"Please, can I join?"

"No, you haven't earned it yet. Go fetch some grapes, berries, any sensual desserts. Hurry!"

Within minutes, but not without a great ruckus, Allistair returned. He stood stark naked at the foot of the bed, holding a tray of food, eager for permission to enter.

"Get over here and feed me."

At the peak of her hedonistic fantasy, she had arranged the boys in an erotic assembly line. Bae sucked her toes while Gabriele's tongue swirled circles around her glistening southern lips. Emmanuel suckled her breasts as Allistair placed fresh strawberries between her teeth. She had never experienced anything like it. All her senses firing, her flesh felt more awakened than the day she was born.

Soon it was time for the moment she had been anticipating: the climax. After all, Deb had instructed her to build steadily to it in those beloved steps. It was time to let loose the stallions to play as they naturally would.

She removed each of the boys' blindfolds and let silence hang in the air. They waited with druggy smiles, their hungry eyes washing over her body like spotlights as she reclined naked atop the fur coat. The room was dark except for a handful of candles she had instructed Emmanuel to light. She could no longer see the moon through the window. The sky was deep black and the glow of lights bounced off the canal and turned it chartreuse. The sound of revelry had ceased. Now there was just the sleepy convalescence of neighbors long retired to bed.

She smiled wickedly. "You are free to serve your queen as you wish."

Stella closed her eyes and sank into the pillows. One by one, the sensation of bodies pressing against her was like the kiss of waves as if she laid on a hot sand beach. She recognized each of them by their scent, their skin, and the caress of their cheeks as they moved slowly across her body. But as the pace quickened, the anonymous touches amplified her thrill. She gave herself over to the cascade of sensations. Briefly opening her eyes, she watched as Bae kissed Emmanuel along the neck. She grabbed at their hard cocks and, wetting her fingers, began stroking them. The men paused as if to rouse themselves from a dream, then embraced in a libidinous kiss. Soon the four Napoleons were a tangle of untapped desires now unraveled like the jute strewn across the floor.

They tugged at each other lustily, their hands grazing shoulders and buttocks and abs. She was their anchor, for they would always return to her. The rolls of her flesh nourished their hands, their mouths, their hips as they squeezed and pressed into her.

"Bondage restricts the mind but frees the subconscious," Veronica had told her.

The cage of four male bodies forced upon her a sensory experience over which she gladly had no power. She was swept up in a timeless euphoria, grounded and floating in the same breath.

As if on a wire attached to the ceiling, her pelvis began to rise. Higher and higher until the sun and moon and stars burst through her loins in some kind of sexual exorcism, and she recalled Barbie's words: "That was just like being on acid."

* * * * *

Stella was the first to wake. Like a pile of snakes in a basket, she was covered with men. They looked so angelic as they slept off the night of debauchery. The tangerine glow of the rising sun filtered through the half-closed curtains where dust danced in their post-coital haze. Stella gingerly transferred the limp limbs back to the torsos of their respective owners and climbed out of bed. She retrieved her dress from the mess of clothes on the floor, swept her cape across her shoulders, and left the villa. Drawing in a mouthful of crisp morning air, she began walking towards the Grand Canal.

Venice still had sleep in its eyes save for fishermen sailing out to the lagoon with their accordion-shaped nets. They buzzed by in their weather-worn boats looking like crusty and determined pirates.

Stella strolled through the empty labyrinthine streets, scanning for an open café.

She looked down at her phone. A text from Veronica.

"What was happening with those boys? They were all so cute in their costumes. I was dying. It looked like a stable. How did you get them to sit like that?"

Stella flushed with pride. Veronica had noticed her. How strange to be a mommy one moment and to feel like a teenager the next.

Something welled up from deep within—pain, relief, and joy—as a rainfall of paper dots pitter-pattered on her head. She heard laughter and craned her head to the sky. On a balcony above, an impish girl let slip handfuls of confetti like a christening. Stella waved and twirled for her like a ballerina. The paper stuck to her eyes and cheeks, wet from her tears.

In that moment, she held herself with compassion, tenderly the way she had held others. The tears flowed stronger. She suddenly felt complete in her arrival. In her metamorphosis.

She pushed back the sleeve of her gown to touch the tattoo maturing on her arm: "I am who I am seeking." It made sense in a different way than when she had it inked months earlier.

Self-acceptance had been so beaten out of her, condemned, and vilified, that a million bullets of love and praise from others couldn't breach her Christian armor, her denial of self, her forced humility, even when humility was not called for. But it was time to start a love affair. A radical act of self-love. Why shouldn't she love herself as others so clearly did?

Stella stepped up to the lip of the water and sobbed from her depths, allowing the grand canals of La Serenissima to store her tears along with all the impediments to self-love that she wore. And she was free. *Truly free.*

ABOUT THE AUTHOR

Sophia Domina is a professional Dominatrix, seasoned filmmaker, and journalist of 25 years who has produced work for CNN, National Geographic, The Dallas Morning News, and Jezebel. When she's not penning erotica, she teaches female domination workshops and produces kinky immersive theater. She resides at her own "Domton Abbey" in Los Angeles.

SOPHIADOMINA.COM

www.ingramcontent.com/pod-product-compliance
Lightning Source LLC
Chambersburg PA
CBHW070636310726
48982CB00001B/298
* 9 7 9 8 2 1 8 4 5 4 2 1 0 *

www.ingramcontent.com/pod-product-compliance
Lightning Source LLC
Chambersburg PA
CBHW070826020826
48982CB00015B/707

* 9 7 8 0 6 4 8 5 2 3 6 3 5 *